MIDDLETOWN PUBLIC LIBRARY
700 WEST MAIN RD
MIDDLETOWN RI 02840

03/17/1994

MIDDLETOWN PUBLIC LIBRARY

P9-DNE-636

WHI
White, Gillian
    Mothertime
MID 7/94   3214800045 7415

DATE DUE

MOTHERTIME

By The Same Author

The Plague Stone
The Crow Biddy
Nasty Habits
Rich Deceiver

WHI

MIDDLETOWN PUBLIC LIBRARY
MIDDLETOWN, R.I. 02842

MOTHERTIME

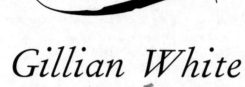

Gillian White

ORION

april 14, 1994

Copyright © 1993 Gillian White

All rights reserved

The right of Gillian White to be identified as the author of this
work has been asserted by her in accordance with the
Copyright, Designs and Patents Act 1988.

First published in Great Britain in 1993 by Orion
An imprint of Orion Books Ltd
Orion House, 5 Upper St Martin's Lane, London WC2H 9EA

A CIP catalogue record for this book is available
from the British Library

ISBN 1 85797 009 8

Typeset by Datix International Limited, Bungay, Suffolk
Printed in Great Britain by
Butler & Tanner Ltd
Frome and London

For Yvette. For everything.

ONE

THEY TOOK Mother prisoner at half past two on Christmas Day morning.

By then they had no option. It was an act of kindness – or defence, at any rate. It was a sad and wisely made decision, the sort most normally taken by civil servants in the way that they have, safe behind reinforced glass.

Midwinter.
Midnight.
Bleak and frosty but with no wind moaning.
'And another thing, Heavenly Father, sometimes I wake up so frightened about what's going to happen to me in the day. Why did You make us the only species able to understand about torture . . .'

Through the comfortable square of curtain, through the draped security of strangers we can see Vanessa Townsend finishing her conversation with God. She has just put down *The Silence of the Lambs*. A winter mist hangs round the old-fashioned street light outside her window, held in silence by the stillness of night. The wide-awake girl has the cloudy smell of Johnson's Powder, she is blameless in white, waiting for Mother to come home, forcing herself to stay alert so that as soon as the house goes finally quiet and Mother drags herself upstairs to bed, she can creep around with the pillowcases she keeps hidden in the back of her wardrobe and then she can turn off her light. And her head. Her dressing gown is laid out on the edge of her bed, ready. Within the walls of the house nothing seems about to happen, the silence is complete.

They hadn't had any sort of Christmas last year and she cannot, will not, she has sworn on her Holy Bible that she will never allow that to happen again. Vanessa is responsible and there is nobody else. It is all up to her and she is sure she's remembered everything ... exactly how it used to be. The freezer is full and there is a Marks & Spencer Christmas cake in the pantry. She's remembered the crackers, even a packet of indoor fireworks.

Dominic – 'the man of the house' Camilla and the twins, Sacha and Amber – well, they're asleep, put to bed with strict instructions not to dare to wake up until seven o'clock at the earliest. That's not surprising. They are all worn out. They lugged the decoration trunk down from the attic and spent the evening decorating the hall, the drawing room, and the sweet-smelling tree that they'd all gone to fetch from Mr Gribble's after tea. It took ages to finish the job properly because the house is a tall one, Georgian and elegant, with high-ceilinged rooms and three flights of stairs. The two illuminated Tiffany pineapples which stand sentinel on their wrought-iron stalks beside the grandish, navy front door are part of Mother's protest against what she calls 'the mediocrity of this blighted world of Boots, Barratts and the Bradford & Bingley' So the house is entirely decorated to Mother's taste now – candy-striped like a chocolate box, lined with padded curtains and bows, jade vases of jelly-bean green are spotlighted in the alcoves and the carpets are so thick you can move unnoticed anywhere.

They have laid Mother's presents under the tree ... there is one with a ribbon, it looks expensive, it must be from Daddy. They have opened the pile of Christmas cards which Mother ignored, or tore from their envelopes with careless indifference, and they have covered the mantelpiece, the bookshelves, and fixed lengths of cotton along the wall to take them all, to display them properly.

There are a hundred and forty-seven cards. So someone, somewhere must have liked Mother once. She always says she is popular.

Once, during the evening, while Dominic was balanced on the stepladder leaning over the tree with the fairy, they were interrupted by Ilse's return.

'My, my!' Her blue eyes bulged. In her gold leggings and padded, silky blue anorak, she looked like a Christmas-card person ... one that would come from a Woolies' mixed pack with a robin on one shoulder. She lifted two dainty gloved hands as though she might start to tap-dance. 'Vat vill Mrs Townsend say ven she zees?'

The children froze and stared. The twins' round spectacles glinted, stonier than the hardest of eyes. Huge tartan bows clutched at the sides of their small heads, shooting out hanks of hair stiff as horns. Their lips moved back, false smiles revealed gappy front teeth. They can afford to ignore Ilse: they know they can get her the sack tomorrow if they feel that way inclined, and Ilse knows it, too. Mother would be shocked if she realised how often Ilse went out – she should have been babysitting tonight – or about the times she brings men back to her bedroom high up in the gingerbread eaves of the house. Ilse has her own tiny balcony but she need not be coy on it like Juliet, she has her own back staircase, too.

'They forecast that it might snow tomorrow.' Ilse inspected the tree. There was one present on the floor for her. Vanessa had signed the label from all of them, Mother included, but Ilse showed not the slightest interest.

'It never snows here, not at Christmas.' Camilla put the Swedish girl straight.

'You know you should be in bed by now. Especially ze leetle ones.' Her lips were swollen, chapped-looking; her collar up to hide what Dominic calls her vampire bites. But she didn't bother to say any more. Sighing prettily she turned and left, and they heard her in the kitchen liquidising some ice for her drink before she took it upstairs. She'd be washing her hair, getting her clothes ready for tomorrow. She'll be off Christmas Day and Boxing Day, too, staying with her new friends in Wimbledon.

Anyway, time has moved on – it's midnight, then one, one-thirty – and now Vanessa is neatly arranged in her place in her bed, settled there, flounced in white like a porcelain child and her legs are straight under the covers with a bump as neat as a sleeping policeman. Oh yes, all the pillowcase presents are wrapped and labelled, chosen with love over the last few months with money Vanessa scrounged under false pretences from Mother, money kept back from outings and school trips, money she'd saved from shopping errands, change she'd hung on to. It was

3

surprising how much cash she had collected; she added it to the large amounts Daddy gave her. It is also surprising how easy life has become since Mother has fallen in love with Bart, a relationship which has lasted much longer than any other her eldest daughter can remember, since Daddy left.

Camilla, aged ten, says that Bart is a man of little substance.

Mother is coming. Vanessa's eyes darken. It feels as if she has been waiting for Mother for years.

From her first-floor bedroom in the mellow house, dimly lit by the bedside light and overlooking the front porch on to Camberley Road, Vanessa hears the whispering engine of Bart's new BMW as it pulls to a halt with opulent lethargy, its fat tyres sucking the gutters; she watches the headlights dip and fade like a reveller's eyes drunkenly drooping. The street is lined with parked cars, neat humps of blackness all the way down, because most people round here stay at home on this special night. Most people want to be near their children. Everywhere else is just as it should be, Christmas-Eve-silent, in that hushed, firelit, waiting mood of the night before Christmas. Not even the trees in the park across the road are sighing tonight and the mist round the lamppost is fixed like a wreath. When she was little she'd thought there were wolves in the park. They lurk on the pathways between the bracken and thorn, they slink in the woodlands of oaks and birches, they howl in the faraway pine trees that stand so lonely against the sky.

Mother is coming.

Vanessa tenses; her wide brow furrows as she waits to discover if Bart is going to come in, or if he'll drive off as he sometimes does, back to his wife in Potters Bar who doesn't know he is going out with Mother but thinks he is with friends at his health club in the City. *Please come in, Bart, please come in!* Vanessa knows that because of the wife, Mother will be alone all Christmas Day. 'Nobody wants me,' she'll sob over the loud and constant TV — Mother loves game shows — with her long red nails bending back on her glass, with her whole self wrapped around her glass and mascara blotching her tear-bruised face. 'Even you kids, you're only here 'cos your father won't have you ... him and his snotty bitch wife.'

The health club will be closed. Everywhere is going to be closed, even Ali's store on the corner, but with a bit of luck Bart will find a phone and call Mother who will talk to him curled tensely over the bedroom extension, the terrible mess of untended clothes littered like overblown petals on the carpet around her. If he fails to do that then Christmas Day will be spoilt, far worse than usual. The best they can hope for is that Mother will sleep until the phone call comes ... that might make her brighter ... that might get her out of her drab dressing-gown.

As time goes by Mother will mutter, 'Ring, damn you,' into the bulging silence that stretches behind the wild television screams.

The nuns at school smile softly and say that Christmas is a time of innocence. Vanessa goes to the Convent of the Sacred Heart because Daddy is a Catholic and pays the fees. Camilla will follow her there next year if she passes the difficult entrance exam. Vanessa played Mary in the nativity although she was one of the youngest, 'because there's a purity about your face that is rare ... a certain sweet serenity, dear, especially when you look up like that,' Sister Agnes told her, lifting her chin with a freezing cold finger as she inspected her profile.

Vanessa treasures Sister Agnes' words. She has written them in the front of her diary.

Mother moans that Vanessa is a plain child who might, with luck, blossom one day, but she doubts it. 'You, most of all, take after your father and there's only so much anyone can do.' Vanessa cannot see what Mother means. She looks nothing like Daddy, she wishes that she did. They say that Mother is beautiful but her children know that underneath the crust of cream there is no beauty there at all. Not even her hair is real; beneath that selection of wigs that sit on the wigstands in her stuffy, scented room, hot like a jungle, what grows naturally on Mother's head is mousey and spikey, cut short and rarely exposed. Mother goes round the house in a scarf like a wartime woman, leaving behind her own, special devastation, the crammed ashtrays and half-empty glasses. Any colour in Mother's face is labelled Clinique, put there with brushes made out of sable and badger hair. Mother might once have appeared on the front of all those old magazines she sighs over, those she keeps in her walnut cabinet, but Mother is no longer glossy or beautiful. Mother is angry and ugly with little red veins behind her knees. This is because she's had so many children ... and that is because Daddy is a Catholic.

They will have to be careful not to disturb her tomorrow.

Mother was on an old advert they put on TV for a laugh last week, pushing a vacuum cleaner in a tight skirt and fishnet stockings. Vanessa smiles between two hooked thumbs as she remembers. Caroline Heaten, as Mother was then, stared at them out of the telly – a stranger with spidery eyelashes and hair stiffly high on her head like an upturned china potty. Bouffant. 'Hush! Shush ... everyone look!' Excited, Mother leaned forward and her face went so thin, her chin went so pointed she looked like a witch. Luckily Bart had not arrived, she was spared the humiliation of that, because they were taking the piss out of the advert; it was so old-fashioned, filmed so long ago that the audience hooted with laughter and when Mother realised what they were doing, lying there on the sofa stroking her arm, she went white and her mouth clamped round her cigarette, wrinkling up like a string purse. Vanessa had felt a sharp stab of sadness then. For a moment she felt sorry for Mother, more sorry than she had ever been; she thought the glitter in her eyes might be tears, but when Camilla failed to stifle a giggle Mother uncoiled, she shot forward and slapped her hard across the face. The ten-year-old gasped. Mother wore no expression at all.

Mother whines about once being famous. Daddy still is.

Mother turns the TV off whenever she sees that Daddy is on it, but Dominic takes the video up to his room and meticulously records every *Update*, even the repeats. The children sit round and watch with a vengeance when Mother goes out, even though they don't understand much of that dry political stuff.

But this is not how it ought to be for the birth of the baby Jesus.

The only thing you can do is to try to make it right.

Mother is coming.

Vanessa hopes fervently that Bart will come in so that Mother's reactions to the Christmas preparations will be eased by his company. She makes an effort to be calmer when Bart is about; she distributes the cold, fluttering kisses she keeps on the ends of her fingers and sometimes pats the odd passing head. But Vanessa hears the curse and the harsh burst of laughter before the car door clicks, before the tap of the high-heel boots as they round the long silver bonnet and approach the pavement. A hollower sound, now, as the boots trip towards the house, towards the cold white pimpled pineapples – Mother always takes those long strides, like a model or a cat — and the window whirrs down, she hears a muffled remark from Bart and then, slurred, from her mother, 'You've said it all, Bart. There's really no need to make it worse. That's it, you arsehole, I know where I stand now and that's just fine so fuck off you jerk.' Her vicious voice pierces like the end of a needle; the sound of her splits the soft silent fabric of night. 'Just bloody well fuck off.'

Shut up shut up shut up! Vanessa's frantic whispers bubble out of her mouth so fast they take all the moisture with them. She licks her lips with just the very tip of her tongue.

In a minute the house will tremble a little as Mother slams the door.

The listening child lifts her head slightly, the expression on her small, drawn face turning solemn and nervous. The bedside clock, with the slither of tinsel she's not been able to resist, says a quarter to two. She slips across the room and fetches the comb from a dressing table which is altar-like, draped in white muslin and decorated with a single, slender, unlit candle. A fleeting glance at the mirror shows unblinking eyes wide and black, there is hurt in them, too, like she's seen in Daddy's, a touch of violet. She makes herself comfortable in bed once more, pushes back the sleeves of her white nightgown — there'd been all sorts of colours to choose from in the shop but she'd chosen white for purity — and starts to comb her straight brown hair, a slow, calming rhythm, obsessive in its intensity. By now the car has driven away and, after a long pause, she hears the fumble of the key in the lock below her; the key drops on to the porch steps with a stony *ping* and Mother stumbles — and over all that comes an odd, gurgling sound from Mother's throat.

Nothing happy ever happens when Mother is home.

Oh God help me. Oh God show me what to do. The Christmas she has planned with such care will be turned into a sickly fraud by the riot and disorder of Mother abandoned again.

The twelve-year-old child grips her hands tightly together, she gazes thoughtfully down to her lap as the fluorescent, pink comb is bent almost back on itself before it snaps in half as if she's been playing too hard with hope, overloving it, fondling it so furiously that it died like that newt she'd once found which was cold-blooded and did not need her love. Did she do that?

It is much better to love than be loved, Mother says, less responsibility.

Silent night, Holy night. Vanessa knows she is crying because she can taste the salt. She doesn't want to cry, to smudge, to be formless and undefended.

Two

THE CRASH on the stairs brings Camilla rushing to Vanessa's room. Barefooted, her ringlets springing about her face, she looks astonished all over, like Goldilocks disturbed by the bears.

'I thought you were asleep.'

'Mother's back.'

'I know. I heard the door bang. She's trying to get upstairs. She'll see what we've done in a minute.'

'Has Bart come with her?' The hope comes shrill with the question. It whistles with the question.

'No. I think she's fallen out with Bart.'

Camilla nods, understanding at once. Her pointed face falls, the slant eyes open wide as they ever do, stretched with worry and difficult questions. If Camilla poses, and puts on her special pouting face, she looks exactly like Mother, dressed to kill in the old magazines, and the colour of her hair is the nearest to gold you can ever get.

'What will she do?'

'I dunno. Depends on how bad she is.'

'What will happen to the tree if we're not there to defend it? Will she spoil it?'

Sick with dread, Vanessa cannot answer that. She knows what she has to say, she might as well say it. 'We'd better go down. Perhaps if we let her open her presents ...'

'It would be better if we were all there. Especially Dominic.' Mother likes Dominic.

'But we don't want the twins to be frightened.'

'Don't be stupid, Vanessa. Sacha and Amber don't get frightened, not any more. Not like you.'

Is that the reason she's made such an effort to create a Christmas? Has she done it because she is frightened – is it an act of defiance or terror? If Vanessa loses Christmas, perhaps she will lose her childhood. Whatever it is, now she feels so terribly weary of it all. She ought to have known it would never work. What had she expected anyway – that Mother's face would glaze over with wonder, that the shock of the Christmas-tree lights would turn her back into something wonderful, tapped by the fairy's magic wand? What she's done, what she's tried to do is ridiculous, and now they'll all pay the price. Planning it all had felt very different.

'And if you go moaning to Robin I can tell you exactly what will happen,' said Mother last year, on the morning they woke up early expecting to see the familiar pillowcases stood at the end of their beds. She made her excuses quickly, annoyed. She was ill, all messed up in the head and how could she be expected to cope after what Daddy did to her? 'He'll be terribly nice,' Mother explained, warning them off. 'He'll commiserate like hell and you and he can berate me together. He'll take you out and buy you whatever you like, to compensate for my bad behaviour. But at the end of the day I can tell you exactly what will happen, because Suzie won't have you at the flat under any circumstances. This house will go, for a start. You won't have a home to go to. Robin will stop paying maintenance and we won't be able to afford to stay here. You'll all be shipped off to boarding schools, God knows which ones or where, he's gone so bloody peculiar, he won't listen to reason.' Mother glared at her children, one by one, each of them wilting under the blast of that direct stare. You shouldn't stare back at wild animals, it only antagonises them and makes them worse. She drew in a lungful of cigarette smoke and blew it out almost gaily. 'So where do you think you'll be spending your holidays?'

'Granny's?' ventured Vanessa, almost soundlessly.

Mother just snorted. 'You should be so lucky! The State makes special provision for children like you. They'd take their forms and go and inspect Isobel's house and conclude that it was quite unsuitable.

Isobel hates children. Robin's mother is so set in her ways, a speck of dust upsets her. She would never cope. No, there's others, special people who'll take you in – people who are trained. No doubt Robin would call occasionally and take you out for treats, just as he does now, when it suits him.'

'Where would you be, Mother, when we were taken in for the holidays?' Dominic's cheeks were flushed. Her only son. You could see that he verged on the edge of tears.

'It wouldn't matter to anyone where I was. It never has mattered, and it wouldn't matter then,' said the crushed thing that was Mother from the raging pain within her. She wandered off to turn on the television. None of the family were dressed. She hadn't been going out with Bart then, there'd been a young boy called Douglas ... dotty, dopey, dirty Douglas, with black greasy hair, and silver studs on the back of his jacket. During this period she took to wearing her long, straight wig with the fringe; it was orange, it clashed with her face. She wore black polo-necked sweaters and skin-tight jeans. Mutton dressed as lamb. She danced with Douglas in the drawing room late into the night, *On the Wings of Love*, difficult to be graceful because of his lumbering boots. She bought him a motorbike so he could get work delivering parcels all over London. Daddy used to laugh about that when they told him. When they told him it felt as if they were snitching. Daddy laughed while Suzie lifted her eyebrows and grimaced. Once, Vanessa looked round and saw Suzie mouth the words, 'Don't interfere,' with her usual, honeyed contempt.

And is Mother a lost cause, like Granny says?

Anyway, no doubt to Suzie's huge amusement, Douglas roared off in a pall of smoke one morning and never came back, but Mother keeps his photograph in the close place, next to the stamps in her purse.

So last Christmas morning, confused and dispirited, they all sat and watched *The Wizard of Oz*. At the point when Dorothy set off down the yellow brick road, a good half-hour later, Mother added huskily, as if they'd been deep in conversation all the time, 'So my advice to you is to keep quiet. There's more to Christmas than presents, anyway. You'll all understand when you're older. I'll give you some money and you can go to the sales tomorrow. It'll be much more fun in the end. I told Mrs Guerney to leave us something cold in the fridge. There'll probably be some turkey, if you're so desperate to taste it.'

'Couldn't we just put a few decorations up? Please?'

'It wouldn't be worth the effort. Not now. You should have reminded me earlier. I'd have got Mrs Guerney to help you. Or Gwyneth.' When Gwyneth left to have her baby, Ilse came to replace her. Mother said it was too depressing, she wasn't prepared to take pregnant Welsh girls again. 'Coming to hide in London,' she said. 'It's time these people with their miserable, grim religions as grey as their blasted little walls faced up to their moral responsibilities, like we have to. To see them just drags me down. And the three flights of stairs are too much for them.'

She'd been blaming Daddy, really; she called his religion grim, too. 'Your father has always loved a martyr – that's why he fell for the simpering Suzie. But he will destroy her in the end. Perhaps,' and here Mother smiled, 'perhaps she'll go up in flames one day. I just hope I'm bloody well there to see it.'

Mother ought not to make jokes about martyrs like that.

It wasn't so bad for Vanessa, who didn't believe, or Camilla or Dom, but it was awful for Sacha and Amber. Sacha came up to Vanessa afterwards and whispered, 'But what happened to our list? Me and Amber wrote one between us and sent it up the chimney.'

'Sometimes lists get lost in the sky, especially at night. But I'll write to the North Pole and say what happened this time so it's not likely to happen again.'

Vanessa considered telling Daddy about their missing Christmas although that would feel like snitching, too. He would phone on Christmas morning, he'd assured them he would. She thought hard and long about it: if she told him, would it really have the effect that Mother warned them it would? Would he decide to send them away, scatter them about in various boarding schools? Sometimes it is hard to get through to Daddy because he is so strongly influenced by Suzie. Maybe he wouldn't listen to their protests. Daddy didn't want trouble – he discussed the situation with them quite openly, saying it was important that they understood. Daddy has not yet dismantled his gym in the basement for fear of upsetting Mother. He'd walked out of the house with only a suitcase full of papers; he'd left the rest of it exactly as it was. Mother had taken everything of his, his clothes, his books and his photographs, she had bundled them up, thrown petrol on top and had a fire in the garden. She poked the smouldering mountain to fury with a garden broom. She danced and made little cries when it flared. Mr Morrisey from next door called from his side of the tall wooden fence; his thin neck rose up over the planks and the shadows did something to his face, making it hollow and long, making it look as if he was wearing a tall top hat, part of the ceremony, flecked with flame like a witch doctor. 'Don't think I'm complaining, Mrs Townsend, but are you sure you have that thing under control? The wind is blowing in my direction.' His false teeth gleamed.

Mother called the children to join her, but they did not want to be party to it. They watched from indoors, huddled together on the window seat in Camilla's room. Dominic, his face shadowy, smokey, dark, kept saying, 'Maybe we ought to ring Daddy and tell him what she's doing.' He hugged a cushion to his tummy as if he had a pain. But they knew it was pointless. Daddy could not get back in time to save anything, and besides, there would only be the most hideous row.

When they told him about the fire he said they had done right to do nothing.

The equipment in the gym, being mostly metal, was impossible to burn. And it was heavy, much of it attached to the floor or the walls, and Mother had not attempted to destroy it. Out of sight out of mind. One day, Daddy says, when things are calmer, he'll make arrangements with a specialist firm to collect his stuff. Until then the basement is kept locked even though Ilse has often asked to use the exercise bike and the weights. Nobody goes down there any more. It is probably dusty, and rusty from lack of use. Vanessa had once climbed down the basement steps to look in, forgetting that the tiny barred windows had been painted white for privacy. Even with your face pressed hard against the bars you can't see anything at all.

Daddy is always sympathetic. 'Your mother is so volatile, she hasn't been able to cope with the change and it's time she got help with her drinking. She does it for attention, for effect of course, and revenge, we understand that. She's never, really, been able to cope. I did her no favours by staying with her as long as I did. But the calmer the waters the better, for the moment. It'll take time, but you'll find that I'm right, your mother will pick up the pieces and get on with her own life again. If nothing else, Caroline is a survivor. I know it must be difficult at home at the moment, especially for you, Vanessa, being the oldest. I depend on you so much. You know you can come to me at any time, don't you? I'm only a cheap tube ride away, and remember, I am always on the end of the telephone. I want to know what's happening, Vanessa. You are my children, you always will be my children and I love you all very much.'

But there is always an edge to Suzie's voice when Vanessa phones Daddy at home.

Mother is home.

'Go and wake Dominic up, collect the twins and we'll go down. Maybe, if we're all together, we can persuade her.'

To do what? What are they trying to persuade Mother to do? Nobody really knows. What is this desire to draw close to the thing which is causing the pain? They want to guard the beautiful tree which is large enough to take two sets of lights.

It does not take long. Following the crash, the house sounds eerily silent. They gather, ghostly, on the dimly-lit landing, not needing to speak or explain any more. They feel very close to each other. Dominic pulls on his manly dressing-gown; he is nervous, his asthma is noticeable. He leads the way, shuffling down the stairs in his hippo-potamus slippers. The twins, half-asleep, squint, adjust their wiry spectacles. They do not ask what is happening. Camilla follows Dominic and Vanessa brings up the rear like a very white angel, the twins' sleepy hands sticking to her own.

Oh no! Mother is ripping the tinsel off, branch by branch. The Christmas tree leans to the right so the fairy's legs stick up in the air — made ridiculous. Mother is sobbing, still with her coat on. She has not bothered to turn on the main room lights so there are just the fairy lights in their glowing glory, so pure, so gentle, a halo round every one. The colours prick the leather of the sofa, a little soft firelight is left in the grate.

'Don't! Don't!' Amber runs forward with her arms outstretched and then she stops dead, sensing the futility of protest. Two small shreds of untouched tinsel wink at each other in the semi-dark.

Mother sobs and then she laughs. Even in her madness she must feel the heavy presence of the rest of her children; their faces make a white semicircle behind her, a primitive nursery rhyme moon. She slows in her task before turning round. She stares straight into Vanessa's eyes and holds them for one second ... two ... before shutting them out again, lost to the darkness. Mother's eyes fade, each one as sad as a pressed flower petal, and quite unable to meet the challenge.

'Don't!' roars Amber again, zipped like a rabbit in her sleepsuit. 'Why are you doing that?' The raging child turns to face Vanessa. With her small fists clenched at her sides she cries out, 'Why is she doing this? Why is she?'

Mother is like a snake ... repellent ... degenerate like a whore.

She struts towards the coffee table where the green bottle is waiting, and the glass. The chink and the glub glub of the gin being poured is the only sound in the room.

'You don't have to do anything, Mother. It's all done. We did it. For a surprise.' Vanessa's voice is firm. There is no fear in it. 'There is really no reason for you to destroy it.'

Mother's face slides as blearily as her voice; it is all pulled down to the side where her lips dribble warm alcohol.

'What's this then? A bloody family reunion?' Her voice is like her, devoid of vitality. She flicks her lighter and moves an unsteady hand towards a bent cigarette, shouts, 'Shit it,' as the flame burns her thumb, and then she sits back allowing the smoke to drift from her mouth, her nose. The smoke is the softest thing about her.

She lies down on the sofa, stretches out her legs and eases off one boot, using the toe of the other. She shakes it off and kicks it aside. She holds up her leg and flexes the stockinged toes.

Somewhere. Somewhere else in the world little children are peacefully sleeping. And there could be a badgers' set underneath one of the pine trees, a whole family of badgers snuggled up in the roots together. Somewhere.

'Well, you put them up, and now you can just start taking them down,' Mother snaps. 'It upsets me to see them. They remind me ... of too much ... hateful stuff and false promises ... Christ, I am sick to death of all this. And I've had it up to here with you, too. It's time you started to see things as they really are ... not as you'd like them to be. The stark facts of life, that's what you need! Are you all so insensitive that you can't understand anything that's ever gone on in this house?'

The children do not move. Vanessa can see that Amber, standing slightly forward, has started to shiver.

Mother's voice is icy. 'Didn't you hear what I said?' She tries to snap her fingers but they are too weak and flabby. Seeing this, she lets her hand drop.

Nobody moves. If they moved they would move as one, as a gas or a liquid, as an essence of misery. They are incapable of movement.

In contemptuous mild tones Mother carries on; you can imagine the shape of her eyeballs behind her closed lids. 'Then I'll have to do it myself. God help me! God help me! One day, so help me, I'm going to get out of all this! And what the hell's the matter with you, Vanessa, you fucking little prude! You played the Virgin fucking Mary, didn't you, and I thought when you told me – how deliciously apt! Always watching me. Always staring with your saintly nose wrinkled up as if there's a smell you can't bear, as if you can't quite locate it! Well it's me, darling, I'm afraid. I am the smell that's too strong to tolerate! I am the leaky sewer, Vanessa. Why don't you come closer and sniff? Between my legs. Under my arms. Christ! Christ!' Mother hiccups. 'As if I haven't had enough already.'

STOP IT, MOTHER, STOP IT! YOU ARE HURTING YOURSELF TOO MUCH AND YOU ARE TOO STRONG FOR ME TO HELP YOU ...

Missing a breath, Vanessa tastes blood. It comes from her bitten lip. She bites harder, surprised to find that she still has the strength.

She is vile! Mother is vile and full of evil! Suffering the wages of terrible sin. She wants to ask then, 'Mother, did you ... was there ever a time when you loved me?' But she knows there was ... memories of that softer time when Mother tried, they threaten to drench her.

An awful kind of laughter grips Mother now, but she stops quickly, as if it is too painful, she cannot cope, she might start coughing. She fumbles to try and get up, with one boot on and one off. Dizzily she reaches for her glass instead, tips it, and the children watch the pale silky liquid drain into her mouth. She swallows and her chest heaves. Her eyes widen. 'I'm sick,' she groans. She brushes her eyes with her free hand which trembles. 'So sick. Christ, I'm pissed as a fart.' There are stains on her coat, and on her skirt, brown stains like old food. And then she leans forward, folded almost in half and vomits harshly on to the carpet. At once the stench overpowers the pine. The stuff continues to trickle out of her mouth, unbroken strands of slime, shuddering her with bitterness. She retches, she moans until there is nothing left but a brown froth on her lips.

Only the children's eyes move; they flicker uneasily from one to the other.

Then Mother, having finally found her feet, turns the colour of milk, sways gently and collapses in a groggy heap on the rug by the fire.

'Oh oh oh oh ...' It seems that Camilla can't stop.

They watch Mother steadily, waiting to see if she breathes or if she has died right in front of them. Is death so easy, then? Mother likes Burl Ives singing *Dippity Doo Da, Dippidy Day*. She says you can't buy wafers any more, only cornets. Aren't these ordinary things incredible? Gradually Mother's chest rises and falls with a regularity. The shuddering stops. Her mouth falls slackly open. Her tongue lolls out like a tired old dog's.

Vanessa looks up. The effort of moving her neck feels heavy. Her shoulders are stiff, as if she's sat in a draught for too long. She steps forward and crushes out Mother's crooked cigarette in the ashtray. Released by her movement Dominic, man of the house, who still wets his bed but nobody knows except Vanessa and Mrs Guerney, crosses the room and lifts one of the heavy curtains. 'We need air. We have to open a window. The room stinks of sick.' And then he turns round with a flush of joy that makes his face round and childish with delight, the secretive curtain flung back behind him. 'Look! Look Sacha, look Amber! Ilse's forecast was right. It is snowing!'

Can you believe how strongly Vanessa envies his enormous, wonderful childishness?

THREE

WHEN VANESSA kneels to wash Mother she feels she is wiping a thin layer of evil away. Mother's eyes cry sooty black smears.

'But we don't want her to wake up,' Amber lisps through the hard, pink gap in her mouth. 'If she wakes up she'll spoil it all. Can't we keep her asleep somehow? Just until after Christmas?'

If Vanessa is plain then the twins are downright homely ... nothing like Mother used to be, or the pretty, ballet-dancing Camilla, or Dom, with his dark, gypsyish beauty. Their little round spectacles do not help, but without them the twins can hardly see; behind them their eyes are pale and speckled – they do not look like eyes that work well, you have to peer hard to find the lashes. Constructed almost entirely of angles, their prominent cheekbones make elves of their little faces, and their elbows are jointed like puppets', sticking out in sharp bony points. Sacha and Amber have short, straight hair, a dull carrot, and their complexions are pale. Their noses are freckled but the freckles are smudged so it seems as if they have forgotten to wash. 'I've never known a pair look so old-fashioned as you two,' Mrs Guerney often remarks, 'with those round-necked Fair Isle jumpers ... not enough colour in them for my liking, except round the cuffs and the neck. With your long stringy necks you'd look better with a collar. A nice bright green would suit you. And kilts! Whoever heard of kids wearing kilts these days?'

Daddy bought them their kilts from the Scotch House. At times like these Vanessa's chin quivered, hurt to hear Mrs Guerney say that, and angry with her because what does she know about anything with her arthritic-y knees and her ugly, misshapen fingers? 'You're okay,' she'd tell the twins, very aware of how awkward they were, of how they lacked the attraction and poise which other children possessed. As she did.

'Sometimes I don't know why I try,' complained Mrs Guerney, 'if I'm always going to be taken literally, and attacked when I give an opinion.'

Vanessa has her own ways of thinking about Daddy, pure ways. She does not like to think of him 'scattering his seed,' as the nuns put it. Daddy is at his absolute best when he comes on TV, so very seriously, in a brilliant white shirt and a dark grey suit. With his eyes large, soft and deep.

Mrs Guerney comes in every weekday morning to clean. She's been coming for as long as Vanessa can remember – she has a photograph of Mrs Guerney pushing her along in a pram in the park. She brings the daily groceries with her in her push-along tartan trolley. As she says herself, 'Why not, I have to pass the deli anyway.' So Mrs Guerney chooses what food they eat. If it is a pie or a casserole she'll prepare it and put it in the oven, timed, before she leaves, with a badly stained instruction note Sellotaped to the tray. More often than not, Mother is not home by seven o'clock, or she isn't hungry, or she's planning to go out for a meal. In any case, concerned as she is with controlling her weight, Mother eats like a bird. She'd much rather open the fridge and pick at the pieces – she does not approve of Mrs Guerney's sturdy cooking. Vanessa is the one then, sometimes Ilse, who prepares and cooks the vegetables, lays the table in the kitchen and dishes up the food. At the weekends they have salad, quiche, or cold meat and cheese, cold apple pies and trifles which Mrs Guerney has thought to provide.

'Dear Mrs Guerney is a perfect boon,' says Mother, when Mrs Guerney is nearby so that she will overhear her. Vanessa thinks the word boon describes Mrs Guerney exactly – comfortable, well-worn and pushed out of shape, like her ancient, down-at-heel slippers. Without Mrs Guerney their lives would be even more wrong, they'd be even more different from other families. At least, although she calls Vanessa 'standoffish', Mrs Guerney continues to treat them like children.

'Mother's wig has slipped over. Someone had better take it off. And it's got ash on it.'

'But don't wake her up! Please, please, please try not to wake her up!'

From her place down on the hearthrug Vanessa looks up at Amber. The fretting child is balanced on one leg, nervously pulling at her bottom lip.

'Mother is not going to wake up. I don't think she'll wake up till this afternoon.' Vanessa isn't sure if she wants Mother to wake up, ever. Vanessa knows that God hears her thoughts. Mother, corrupt, contaminates everything. Mother drives her to a wickedness that is too extreme to confess. Such violence. To want someone dead is as bad as killing them. Vanessa secretly reads fairy tales like *The Sleeping Beauty*, *The Little Mermaid*; she fights against the bestsellers, the frightening books which she forces herself to read because she ought to. She wants her breath to smell forever innocent – of tinned rice pudding and Bird's custard and the house ought to smell of freshly baked bread and sweet peas in china-blue vases.

'She might have hit her head on the firedogs, and split her skull open. She might have fallen into the fire.'

'But she didn't, Dom, did she? And now we've got to move her to somewhere more comfortable.'

It is at that precise moment that Vanessa makes up her mind. It is something akin to a miracle because one minute her brain is dead, the next she has decided exactly what they should do, a blindingly golden idea, more like a vision. And it is so simple! It means that everything will work out okay and in some ways it will be kinder for Mother. She will not have to endure Christmas, or wade through any more agonies with Bart. She will not have to torture herself over what to wear or worry about presenting herself at any more tormenting auditions which leave her a little uglier every time, a little more spiteful, a fraction more angry. Blaming. Blaming. Blaming the children. Blaming poor Daddy for the destruction of her talent, her looks, her mental abilities, driving her into a black depression so the magic goes out of everything.

Vanessa is only twelve. A child still, she should not have to cope with this. Isaiah said, 'Prepare a way for the Lord; clear a straight path for him.' *Okay, then I will*. Mother's mouth is clean now, and most of the make-up that stuck up her eyes is on the flannel. She looks pale and thinner than usual, as if she's been very ill. Slowly, without dripping,

Vanessa replaces the cloth in the bowl. She stands up, staring down all the while at Mother, fearful that she might wake and move before the plan can be put into practice.

'We must make her comfortable. Yes. Somewhere where she'll be quiet and not have to put up with interruptions. We can move her more easily if we wrap her up in her coat. We don't want to bump her.' Vanessa is breathless. Her words tumble over each other. She sounds hysterical.

'Where will we put her?' Camilla asks, interested.

'In Daddy's gym. It's the perfect place.'

'Brrr. It'll be cold down there in the basement.' But there is a glint of excited expectation behind Sacha's glasses.

'Not if we make up a bed. Cover her with lots of blankets.' Stubborn, knowing she is right, Vanessa refuses to yield now.

'Mother would not like that. Mother would want to be put on the sofa, or carried up to her bedroom.' Camilla looks as uneasy as she sounds. 'Daddy's gym is a spooky place. Vanessa, I think you've gone mad.'

Vanessa, defiant, doesn't care. 'In the sauna.'

Where, as children, have they all gone wrong? The mourners at this ceremony are all dry-eyed, faced with the death of love. They stare, baffled, unsure if they understand what is happening. Then Dominic licks his lips; staring down at his fingernails he says carefully, 'We could lock her in the sauna. Just until after Christmas.'

'But what about when she wakes up and sees what we've done?'

Nobody answers Camilla's question. They are all quiet, imagining the look on Mother's face, imagining her fury, the violence, the curses.

'If we kept her down there for long enough maybe we would be able to talk to her. We could explain why we'd done it. She wouldn't be able to drink. She'd be sober,' Dominic reminds them all. When he tries, Dominic can make anything he says sound reasonable. He is good at steadying nerves, Mother says. 'She'd have peace. And it's peace she always moans that she wants.'

'She would have peace, but no dignity. What about Ilse?' Camilla has crossed to the window to watch the snow. Against the dark night they can all see the flakes, drifting dreamily down past the window, cutting out sound as it sinks, closing them off from the rest of the world, from grief, wrapping the house in white blankets.

'Ilse won't know anything. Ilse is asleep and she'll be off before breakfast. She won't come back until late tomorrow night and by then everything will be all right again. Mother must not be allowed to spoil Christmas.'

'But what if Mother starts screaming?' The idea takes on a nightmare quality.

'No one will hear her down there.'

'What about when Daddy phones?'

Vanessa sneers to cover her fear. 'He won't expect to speak to Mother. We can say she's still in bed. He'll be relieved if he doesn't have to speak to Mother. He always is. He tries to avoid seeing her. Suzie doesn't like it.'

'What if Bart comes round?'

'It's Christmas Day. Bart won't come. Anyway, they argued last night. We all knew that Bart wouldn't last.' Vanessa's heart beats faster. She fights to stay cool.

Mother lies prone while they discuss her, prone and gross, still as a dead body, wearing her shaggy fur coat and one shiny black boot. Vanessa shudders, unable to help it. 'She was too damaged,' she says of Mother, throwing the first clod of earth because no one else dares. 'She should never have had any children.'

'Who said that?' Camilla asks.

'Suzie. She told Daddy. I overheard her.' There is a new hardness to her voice. A flat certainty.

'That's easy for *her* to say,' says Camilla.

'Get her ready,' Dominic says suddenly, 'while I go and find the keys.'

And so the decision is made and the first tentative actions taken. On his way out Dominic turns on the light and for the first time, the children see the position clearly. The room is still beautiful, startlingly bunched with Christmas colour; tinsel twists softly, the paper chains twinkle above the mirror, over the fire. The only ugly thing in it is Mother, lying there with her head thrown back and her wig askew and her skirt rucked over her knees. There is something terrible about her limp, jewelled fingers. Rank all over, gin and nicotine, but still, one of God's creatures.

'There is no option,' says virginal Vanessa in her white nightgown, simply, disposing of all doubt. 'There is nothing else for it. We have to do it. Let us prepare her.'

So they follow her instructions obediently.

FOUR

DEEPLY UNCONSCIOUS, yet Mother is resistant to movement; a rubber bendy doll coated in tight black lace, her arms and legs keep springing back. And she is heavy.

When Vanessa removes the chestnut wig — a smooth, silky bob that reaches Mother's shoulders, she passes it to Camilla who passes it to Sacha who gives it to Amber who drops it. Smelling of dry skin and unwashed brushes, it is warmer than Mother herself, as if all her energy has left her body and gone up to her head and onwards through her hair. Vanessa knows that Mother's false hair comes from poor people, like transplant kidneys and donated blood and starving babies.

'I keep thinking she's dead,' cries Amber. 'Perhaps we should put her wig back. She looks ... awfully rude ... without it.'

'She looks as if she's been radiated.'

Baffled, they turn to Camilla who quickly explains, 'Radiation treatment, for cancer. Perhaps Mother was secretly ill and never told us.'

'That's nonsense. If Mother had cancer everyone would know. We know when she's got a sore throat, or a headache, or aching feet. If Mother had cancer Daddy might even come back.' This is Amber's greatest hope. She lives with it night and day; she carries it around with her everywhere she goes, poking at it occasionally, treasuring it, like a baboon carries its young. She never leaves it out of her prayers and whenever she sees Daddy, she asks him. She asks him when Suzie is out of the room, she arranges herself like a kitten on his knee when she asks him, she plays with his silver watch-strap — although Vanessa has warned her often enough to leave the subject alone.

'It's a waste of time. It is difficult enough for Daddy at the moment without you adding to the pressure,' she says. 'He is not coming back, Amber. Daddy loves Suzie. And if you were Daddy, would you ever want to come back to Mother?' She remembers the flaming rows: Daddy's strained face, the broken porcelain, the food on the walls, hysterical, drunken laughter when Daddy's friends were round, the head-in-hands humiliation of Daddy's life with Mother.

His new flat is calm and peaceful. Suzie is neat and contained. Suzie has Daddy and Suzie has everything. Vanessa hopes Suzie is barren.

When Amber asks Daddy her awful questions he leans back his head and his eyelids seem huge as they drop down to shut out the pain in his eyes.

Vanessa . . . all of them secretly strain to listen. 'Oh poppet,' he says, sighing deeply. 'If only you were old enough to understand.' Daddy always makes sure his children have money when he takes them back home again. He tries to drop them off without coming in. He went so quickly, he visits so rarely, that after Mother's furious bonfire his smell soon left the house.

So Amber asked Vanessa, 'Well, why didn't he take us with him? If he loves us so much?'

'There are too many of us. And Daddy lives in a flat.'

'Only because he's a Catholic. Mother says that's his fault.'

'I don't think that any of this is Daddy's fault,' Vanessa said firmly, in a cold and unreasonable voice, an intolerable pain in her heart. 'I think, like the rest of us, he is a victim. Don't you?' Yes. Snivelling victims who don't fight back.

If they long for love none of them know it. Mother is quieter since Daddy left. She goes out a great deal more — some days they never see her — and of course, she has her little job.

When the fur coat is off they lay it flat on the floor and roll Mother so that she lies in the middle. Once, she opens her eyes wide. The children gasp, backing away from her, terror-stricken. Vanessa's heart almost bursts . . . the sound of beating fills her ears, blood pounds before her eyes, her head is about to burst open. No! No! No! She wants to suffer for Jesus' sake but not like this! Murder would be a mortal sin, making her loathsome in the sight of God. Her frightened eyes fix on the poker but she knows that she could not hit Mother with that. Could she? Would she? She never finds out, because Mother slobbers slightly, her nose twitches, then her eyes leer into her skull before drooping closed again. Wretched, faced with the danger of hell, Vanessa will do penance for her wicked thoughts afterwards.

'Phewee! I thought we'd had it.' Amber giggles, then whimpers.

'If she woke up now she wouldn't know what we were doing. We could say we were only wrapping her up so she'd keep warm.' Sacha is much more afraid.

'Perhaps we should tie up her hands.'

Camilla says no, but Vanessa gets up and makes straight for the Christmas tree. In spite of her smile she is almost crying. She kneels by the pile of presents, scanning the labels. She picks out hers for Mother. She tears off the wrapping so beautifully done, she rips off the bow, she tugs at the bright red scarf to test it for strength. Mother would not have liked it anyway. Camilla is still saying no when Vanessa carefully brings Mother's arms from her sides, across her chest, and, gritting her teeth, she binds them. She stares down at Mother intently, at Mother, at what she has done to her. The lambswool is soft, it won't hurt, even if Mother strains against it. 'We can't go back now,' she tells Camilla, softly, earnestly. 'From the moment we first decided, we knew we must not go back. Mother must be disposed of.'

'Just until Christmas is over,' says Camilla, almost pleading, but Vanessa does not answer.

'It's cold in the gym.' Dominic returns with his dressing-gown sleeves purposefully rolled up. 'I have taken the electric fan-heater down there, but we're going to need blankets. Are you ready?'

'Are you sure Ilse is asleep?' This is not a serious question because everyone knows there is no threat from that quarter.

The brown fur coat makes an efficient sledge. Dominic rolls the rug up out of the way and the children pull Mother along by her coat hem. She rides with a melancholy dignity over the wooden floors, while the children pull like a team of puffing husky dogs. The process is quiet, the only noise over the sound of their breathing is a thin sheeting sound as the fur slides softly along, and the squeak of the odd floorboard. Mother's head is propped up on a Liberty cushion. When they turn round it looks as though she is directing them, calling out orders.

In this same manner they slide her downstairs; Dominic holds her head up and the thick carpeting makes movement easy. 'Always the considerate one,' Mother says of Dominic. 'He will make some woman a wonderful husband one day.' In happier times sliding down the stairs on Mother's fur coat would have made a fantastic game. Down in the hall they are back to the wood once again. The time on the grandfather clock says half-past two, and yet Vanessa feels no time passing on this, the morning of the Holy Child's birth. They slide Mother towards the basement door which Dominic has already unlocked. It stands open, inviting them in. Mother does not groan, or stir. Mother is well out for the count. 'She must have drunk one helluva lot,' says Dominic. And then he adds, 'Bitch!' The curse, so placidly spoken, coming from someone usually so mild, is startling.

The cold streams up, its frosty breath disturbing the fussy paper bell they have pinned high up on the hall light. The cold and the stark of the atmosphere are beamed up from the basement together on shafts of fluorescent lighting. Vanessa is glad it is cold down there, for cold is clean, but her own face feels wickedly hot.

This just has to be done. When this is all over, Vanessa will go to her room and sing a solemn Te Deum in thanks. But God must stay with her now, just for a little while longer. Manhandling Mother down the spiral iron staircase which drops so steeply to the basement is a different matter entirely. Now they have to work hard, half-dragging, half-carrying their load, making sure the coat does not slip through the gaping, tapering, tinny steps. They have to force her to bend. Her skin is cold and clammy like clay. Vanessa's eyes fasten on Mother's face, but it keeps that same sozzled look, slack, unaware, as if the mind has temporarily abandoned the body. Perhaps Mother's soul is already in purgatory. As a good Christian Vanessa ought to be praying for her, not hiding her away. She feels dizzy, sickened with guilt. She has to hang back, she stops helping for a while. Somehow, eventually, with as much effort of will as of body, the five of them manage it.

Mother slides down the final three steps with her arms crossed over her chest, like a corpse on its final journey for consummation in the crematorium fire.

Even when it was in full use, this room never felt other than empty. It is a machine room, silently waiting for legs and arms to pump it alive, waiting for the grease of human sweat to oil it. The walls down here are of brick, painted white, with a floor of dull red lino. The central-heating boiler is kept down here; it gives out a constant, low rumble but no warmth. Massive old pipes lead off it; heavily lagged, they take a turn round the room before they snake up the wall by the door and disappear through the ceiling where the flakes of plaster are loose. A smell of wet animal comes from the leather vaulting horse, the small trampoline, stacked neatly beside the back wall, is dappled with patches of what looks like damp; there are prickings of black on its thin metal parts where it has corroded. Fitted out by rails of silver and chrome which glint with splinters of light, the area is sterile, serviceable as the inside of a fridge. If Vanessa has expected to find something of Daddy left down here she is disappointed. There is not even a twinge of his familiar old B O.

'It's echoey down here. It looks as if the snow has covered the windows.' Camilla checks the door to the street and tries to peer out of the glass beside it. It is locked and bolted, the hinges rusty from lack of use.

'Daddy had them painted over, don't you remember, so nosy neighbours couldn't stare in to watch him. And the bars were always there. I suppose, years ago, they kept food down here. Come on. Let's hurry.' Vanessa's heart still pumps but everyone else seems remarkably calm.

Mother slides easily over the lino, casting a looming shadow on the walls. They make for the largest, most colourful thing in the room. The sauna is of Swedish pine, pleasingly constructed like a Scandinavian log cabin. The stripped wood is a pale-ish beige, Mother's most hated colour. It stands hard against the furthest wall, right in the centre, like a little house that a child might draw, with the rest of the gym like a frosty garden of ropes and coils spread out around it. The vaulting horse, thinks Vanessa, might be a grazing cow, head down, beside a railing fence. The sauna has its own light inside, a bare 40-watt bulb which Dominic has already switched on so it looks almost inviting, nearly cosy. 'I thought she'd want a light on,' he tells them casually, 'for when she wakes up. I'll turn the electric fire off now and we'll turn the sauna heat on when we leave, just a gentle sixty-five degrees.'

Dominic is beautiful. His black hair curls at his neck, his skin is the shade of a creamy coffee liqueur so that when he smiles his teeth look an almost translucent white, mother of pearl. Sometimes he needs his puffer, but not tonight. His asthma gets worse when he concentrates on it and he hasn't had the time, he's had far too much on his mind. The pride in his voice makes it sound as if he wants approval for completing a Lego windmill, or mending his remote-controlled Ferrari without Daddy's help.

Dominic has moved the padlock from the basement door, and hitched it round the double handles of the sauna. When the metal is snapped together there is no way that stout wooden door will budge.

They heave Mother up so she lies neatly along the slatted wooden bench. Amber is shaking all over with exertion and excitement. Dominic approaches Mother; he stares at her carefully before untying the scarf from her wrists. Sacha and Amber bring down the blankets they've been sent to fetch from the airing cupboard, so Mother is fine ... if she finds it chilly she has not only her fur coat, but fleecy pink blankets to snuggle in. Because of their concern it does not feel as if they are doing anything so dreadfully wrong. While they take care of their charge, surely God will forgive them? But Vanessa knows. Is it only she who is aware of the enormity of what they are doing?

Before they leave her they make sure the bucket on the floor is filled with fresh water from Daddy's shower; they use the shower tap. She will be able to drink from the wooden ladle. She will not need anything to eat.

'What if she wants to pee ... or something.'

'I haven't the faintest idea,' Vanessa says coldly.

'She'll have to lift up the grating and do it in the drain. She can sluice it away if she uses some of her water.' Dominic has had time to work it out. Vanessa gives him a grateful look, for in all the horror of the last terrible hour these thoughts have not crossed her mind. All she wants, her frantic desire, is to get Mother out of the way.

'That means she will have to squat down in the middle of the floor.'

'We can't do anything about that,' Vanessa snaps at Amber. 'Unless you want to go into the attic and find your old plastic potty.'

'I was only asking! Can't I even ask?'

'We can push her food through the hole where the pipes travel through.' Even Camilla is with them, concentrating on the practicalities now. 'That hole is big enough for a plate.' But nobody enjoys the thought of this. The silence comes; it tightens. When they push a plate through the sawn hole, it looks like a cartoon mouse-hole, Mother will be wide awake ... But they've come this far. There is no turning back. They have to go on.

It is Dominic who turns the key in the padlock. He gives it to Vanessa who passes it to Camilla who gives it to Amber. The key moves quickly, with a life of its own, like Mother's warm and tingling wig. Sacha takes it out of Amber's hand. She starts back up the twisting staircase, fluffy as a snowman in her sleepsuit and slippers. In her chirpy, high-pitched voice she says, 'I'll hang it on the hook in the kitchen, beside the key for the garden shed. Mrs Guerney can look after Mother now. And then why don't we all have some cocoa?'

What? Does Sacha think Mrs Guerney's going to come and scrub this away as if it's a mess they have made with their paints? Does Sacha believe she's going to come with her dirty great floorcloth and turn all these colours of fear into a watery grey before disappearing them all together — with her Flash? Vanessa turns crimson. She takes her horrified gaze to Camilla who hesitates beside her at the foot of the steps. Filled with a fearful dread, she wonders how they are going to get through this. Her tired eyes sting, they feel as if they've been filled with sand. Her will almost collapses as she realises — they must have imagined they'd been playing some game! The twins — Sacha and Amber — like the men who crucified Jesus, oh God they do not even realise what they have done.

They will have to be told. The twins will have to be bribed to keep their mouths shut.

Wearily she climbs the spiral steps to the hall and closes the basement door behind her. Heavy and solid, she thinks of a headstone. Angry now, for the relief she had hoped for has not materialised, she would like to scrawl on the door with a squeaky chalk, 'Grant her Thy peace'. She wishes she'd been able to bury Mother absolutely.

FIVE

WHILE ROBIN TOWNSEND'S five young children are sleeping the sleep of the just, two good wives come down to their kitchens in order to put their turkeys in.

Down in their South Kensington mews, Suzie and Robin are trying for a baby ... well, obviously not at this actual moment in time, but a great deal of their energies are directed towards this objective which is understandable because they have only been together for eighteen months so the bedroom is not just somewhere they go to sleep and change and dry their hair. Naturally not.

Does Suzie believe she can redirect Robin's affections once he has a new child, by her? Does she think a baby will take away some of his guilt? She sat and stared at the sky last night and thought that the biggest star shone directly over her roof ... a sign, perhaps?

Suzie Townsend's turkey is a twenty-four pounder because, although there will only be six for dinner, she only has turkey once a year to keep it special, and she likes to eat it cold. She also enjoys cooking home-made soups and curries. She enters the pine-shuttered, plant-strewn kitchen with its walls of exposed red brick in her negligée, tying the tapes of a frilly waist-pinafore round a middle which is nicely proportioned. Barefooted, her toenails are painted a pretty pale coral.

She turns the radio on in order to get the carols. She pulls up the blinds. How wonderful – it is snowing! She cannot remember how long it is since she's seen snow on Christmas Day ... the last time she'd been skiing, surely?

Maybe the roads will be too dangerous for travel.

Robin's parents, and her own mother, Eileen, are arriving at lunch-time today. Because of the Townsends, no matter how much they have to drink, the whole thing will be terribly formal. Suzie, of course, as the hostess, will take the strain. Never mind. She laid the dining-room table last night, after their return from the opera, and it looks superbly festive in a muted, tasteful way ... mostly tartan. That is one blessing, she considers, as she struggles manfully with the huge bird, remembering Delia Smith's instructions to make a tall parcel of the foil. Starting again means you can choose the most up-to-date decorations from Harrods; you do not have to drag all the old tatters along for sentiment's sake.

Yes, she has laid the table and the various stuffings are in their dishes under foil in the fridge, as is the bread sauce, the cold consommé and the brandy butter. Suzie does not stuff her turkey. She dislikes inserting her hand. As she waits for her split-level cooker to warm she returns to the old problem, the one she spent so many wakeful hours trying to tackle last night, pondering deeply into her pillows.

Robin's kids. Hell. She had a dreadful struggle to get him to take the presents over to Camberley Road last week. 'Just in case we don't get around to it ...'

'What do you mean? I thought we'd decided.' He looked suddenly crestfallen, like a child. His serious face puckered up like a baby's.

Suzie hastened to say, 'I know, Robin, I know, but the best-laid plans have been known to go wrong and how awful if something happened which meant that you couldn't fetch them here after all. Imagine! If they thought you had forgotten them! Go on, deliver the presents, just in case.'

'The tragedy is that everything has to be caged in this sort of ridiculous secrecy.'

'Well, if you'd asked to have them on Christmas Day, Caroline would have refused – everyone knows that. I mean ... "how cruel, to deprive me of my family ... you have taken everything from me and now it's the children on the most sensitive day of the year". I can actually hear her saying it! But if you call round unexpectedly she'll probably be out, or in bed, an entirely different situation.'

'Yes, but I could have delivered the presents in person. You don't understand, Suzie, the whole joy of giving is to watch the children open them. I missed that last year and I am just sorry, that's all, just very, very sorry to be missing out once again. I am extremely uneasy about the whole situation. Ilse won't be there and neither will Mrs Guerney. We should have kept the presents here as I originally intended.'

Suzie thought, *They will open the stable door and go and play in the garden. They will trail mud into the flat. They will knock the pot plants over. And if I attempt to quieten them down they will pester Robin until he plays the old videos. We will sit and watch old videos all through Christmas afternoon.*

Suzie edits gardening books. She is a specialist on orchids. She is at her happiest when fiddling in the greenhouse, or out in her borders cutting and pruning.

She said, 'I still think you have done the right thing by taking them round. You worried yourself silly last year but it all turned out fine. Caroline is an actress, and when she hasn't got anyone to perform to she manages to behave perfectly well. She has taken you in for too long ... you and everyone else. She'll probably be absolutely contented cuddled up under the mistletoe with her latest man.'

God, if it wasn't Christmas it was something else. And the flat, though larger than most people's houses, is hardly the size happily to accommodate five excited children, the stodgy Townsends and Suzie's own homely old mother, hot and disgruntled after gorging themselves silly. Halfway through the ghastly performance Robin will probably crack and disappear off to his study, leaving her to cope with the mess.

Suzie has promised to do a special, child-orientated tea with paper hats and crackers, something light, just a fun meal really which can be eaten at any time of the day though she prays she will not need it. She had battled through overcrowded shops, staggered home over people-heavy pavements to fetch it. Most of it is in boxes – packages of stuff from Marks. She looks out of the window again with a wry smile she uses often, familiar to her face. Suzie is small, unlike Caroline the model, everything about her is small, even her well-controlled, silky voice. She is pretty and lithe as a cat with fascinating green eyes that slant provocatively when she smiles. Perhaps it will snow harder. Maybe it will continue to fall, thickly like this, all day, and stick. Contrary to what Robin imagines, Suzie understands his need to see his children, she just wishes things were different so he could go round to Camberley

Road and be with them there because surely, from their own point of view, the children would prefer to be in their own home on Christmas Day.

Coldly polite, Vanessa, Camilla and Dominic do not approve of Suzie. They make their attitudes quite clear when Robin's back is turned. The twins, Amber and Sacha, are too young, thank God, to play those jealous games. No, Suzie is determined to do everything she can to prevent the threatened visit of her new husband's children. It is guilt that drives him, poor Robin, yet of any man she knows in the world, he has the least to feel guilty about. Awesome in his remorse and self-recrimination, yet surely a phone call will reassure him? A well-timed phone call will relieve his suffering.

So would a new baby.

Gracefully as in all things, and quickly, Suzie removes the toast from the toaster and slots it in the toast rack. She unplugs the percolator and sets it on the tray beside the milk jug. She crinkles her catty eyes as she prepares the grapefruits. All these loving little services are quite new to Robin. Caroline had never, ever, brought him breakfast in bed ... and when Suzie first moved in with Robin he had tried to behave in the same way with her, from habit, as if she had to be consoled before he approached her ... babied, wrapped up in cotton wool in case she would break into sharp pieces and cut him. It was pathetic. The whole sorry story of Robin's marriage is pathetic, although friends confide that Caroline had not started out like that. 'Well, think about it,' said one. 'Why the hell would he have married her if she'd been that bad? Things happen to people, Suzie, they change.'

From the heights of her superior knowledge Suzie smiles briskly. For a while, when Robin first left Caroline, Suzie had been forced to pretend that she did not even exist, and her protestations, 'But Robin, this is all perfectly ridiculous,' fell on deaf ears. 'Just for a while, Suzie, for me, please!' He begged her so pitifully that she was embarrassed, glad to comply for his sake. For the first time she saw another side to her lover, for this was not the man who clicked his fingers at waiters, who appeared so suavely and intelligently, the presenter of *Update*, who dealt with dictators and foreign ambassadors with such wit and cynical charm, deferred to in all things during the Gulf War.

Caroline loomed large in those days, not so far off, only the year before last. Such pathetic, childish behaviour! Such a silly woman! She turned up at the BBC and contrived to cause the most scandalous scenes until the doormen were instructed to alert the security department whenever she was spotted anywhere in the vicinity. It was ghastly. Robin's terror was contagious, and Suzie, normally such a philosophical person, caught herself creeping around, afraid to pick up the morning post after the first banger went off, nervous of taking Robin's car after Caroline penetrated the cavernous vaults of the underground car park where he normally left it. Mercifully, knowing nothing about cars, she ripped out anything from under the bonnet that could be moved. At least he had not driven off in it because of course it had failed to start. He might have killed himself.

And the money she'd spent on that private detective – Robin's money! Robin's money flows like water through Caroline's hands.

Christ! What was all that about?

And all this was before Caroline realised that Robin had left her for another woman!

The Christmas bells are ringing. The snow is softly falling. Poor Robin. Those poor little kids, what chance have they ever stood with a mother like that? Hopefully they were too young to realise, kept in the dark during those early days.

Caroline is quite without shame. Suzie, stretching to reach the grapefruit dishes, supposes there must be a funny side somewhere. One day, perhaps, they will look back and laugh. There was one incident, when fascinated viewers watched open-mouthed as the camera zoomed close in to Alan Bean, with his mike and his herringbone coat, and a wild-looking woman chained herself to the railings behind him while he was giving his live report. Robin, back at the studio with his list of relevant questions, recognised Caroline immediately, you could see he did. His expression did not flicker but he did a half-twirl in his chair when Alan Bean, unable to ignore the disturbance any longer, remarked, 'Here is a lady who is clearly violently opposed to the Prime Minister's visit to China. Perhaps we should ...'

Apart from the country's lip-readers, it was impossible for anyone else to catch the obscenities that Caroline was shouting. *'Look what he's done! Look what he's fucking well done! Look what he's done to me!'*

How ridiculous! No one can do that to anyone else!

'No, no,' said Robin calmly, straight-faced in front of twelve million viewers. 'Just speak your piece, Alan, just carry on.'

But two deaf viewers wrote in to the programme, demanding to be told who Caroline referred to, and why. You always get your insensitive cranks. Quite rightly Robin instructed his lackeys to ignore them.

Suzie gives a little barking laugh. There is absolutely nothing anyone can do but wait for time to do its healing. Caroline is massive, terrifying, still beautiful in a brutal sort of way, and seemingly inescapable. There was a period when Suzie feared Robin might take to drink to survive. The large attic space in the Kensington flat remains empty, waiting for Robin's beloved gym. Suzie does not question his need although she could do with a study of her own. Nearly forty, keeping fit is important to Robin – he is absurdly pleased with himself for completing last year's London Marathon. Every weekday morning he goes jogging and three times a week he plays squash. On a Sunday he brings her breakfast in bed and then goes off to church. When the time comes, when Robin finally decides that the time is right to send for his precious equipment, so cruelly denied him, Suzie believes the worst of the trauma will all be over, they can all start behaving sanely again. Suzie gives a hopeful smile. He will probably send for it this year. Caroline has gone quiet recently and the children appear more cheerful, almost normal. Suzie tells herself she must be more relaxed; it is Christmas, she should be more charitable.

But thank God Caroline is promiscuous. Thank God for all those other men. Dreadful though her behaviour undoubtedly is, and no kind of example to her children, while Caroline is otherwise occupied Caroline is calmer. With a bit of luck one of them might take her on, relieving Robin of his burden for ever. But then again – Suzie receives a sharp image of Caroline's face in torment, suffering so, she sighs – maybe not.

Suzie Townsend fiddles anxiously with the piece of holly she has arranged on the breakfast tray. The whole effect is crisp, clean and healthy. The blood-red berry of the holly detracts from the freshness of the greens and whites and yellows she has made. 'Oh the holly bears a berry,' she hums smugly to herself as she removes the distasteful sprig between finger and thumb. 'Happy Christmas, you old sleepyhead,' she calls as she pads eagerly up the stairs and towards the bedroom. She smiles her sexiest smile. There are ways and means of persuading Robin to miss Mass this morning and, a powerful woman in spite of her size, a firm Unbeliever, she fully intends to use them.

SIX

THE ATMOSPHERE is quite different over in Potters Bar.

In the kitchen of a heavily mortgaged terraced house painted a wild canary yellow, Ruby Dance steps over paper, unopened parcels, children, nappies and feeding bottles in an effort to reach her bird and stuff it.

Ruby has been up since six-thirty, dealing with over-excited toddlers, trying to keep them quiet, bundling up the piles of paper so there is somewhere to walk in safety. Earlier, passing through the hall, she heard the distinctive *ping* of the bedroom extension but she walked on, determined, yet again, to ignore it. There is far too much to do in her life than allow her imagination to play the kind of tricks that her present mental state will not tolerate.

She is catering for Bart and her four small children. Her sister Elspeth and her boyfriend makes eight, and Bart's parents and strange brother, Lot, out from his hostel for the celebration, makes eleven. An odd number, difficult to accommodate at the oblong dining-room table. Where has she put the Christmas cloth? Is it out of the ironing basket yet, or still lying there crisply, abandoned at the bottom since last year?

'Count your blessings,' she yells savagely at herself, into the mayhem, 'and you'll bash your skull in, Naomi, if you try to balance like that.'

She will put Damian's high chair at the end of the table so she can roam more freely to the kitchen and back and, at the same time, deal with her thirteen-month-old baby. She, like one of the foolish virgins, has not done her preparations previously; she has ignored Delia Smith's countdown and now look ... chaos! Phew! She blows up her scattered

38

fringe of hair – it is like a panful of burnt scrambled eggs which have spilt all over her head – she sits down in the mess with her first cup of coffee of the morning and lights up her fifth cigarette.

She digs the traces of sage and onion from under her fingernails with a cocktail stick. Bart had flopped into bed beside her last night. Ruby had only just settled Damian and she was slipping, relieved, into her own dreams when the cold of the flapping duvet disturbed her, and the click of the bedside light.

'You're surely not going to read,' she groaned. 'Not at this hour. It's terribly late.'

'You know I can't get to sleep unless I read first.'

'That's crap. You should come to bed earlier, then.' Already she was worrying about the ham.

'I couldn't get away. There was a party at the Club.'

'A party at a health club? Huh! You'll get yourself talked about. What did they give you to drink? Kiss me properly, Bart.'

But his kiss was so hard and dry his teeth scraped against hers. The bed creaked, putting her in mind of a frozen lake. 'Wine,' he said. 'There is nothing wrong with the odd glass of wine. And I did phone you.' His hand slithered down her thighs but she pushed him off, exhausted.

Yes, he phoned her, and she had sat down on the floor and wept, feebly and forlornly, because he had promised to be home to help her. She finished the last of the parcels with tears dripping off the end of her nose which she had to lick off with her tongue because both hands were busy holding down uneven edges and manipulating the Sellotape. But it was understandable, she told herself. He worked so hard he needed his leisure time with his friends, and the Club was a useful place to meet clients and that is important, *it really is*. Being home, these days, is hardly relaxing. Everywhere you look there are demands – to clean, to console, to mend, to wipe, to pick up, to cuddle. Everything is slightly easier now that Naomi goes to school, but Ruby still has three at home, and she has to struggle over three main roads with prams and reins each afternoon to fetch her.

'It can't get worse,' Bart often assures her. 'Chin up, old thing. At least we stand a good chance now, of getting through the eye of a needle. When things get better we'll move, maybe to the country. You can lie on the grass and sunbathe all day. What do women think about when they sunbathe?'

'What do men think about when they are driving? But for now get your hand out from under my skirt.' But Ruby can't see how a change of scenery would help her. It is time she needs, and a serenity which seems to have abandoned her.

Good Heavens, she can't complain. If they had been invited out, if there'd been a party, then Bart would have taken her, they would have found a babysitter. Somehow Ruby would have made an effort to make herself presentable, dug out her old black dress. If only they had not bought that expensive car ... She knows that image is all important, but things were looking up at the time they had made the commitment. Now, only months later, poor Bart is gripping on to his agency with white knuckles and broken fingernails. He's already been forced to make two of his best designers redundant.

They are going home to Esher for the New Year. Ruby has made up her mind to ask her father for help. She knows he will give it because she is his favourite daughter. Mummy will say, 'I told you so!' but there, the Dances are in no position to pander to pride. A child screams – not seriously. Ruby jerks, a puppet in a cherry-red dressing gown, she sees the mess on the floor and automatically reaches for the cloth.

When the phone rings, Ruby curses. What now? It is impolitely early. She moves a tricycle in an effort to reach the hall, with a mutinous child still clinging to the handlebars.

'Hello?' The chair beckons invitingly because it has nothing on it. She crosses her legs and the dressing-gown flap falls back, revealing them, shockingly unshaven.

'Is that Mrs Dance?'

'Yes it is.' Once again she puffs at her overgrown fringe, surveying her violent surroundings.

There is a short silence, during which Ruby's eyes take on their darting anxiety again. Where is Damian? Oh no, not upstairs. She wants to call Bart to get him to keep an eye, she has forgotten to put the damn gate up.

'Yes,' she says again with impatience. Hurry up, she wants to add.

'I have something very important to tell you.'

What a very strange way of speaking. Canvassers could not possibly be working on Christmas Day, could they? Ruby frowns, covering her legs again. She ought to have shaved for Christmas. She waits. She does not know the owner of this voice.

'Mrs Dance, I am afraid that your husband is having an affair with a divorced actress in Highgate. It has been going on since October. I thought that you ought to know.'

Ruby tenses. Her body thunders with fear. 'Who the hell is that?'

'I am a friend. But who I am does not really matter.'

'But it's Christmas Day!' cries Ruby, shrinking.

She clutches the receiver long after the caller hangs up. By the time she realises what she is doing she is cradling it like a baby.

She knows, of course she does. She has chosen to pretend – but now that option is closed to her. She knows that this was not just an abusive telephone call, she knows that the stranger spoke the truth. She looks around, bewildered, at the turmoil that is her house, startled into extreme sensation. Before she became a mother she had imagined none of this ... Christmas Day should be happy ... she wanted to enjoy the children at these most precious times.

'Bastard. Bastard,' she mutters under her breath.

'Mummy! Mummeeee ...'

'Wait a minute. I'll be there in a minute.'

'But James has climbed on your chair and now he is crawling across the kitchen table!'

'All right, Naomi, I'll be there in a minute. It's okay. It's okay. I just have to go upstairs for a moment.'

To the sound of a bloody battle from her kitchen, Ruby climbs her balloon-strewn stairs, tucking her pale hair behind her ears, determined to be able to see her way quite clearly. She pushes open the door to her bedroom. Bart is sitting up in bed, wide awake, watching some mindless cartoon on his miniature T V. She stands in the doorway and stares at him hard ... handsome, even at this worst hour of the day, but debauched, slightly paunchy round the jowls, eyes sinking greedily into his head as the pursuit of money possesses him. A pig. Betraying her, even while he grunts on top of her, imagining the other woman, the actress in Highgate, my God!

'Get out of bed,' says Ruby, terribly calmly.

'Sorry?' Bart's guilty eyes widen and he seems to crouch deeper into the covers.

'Look, I'm not at all sure that I can bear this so I'm not going to stand here repeating myself.' She clenches her fists, and finds she is holding a tinfoil star. Lost and sickened, Christmas is only a wilderness of trash. Once, she had picked up a snowball and found it to be a frozen blackbird. 'I am unreal, Bart. I am unreal and this house is unreal and you are unreal. Get yourself out of that bed and go and find Damian. Then there's the spuds to be peeled and the table to lay. When you've done that you can get on the floor and start playing with your blasted children! Do you hear me, Bart? Have you understood?' Ruby's tired voice rises to a scream.

'Whatever's the matter?' But he leaps out of bed. He must know!

'I have just dealt with the most extraordinary phone call. The woman on the other end told me ... that's what has happened, that's all. I know everything, Bart. The only thing I don't have is her name and I think I can live without knowing that.'

'I don't know ...' he tries to protest, stupidly fiddling with the tie of his scarlet silk pyjamas. She cannot watch. She cannot bear to take her eyes to anywhere below his waist. His face is painful enough. Ridiculous.

She cuts him off crisply. 'If you speak one word in your own defence then I'm going, and you can go to her. I am taking the children, the car, and I'm going home. It is up to you, Bart. From now on it is entirely up to you.' Without Ruby's father's help Bart's firm will collapse and he knows it. Ruby shrugs. 'You see, I am much too tired to play any more of your games. If you want to telephone the cow and explain then carry on. But I give you ten minutes, that's all, and if you're not downstairs, dressed and ready by then, I am leaving this house. You won't sell it. Not now. You'll be bankrupt in two months.'

She leaves him alone; she listens hard but he does not pick up the extension.

She pushes the crushed tinfoil star down the waste disposal. Ruby stands at her sink and stares blindly at every sprout she handles. The cuts she makes are deep and precise. She handles the knife with relish. She is weeping softly from pain and frustration and one of her nails has broken. Wronged, wronged, horribly wronged in so many ways. She keeps her back to Bart when he comes down and sidles sadly to the drainer beside her.

'It was over anyway,' he tells her sincerely. 'I don't even know why it happened. I can't explain.'

Suspicious of gifts, any gifts, slowly, Ruby turns round, not looking at him. Expressionless as she surveys the mess about her she says, 'I know why. I know very well why. But I didn't ... and I could have. Many many times I could have. Bloody hell, only last week I could have screwed the Bendix man. Well, don't just stand there. For God's sake open the sherry.' And then she says quietly, 'You bastard, you know it is going to take years. Was it so wonderful? Was it worth it?'

'No,' says Bart. 'She was a bitch.'

At 14, Camberley Road Vanessa and Camilla are still laughing. 'You did it so well! I wish we had someone else to phone, I want to hear you do it again.'

'Well, that's sorted Bart out. He won't be phoning again this morning – or ever!'

'But what did she sound like when you told her? Did she shout? I wish I could have heard.'

Vanessa thinks hard. Her telephone hand is still sweating. 'She sounded just like anyone else. She was quite calm. Not hysterical. She sounded as if she already knew,' says Vanessa. 'It was quite disappointing in a way.'

'She can't have cared, then.' Camilla is surprised. She fingers Mother's address book.

'Oh no,' says Vanessa. 'We are all right. I am sure that she cared very much.'

SEVEN

'OF COURSE you realise that we will have to go down soon.'

'Why do we have to?'

'If we want to keep Mother alive we will have to go down. She will need feeding.'

This — all this — everything they are doing ... they are merely beating time. Hardly aware of what is happening, as if some vast net has been thrown over them and dragged them along, they have stepped over some boundary and Mother might be snarling down there in the basement by now. Vanessa is frightened and fascinated by the very idea.

Last night Vanessa listened to the soft sift of snow against her window and tried to remember only loveliness. She tried not to hear the wind which bore the howls of the wolves in the park, like a living thing, breathing unceasingly, with a breath as cold and frightening as death.

Throughout all the giddy excitement of the morning — Camilla helped Vanessa to distribute the pillowcases, Dom and the twins went to sleep extraordinarily quickly after the gruelling events of the early hours — there wasn't a moment when Vanessa was not conscious of the time they would have to open that basement door and descend to the gym. It was the thought of *speaking* to Mother which slayed her: not so much what Mother would say, but what she would say to Mother.

Vanessa and Camilla did not get to bed until after three. The younger children dragged their pillowcases into Vanessa's room at seven-thirty on the dot, 'Although we've been awake for hours.' She imagined Mother's livid face, rammed against the round porthole window, flattened by the pressure, puce with anger – the window which is not made of glass which would steam up in the damp heat when the sauna is in use, but designed out of a cloudy kind of reinforced plastic. The window is at the top of the door, just the right height for Mother's face.

This morning Vanessa's hair is pinned into a simple knot on the top of her head, pulled back starkly from her face. She refuses to use Mother's toggles and ribbons. She wears a bottle-green velvet dress from Laura Ashley, the one with the nun-like collar, and the starched white sleeves grip her wrists. Mother says it is too long; she says that it throws her head and legs out of all proportion. 'You're all body in that,' says Mother. 'Especially with those black tights underneath it. You look like a praying mantis.'

Is Mother awake yet?

How important it is, now, that they should love one another.

Bart's unexpected, early-morning phone call frightened them.

They meet Ilse in the kitchen. She is squeezing fresh oranges into her glass; already with her coat on she is planning an early start. 'Did Mrs Townsend approve of your beautiful work? I did not hear her come home. She must have been very late.'

'Mother loved it.' Vanessa frowns a warning at the twins. At the lie Sacha squirms against her, trying to bury her head in her dress but Amber doesn't seem to notice. There's been no opportunity to prime them yet. She tries not to sound anxious when she asks, 'Will you be able to reach your friends' house with all the snow?'

'They are picking me up on the corner. I will probably have to wait hours because of the snow. I will just have to hope they can run me back safely by tomorrow night.'

'I am sure Mother won't mind if you don't make it.'

Dominic is being far too reckless but Ilse doesn't appear to notice. 'I can only do my best,' she says. 'I suppose Mrs Townsend is still asleep.'

'Why, did you want her?'

'Just to let her know I vas leaving, that's all.'

Amber bongs about the kitchen on her new pogo stick. Over-excited, it is difficult to tell if she even remembers the capture of Mother. 'You've got a present, Ilse,' she jabbers, face flushed, hair tangled. Already she looks like a motherless child. 'And it's waiting for you under the tree!' There are chocolate stains dribbled all the way down the front of Amber's sleepsuit.

Oh no! Oh no! Ilse was on the point of leaving but now she hesitates, and they've forgotten to straighten the Christmas tree. Pieces of tinsel are still hanging off it.

'Camilla, why don't you go upstairs and fetch Ilse's present down for her?'

Ilse likes the flashing earrings. She even takes time to put them on. 'I want them,' Sacha says, climbing on a chair in order to finger them rudely. Ilse gave the children their presents last week because they were partly Christmas cards ... Boots tokens ... yuk. 'Tell Mrs Townsend that I am most grateful and vill thank her ven I return.' Mother would never have chosen such a gift. She would have called the earrings common, pandering to the lowest taste.

Ilse zips up her anorak, she draws the strings of the hood and ties them. Everyone calls 'Happy Christmas,' and they wave and smile as, in the distance, her colours turn dark in the snow. When they close the door it feels as if some vital link from the past has been severed and gone stamping off into a pristine, untrodden future.

What is Mother doing now? Is she awake, down there in the gym? Vanessa listens hard for any signs of disturbance from Mother because the basement steps lead into the drop directly to the left of the front door.

It is after Ilse's departure that they carry out their plan and telephone Bart's wife. Vanessa makes the younger ones leave the room, 'because I've got to be serious and you'll only muck about and start laughing.'

'But what are you going to say? What are you going to say?'

'I don't know yet, Dom, I haven't decided. You could make yourself useful by fetching some wood. We ought to have a fire.'

Vanessa still has not decided when she picks up the telephone, but when she starts it comes easily. After all, the message is a simple one. Bart's number is in the front of Mother's address book. Above his are several other names, angrily scribbled out.

'Don't let's put the television on. Let's have it quiet – would anyone mind?' The flames leap in the grate ... it is just like a Christmas card. So they struggle to reset the tree in its bucket, replace the torn-off tinsel and sit round in a circle to open the parcels from Daddy and the Grannies. Sacha, cross-legged, sits with a drink on the carpet beside her, something that is never normally allowed.

'It's so strange. You would not guess that Mother was anywhere in the house.' Camilla brings up the subject shyly. 'Even when she's upstairs in her bedroom there's an atmosphere. You're always waiting for her to come down, you're always listening for her, but this morning I can't feel it.'

Vanessa has not spoken of her secret hope, not to anyone, but this year she's dreamed that Daddy might arrange to have them with him on Christmas Day. After all, he and Suzie are 'settled in' now — that was one of his old excuses. 'We haven't got enough plates,' he used to say, laughing. 'For all you lot!'

So her heart sank when she discovered the parcels he had delivered on the last day of school. He must have called late because otherwise Mrs Guerney would have moved them. They were stacked in the hall, where he must have left them. Mother must have let him in and told him to leave them there. 'Your father called with his usual expensive love-bribes,' was all Mother said scathingly when Vanessa asked, her sticky scarlet lipstick adding malice to her words. 'You'd better take them upstairs and put them somewhere safe until Christmas Day.'

They were in four bulky Hamley's carrier bags, and Vanessa didn't look any further. It wasn't until she'd placed them round the bottom of the tree last night that she'd noticed the one with the bow, the one for Mother. Now, as they opened Daddy's presents, she wonders if anyone else has been hoping for the same thing ... that Daddy will come like a knight in white armour and whisk them away. He could help them to build a snowman. Vanessa wonders in secret because of course the question is much too painful to ask.

In a similar way she finds Daddy's presents almost too painful to open. The suspicion lurks in Vanessa's mind (she hates herself for it) but has he bought them, or has he sent Suzie? Daddy loathes shopping. And even worse than that, if he has sent Suzie, would Vanessa know? This is a complicated matter because she will shun any present bought by Suzie but she will adore anything chosen by Daddy. She is old enough to know how ridiculous these feelings are, but not mature enough to dismiss them.

'Wow! Brill! Nintendo!' Dominic falls back, triumphant, with the wrapping paper balanced on his head.

But how will Dominic cope with his new computer game without

Daddy to help set it up? Last year he spent hours battling with his camera instructions himself, and by New Year's Day he'd been sobbing with frustration. Perhaps Daddy isn't coming to fetch them, maybe he is planning a visit instead. And from Isobel and Joe – Granny and Grandpa Townsend – he opens a child's carpentry set from Galts, quite inappropriate. Dominic has used adult's tools since he has been able to hold them. Vanessa imagines Mother's response if she'd been with them; 'How absurd. Quite loopy.'

Daddy has chosen – or is it Suzie? – a puppet theatre for Sacha and a doll's house for Amber. Both the theatre and the doll's house are full of packages of props, furniture and little people. You can tell they are delighted because the twins just flush, clasping and unclasping their hands; neither of them says anything at all but Sacha manages to knock her drink over. Nobody takes the slightest notice as the blackcurrant stain moves quick as mercury across the thick Chinese carpet.

What is Mother doing now? Malicious? Or insane?

Vanessa puts her own presents down, suffused with sorrow and shame because, what if she doesn't like them? How hurt Daddy would be. 'I think I ought to put the turkey in the oven. You can open mine for me while I'm gone.' She cannot bear to be the focus of everyone's attention. She feels hemmed in, weighed down with responsibility, not just for the children, now, but for Mother as well. For a while she stands motionless in the middle of the kitchen floor. Deliberately she inhales and exhales with deep breaths until the pain and anger in her chest is eased, then she goes to the sink and holds a wet dishcloth against her face. But she need not worry because while she is heaving the frozen bird into the roasting pan, holding back tears from a source she cannot identify ... anger, remorse, sadness ... Camilla comes into the kitchen, saying, 'Close your eyes while I put the box into your hands. Close them, go on, then open them. Like they do on films.'

Vanessa pretends not to hear her.

'It's all right, it's all right. You will like them, I swear. And Suzie would never have chosen these.'

She has to trust her sister although she is only ten. The jewel box is tiny. There is cotton wool on top of whatever is waiting for her inside. Something exquisite ... must be! Vanessa lifts it cautiously, looks, and raises her shining eyes to Camilla's.

'It is covered with real diamonds. They must be real,' assures Camilla, 'or Daddy would not have bought it.' The glittering crucifix sparkles in the lights. It is attached to a silver chain, and the other present from Daddy which Camilla has also thought to bring down is a white leather Bible. But Vanessa is not ready to give her feelings away. So special! So special! This is something very close that she and Daddy share, faith and devotion ... but it's so grown up! She pretends to Camilla as hard as she can but it is the *wrong present!* She is not a nun, she's a little child! Why does he go on, buying her off, trying to give her away to God? What will he give her next year — a couple of candlesticks? Knowing that there is no nobility in her she turns back to the turkey and asks Camilla, 'What did you get?'

'Come and see! A tutu and a record of Swan Lake! I am going to put it on, see if it fits. Dominic's waiting to take a picture. If it does I am going to wear it all day.'

'We are going to have to go and see about Mother.'

'Not now.'

'Yes, now.'

'Oh, let's wait just a little bit longer.'

And then the twins walk in. Vanessa stares, astonished to see them so quickly changed out of their sleepsuits and dressed in crisp new nurses' outfits with red crosses on their elasticated caps. The smocks are still undone at the back, they have not bothered to press the studs together. 'Smile,' says Dominic, following on, crouching behind his camera. 'Don't sulk, Sacha, smile!'

Their childish nakedness is vulnerable; they look so skinny and pink from behind, like plastic baby dolls. 'Granny sent them. D'you think that Boots sells doctors' kits?' Sacha asks Vanessa. She prods the turkey's hard humped back. 'Are we going to be eating that?'

'It looks awful,' says Dominic, his face taut with distaste. 'Don't put it back yet, tip it up towards me, let me take a picture.'

'I think I should have taken it out of the freezer last night, but never mind, we'll just leave it to cook much longer. There's no hurry.' In all sorts of ways the Christmas she's planned is eluding her. She is failing with the food as abysmally as she has failed to deal with Mother. And then she sits wearily down on Mrs Guerney's cushioned chair and her voice is serious. She sounds as devout as Mother Augustus giving out

49

notices in assembly when she goes on. 'Now that we've opened the parcels we're going to have to go down to the basement and see if Mother's all right.' She includes Amber in her gentle reminder. 'Now this is going to be extremely difficult for you, for all of us. You two have got to understand that this is our secret. It is terribly important to remember that whatever happens, whoever asks, we must not tell anyone where Mother is.'

'Not even Daddy, if he asks?'

'Not even Daddy. We would all get into the most awful trouble.'

'Perhaps we should leave the twins out of it. They might be too young.' Camilla turns away from the group at the table, and fiddles diffidently with the oven's switches. Vanessa sees that her sister is more frightened than she is herself.

'You can't leave us out,' Sacha proclaims in her most argumentative voice. Her tiny spectacles flash with reproof. 'Granny has sent us something suitable for once. We've dressed up specially. We are the nurses. Now that we're dressed like this we can look after Mother properly.'

'But Mother's not sick,' says Vanessa too quickly, hating to think of her needy and ill. But Mother *is* unhealthy. With her rasping cough and her tense, nervous movements, she hasn't been well for a long, long time, and Camilla's troubled backward glance confirms her sister's lie.

EIGHT

THEY MAKE a strange procession – Vanessa in her formal green carrying the menu, Camilla, a fully-kitted ballerina, Dominic, who hasn't dressed yet but whose precious camera hangs round his neck, and Sacha and Amber, two miniature nurses clinging to the hand-rails, fingers thin and taut as the iron itself as they climb down the steep black steps of the spiral staircase as if they are cautiously lowering themselves into some deep, unknown water. But this river is full of rapids and the bottom is covered with jagged rocks.

Nobody speaks. Vanessa's eyes fix on the porthole window. Shocked to see it clear, she blinks nervously. And there is no sound. No raving. No cursing. If it wasn't for the dim glimmer of light from the sauna you would not know there was anyone in there. This is nothing like Vanessa had expected.

They plan to push the menu through the pipe-hole because this will avoid the problem of trying to talk to Mother if she decides to be difficult. She can have cornflakes, toast, scrambled eggs or boiled eggs. She can choose tea or coffee.

'Do you think we need to give her a choice?'

'She's always liked a choice. You know she prefers a choice, Dom. We're not trying to punish her.' Vanessa endeavoured to explain something that threw her into confusion herself. 'Just to contain her.' So they drew up the menu on Mrs Guerney's fat shopping pad. *Have a nice day!* is printed across the top. Sacha is carrying Daddy's present, being the keenest of them all to discover what is inside it.

They wait until the last one is safely down before they cross the floor. Vanessa never moves her eyes from the porthole window. Adrenalin is pumping, she is prepared for a terrible shock, she feels this way when she has hiccups and is expecting one of the others to shout suddenly, or spring out of hiding to cure her. That always works but she's never liked it; she'd far rather drink water upside down. She wipes her warm, wet hands on her dress.

The nearer they move towards the sauna the more uneasy the children become and the more Vanessa experiences a feeling of strange, faraway unreality. They gather outside the pinewood door, staring expectantly at Vanessa when they realise she is the only one tall enough to peer through, and even then she will have to stand on tiptoe. She sighs and shakes her head in confusion. She murmurs, 'Oh, this is awful.'

'Go on,' urges Dominic, his smooth eyebrows arched. 'She can't hurt you. She can't get out.' The brightly lit room throws an echo back with every word that is spoken.

'No, wait, hang on a minute,' because there is this unnerving feeling that Mother, so dominant, so powerful, could have escaped already, could even be hiding somewhere in the gym, behind the horse, or over there in the corner behind the stack of shiny weights.

'Go on.' Camilla shivers and her voice is only a whisper. 'It's cold down here.'

'You've hardly got any clothes on,' Sacha points out.

As she takes her position before the door Vanessa fingers her crucifix. Cool and hard in her sticky hand, it is full of commonsense and courage – admirable traits which Daddy clearly believes are naturally hers. *'Think not that I am come to send peace on earth; I came not to send peace, but a sword.'* Dominic is right, she is quite safe. Mother, however hard she tries, really cannot reach her.

'I am never allowed a moment of privacy.' Mother used to weep, when someone inadvertently stumbled across her changing, or talking, or listening to her music. Now Vanessa thinks of a bad-tempered budgie, and someone's coming to stick a finger right into its cage.

Mother is sitting, slumped, on the bench. She is draped in her fur coat. She cannot have heard the children arrive, she can't have noticed the gym lights go on. Vanessa's knees start trembling. But surely she must have ...

'I hope you realise what you've done.' Mother continues to sit there pretending to file her nails, not even bothering to lift her head, not addressing Vanessa directly but knowing full well she can hear her. Every one of her gathered children can hear her. Her voice is hoarse and gravelly after her evening of heavy drinking, and she drones along on one bleary note in the way that she does when she's pissed. 'And I hope you fully understand what the consequences of this are likely to be.'

Through the porthole Vanessa watches the menu, with the pencil wrapped inside it, being pushed through the hole in the wall like a special gift being posted. From between Mother's fingers smoke spirals from a smouldering cigarette.

'There are only a few special units for disturbed children in this country. I believe the places are scarce but they will certainly manage to find one for you.'

What? What is this? The floor is hard and ungiving on the balls of Vanessa's feet. Her heart pumps so violently she thinks she is going to unbalance with all the banging going on inside her. Her mouth is dry and she swallows hard to dislodge the lump in her throat.

But Mother can't stop. She rolls on, as out of control as a dirty snowball enlarging itself as it crashes along. 'There is no time limit. It isn't like going to prison. The courts don't fix a sentence like one year, or two, or three. In cases like yours those decisions are left in the hands of the doctors. The experts.' Although she looks limp and dejected, although she is quite helpless, Mother spits out her words with venom. 'They will probably be quite kind to you,' she adds, 'in their way.'

'Mother, you were drunk. You were ill. You might have hurt ... I could not think of ...'

'If we are talking about sickness, Vanessa, then I think it is essential that you sit down by yourself, somewhere quiet, and consider carefully what you have done. You and your father together, your sinister beliefs tell you that you will be purified by pain, even if it is pain you have brought down on yourself. Certainly you influenced the younger ones, as usual. They are innocent of this. They would not have dreamed of doing such a wicked thing without your encouragement. What on earth did you think you were going to achieve? Or did you think? Did you give any thought at all to the consequences of your actions?'

Mother, calm and oiled by the booze like this is far more sinister than

Mother enraged. Vanessa speaks through tightened lips. 'We came down to see if you wanted something to eat.'

'Don't be silly, Vanessa.'

'And we brought you Daddy's present.'

'You are utterly ridiculous!' Mother drags on her cigarette.

'Don't you want it, Mother?'

There is no answer, and when is Mother, still strangely in command, going to demand that they set her free? She does not need to ask, she just expects it. She looks quite settled in the little cabin, sat back, spreading her legs out smugly as if she owns it and has always lived there. It is a shock when Sacha speaks up. 'Mother, if you don't want it can I open it?'

Once again there is no reply and on her bench Mother makes no movement.

'She can't be hungry,' says Dominic. 'We'll have to come back later. Perhaps she'd rather skip breakfast and try some turkey. What does she look like?'

Trembling, Vanessa lets herself down to rest on her heels. Her face is white when she turns to reply. 'She just looks the same, exactly the same as always, although she isn't wearing a wig. Or make-up. She looks quite pale.'

'And angry?'

How can she answer that? Mother looks far worse than angry. Coldly furious would be closer to the truth. She thinks of that tattered, unkempt head, obscene without its scarf. 'Mad,' states Vanessa, still shaking.

Amber is disappointed that the menu has not been filled in and returned. She's been crouched at the pipe-hole, waiting. 'I want to do the next one,' she demands, quite unmoved by the tense atmosphere. She is merely slightly excited.

None of them know, thinks Vanessa, none of them fully realise what is happening except for Camilla, and Dominic perhaps. Her brother is old for his eight years. They are all wise for their ages. Vanessa has to ask them: she is the oldest, she is to blame, but if they are to keep Mother prisoner for longer than one night it is only fair that they be given the choice.

'Well,' she says. 'Mother seems to be all right. What shall we do now?'

'I don't know what you mean.' Dominic has moved to the bottom of the staircase to inspect the sauna's heating controls. 'Why do we have to do anything? What do you think we should do?'

'The longer we keep her down here the more trouble we will have to face.'

'How can we let her out?' The frightened look on Camilla's face proves that she understands the implications. 'She's already told us what will happen to you. They will take you away and put you in a special unit. Is that true? What if it is? How can we let her out? Why would we even want to?'

'But we can't keep her down here indefinitely!'

'Why not?' asks Dominic, with a strange little laugh. 'No one will miss her.'

'What about when she doesn't turn up for work?'

'We'll make up excuses. We'll say she's gone back to her clinic, or the health farm.'

'She would have given them prior warning.'

'Then we'll have to make it sound as if she is giving them warning. That's not impossible. Camilla can do her voices, she's brilliant at imitating Mother, and if we practised long enough we could copy her writing.'

Vanessa listens, amazed, as Camilla and Dominic sort out the details between them. They make it sound so simple, as if they are merely working out the rules of a new board game. There is no doubt that Mother can hear them, too, but she does not interrupt. There is no sound from the sauna but the low, almost indistinct hum of the heater.

What they are saying is certainly possible. They have Mother's voice on the answerphone, so that would deal with most incoming calls. In honeyed tones the message says: *'Caroline Heaten is unavailable just now so if you would like to leave a message followed by your number she will call you back later.'* It sounds like an invitation to the bedroom in black and white, the way it is done on very old films with fox furs, pillbox hats and shoes with little straps. They could stick with that one or they could change it. Daddy's money goes into the bank every month and Mother carries her Access card in her handbag which is still upstairs in the drawing room exactly where she dropped it. Between them they could regularly draw out any cash they might need and Mother has accounts at all the large London stores.

Daddy pays the school fees. Bart has already been dealt with and Daddy, understandably, does everything in his power to avoid meeting Mother or speaking with her. A phone call from Camilla would satisfy the child acting agency — DOTS, which stands for Daughters On The Stage — where Mother works three days a week. She'd got the job — it did not pay well — because of her old press cuttings and publicity photographs, and because she informed them that she had 'connections' in the theatre. She used to tell people she enjoyed working there because it kept her in touch, but Vanessa suspects that she hates the clients ... she loathes the talented kids who succeed despite her, those that gain the kind of acclaim that Mother only dreams about.

For many years Mother bullied Camilla; she tried to live out her dreams through her second daughter who was pretty and clever and natural on the stage. All the children had endured that — every single one of them, including the gauche and plain Vanessa had done their time in pantomime, and the tiny twins, led on, bewildered and snivelling, at three years old, were a triumph in *Cinderella* at the London Palladium. 'RADA for Camilla,' ordered Mother, long before the child could walk. And Camilla, obedient and sweet, pranced and simpered for Mother, plié-ed and pirouetted for Mother, went to the local dancing class and was told by the crippled prima ballerina, Ceci Koch, who ran it, 'This child was born to dance.' Mother glowed. Then, one day, for no apparent reason, to Mother's rage and incomprehension, Camilla had simply refused to carry on. 'I want to dance in my bedroom, alone.'

'But there's no bloody point in dancing like that. Don't be outrageous. What is the point in dancing if no one can see you, you fool!'

'I can see myself in my mirror,' said Camilla.

Last year, when Camilla grew out of her leotard, when her worn-out shoes became too tight to put on, Mother refused to replace them. 'Because there is absolutely no point,' she said grimly. Vanessa does not think that Mother will ever forgive Camilla for letting her down like that. And on the rare occasions when Daddy and Suzie take Camilla to the ballet ... it was *Swan Lake* the last time ... Camilla says she enjoys it. But she goes very quiet the day after, and once Vanessa found her crying in her bedroom.

Ilse is paid by banker's order — a fact of which Vanessa is well aware because Mother often grumbles about not being able to dock the odd hours when the slovenly Ilse arrives home late and Mother is there to notice. 'I ought to pay her cash, weekly, the same as Mrs Guerney. You have so much more control over cash,' Mother says. Yes, she'd even tried to deduct money, once, for Mrs Guerney's breakages, but Mrs Guerney wasn't having that. She removed her floral overall, she picked up her slippers, she put her hat on there and then and threatened to walk out so Mother crossly backed down.

'Your mother's not stupid. She knows she couldn't cope for a minute without Mrs Guerney,' Daddy says.

They can find the key to Mother's desk and write cheques to cover the monthly bills ... they can send for a new chequebook when Mother's runs out, they need never show themselves at the bank.

Mother does not have a car so its lack of use will raise no suspicions. Mr Morrisey next door, who has three, asked if he could rent their garage but Mother thinks renting out anything is common and anyway, why should she do anything to accommodate 'that nasty little man with boils on his neck. He would probably overstep the mark and store things in it.' Since her last heavy fine and disqualification she says it isn't worth running a car. 'Frankly I'd rather use taxis. London is getting impossible and you can't park anywhere.'

Oh yes, there are ways of thinking about the situation which do make sense; they are called daydreams. They are easy, they are lovely, but before she allows them to carry her completely away, in a low voice, Vanessa points out the screamingly obvious. 'Mother's not going to stay quiet for ever. If she starts banging or shouting then Ilse or Mrs Guerney will hear her eventually. If she screamed loudly enough she could probably be heard by people walking past on the pavement.' With the snow lying on the ground outside it is hard to tell how clearly passing footsteps can be heard and Vanessa cannot remember. The children rarely visit the gym. Even in the days when Daddy lived at home it was his place, and he preferred to exercise alone.

Dominic frowns. His mouth, which so often trembles, is not trembling now and he says in a voice soft and high, 'If she starts doing that then she must be punished. If she behaves herself then she will be rewarded.'

'Dominic! How can we punish Mother?' Intimidated by Mother's close proximity, there is still room for shock and surprise over Dominic's vicious determination. He should not be taking photographs either, not at a time like this. Pretty, more like a girl should be pretty, he, in spite of the rigid self-control which he will not break, seems far more angry than frightened. He shrugs but does not answer her question. Vanessa shivers, and Camilla, nearly naked in her layers of pink netting and her satin shoes, must be frozen. 'Come on, let's go upstairs and talk. We should not be discussing these matters here.'

It is as they are leaving the basement that Vanessa notices her brother turning up the sauna heating to an exact 78 degrees. A considerate, sensible boy, he must assume that Mother is cold. She must be cold because why else would she be wearing her coat? Dominic, of course, having not seen her, cannot know that.

NINE

'CAN ANYONE ELSE hear the thudding of my heart?'

'Why, Vanny, are you frightened?' With her small, quick hands Sacha has Mother's present on the kitchen table and is opening it gleefully, while Vanessa and Camilla peel the potatoes. 'I am going to keep this bow. Why do you think Daddy wasted a bow on Mother?'

'The turkey ought to be smelling by now,' says Camilla gloomily.

When the doorbell rings the five of them freeze. They stare at the unwrapped present – just a nasty glass fruit bowl decorated with fragile flowers – as if it is the object itself which has sparked the fear. Gradually, sitting rigidly on their chairs, the younger ones tear their eyes from the bowl and turn them on Vanessa. Who would call on Christmas Day morning without being invited? On Boxing Day, when Daddy was living at Camberley Road, everyone came ... it was open house and visiting children, tired and excited, brought their best toys and showed them off while Daddy's friends laughed and drank downstairs. Mother adored occasions like those, and it wasn't until later, towards evening-time, when she'd drunk too much that her mouth fell slack and her eyes turned vacant and she caused her embarrassing scenes. Once, Vanessa remembered, Mother turned into a dog and went crawling along on the floor between everyone's legs, and the drips of passion-fruit sorbet. She was wearing her curly brown wig, like a spaniel's hair. It was on all fours, that day, and with snarling teeth, that she waged war on her husband. Daddy and his co-presenter, Alex Graham, tried to get her upstairs, but she growled at them; she would not go, not even when some of the women in their tight cocktail dresses scuffled about on the carpet trying to persuade her. She pulled and hung on to her shame like a bone. None of the children said anything but Vanessa, a tight bundle of sorrow and distress, could see they were hiding cruel little smiles.

But on Christmas Day only the select few were ever invited.

Perhaps Mr Morrisey next door has some weird, boring idea about clearing the snow ...

The bell rings again, viciously, like an alarm. Surely, down in the basement, Mother, awake and alert, will hear it. To ignore the caller would cause too many problems. Even if whoever it is goes away, it is essential to know who is ringing that bell; Vanessa cannot endure not knowing. There is no time to run upstairs and spy from the window. There is no time to remind the twins to keep their mouths shut. So, with aching legs and a set expression on her pale face, feeling dead, she goes to open the front door.

Out on the step, with the silent blankness of snow softly falling, there is no sound from Mother.

'*Daddy!*'

No longer an outcast, Vanessa is safe in Daddy's arms, just his little girl not rotten and growing up any more, mewing into his snuggly fawn duffle coat. Over his shoulder his dark blue Jaguar is crouched in the snow – ROB 1. 'How very bourgeois,' Mother would sneer. 'What vanity!'

Daddy says, 'Happy Christmas, my darling!'

Bless me Father for I have sinned.

Oh Daddy help me. If only he knew what they'd done. Maybe, handsome, rich and powerful, he of all people can still make it right ... There is no sound from the basement. Is Mother, lying quietly in her dark pool of self-pity, trying to worry them, feigning death?

'Where is Caroline?'

'She's gone back to bed.'

'Is she ill?'

'No, no, we made her! We're cooking the dinner for fun ... it ought to be ready by tonight. She said we could. There's a programme on TV she wanted to watch.' The lie is out. It sounds excited, it feels elated like a streamer being thrown.

Daddy's clear grey eyes are wary. 'She's been up, then?'

Vanessa forces what she hopes is a natural smile. 'Of course she's been up. She watched us unwrap our presents. Why didn't you say you were coming?'

'Because I didn't want to disappoint you if anything went wrong, and then I saw the snow and decided it was now or never.' He bangs his cold hands together as he follows his daughter into the warmth of the house, to the warm light of the kitchen. 'I didn't see you last year so I was determined to make up for it this time.'

They both know that he had risked more than snow to get here. There'd be Suzie's disapproval at his end, and Mother's scathing condemnation at this. So Daddy is capable of courage and action, in spite of Mother's tauntings, her crass insensitivity. Vanessa should have kept faith. He would not have given Dominic Nintendo if he hadn't been meaning to come all the time!

Daddy, blowing cold balloons of white air, braces himself with his hands to a point above his head as his children throw themselves at him and hang for a moment like wild decorations.

He seems to make his decision immediately, right then and there, filled by a sudden magnificent burst of assurance. 'What do you think Caroline would say if we popped to the flat for a couple of hours? Would your special dinner survive in the oven for that long? Isobel's already arrived, and Joe.' He is careful not to mention Suzie.

'I don't think she'd mind.' Dominic sounds far too certain. 'And dinner won't be ready till very late.'

'I could ask her,' puts in Camilla, too readily, with a clever and knowledgeable look. But it's all right, Daddy doesn't notice.

'Go on then, my pretty ballerina. I'm glad it fits you. Dance your way upstairs and go and see. But be careful now, make sure you don't upset her.'

'I'll go and get dressed,' says Dominic. 'And can I bring my Nintendo?'

Daddy hardly hesitates, hardly thinks of Suzie before he agrees. Catching sight of Mother's present still lying in its remnants of paper he smiles wryly, 'She didn't like it, then?'

'Oh, she did! She did!' Vanessa can't bear that violet shade, she hates to see it fleck his eyes just like a cry of pain – and what if he guesses that she didn't like her crucifix? 'She left it there because she said she wanted to fill it with fruit.' Vanessa clings to her crucifix. It is so much more pleasant to make Mother up, it is so much easier to turn her into a fantasy person.

'And she loved the bow!' It is Amber's turn; she is delighting in the game. Everyone knows she is lying but the rules have changed; it no longer seems to matter. She sounds quite unaware of the lie. 'She put it in her hair, didn't she, Sacha?'

Daddy raises his furry black eyebrows but makes no comment. He just looks very relieved to see everyone so relaxed and happy. So they have done the right thing. By locking Mother away from Christmas they've made sure that even Daddy, so safe and respectable, so worn out and troubled, can enjoy himself ... like the time they'd found the lewd pictures and hidden them away so he wouldn't see and be hurt – a very young Mother, abasing herself, posing naked, perverted and abnormal in her desperate attempts to be noticed and admired. Taking deep breaths after studying them intently, shocked by the way her own thin body was growing, Vanessa burnt them one by one in ritualistic fashion over her single white candle. The smoke turned dark and putrid. The smoke stung her eyes.

So the more she thinks about these things the more she convinces herself of the rightness of what they have done. It is not up to her to pass judgement, but it *is* up to her to protect Daddy from pain. It is up to her to guard all of them from Mother's extremes of behaviour. Vanessa has often wished morbidly that Mother would die, or have an accident which would confine her to a wheelchair, helpless, dependent and therefore *good*. She would have looked after Mother, a placid and obedient daughter, happy to carry out her filial obligations. But now she is free of those wicked thoughts, made righteous by newly acquired courage, instead she wishes that she had bought a present for Daddy from Mother, but then that might be going too far.

However, Mother is right about one thing – Vanessa shouldn't be so old-fashioned, she should relax more, and let herself go. Well look, even now, on this Christmas morning when she ought to be happy, she is worrying about leaving the house with Mother still in it, imprisoned and alone. Maybe ill. Vanessa suffers. It is rumoured that Sister Agnes never sleeps without a bottle of gall under her pillow; she rubs her eyes and mouth with it every morning. Vanessa looked up gall in the dictionary and it said, 'something bitter to endure'. She took a lemon to bed and tried it, a sticky, unpleasant, stinging business, but after three days of that Vanessa concluded she did not yet hate herself as much or as magnificently as Sister Agnes.

More bitter than the lemon, Mother attacks Vanessa's looks, her behaviour, but worst of all she attacks her beliefs and her love for Daddy. 'Not only have you inherited your father's looks and temperament, but also his instinct for mindless worship. And that, to my mind,' snaps Mother, 'is a particularly dangerous trait.' For months Vanessa convinced herself that she must swallow the gall. Mother's tortures would make her into a better person, fitter for God in the end, for, 'he that endureth to the end shall be saved'. But the others? Daddy? What about them? No, the situation could not have been allowed to continue any longer.

After a reasonable five minutes Camilla returns to the kitchen. 'She says that's fine.' But then, quickly, hitching herself and her layers of pink netting up on the kitchen table, Camilla corrects that statement to the more likely, 'She says if that's what we want to do then she honestly doesn't care.'

Daddy runs a nervous hand across his stubbly chin. 'Maybe I ought to go up and check ...'

'She really would not like that.'

He bows his head in acknowledgement. 'Yes. You are quite right, of course. Sometimes, you know, I forget ...' His smile is a false one and everyone ignores it.

'She is watching her programme, but she did say to wish you a Happy Christmas.'

'Oh?' Daddy brightens, relieved again. Borrowing his children will be all right. He claps his hands, 'Come on then, but dress up warm, we might even get stuck!' How can this loving, intelligent man, this father who loves them and foists no thwarted ambitions of his own upon his children, how can he possibly consider ignoring their needs, splitting them up and sending them off to boarding schools? It is just another of Mother's lies made up to keep them quiet. Unless Suzie ...

But is Mother's talk of special units based upon truth? Diminished and vulnerable as she remembers, Vanessa fears that it might be. Daddy would know but how can she ask him?

Vanessa closes the oven door on the turkey after a brief, humiliating inspection. The roasting pan is almost overflowing with water so she spoons some of it out. It probably will not be ready until this evening, and now they are going out she'll leave it roasting on a low heat. After all the sweets they've already devoured nobody can be hungry. The plastic bag with the giblets still in it is possibly still stuck inside it. She will haul it out later when no one is looking, pretending she has not forgotten. Or maybe there is no bag.

No one discovered the presents she'd hoarded, but she'd nearly been found out with the food. When Mrs Guerney spied the Christmas provisions she'd vibrated with surprise. 'Well,' she said, 'there's a turn-up for the books. What has got into your mother all of a sudden?' Vanessa did not tell a lie. She simply said nothing, staring at Mrs Guerney blankly, praying that the woman would not give the game away. They'd flown really close to disaster one morning a week before Christmas, when Mrs Guerney, chatting away with her usual terrifying loss of control as she bustled about with her duster somewhere between osteopaths and orgasms, said, 'I see you're going over the top this year then, Mz Townsend, splashing out on your festive fare.' Vanessa's hands gripped her book tightly as she sat by the fire pretending to read but she itched with concern all over. Mother was in a hurry as usual. With controlled impatience she said, 'Mrs Guerney, there are some items I've left on my bed for dry-cleaning and I'm not going to find the time. Perhaps you would be an absolute dear and drop them in for me?'

Mother rarely listened to anything that Mrs Guerney said and Mrs Guerney knew it: 'That's why I leave a note when there's something important to say.'

Before they leave, Daddy must go upstairs to the drawing room and admire the tree and the decorations. 'It is quite like old times,' he says with a smile of nostalgia for something so long ago Vanessa cannot remember. Can he? 'Perhaps things are going to start getting better from now on. Maybe we've all been through the worst.'

The children smile and cling to him, especially the twins, relishing his happiness and his company.

Five minutes later the twins slide towards the car, glorying in the brand new snow and squealing. They look like little dancing gnomes in their bobbing bobble hats, creatures up from an underworld.

As she closes the front door and crunches across the pavement Vanessa listens hard for screaming curses from the basement or a crashing of fists on the sauna door. The dread is mixed with a strange excitement, almost euphoria. The silence is sinister: perhaps the walls are so thick that no sound can penetrate. Why does she imagine that Mother is smiling? She glances at Dominic so flushed and excited, cradling his Nintendo, looking as if he hasn't a care in the world. At least he's made sure Mother will be quite warm enough, they need not worry about that. She thinks about the turkey in the oven, sweating out all that bloody water.

She scans the house once again, afraid that somehow it might be giving away its secret. But no, no one would ever guess.

Inside Daddy's car feels like the safest place in the world. She is once again the beloved daughter taking her place on the front seat, driving away from her strange and dangerous house with the rottenness in the cellar. The opulent interior smells of leather, the engine purrs with pure pleasure for the times they have spent together.

Camilla wears her coat over her tutu, she carries her ballet shoes and her face has lost its earlier strain: she looks radiant. The snow adds to the feeling of safety. It cocoons them in love as they creep along the deserted streets in case they skid, their fears and doubts put to one side as they concentrate on the wheel-tracks and judge other people's Christmas trees.

'Have you got a tree, Daddy?'

'Yes. But it's silver.'

'Oh.'

'Suzie chose it.'

'Ah.'

No one else notices, but, with a surge of pity, Vanessa sees how his black-gloved hands tighten on the steering wheel.

TEN

OH DEAR, SUZIE. Why is everything going wrong and why is life so terribly unfair? How come you were not persuasive enough to prevent Robin from going to fetch his children? All Suzie wants to do is edit her books, nurture her orchids and bear Robin's baby, probably in that order, I'm afraid. But while her orchids are snuggled down in the greenhouse at a constant, carefully controlled 60 degrees Fahrenheit, what is happening to the struggling seed in the moist, dark depths of her womb? How is that coming along, or did it slip out in the bath last night and wiggle off down the plughole?

Life is so unfair, because Suzie would make a far better mother than Caroline, who manages to breed like a rabbit.

Dominic, that beautiful, precocious son of Robin's, told Suzie exactly what Caroline said when she first heard about his mews flat. 'Isn't it sweet?' Dominic stared levelly at Suzie as he relayed Caroline's comments on a note of cocky triumph. 'And how typical that your father should end up sharing a stable.'

Suzie drew herself tightly up. 'Well, Dominic,' she calmly replied. 'Do you think it looks like a stable? Does it feel like a stable?'

'No, it looks more like a pub.'

Robin laughed uneasily. He gathered his new wife consolingly into his arms. 'He is talking about the low ceilings and your antiques. All the rooms at Camberley Road are large and square.' Suzie has never been to Camberley Road so she wouldn't know about that. Yes, Suzie supposes, all the rooms in the flat are quaint, apart from the one on the top floor where Robin has raised the ceiling, installed roof windows and strengthened the floor, the room which lies empty now, waiting for his apparatus.

There is something unnerving about the sly way Dominic looks at Suzie ... she catches his glances when she turns round quickly, long black lashes over those dark, haunting eyes, the slanting smile, so knowing. And yet he is an innocent child, only eight years old. Suzie supposes she has a problem when it comes to Caroline's children and she works hard to conquer it, without much success.

Now she watches from the diamond-paned window as Robin's car moves silently up the narrow road over the snow-humped cobbles and in through the whirring garage door. She is suddenly horrified, aware of what she must look like to anyone watching from below ... chewing her lip ... twisting her fingers. The branches of the wisteria that clads the front of the flat, wispy and bare only yesterday, are padded now and swollen with snow and she thinks of her butcher's fingers. She stares down at the roof as the car moves inside, a carload of kids on top of everything else, for God's sake!

Not only was Suzie forced to hide from Caroline when she and Robin started living together, but she endured the humiliation of having to hide from the children, too, because they were invited round to Ammerton Mews on the occasional Sunday or Saturday afternoon. 'But surely the bedroom is safe? Can't we lock the bedroom door?' Suzie would ask, exasperated, with her private belongings gathered in her arms, a celery stalk between her teeth, on her way down the narrow staircase to her Peugeot GTI which waited with its boot propped open. Again. 'Christ, I feel homeless, like a refugee. This does nothing for my morale you know, Robin.'

'I'd rather be on the safe side, Suzie. When I tell them about us I want to make sure it's done properly. They have suffered enough already and I don't want it coming as a shock.'

The black dustbin bags full of her clothes were already worn and tattered by then. She had shoved as much as she could out of sight under the bed. 'But couldn't we tell them now? We could tell them to keep your secret, to keep quiet in front of Caroline. They know her better than anyone else, they would understand.'

'That would be grossly unfair. They are far too young to cope with those sort of confidences, and Caroline is so manipulative she could squeeze water out of a stone if she thought there was something going on – particularly where I am concerned.'

'They probably know anyway,' said Suzie, whose own childhood has been so happy she remembers very little of it except long, warm summer days and dens she built in her garden. Dens to nest in; she filled them with dolls, practising for her future home ... no one would ever have dreamed of turning Suzie out of one of her dens. And all those things she had promised, as a child, never to do: give up her name, for a start, and end up with nothing more than an S on an envelope; be penetrated by a man – she resolved that if she must have a baby she would conceive by test-tube and thereby achieve perfection – share a television set or a bedside light.

So, in the face of all that, it is quite understandable that Suzie still harbours some resentment. It is natural, surely, after such a nerve-racking start.

'Have they arrived? Did I just hear a car?'

Suzie adjusts her face and turns round smoothly. A bleak white light fills the room, unbroken save for the orange flicker of the fire and the prick of the candle wall-lights. 'Yes, Isobel, they've arrived. I'll go down to the kitchen and welcome them.'

'Are they going to eat with us? What time did you say that dinner would be ready, Suzie? I am afraid that I have forgotten.'

Suzie flexes her shoulders. Oh, but Isobel has not forgotten. She is making her point again. Suzie and Caroline, so unalike, would agree on this description of Isobel – Robin's mother is suffering from a terrible reverse kind of senile dementia where, instead of letting herself go all messy and higgledy-piggledy as she moves up through her seventies, she has become abrasively fastidious, laundered and trim, and instead of embracing a relaxed absentmindedness, she is acutely alert with a predatory kind of vigilance. Absolutely terrified of losing control, she conducts her life by way of lists and orderly bowel movements.

Robin's mother does not approve of meals being served in the middle of the afternoon, even Christmas lunch. She would prefer it – she *expects* it – to be dished up at one o'clock on the dot. Suzie, so organised, so controlled, is a far more suitable wife for Robin than Caroline could ever have been, so why does the woman persist in her resistance to the change? All right, she does not approve of divorce, especially when there are children concerned, but she certainly never accepted the sluttish, disorganised Caroline and she knows very well what Robin has gone through during his fourteen years of married hell.

Isobel sits stiffly beside the blue flames of the coal-gas fire; massive dried floral arrangements of Suzie's stand either side of the great burnished canopy. Her soft jersey-wool suit is what you might call an eggshell green, but Suzie thinks of stained birdshit. Joe, her large and comfortable husband, crammed into a smart suit, is playing solitaire, the tiny white pegs really too small for his fingers, at the other end of the room beside the silver Christmas tree. Joe always manages to find the backs of rooms. A shy man, familiarity alarms him. Two cotton-wool puffs of snaggly hair grow above his ears, like headphones. He listens but does not join in the conversation that Isobel is having with Suzie's mother, Eileen, who is happily draped in the soft armchair with her stockinged feet on the antique fender.

Both women had encouraged Robin to fetch the children in spite of Suzie's desperate signals to her mother. She put forward every argument she could think of: 'What if you can't get them back? What if they can't get the road-sweepers out? What if the streets get impossible and they have to stay the night?'

And then, 'It would be awful if the twins got upset again when it was time to leave, like they did last time. It would be cruel to make them unhappy on Christmas Day.'

She whispered, 'You will have to cope with the added strain of making sure they behave properly in an enclosed space, with Isobel.'

'Do you want me to postpone lunch?' she asked him eventually, close to despair, thinking that this device might change Isobel's mind.

'No,' said Robin. 'Good heavens, of course you needn't postpone it. We can eat at the same time, according to plan. The children will be quite happy playing while we eat. It's not that important, Suzie. The essential thing is that I see them on Christmas Day, and I would like them to stay for tea, as planned. Is that so strange?'

'But you won't be gone long, dear, will you?' asked Isobel, alarmed by the prospect of time alone, abandoned by her son and left to Suzie's ministrations and Eileen's slovenly conversation. 'It would be better if you brought them here rather than stay over there.'

Joe merely watched and listened and said nothing. Eileen did not care either way although 'it would be a shame to waste that lovely tea'. She was thoroughly enjoying herself, 'being looked after, treated like a Queen.' Dear Mummy, she puts Suzie under no pressure, an easygoing, cheerful person, happy with her fatness, in her orange trousers and navy top, although she is finding conversation with the stiff-necked Isobel hard going. She thinks she might have to sell her cottage. She feels she can no longer cope with the garden. She discusses all this with Isobel and you can see her thinking – with a mother like this, no wonder poor Robin is so serious, such a responsible person.

So that's how it happened. Nothing has worked. As far as his children are concerned Robin rushes here and there and gets nowhere, driven onwards by guilt.

Up until the moment she'd seen the steamy windows of the car, Suzie had clung to the very great hope that Caroline, so unpredictable, so determined to thwart Robin at every turn, would refuse to let her children go on this special day. Not so. Engrossed in her latest affair, muses Suzie, Caroline has apparently seized the opportunity of a day in her house, alone, with her man.

A couple of hours with the children would be bad enough, but all day! Damn the snow! In a minute the midday peace, all Suzie's careful organisation will be shattered.

Foiled. And full of foreboding, Suzie leaves her guests and heads downstairs. The flat, comprising three small cottages knocked together by the previous owner, is really nothing like a flat but that was how it was described on the brochure when they bought it. To one side of the garage remains the original great arched entrance with the studded, oaken door still intact, but now, instead of leading into the old cobbled courtyard it opens on to Suzie's well-tended garden, and her greenhouse leans against a sunny, south-facing, ancient wall. The whole effect is picturesque and pleasing. Even Caroline, when she finally traced the place and arrived to cause trouble, even she had to admit that it was a dream house, although, she insisted, 'Still very much a stable. A conversion is always a conversion. You never get it to feel like a house inside, no matter how old it is.'

Bitch.

The kitchen that Suzie loves is a mass of creeping greenery, pine shutters that actually work, and a stone-clad plinth houses her hob, standing squarely and dramatically in the centre of the room. What a very good thing she is a good cook, an inadequate cook would be intimidated by this kitchen. She opens the stable-door to the garden; her face cracks into a smile as she lets everyone in.

'Happy Christmas!' calls Suzie, five times and fading, using a happy knack of plunging into a nightmare without even changing expression. But having no children of her own – not yet not yet – not being an aunt, or a godmother, or anything to do with other people's children, she finds it difficult not to talk down to them. Of this she is very aware.

But with a child of her own she will be quite different.

They are polite, as usual. They are introduced to Eileen for the first time. They present themselves one by one to Isobel, gravely thanking her for their gifts. 'I am glad to see you liked the nurses' outfits,' she tells the twins. 'Although I would have thought them hardly suitable in this sort of weather, Robin, and wouldn't it have been nice to dress them in something smart on Christmas Day?'

Robin, having got his way, can afford to smile benignly. 'Let me top up your sherry, Isobel.'

'I have had quite enough already. Aren't we eating yet?' Isobel bites an olive in half and the bitter pimento catches between her two front teeth and hangs redly there, unnoticed.

'How is your mother?' Isobel asks Vanessa. The serious child sits as neatly as her grandmother, tall, pale and green tucked into one end of the sofa stroking her crucifix. She seems to like it, thank God, thinks Suzie. It was difficult to know which one to choose. Of all Robin's children, this is the one Suzie would most like to know. Veiled and impassive, what lies behind that protective veneer? If Suzie found favour with Vanessa, she would be well on her way to acceptance by the others but Suzie has tried and tried and every time that quiet, pale child politely rebuffs her. Suzie is hurt every time. It is just not fair.

'She is very well.'

Isobel frowns and her eyes turn an eerie light green. 'Everyone always tells me that when I ask and it is, quite blatantly, untrue.' She crosses her thin hands on her lap, unconsciously mimicking the child herself when she goes on, 'People persist in telling me that Caroline is fine, I don't know why. But then I have never understood that particular situation. Even when your parents were married I could never quite grasp what was going on under the surface. But there,' she smiles confidentially at Eileen who returns a sherry-sweet leer. 'Different generations, I suppose. I really ought to have kept in touch, I know. Time and time again I have written, "Ring Caroline" on my daily list, but your mother can be so difficult. Perhaps when Christmas is over.'

The silence is an empty rushing of air. From the far end of the room Joe gives an abrupt wheezy chortle. Everyone turns but he is engrossed in his solitaire.

Eileen is moved to ask, 'Are you quite sure there is nothing I can do to help, lovey?'

'No Mummy, really, I did most of it earlier. You just relax.'

'I think that Mother has plans,' Vanessa says suddenly, rather loud.

You can actually see Robin turn pale, as a soldier might turn and gape at the battle he thought he had won, only to find that behind his back his opponents have started to scuffle again.

'Plans?' He is concentrating on the Nintendo, down on the floor amongst the aerials and wires with Dominic, the boy whistling through his teeth in a most infuriating fashion. Everyone else stares at Vanessa, waiting for her to explain.

'I don't think Mother will be at home after Christmas. You see, she was talking about going to Broadlands again. I think she has booked herself in for a fortnight.'

'There, and yet when I asked you a moment ago you told me your mother was well. It is terribly unfortunate, this drinking problem of Caroline's,' Isobel mentions to Eileen, who nods in boozy sympathy. She is quick to explain that she knows all about it, and she adds reassuringly, 'Most families have one hidden away somewhere.'

'Sorry?'

'An alcoholic, lovey,' Eileen says doggedly. 'Most families do, like homosexuality and bankruptcy and mental illness.'

Suzie manages to stop herself from contributing thoughtlessly, 'But we don't, Mummy. We never knew anyone like that.' With the children sitting round listening so intently it would be a silly remark to make. Instead she asks, 'But she'll wait until you are back at school before she goes, surely?'

Robin's impatient with her. 'It doesn't work that way, unfortunately, Suzie. It's not that neat! You can't just pick your time and book in as if you're planning a nose job.' He asks his oldest daughter, 'Is there any particular incident which has triggered this emergency off?' Lying on the floor, reading instructions, Robin's voice is distant, coming from a faraway place. How much easier life would be if everyone's ups and downs could be controlled by a button, like Mario, so you got another turn, and another, emerging unscathed from the crisis each time. Broadlands is cripplingly expensive, double the price of a luxury hotel, and yet how can he refuse to cater to his wife's urgent needs, especially when her well-being is so central to the happiness of his children?

'She has split up with her friend Bart.'

Robin groans and shoots Suzie a brief, knowing look. 'It had to happen, I suppose,' he says lamely. 'Rather bad luck over Christmas, though. Is she drinking very heavily?' Poor Robin, he truly does not want to know.

'No,' Vanessa assures him, her pinched little face deadly serious. Christ ... she is only twelve years old. Eileen is shocked by this discussion, so obviously familiar to these young children, so casually conducted.

'No, she's not too bad yet, but I heard her telling someone on the phone that she thought she could cope with it all the more easily if she had the support of the staff at Broadlands.' Vanessa stares glassily into the fire. 'Mother doesn't want to slip back, you see.'

'Well, at least Caroline has the right attitude at last, that's a blessing at any rate.' Isobel, aware of the red fleck between her teeth, picks at it with a white fingernail, concealing the action behind her hand.

Suzie knows that the other undoubted blessing is that when Caroline goes to Broadlands there is far less likelihood of disturbance. There will be a fortnight of uninterrupted peace, and life at Camberley Road runs more smoothly when the mistress of the house is away. The children will be back at school and thank God for that gem Mrs Guerney. That the woman stays to tolerate Caroline's insults, the abuse, is certainly one of life's miracles. And Ilse, of course, however inadequate the girl might be, at least her presence gives some peace of mind. And the children are capable, not babies who need twenty-four-hour attention.

Every now and then, when overstressed, Robin plays with the vague notion of boarding schools for his children. He has broached the subject with Caroline who said that the children would hate it. 'Too many changes in their lives, too soon,' she said pointedly. Guilt. Guilt. Guilt. Suzie is careful not to comment but she sees the problems ... these children, so close, would be split. Robin considers the twins too young to leave home and he says, 'How much more hellish life would be for them at Camberley Road without the older ones to protect them.'

Suzie knows what the children want. They want to come and live here! And Robin ... what does he really want to do? A few weeks ago he dropped the hint casually, 'You know, Suzie, there'd be plenty of space for three bedrooms up here if I jettisoned my gym.'

My God!

Once, Suzie dreamed that Caroline died and the children hovered round the flat in pyjamas, like ghostly Peter Pan people.

But now Robin is slipping away, his eyes glued to the television screen ... an infuriating trick of his. He can read a book in a room full of people, at a party he will closet himself away with one person and leave it to Suzie to mingle. 'You worry too much,' he says, when she tackles him. 'Nobody minds.'

'Of course they mind,' says Suzie, furious. 'When people come to the flat, they expect to see you – to talk to you. You're the celebrity, not me!'

The monotonous ditty of the computer game is worse, far worse than the flickering distraction of those old, overplayed videos she's been forced to watch on past occasions, hour after hour. What should she do? Suzie is aware of Isobel's mounting irritation, the twisting handkerchief, the tight-lipped, steely stare. If she is so aware of his mother, why the hell isn't Robin? And the children, particularly the twins, are growing restless.

'Why don't you all go outside in the garden and play in the snow,' trills Eileen brightly.

'But they haven't brought their gloves ...'

'Oh fuss and fiddle,' Eileen insists. 'They don't feel the cold at their ages! And we can string all their clothes on a horse round the fire to get them dry before they go home.'

Isobel tenses but Suzie smiles bleakly. Her precious garden ... The snow has slyly covered the beds, so it is impossible to detect some of her rarest, most vulnerable shrubs. Even she would have difficulty in keeping to the path through the rockery.

'That's right ... off you go, lovies!' shouts Eileen, red in the face and clapping her hands with seasonal joy. 'Really, it does my heart good. Do you remember, Suzie?'

But Suzie's head is clogged with a myriad other thoughts; strangely, she can remember absolutely nothing at all.

'Don't go in the greenhouse whatever you do, will you?' she calls after them faintly.

ELEVEN

Despite their monetary problems the Dances have switched their heating full on – because it is Christmas Day, because they are expecting guests, because it is snowing outside and because two-timing Bart wants Ruby to be as warm and comfortable as possible. He loves her. He does not want to lose her. And her father is a very rich man.

She has only just stopped shivering.

Ruby Dance cannot remember a Christmas when she has been so pampered. Bart is behaving like a real father should and they are ready before their guests arrive – table laid, food prepared and under control, kids bathed and dressed and sitting room fairly neat and tidy.

But Ruby, who never drinks before noon, is already on her third sherry.

Before she knew, before she allowed herself to accept the fact that Bart was off screwing somebody else, she had pushed the horror to the back of her mind and buried it. How could she cope with the turmoil of that massive betrayal, with everything else that was cluttering up her days and nights? With her broken nights and her child-filled days, with all the worries about money and Bart's business going under, Ruby spent most of her time on her knees like a down-and-out, exhausted. She is tired of all the scrimping and scraping, she is fed up with using buses and never having the car.

But now she does know. And the knowledge gnaws away at her, like a rat with a long, grey shiny tail, into garbage, down and down into all the litter and trash of her subconscious fears. It reaches her self-esteem, her competence as a wife and mother, it worms its way down to her image of herself. Is she still a young and attractive woman? Apart from the Bendix man, would any other man want her? If she was abandoned, would it be possible ever to find anyone else? What with the kids and everything . . .

And anyway, this thing of Bart's, he says it was unimportant but how serious was it? In spite of the fact that it hurts her, she cannot leave the subject alone. Bart has already confessed that he tried to ring the bitch this morning in a misguided bid to try and patch up some misunderstanding they had last night.

'But you said it was over!' whines Ruby.

'It was over. But I tried to phone to make sure she was all right. I thought it was odd that I got the answerphone.'

'Why's that?' Ruby sleuths.

'Because she has five children and I doubt they would all be out at that hour.'

'Five children! She's a goer, then. What is her name?'

'Ruby, can't you leave it? This conversation is only damaging us both.'

'No, Bart, I am very sorry but I cannot leave it alone. I know it makes no sense but I have to know her name.' Ruby is terrified it might be a friend of hers, or even some acquaintance at whom she might nod and smile.

'Well, her name is Caroline.'

'Caroline who?'

'Oh Ruby, please don't.'

Ruby's eyes are madly bright. She sits and watches with her fists clenched while Bart kneels on the floor, inexpertly changing Damian's nappy. 'Caroline who, for God's sake?' Bart is forced to abandon Damian and rescue the chocolate tree decorations from James' clasping fingers.

'Her surname,' says Bart sadly, a safety pin clamped between his teeth and his hair wild and desperate, 'is Townsend.' He raises his red-rimmed eyes from his submissive position on the rug in front of her, like a slave to an empress. But Ruby does not feel like royalty this morning. Damian drags at the hem of her tartan Christmas skirt, exposing her worn-out, two-year-old boot.

'And why were you worried that she might be upset?' You see, the more she learns about Bart's affair, the more she is seized by a masochistic craving to know more. And yet every fact she learns makes it worse, leaves her more dissatisfied. She is trying to make him take away the pain but this is not the way. It's not working.

'Because I said some unkind things to her. I told her I wanted to call it a day and she was hysterical in the car on the way back ...'

'On the way back from where? Where had you taken her?'

'We spent the evening at a nightclub.'

'Which nightclub? Were you alone?' If they'd been alone that would be terrible; if they had been with other friends it might even feel worse. Ruby is far too impatient to wait for Bart's answer. 'Did any of our friends know about this?'

'No, Ruby. Nobody knew.'

'David must have known.' David, Bart's partner.

'Dave might have suspected, but I never told him.' Bart is wrestling with the baby, he is trying to send reassuring smiles to the child and talk to Ruby at the same time. He is losing the battle on the carpet.

'Oh come on, Bart! You kept the whole sordid business to yourself, did you? You are actually trying to convince me that you did not confide in anyone else?' She cannot believe that. Somebody knew, surely? Somebody is sneering at her abysmal ignorance. 'So this woman, this Caroline, did she want to carry on?'

'She was lonely, Ruby. She's just been through a difficult divorce. Her husband walked out on her.'

'My God!' Ruby startles the baby, Damian, who staggers across the room in his slipping nappy and flings himself into her arms. She coolly disengages him and passes him to her husband. 'My God, my God, how absolutely appalling for her! Christ, how my heart goes out to her at this most difficult time of her life! How considerate of you, Bart, to ring her up and make sure she's all right once I was up out of bed, down here and out of the way, taking care of your kids and drudging away trying to create some kind of fucking Christmas ...'

'Don't, Ruby, please stop ...'

'She never said that to you, did she, Bart? Presumably she was never too tired!' Ruby's eyes narrow, her face turns scarlet. Through clenched teeth she asks him the dreadful question: 'Who paid? Who paid, at this nightclub, and at all the restaurants and pubs and wine bars and dark little underlit venues with satin button-seating where you made your amorous assignations! WHO FRIGGING WELL PAID?'

Bart hides his face in his hands, as well he might. 'I did.'

Ruby sits back now in agonised triumph. 'I see,' she says to nobody in particular. 'I see. I see. I see.'

'I used the business account. It came out of expenses.'

'Tax deductible' Ruby gives an awful smile. 'That's all right then, isn't it? While I trudged around the sales trying to find ways of giving the children some kind of Christmas.'

'What can I say?' groans Bart, surrendering and utterly defeated.

'Just tell me how long.' Ruby is like an automaton, but she is winding up, not down.

'Sorry?'

'When did you first meet her?'

'In October.'

'How, in October?'

'I stopped in a pub on my way home from work. It was the day we lost the Barker account. She was sitting at the bar . . .'

'Available, and probably poxed. I can only pray that you took precautions. Just like an old western, really.' Ruby conjures Caroline up, a long-legged moll with scarlet lips, a drooping cigarette and world-weary eyes. Quite an accurate picture in fact, apart from the wig.

'I needed someone to talk to who wasn't involved. I was dreading getting home, telling you.'

'Oh? Now you're shoving me into the convenient role of shrewish, nagging old wife. Go on, then. This is crap! This is the sort of thing you bloody well read about!' Ruby's lips draw tighter together.

'You know I don't mean it like that. I knew you'd be desperately worried and upset.'

'And did she help you . . . in ways that I could not have done?'

'She listened.'

'And then you fucked her.' Bart fails to answer. 'Where did you fuck her?'

'I went back to her house.'

'Ah, yes. The house in Highgate.'

Bart is startled. 'How do you know?'

'The phone call told me that. Who would have made that phone call, Bart?'

'God knows.'

'What does she look like? Tell me exactly!' It is in the middle of all this drama, as it usually is, that the doorbell rings, a melodic chime that ought to signal happy arrivals, especially as Ruby has hung a wreath on the front door, a wreath for life when inside the house at Potters Bar it feels as if there is only death, long and lingering and everlasting.

Eleven for lunch. Ruby, on her fourth sherry now, knows that it does not really matter if the turkey is raw, if the spuds are white, if the gravy goes grey and lumpy. All these fears are negligible now ... and always were, quite honestly. This might well be the last Christmas the family spends together. Certainly if Ruby goes on feeling like this she won't be able to bear having Bart in the house, let alone at the dining-room table, let alone in the bedroom.

It is the snow that is making this Christmas so horribly realistic.

'Happy Christmas, Happy Christmas, Happy Christmas.' The greeting goes on and on and on because all the Dances' visitors have managed to arrive together. Ruby gets up, she moves toys and takes coats; she makes her mouth smile and takes part, but at the same time Ruby is utterly excluded from everyday life and feelings. Inside herself she's not there. Stunned, Ruby watches.

She is easy with her pretty little sister, Elspeth, and her latest boyfriend, Kurt. She is easy with Bart's gregarious parents, who have always loved her and make sure she knows it. 'I hope Bart realises what a lucky bloke he is,' said Harry Dance from somewhere under his tipped top hat, making his speech at their wedding. She is equally easy with Bart's brain-damaged brother, Lot. She has all the time in the world for Lot, who lives in a hostel in Kentish Town, folds gift-boxes at the special workshop and is made very welcome at Potters Bar on high days and holidays. Lot was a page at Ruby's wedding. Lot adores Ruby and is far too guileless to conceal it. Lot's blatant worship of Ruby is a sort of family joke, kindly done. Lot was damaged by a forceps delivery in the days when they were so fashionable, in the days when highly paid men wouldn't wait for women to push their babies out, too keen to return to their golf-courses and their gins. There was no compensation for poor Pat Dance when that awful light dawned and she slowly realised that Lot was failing to meet the targets set so brilliantly by her bright-as-a-button little blond-haired Bart, ten years the elder. But they loved their gentle, different child just as much, if not more. Their lives were taken up by the wickedly essential everyday battle for his rights. Oh yes, the whole day would have been quite fun in a chaotic kind of way – if Ruby still felt easy with Bart.

But she bloody well doesn't. And who can blame her?

The only one of Ruby's guests to sense that something is wrong is the brain-damaged Lot. Still in his twenties, Lot is the Jesus in every epic, the disconcerting presence, the divine man with the piercing Robert Powell eyes and the faraway smile. Long and loping and gaunt, his clothes and his jet-black hair flow smoothly behind him and there is something distinguished about his pain. Once he was wrongly diagnosed as schizophrenic but Lot does not fit any labels, he goes his own strange way. Hauntingly beautiful, uncannily graceful, Lot is uneasy this morning; he knows there is something wrong, and he sends Ruby long worried looks.

Christmas lunch is a tremendous success because of the effort put in by the mortified Bart. The children behave quite wonderfully. Naomi sparkles, her lovely, almost-white crinkly hair is the fine-spun silver of the fibre-glass decorations. She is just like a fairy.

Afterwards Harry suggests that they take the children outside to play in the snow, and 'Give you a well-deserved break, Ruby Tuesday.'

Ruby sighs. 'I'll clear up while you're gone.'

'I'll stay and help you,' says Lot, and everyone gently smiles.

'You go out and enjoy yourself. I'll stay here and do that.' Someone will notice there's something wrong if Bart isn't more careful.

'I would rather stay indoors in peace, for a while, and Lot would prefer to stay in the warm, I think. He's not too happy in the snow. He hates it if people chuck snowballs at him.'

Ruby throws all her efforts into pretending. She could confide in Elspeth, but it is impossible for the sisters to spend that much time on their own today without attracting attention. She could probably confide in Pat Dance, because she has known so much pain in her life Ruby's mother-in-law virtually bubbles over with genuine kindness and understanding, but that would spoil everyone's Christmas. Pat would have to have it out there and then in front of everybody, no messing. No, Ruby will just have to bide her time and wait to attack Bart again the minute that everyone has gone. But in the meantime Ruby is forced to endure as the intolerable pain bites deeper.

Lot and Ruby stand alone in the kitchen of the silent house. Lot stares at Ruby, trying hard to understand. He waits patiently beside her, his deepset features in shadow, holding the tea towel, while her fair face steams in the running hot water. She tries to put him at ease by smiling, but she sniffs forlornly and fails. Even the Fairy liquid has taken on a merrily malicious Christmas gleam.

One warm tear trickles down her cheek. She brushes it off with the back of her hand, afraid in case Lot will see it and become upset. She must pull herself together, just for a little while longer; she must, she must.

But she cannot, she seems to have lost all control. If she doesn't talk to somebody soon she is either going to choke to death or throw up all over the greasy dishes. Lot sinks down beside her, the perfect, patient listener. His whole body stiffens as he hears the hurt pour out of his idol, his dream woman and his queen.

'She must be a very wicked, evil person,' he says eventually, when she has finished, his eyes impassive as a camera lens. 'She must be the most wicked person ever to be born on this whole earth.'

Ruby sniffs a little hysterically. 'Well, hardly that bad, Lot. After all, Bart had something to do with it. It does take two, you know.'

But it is too late; Lot fails to hear her. He has sunk into one of his deepest trances and when Ruby, slightly better, gets up to tackle the dishes again he stays at the table with his head in his hands, sunk in the deeply bewildering world that is his own.

It's as simple as constructing boxes, really; you flatten, bring up, stick and fold over. A to B to C. He is going to find this wicked person and throw her away so she'll never hurt anyone, especially Ruby, again. Dispose of the dirty sweepings.

Because Lot knows, oh yes, Lot understands what has happened. And he might view the world through unusual eyes but he has certainly arrived at the right conclusion.

In essence, Ruby Dance's heart has been broken.

TWELVE

WHEN DADDY GETS UP, stretches, and declares that it might be time to start thinking about going home, Sacha's outburst gives Vanessa real pain. It seems somehow to reflect on her – the temporary substitute mother. The embarrassing silence that follows is difficult, the fuss made worse because it takes place in front of a stranger, Suzie's nice fat cuddly mummy.

'I want to stay with you!' The demand is childishly direct as usual. She clings to the back of Daddy's old hacking jacket, faded and familiar with the sticky old Nuttall's Mintoes of days gone by glued to the inside pocket; it smells of him. She tugs it. Daddy's daunted eyes find Suzie's. She closes hers slowly. She's saying, 'Oh no, surely not this again,' easing out a long steady breath.

'Just for Boxing Day!' Sacha's head swivels on her babyish neck, she embraces the room, trying to grab with a clumsy, hysterical gesture. 'Anywhere!' she cries, her glasses flashing. 'We don't need beds, we sleep anywhere, don't we, Amber? You tell them! Ask anyone!'

Daddy's kneebones click and he hitches his trouser-knees to adjust himself down to the small girl's height. He is calm and gentle. 'That would be quite wrong, Sacha, don't you understand? That would be taking advantage. That would be breaking all the rules. Because of the snow I've had you all day as it is, and now Mummy will be waiting for you at home.'

'What rules?' It is useless and Daddy is silly to persevere. No one can argue with Sacha in this frame of mind, she's not old enough to listen to reason, she continues to shout her demands while her voice grows higher, choked with sobs as she reaches a state of absolute despondency.

'It is getting dark,' Daddy gallantly tries to persuade her, 'and I'm worried about the state of the roads. If this lot freezes . . .' his voice, threaded with lies, goes dotting away to an icy nowhere, trailing off as in a book.

Suzie is watching with a strained face, and tension lines web the edges of her eyes. Everyone's on the watch. You can see that Eileen would love to speak. Her dumpy body leans forward, her elbows rest on her knees but her restless hands want to stretch out, to mend, to cure, to be helpful. Through a kindly face and soft blue eyes she stares at the audience of agitated faces, she licks her lips, ready to speak, but says nothing. Isobel, frail and grim, who so disapproves of divorce, would dearly like to remind everyone, 'You see? You see what I mean? Such selfishness brings its own rewards.'

What is happening here? Surely what is happening cannot really be happening! Vanessa blames herself; a sense of powerlessness raises its head so suddenly it is terrifying. *What about Mother?* How can they stay here and leave Mother alone all night without food or supervision? She certainly should have foreseen this reaction.

'We have all had such a lovely day, poppet, playing in the snow, pulling the crackers, now please don't go and spoil it.'

But Sacha just goes redder than ever as her anger boils over, impervious to reason, and now Amber, disturbed and afraid, starts her habit of repeating her twin word for word as she always does when she is over-excited about something.

'I'll run away,' shouts Sacha.

'I'll run away,' says Amber.

'And then you'll be sorry!'

'And then you'll be sorry!'

Sacha flings herself on to the sofa and buries her wet face under a huge floral cushion. Her 'somebody is being very naughty' is too muffled to hear until Amber interprets it as she stands there stiffly with one small hand on the sofa arm. 'Somebody is being very naughty.'

'Listen to me, poppet.' Daddy places exasperated pats on the hot, shaking, uniformed back of his weeping child. None of his kisses quite touch. In the *Radio Times* they call him thrusting and penetrative. Some people say that to be interviewed by Robin Townsend is better than getting a puppet of yourself on *Spitting Image*, or being invited to take part on *Desert Island Discs*. 'I understand why you think we are being naughty and not realising how you are feeling, but that's really not true at all, is it, Suzie?'

Suzie, on the very edge of her chair, nods 'we've all been through this before haven't we' encouragement.

'You see, if we let you stay here for Boxing Day we all know what would happen. We would have to go through this very same tantrum tomorrow night.'

'No, you wouldn't! No! No!' Sacha's words are difficult to decipher as they come through the cushion, punctuated by shuddering sobs. 'I would promise on my honour that I'd go quietly tomorrow. I would probably get in the car at six o'clock without even being told.'

Poor Sacha. She has sensed a hole in the forbidding wall of adult disbelief. She is trying to push herself through it.

'I don't think so, darling ...'

'Oh dear,' exclaims Eileen, her gentle coil of white hair listing dangerously as she follows the drama, resting on one arm, then the other. And then she mouths with her lips alone, 'Oh, lovies, this is quite dreadful.'

'It is quite understandable.' Isobel stirs the chilly undercurrent and her closed eyelids are white and fragile as communion wafers. 'After all, there is nothing for them at home.'

'Oh Isobel, please!' snaps Robin.

'I hate you all!' screams Sacha, from underneath her cushion.

'I hate you all,' says Amber automatically. Her handle of orange hair sprouts from the elasticated edge of her nursing cap and bobs up and down like a question mark and her freckles darken her face.

Vanessa speaks out with as much force as she dares. Sacha must be made to back down. She can't think of anything with which to bribe her, except for an unabridged reading of her favourite story about the skin horse who is LOVED and therefore becomes miraculously REAL, unlike the expensive mechanical toys or the doll with the golden hair. 'Sacha, remember we've got our special meal and it's cooking in the oven at the moment. We are going to need your help to get it all ready nicely *as a treat for Mother.*'

'And I hate Mother,' shouts Sacha. 'I do not want to give her any treat.'

At any moment now, Sacha, delirious in her agony, is going to blurt out the awful truth. Of course there is always the chance that nobody will believe her, but . . .

'Oh Robin, all right, let them stay.' Suzie drops her bombshell in a fast, gruff voice as she stalks over to the window, and the extraordinary thing is that she means it. She is standing, holding the curtain and she might also be holding back tears but you can't see her face. More likely she's just sneering. Vanessa noted with interest that throughout Sacha's performance Suzie never lost her quiet confidence, her self-assurance. Suzie's doing this for Daddy; she wants him to see what a martyr she is, how she's pained by his children. She stares through the small panes, through the thickly distorting glass; she stares out into the fading light.

Everybody is stunned.

Sacha goes instantly still and is silent except for the odd wet sniff. They all stare at Suzie's straight back and Joe coughs lightly from the far end of the room, not making any particular point, only clearing his throat. You can sense Isobel's constant impatience with him. He has stayed inside himself all afternoon, tucked in like a tortoise.

'D'you know, I think that's a jolly good idea,' says Eileen, glowing all over.

'I suppose I could telephone Caroline and see what she says. I would have to telephone anyway, to remind her to turn the oven off.'

'Oh yes, Daddy, yes!' Sacha jumps up and down, crazy now. Her pink tongue pokes wildly through the gap in her teeth and her tear-stains already look dry.

'I do not want to stay here. I can't stay.'

Oh thank you, Jesus! Vanessa stifles the urge to cross the room and kiss Dominic hard, to take her cool and calculated hero into her arms and hug him.

Daddy stares. 'You don't want to stay here for the night?' His eyes are flecked with violet, his voice is tired and old. 'Well why not, Dominic, for God's sake? Why can't you?'

'Because I have forgotten my puffer,' he replies, head down, peering furtively out through his eyelashes at Vanessa.

'It would be awkward if we stayed here, really, Daddy. I know

Mother would be upset if we didn't give her notice and she is going away. She is waiting for the meal we promised, we've been here all day and now we really ought to be with her.' Vanessa thanks God for finally giving her back her voice.

Daddy simply nods. 'You are absolutely right, of course. Some other time perhaps.'

Sacha sucks at the finger she's stuck in her mouth, her ankles are crossed, she doesn't understand what is going on. She pleads, 'But Suzie said we could, didn't you, Suzie?'

'It was never a very sensible idea,' Daddy puts in quickly.

The sulking child raises her eyes and meets Vanessa's direct gaze. She has forgotten all about Mother and now the memory flashes back. It's to do with secrets she must not tell, happenings she must keep hidden or there will be a very great deal of trouble. She purses her lips and keeps them tight together, ashamed of herself suddenly, and aware how near she has come to letting everyone down. Her abrupt change of attitude is astonishing, enough to stir the mildest curiosity but of course none of these adults have the slightest idea ... Vanessa must stop worrying, but how easy it is to believe they are blessed with special powers, like God, and are watching and waiting to see what she'll do.

'If we go back, please can you come and get us again? Can we come back tomorrow?' Sacha wheedles, twisting with guilt and remorse as she fumblingly replaces her glasses.

'Well, actually poppet, that would be difficult, as you see we've arranged for some people to pop in tomorrow. It would be very boring for you. You wouldn't like it.'

'All day?'

'Yes. All day, I'm afraid.'

Open house on Boxing Day, exactly the same as it used to be at Camberley Road when Daddy lived there but now how strange it is, life goes on exactly the same for some people while for others − Vanessa glances at Sacha − their worlds are turned upside down. She will read her sister the whole of *The Skin Horse* this evening; she won't skip even half a page.

'Will these people be bringing their children?'

'Oh no, I shouldn't think so.' But even Sacha is astute enough at six to know that Daddy is lying, even if his half-truths are clever like a conjuror's, snaking down his sleeve so he has to wipe his hand. He forces himself to brighten. 'Come on, gang, let's find your coats and say our thank yous to Suzie.'

Vanessa is angry with Daddy. Can't he see Sacha's crumpled face, doesn't the sight of so much pain hurt him? 'Thank you for having me.' 'Thank you for such a lovely tea.' They are forced to smile at Suzie because she holds their happiness in her hands but Vanessa's is the smile of a ceremonial Madonna carried through the streets on religious holidays, pale and waxen, moulded to her face.

They help Daddy to find his spade and he puts some sacks in the back of the car. Outside the garage Sacha whispers to Vanessa, 'It's not fair that Suzie's got a mother like that.'

'What – Eileen?'

It seems that Sacha's ashamed of her disloyalty; she doesn't want to say much more. 'Yes, why can't we? And a cottage called Poppins, cats, and a lovely wild garden?' And then she looks down, trails her small red boot in the snow, unable to find the words that she wants. 'We would be different.' She runs away to find him, she clutches a toggle on Daddy's coat. 'You should have a bar of chocolate, too, Daddy, in case you get stranded.' Sacha's concern is desperately real – how can she forgive him so soon, and how can he let her?

Would we be different?

The white of the snow soothes Vanessa's head during the journey home.

Dominic can't stop talking ... about silly, ridiculous things that don't matter and probably are not true. Anyone would think that his life was happy and normal. 'D'you know, Daddy, that they have to have a proper funeral ceremony even if they find someone's leg?'

Daddy concentrates on the hazardous driving. He says, 'Is that so?'

'Yes, Westminster Council had to call in a priest last year when they buried a woman's leg they found floating in a canal.'

'Really?'

'Would they dig it up and bury it with the rest of her if they found her?'

'I expect so. But you'd think they'd have burnt it.'

'Oh no, they might need it later, in case there was foul play.'

Vanessa looks to see if the ribbons are still round the trunk of the tree ... she sits back and sighs, relieved to see that they are, although they are wet and drooping, and have lost most of their colour. She is saddened to see there are no flowers any longer. This is the spot where, back in the spring, a sixteen-year-old joyrider crashed his stolen car and died, and the tree where it happened was surrounded by flowers until recently ... all sorts of flowers, from stiffly posh bouquets to soft little posies. The number of bunches dwindled as the year went by. Every time Vanessa comes past she stares with a sinking heart. 'The boy's mother might think that people have stopped remembering,' she confided to Daddy one day. 'What will happen when the ribbons rot? She'll think that nobody cares any more and be even more unhappy.'

'No she won't.' Daddy is wise; he understands terrible things like death. 'She will know that the giving of flowers is just the beginning of mourning. When the flowers die, Vanessa, they leave room for something more permanent to grow in people's hearts.'

'You are so morbid sometimes, Vanny.' Camilla is far more competent at dealing with the sad facts of life.

There are no flowers there today. Morbid or not, Vanessa is going to pick some snowdrops one day during the holidays and take them along all the same. She tries to see through the windows they pass and wonders where that poor boy's mother lives.

All the other houses are flooded with light, while number fourteen is dark and frowning. It is a kind of prison now and it has taken on the menace of a prison. You can almost imagine you can hear the ghost-wolves howling from the high pine trees over in the park. Her breath catches – she can't breathe: what about the 40-watt sauna light they've left on? Can it be seen from the road?

She shivers with relief, like when she's waited too long for a pee. Thank goodness the sauna is against the back wall of the gym, and the white paint on the windows is thick. In future they will have to think far more carefully about such details. The ordeal has only just begun and already they've been dangerously careless, they could easily have been found out.

'Your mother must have been very tired,' says Daddy. 'She's not up yet. Do you want me to wait? I really think I ought to come in.'

But he does not want to wait ...

... so they say, 'No, we'll be all right.'

The snow still falls but is barely noticeable because the flakes have turned light as icing sugar sprinkling softly down through a sieve. But the fresh snow lies thickly, crisp and shining on top, hardening as evening comes and a cold breeze ices the top layer over.

Getting out of the car is difficult, leaving all that warmth outside on the road, leaving Daddy's smile, and his promise to phone in the morning. 'Say thank you to Caroline for me. I won't come in,' he calls through the crack of the open window. 'I don't want to get stuck, I'd rather keep the engine running.'

Thank you thank you thank you — everyone always has to be thanked, everyone seems to be doing them a favour as if they are beggars with nothing to give of their own, the kind of children who get sent out into forests in order to gather sticks.

Camilla closes the car door and says nothing. Vanessa watches Dominic's lurching run, so eager to get away from the person he most loves. She knows that the minute the twins get inside the house they will ignore all their new, expensive presents and get out the box of catalogue paper dolls.

'Phone me, darling, if you need to, won't you?'

'Yes. I will. Goodnight.'

'Enjoy the turkey, and Happy Christmas!' calls Daddy as, in his own protected pool of light, he drives cautiously away.

Thirteen

It is armed with the wig on the end of the Hoover extension tube that the five children pay their second visit to their mother. Dominic follows with his camera, carrying the torch, because Vanessa says they don't want to attract attention, and if neighbours notice the lights being used after so many long months of darkness they might wonder what's going on. 'I doubt that the torchlight will show from the road,' she says, 'if you shield it with your hand and be sure to keep it pointed the other way.'

It is already seven o'clock and there is no point in waiting around for the turkey. None of them is hungry after Suzie's tea — nothing home-made, not even the sandwiches, Eileen wouldn't have treated them like that — and the bird isn't even tempting, but white and watery with strings of bloody mucus inside. They decide to turn the oven full up. The fan whirrs; it will not be ready until much later this evening.

Vanessa raises her palm in a saintly gesture as they reach the basement door, and they stand for a while, she praying silently while the others listen.

They had argued over which wig to bring, although not over the basic idea. They were all agreed on that. Without this essential cosmetic device, Mother would feel stripped and humiliated. It would be more cruel than depriving her of her clothes. But which wig? Going, alone, into Mother's bedroom was an unnerving experience. The sense of her spilled from every half-opened drawer, from the talcum-powder-strewn shower floor, to the sticky dressing-table jars and the wilted flowers with the message balanced on the browning petals that had not fluttered down to the royal-blue carpet already – from Bart. The atmosphere in here was enraged and unpredictable; it was puzzling, it had something to do with experience of life, with being knocked down, and being grown up. Inside Mother's room Vanessa always feels like a strict spinster aunt.

'We must be careful to keep it exactly like this for when Mrs Guerney comes.' Dominic is good at thinking in advance. Assaulted by the mess, Vanessa was on the verge of tidying up in an effort to calm the calamitous disorder that was hemming her in again as the visit to Mother drew nearer. Flustered by the suffocatingly hot, exotic room, yet she must keep her wits about her.

Ashes to ashes. Dust to dust. Daddy's things went up in a sacrificial blaze and the day after Daddy left, Mother did two things: she took to the telephone and she ordered the decorators in. Daddy's departure heralded a whole sequence of disjointed, peculiar events. It was a time for keeping your head down, it was a time for drifting and flowing. The whole of the house was redone, even the kitchen. For months they lived amongst dust sheets, they moved between galvanised stepladders, they inhaled the intoxicating smell of paint and they moved from bedroom to bedroom as their own rooms were stripped and transformed. Nothing was sacred. Nothing was permanent. Mother was obsessed. One minute she was talking of waging revenge to her friends on the telephone, the next she was supervising the cowering workmen.

'No warning! No – nothing! I still find it impossible to believe.' The friends she chose were women who'd been abandoned themselves ... and Mother knew several. She used to despise them for what she called their martyrdom but now she needed them. 'I wouldn't have him back if he begged me on his knees,' she said, caving in on herself as she settled down in the telephone chair, frowning, examining each long nail in turn, her cigarettes and her lighter in her lap. If one of the children was on the phone already talking she'd press the disconnection buttons and say, 'Move, please!'

Even while she talked she studied her reflection in the hall mirror.

Daddy predicted the recession a whole year before it happened. Privately he still says that it is bizarre the way the West is holding out hope to the newly freed Eastern countries, offering them a way of life that is already quite obviously doomed. 'Unless there's a brand new system, a whole new way of thinking, there is no alternative except absolute catastrophe. But there's no one with the vision to give a lead.'

Vanessa felt glad that everyone else was about to experience catastrophe. Why should they be suffering catastrophe in frozen isolation, almost unnoticed in Camberley Road? But then she felt guilty; she remembered Our Lord and His wounds, and at school she learned how important it was to suffer. Every night when she undressed she looked hopefully over her body for signs of stigmata but found only the vile lumps and bumps of adolescence.

When she turns into a woman she's going to lose Daddy.

'Would we know if Daddy died?' asked Amber tonelessly. 'Would anyone tell us?' Mother pushed her aside with a steely glare and nobody else could answer. Amber went straight upstairs and deliberately overfed her two goldfish; she showered the fish-food into the tank. In the morning they floated, fins up and silvery, on the peppery surface of the water. They buried them in a shoebox in the garden and Amber made them sing *Greensleeves* because it was sadder than any suitable hymn. 'At least I know exactly where they are,' she said, satisfied. 'And now, if you wouldn't mind, I think I would rather be alone.' The children left her and watched beside the back door. She knelt at the edge of the grave and her hank of hair shone red as the Little Red Rooster as the dying sun caught it.

It never appeared to cross Mother's mind that she might have driven Daddy out. In her telephone act she'd be gayer than ever, betraying the tension in her face, 'No,' she said, 'it's extraordinary. As far as I know, there is nobody else. He says he wants his own space ... can you believe that, Jenny? I never used to believe in the male menopause but you have to wonder. He'll be growing a beard and turning up at a men's support group next, there's bound to be something in Hackney. No dear, of course he hasn't taken the children. Do they ever?' And her loud, crowing laugh could be heard all over the house.

She twiddled the diamond in the huge claw of her engagement ring. The children lowered their eyes when they went by, making it look as if they weren't listening, and sometimes she'd crook the receiver in her neck and mime the pouring of a drink, opening her eyes very wide to communicate great urgency. Then someone would bring her a glass and the gin. But these conversations were so repetitive that eavesdropping soon became boring.

She went to an exclusive shop behind Harrods where she bought thick carpets and enormous curtains that were so long that they trailed across the floor; she had the furniture re-upholstered and even the window seats got padded and the food tasted of turpentine.

It was summer-time and the smell of mown grass was hot and sweet. Daddy came and took them for a walk in the park right opposite the house. There'd been so many questions she'd planned to ask but then Vanessa could think of nothing. She had never felt so dull and stupid in front of Daddy before.

'Why are we all walking along like this?' Amber asked them, small and straight, going along in front bearing the precious jar of beads from which she would not be parted. In her little sundress she looked just like a lavender painting. Daddy plodded heavily along, affected by the heat.

They stopped by the lake to watch the boats and the people fooling about. They sat on the grass, a wasp wouldn't leave Daddy alone and he flapped at it with his printed list of telephone numbers. He gave them to Vanessa ... all crumpled to the shape of his grip ... and he told her solemnly, with great effort, 'If ever you need me, even in the middle of the night, I will be at one of these numbers. If I could have told you I'd be leaving, I would have done, but it just wasn't possible. I didn't like the way it happened any more than you did, but there was no other way. Just because I'm not at home any more does not mean that I love any of you less, or care any less, or think about you any less ...'

'Daddy, look, the wasps are coming from that litter bin.'

'Do you understand what I'm trying to say, Sacha?' Hopelessly he tried to capture her attention with the seriousness of his eyes.

'It's that can of Coke – that's what they're after.' She would not listen to him. She picked up a stick and started to stir up the malodorous contents of the litter bin.

'Amber's fish are dead,' said Dominic stolidly. He had turned his usual coffee-brown which made the whites of his eyes and his teeth shine. 'Daddy, did you know that farmers commit suicide more than any other group of people except doctors?'

Harassed and hot, frustrated by his inability to communicate, Daddy endeavoured to humour him.

'Oh, and why is that?'

'Because they are used to putting their animals down when they're no use any more. If a farmer fails he feels useless, and so he puts himself down, just as he'd put down one of his animals. Usually they shoot themselves.'

Very often the things that Dominic comes out with don't make much sense, but Daddy was trying hard to understand. 'Am I useless now, Dom? Is that what you think, because I don't come home any more? Would you rather I was dead?'

'I never said that.' Dominic strutted about on the edge of the lake, looking very foreign in his gaudy knee-length shorts and bright yellow T-shirt, like one of the tourists. He pointed across the sparkling blue water. 'I'd really love a remote-control boat like that. Josh Collins has got one of those. They're divorced.'

Daddy looked sad. He didn't answer.

There was a great fuss because Sacha got stung and Daddy had to buy her a green ice-lolly to hold against her arm – she insisted that only a green one would cure it. Camilla, who'd been quiet all day, said she'd done it on purpose in order to get more of Daddy's attention.

It was not a good day. That first, serious talk didn't make anyone feel any better, in fact it was all very uncomfortable.

Vanessa drew her knees up tight. She sat on a dust-sheeted chair and watched the television pictures of the starving children in their flat, brown land. There was an appeal but Mother said it was no use sending money which would only end up funding more wars. Vanessa stole a five-pound note from Mother's handbag and put it in the collection box at St Mary's. She lit a candle and prayed for Mother's soul as well as her own. Amber looked round at the new, strange drawing room and said at the time, 'Daddy won't come back now, will he?'

Camilla came back from a day with a friend with her ears pierced. Mother came out from her wallpaper book and went mad. 'How dare you! How dare you do such a common thing! You will never be the same again! You have mutilated yourself, and you didn't even ask me first!'

'Did it hurt?' Vanessa was terribly impressed.

'Yes,' said Camilla. 'It was agony. And I enjoyed it.' Just like Vanessa felt when she stole that fiver.

'Don't tell me you're another one with your father's perverted ways, it's bad enough putting up with your sister,' snapped Mother, taking a sip of dry Martini as she turned one more of her monstrous wallpaper pages.

'Every day we must come in here and muck it up after Mrs Guerney's gone. Every day we must dig out some suitable clothes and drape them around to make it look as if they've been worn. Mrs Guerney has eyes like a hawk.' Mrs Guerney, of course, was nothing like a hawk, more like an ordinary brown female blackbird, far too busy with the essentials of life to be preening her feathers or flaunting her colours. Dominic pushed a finger into a jar of cold cream. He sniffed it and read the label; he looked like an expert wine-taster. 'Nourishing,' he said with disapproval, and then he wiped his hands roughly clean with a tissue as if it was Mother herself that he'd inadvertently got stuck on his fingers. 'We must even try and make it look as if the make-up has been used. And the bed. Detail is all-important.'

Whenever he's been with Daddy, Dominic begins to sound like his father. He tries to use his words and expressions and this is what makes people who don't know him believe that he is precocious. To Vanessa he sounds much more defenceless when he does it, much younger than when he is being himself. Dominic's not tough, he's not tough at all.

The twins stood on the threshold of the bedroom looking tired, with their fallen white socks exposing the sharp little shinbones of their stork-like legs. Sacha's gaze was glued to the floor under the bed as if she was afraid that Mother would spring out, screaming a witchy shriek, and pounce on her.

Vanessa drew them inside. 'It's okay, Sacha, don't look so scared, it's perfectly all right. You know that Mother's not here, she can't see what we're doing.'

'I know, but it feels as if she can.' Sacha's face was clenched tight, determined to survive no matter what Mother did.

'Which wig?'

Camilla had already opened the wardrobe where the wigstands stood on the shelf inside, six of them, heads stuffed with straw, stiff beige heads without eyes ... one of them bald. They must remember to put the chestnut wig back.

'Well, which one is her favourite?'

'Which one is most likely to suit her mood?'

There was a silence as they all considered this last point. Eventually Dominic said, 'The black one.' He picked it off the wigstand. It was well-brushed and cared for; out of all her possessions, her wigs were among the items over which Mother always took pride.

'And what about a clean vest and knickers?' When they turned to stare at Amber she said with her sweetest smile, 'Well, she's been down there for a night and a day.'

'I suppose we should,' said Vanessa to Camilla.

Mother's underwear was made out of silk, slippery and warm to the touch, lots of thin straps and lacy fringes. Sorting through it felt worse than anything they had already done, as if they were touching something far too personal, like Mother's own naked skin, the cold, paper skin which Vanessa had run her fingers along when she'd found the rude pictures, before she'd burnt them. 'Nothing too sexy,' said Camilla. 'After all, she's only going to be stuck down there. She's not going anywhere. Nobody's going to see her.'

'Unless we have to call the doctor!' Sacha was hopeful. She sounded pleased, standing with her hands in the businesslike pockets of her white, starched apron.

'Don't be so silly, Sacha.' But Vanessa has made this remark before, and it sounded as weak as it did the first time, 'Mother's not sick.'

Behind her glasses Sacha rolled her eyes. 'Well, she was jolly well sick yesterday. All over the carpet, too. And I was only asking. Can't I ask?'

With all the sedateness of a six-year-old child Sacha leads the procession towards the door of the basement, holding the black wig aloft on the end of the Hoover extension tube. She looks a little like Mother Augustus with that flapping white seagull cap on her head. She could be the chorister who wears white gloves, leading the choir at St Mary's, carrying the cross.

Vanessa is unaccountably upset. 'Don't do it like that. Don't mock.'

'I wasn't mocking anything, silly. We're having a ceremony and somewhere an organ ought to be playing.' Yes, a deafening, minor chord striking deep into her heart. Vanessa can almost hear it; her ears are roaring.

'I think we should ring a bell, the next time,' said Sacha with proper solemnity. 'For Mothertime. And it probably ought to be silver.'

FOURTEEN

IT IS MOTHER who is confined, so why does Vanessa suffer the angry, helpless frustrations of a prisoner, someone who has slipped off the edge of life? Trying so hard to make sure that everything is forgotten but hatred?

They follow their leader with eyes like spies unsticking envelopes. The heels of their shoes clang round and round on the metal spiral steps.

Amber holds the new menu preciously, close to her chest. Dominic allowed them to tear a page out of his new art book so the menu for the evening is on smart, stiff paper with an oval border. Decorated with pen and ink holly leaves, red and green, there are two choices crayoned upon it in letters alternately blue, green and yellow: she can have ham salad and Christmas cake, or sausage roll and green salad followed by mince pie with cream.

Amber is holding her breath and her cheeks balloon out as though she is swimming underwater. She crosses and uncrosses her legs, and shakes a frantic head in reply to Vanessa's worried enquiry. 'I've been! We can bring down some turkey later for a midnight feast,' she whispers, puffing air between gritted teeth, letting the tension go.

Camilla carries Mother's change of underwear. She has folded it neatly and now it is in a carrier bag but she holds it out at arm's length, not in the way you would carry ordinary shopping.

Vanessa is aware that they bring their gifts like offerings and that Mother is sitting there encased in pinewood, hidden from the eyes of all but the chosen, a holy relic like the Shroud of Turin. Or poor, poisoned

Snow White. Preserved behind glass and all the more powerful. But where do you draw the line between an acceptable relic and a graven image? The first, she supposes, exists to satisfy curiosity, but the second is a replacement of God. At the moment Mother seems more like the first ... yet their world is already revolving around her.

The atmosphere is as stale and ominous as the crypt that runs under the vast stone floors of St Mary's, and you have to pay fifty pence to look at the old bones entombed there. This is sacred ground, too, where you might find bones, a place where evil has been done. Dominic prefers a trip to the vaults at St Mary's where the air is the colour of hymn books to a visit to the London Dungeon, and he says the spooky word T O M B till it echoes off the crumbling walls. The gym is eerie in torchlight. Dominic directs the beam like an usherette at the cinema; the yellow cylindrical sphere exaggerates the metal and chrome, it picks out the cold stainless steel of the apparatus which takes on the menace of a torturer's tools. Footsteps echo. The sauna hums. A dimmer light shines out through the porthole window, not nearly strong enough to be seen through the window out on the road, thank goodness. Sacha steps forward and kneels beside the pipe-hole, her nursing cap almost touching the floor as she calculates the angle and, like a chimney sweep shuffling his rods through his hands, she licks her lips in concentration as she pushes the wig through the hole on the end of the extension tube.

'It is like the arched window in *Playschool.*' Amber lines up breath-lessly behind Sacha with the menu rolled up in her hands like a scroll. 'Only it's not big enough to see anything through it, not quite, just the floor.'

Vanessa, who has no gift to bring except words, touches her crucifix as she raises herself to the level of the clouded window. She takes a deep, troubled breath, murmurs a silent prayer and then:

'Mother, are you all right?'

Mother has removed her tight black dress and you can see her ivory petticoat peeping out from the flaps of her fur coat. Where is the dress? Screwed up over there in the corner along with her tights where it looks as if she has thrown them. Mother is screwed up too, all in a huddle with her arms wrapped round herself, shivering, with wet, spiky hair as if she's just come out of the shower, and they can't have removed all the make-up because her eyes look bruised and black — dead eyes in a crumpled face. The rings on her fingers flash. When she smiles it is hideous. Even her skin, something has happened to her skin! Her skin has gone the wrinkled brown of a Choc Chip Cookie.

But Mother's attention is fixed on the wig as it slithers across the floor and comes to a halt not inches from her bare feet. Her toes curl. She watches the wig as if it's a deadly spider, while horror spreads over her like a sheet and she hunches completely into herself, bringing up her knees, hiding her head in her arms. She is like those pictures of unborn babies tied up in knots in women's wombs.

'We looked for peace but no good came: and for a time of health, and behold trouble!' Dear God, what have we done to her?

'It's the black wig, Mother,' Vanessa is quick to explain. 'We thought you might feel better if you ...'

'More worms crawling out ...'

What? The shock of Mother brings on that dreamy, floating, unreal sensation and for a moment Vanessa forgets where she is. She feels a crushing kind of exhaustion as if someone is pushing a pillow down on her head. She cannot make out exactly what Mother is chattering through her clacking teeth.

'MORE WORMS.'

The waiting children start violently. They glance at each other with round, startled eyes, terrified by the harshness of Mother's scream which reverberates and pings off every piece of apparatus.

'Quick! Quick! Try the menu!'

But Amber's hand is trembling as she pushes the scroll through the hole.

Vanessa comes back down for a moment. Her shoulders droop. She stares at Camilla. 'Oh dear, I think there's something the matter with her.'

'Let me see.'

All in a flurry they bring the small, round trampoline and push it in place underneath the window. Vanessa and Dominic hold Camilla's hand, steadying her, as she balances on the springy surface with her waterfall of golden curls gushing down over her face. Camilla is still in her tutu although now she's wearing an almost knee-length mohair cardigan over the top. As she rises and bends forward she looks rigid as a plastic ballerina on the top of a cheap musical box, easy to snap off if you weren't careful. She takes a quick look through the porthole with a fascinated expression on her face before one hand flies to her lip. She needs help to climb down, her hand, with its chewed fingernails, feels bony and icy-cold. She has always suffered from chilblains because of her poor circulation.

'She is shaking like a jelly. And huddled up.'

'Let me look.' Dominic climbs on the trampoline and everyone switches their attention to his face. He watches Mother for as long as a minute, his two palms flat on the door. His brow clears and hardens. 'Mother?' he calls, unexpectedly so the children jump. And then he repeats more loudly, 'Mother, can you hear me?'

'What's she doing now?'

'There is no need to whisper, Camilla, she can't hear you.'

'But what was she shouting about worms?'

Dominic peers through the window again. His camera dangles round his neck. 'She's not shouting now. I can't see her face at all now, she's got it completely covered up.'

'I want to look!'

Vanessa snaps, panic rising. 'No, no Sacha, not now. Next time we come, perhaps.'

'That's not fair!' The child's voice quivers.

'Don't start, Sacha. I'm not Daddy, and I'm not in the mood to be bothering with you.'

'I can ask!'

Dominic's report lacks real concern; he uses the same crisp air of authority that Daddy does when he talks about terrible things on the television. Whenever Vanessa questions Daddy he says, 'What I am saying is bad enough, they don't want me to break down in front of them as well. That's not my job, darling, and nor would it help anyone.' Dominic says, 'She is huddled in the corner with her coat right round her. But she's still shaking all over. I think the sudden appearance of the wig must have frightened her. Perhaps we should have knocked first and told her what we were doing. Maybe we should have given her some warning. And I think she is still cold.'

'How can she possibly be cold?'

Dominic takes another look. 'Well, we don't know that the heating controls are working. It must be ages since anything down here has been serviced. It can't be working. If she was hot she'd be red in the face but she isn't, she's sort of pale and crinkly.'

'But we daren't turn it up any higher, Dom. It is seventy-eight degrees already.'

His reaction is as cool as the stainless steel that surrounds him. As if he is nothing to do with any of this, he says, 'It won't hurt. And anyway, I think she might be trying it on. Hang on a minute, I'll see how she reacts to the flash.' And he brings his Instamatic to his eye, pausing briefly before clicking the shutter.

'No reaction, nothing at all,' he reports, the film whirring on. 'But I still think she's trying it on.'

'How do you mean?' All this would feel so different if they had chosen a warm, sunny room.

'She wants us to open the door and this is her way of trying to frighten us. She might well be pretending she's ill. If we give her another burst of heat she'll learn that behaving like this won't work.'

Reward and punishment? Can this be the gentle, sympathetic, soft-hearted Dominic, Mother's considerate child, who would give his last coin to a beggar?

'I told you she would be ill.' Sacha puffs up with glee.

'But she's not ill, Sacha, that's just it. She wants us to think she's ill so we open the door. And then what do you think will happen?'

'She'll go mad.' Sacha's mouth goes down and tightens. Her chin sticks out in a knob like a little old woman's.

'Something bad will happen to Vanessa.' Amber is close to tears. Mother's scream has frightened her badly. 'You heard what Mother said last time we came down – don't you remember, Sacha? Vanny will be taken away and they won't even tell her for how long. To a special unit. We might not see Vanny for years, probably not until she's grown up. All wrinkled and old and not even knowing who we are any more.'

Sacha gives her bullfrog pout. Her bottom lip trembles as she throws out the shrill accusation, 'And I suppose Mother won't even want her clean knickers now.'

Camilla stares aimlessly down at her carrier bag. 'No, I suppose not now.'

'We have to start as we mean to go on, don't you see?' Dominic is the only one to remain unmoved by the drama. His impatience shows.

His breathing becomes more laboured as he presses his point home. 'Mother has got to know where she stands. When we go back to school this house will be empty during the day, apart from Ilse and Mrs Guerney. We won't be around to keep an eye on things down here. So that's why we've got to teach her who is in command in the few days we have left.'

'This isn't Dungeons and Dragons, Dom, and she doesn't look as if she is pretending.'

'Vanessa! Mother is an experienced actress!'

'Well, I think she looks ill.'

'All right, so are you prepared to take the chance?'

Unconvinced, and yet it would be such a relief to believe that Mother is merely misbehaving. Vanessa can't argue any more, and why should she, anyway? Why should she spring to Mother's defence? Why should she feel responsible?

Dominic says smoothly, 'Why don't we give it a little more time? There's no need to make any decisions yet. We'll keep coming down to see what's happening but I think I'm right. She's not ill. Mother is never really ill. Even when she says she's got a migraine she's up there reading or watching TV in her room. Guzzling chocolates. She gets better quickly enough if someone asks her out. It is important that we don't become over-emotional in all this.'

'You are talking as if this will go on and on. We can't keep her down here for ever, can we?' Vanessa's heart flutters as the thought strikes her, as she asks the unsettling question, as she is engulfed by the brief, unpleasant vision of the years that threaten to follow ... Herself, unable to move away from this house, forever living with this terrible secret, waiting for the police to find out, knowing that one day she will be taken away with a blanket over her head and cameras outside the front door and furious old women knitting and spitting. Her life in ruins ... *and all because of Mother.* 'Move away a minute, Dom, let me have another look.'

Mother raises her head, frowns, and disconcertingly slowly her narrowed eyes focus on the face through the window. She can see Vanessa, it's as if she failed to recognise her before. She looks – ravaged, with clenched teeth. It's horrible. And then, much worse than that, she slowly acts out a parody of the mime she uses when she is on the telephone, the mime she uses to attract the children's attention when she wants a drink. Vanessa cannot remove her eyes no matter how much she wants to. In awful slow-motion Mother's shaking hand comes up to form a claw round an invisible bottle. She watches it to make quite sure the final effect is correct. Then she turns her head to concentrate on the other hand which snakes out from the furry depths of the coat in order to cup a fantasy glass. Vanessa stares at Mother's eyes. Here they go ... they open wide to communicate urgency, but they're not like Mother's eyes any more. Empty of command, they are lost and far away and more like the eyes of a terrified child. Begging eyes. Begging hands. Like someone starving might pray in a famine, kneeling in rags beside the walls of some biblical city.

Her coat slithers off her shoulder. The shoulder-strap of her slip follows the trailing fur, exposing those bony hollows in her chest and then ...

'One of Mother's bosoms has come out!'

'Oh no!'

'Let me see!'

'No, Sacha! And you certainly should not be giggling!' Vanessa backs away, pale, trembling, clutching her magic crucifix.

Dominic looks furiously disgusted. He gasps, 'She is doing this on purpose, can't you see!' He is nearly in tears. 'Let's go upstairs. I need my puffer. Let's just leave her. When she's had enough she will settle down.'

'Has she got enough water? She will die without water but you can go without food for days.'

So Vanessa must look through the porthole again. She rises in trepidation only to find Mother still holding her terrible pose, imaginary bottle in one hand, glass in the other, begging for a drink with her clothes half off her like people you see in shop doorways. Oh, poor, poor Daddy.

'Yes, the bucket is still almost full but that old water must be stale by now.'

'We can't help that,' says Dominic, very upset but still able to think more practically than anyone else. 'Next time we come down we can push more water through the pipe-hole. We can push it through in a sealed ice pack.'

'She's not going to want any turkey, is she, Vanny?'

'No, Amber.' Vanessa remembers that steaming white bird. 'And I don't think I'm going to want any either.'

Dominic turns the sauna heat to ninety-five degrees, muttering as he does so: 'That'll fix it,' and in the face of Mother's shocking behaviour, no one can contradict him.

FIFTEEN

THE TELEPHONE RINGS as they are sitting, picking listlessly at the turkey – they didn't bother to carve it, they just pulled the crispy bits off – round the kitchen table, smiling at Vanessa while eyeing the mushy frozen sprouts and pushing them around on plates made wet with Oxo gravy. 'Ugh! There's still blood in the middle of it!'

'There is more cranberry sauce,' Vanessa urges, her green paper hat giving her a plumpness she does not possess. It makes her look like a motherly cardinal. 'Just help yourself.'

It is always a bell that signals alarm. Amber is right – they should ring a bell the next time they pay a visit to Mother.

'We'll have to answer it. It might be someone who's been trying all day.'

'We can say that Mother is out, or asleep.'

'That depends on who it is.'

'Leave the machine to answer, then we can decide what to do.' The urgency of the bell is driving them mad. It grows louder and louder until the click of the answering machine brings temporary relief. 'Caroline, don't worry, it is only me!'

'That's Charlotte!' Camilla's heart sinks. 'You'll have to answer it, Vanny.'

People are more like their bags than their dogs; you can tell an awful lot about people by the favourite bags that they carry. Mother most often carries a flat zip-up purse made out of crocodile skin, brown, crisscrossed, dotted and snappy. Charlotte is a large, messy, disorganised woman and she chooses a sealskin shoulder bag crammed full so the flap won't close, while Mrs Guerney, who has seen the Queen in the flesh, and Princess Margaret and the Queen Mother, uses a plastic Union Jack holdall and her things are packed away neatly inside. Vanessa picks up the kitchen extension, leaning against the wall fiddling with the pen just as Mother does. She presses the machine to the off position and it feels like diving off a high board because now there is no turning back.

'Hello Charlotte.' But her frightened gaze rests on Camilla.

The tinny voice on the other end grazes the silence of the kitchen. 'Is that you, Vanessa? Happy Christmas, darling, and are you having a wonderful day?'

'Yes thanks, Charlotte. Mother is upstairs at the moment.' She wipes one sweaty hand on her dress. Should she say she's asleep?

'Well, be a dear and call her for me, will you?'

Mother always talks to Charlotte. She would never shout downstairs crossly as she does for so many people, 'For goodness sake, Vanessa, you know by now how to say that I'm out!'

'I'll just go and get her.'

Vanessa can hardly see for the throbbing behind her eyes. She covers the receiver with her hand and beseeches, 'Camilla, do you think you can handle this yet?'

Dominic the perfectionist protests hysterically, 'But she hasn't had a practice!'

'I know she hasn't, but what else can we do?'

'We could say that Mother is in the bath and will call back later.'

'And then what, Dom?' Vanessa's heavy sarcasm goes unnoticed, there just isn't time.

'Well, then we could just leave it and see if Charlotte calls back.'

'That's just putting it off. We're going to have to do this at some time, you know that.'

'But Charlotte is going to be difficult – a long conversation talking about all sorts of personal things.'

'It needn't take long. Mother could say that she's not very well.'

With a face completely devoid of expression Camilla steps forward deliberately as a rehearsed ballerina, and she takes the phone. She clears her throat before she speaks, her determined eyes fixed on Vanessa's. 'Oh Charlotte, I wondered if you'd call.'

'I've been trying all day, darling, where have you been?'

'I can't have heard it. The kids have been over at the Dude's, wined and dined by the Lady who is doubtless even now sobbing into her pillow as she contemplates the damage ...'

Vanessa stares hard at her feet, at her two splayed feet, overlarge, strapped into what Mother calls 'a lady cellist's shoes. And you sit like a lady cellist, too. Do try and be more modest, Vanessa.' Talk about the pot calling the kettle black.

Charlotte is coy with sympathy: 'Oh sweetie, and they left you there all on your own?'

Camilla answers brilliantly: 'Since when has anyone round here given a thought to my feelings? Charlotte, you know better than that. I have been enjoying myself in my usual solitary fashion ...'

'Where's Bart? Stuck with the little woman in Potters Bar, I suppose, playing Santa Claus?'

'Charlotte, I'd far rather not go into that at the moment ...'

'Nothing has happened, surely?'

'Well yes, I'm afraid a great deal has happened,' Camilla replies with no hesitation, 'and I'll tell you about it when I'm more up to par. But I had rather a skinful last night and it's taking its toll. My head feels like a number one runway and my mouth tastes like an ashtray. I was lying down with a mask on my eyes when you called and I think I'd rather return to that prone position as soon as poss. I know you'll understand.'

The children listen open-mouthed as, not only does Camilla sound exactly like Mother but she looks like Mother, pouting, pointing to the crumbs on the floor with the toe of her ballet shoe, flinging her hair back every now and then and running her fingers distraughtly through it, just as Mother does. Her voice is low and confidential, exactly the right tone for talking to Charlotte. She sounds as if she might be disturbed at any moment, she talks quickly and tightly, telling great secrets which might be overheard. But those are tiny bumps of fear on her arms.

'Oh Caroline, I am so, so sorry!' Charlotte's enthusiastic sympathy betrays its underlying pleasure as usual. How can Mother possibly keep this woman as a friend, how can she be so blind and not see ... Charlotte, who looks like a sucking fish, feeds off other people's misery. She loves it ... that is surely why she phones. Pain manifests itself in so many extraordinarily different ways. 'That terrible woman,' Daddy calls her, 'that parasite with a bloodlust for pain! Is she still hanging around?'

But this evening Caroline's misery comes over as so unaffectedly genuine that even the shameless Charlotte cannot pry further at this painful stage. Still, she's been given her fascinating Christmas present; she cannot unwrap it, but it's waiting for her and the anticipation of what it might be when revealed is even more enticing. So she sounds quite happy when she chats on, 'Caroline you poor, poor thing. Of course I understand. Remember, all men are wankers and as I always said, I told you, you were demeaning yourself playing around with that little prick. I know it doesn't feel like that now, but in a few weeks' time you'll wonder whatever you saw in him.'

'I dare say I will, Charlotte. But I've booked in for Broadlands and I expect to go down there on Wednesday or Thursday so I might not be able to get back to you until I return ...' There is even a choke in Mother's voice and for a moment Vanessa, her eyes still glued to her feet as if they're the safest thing about her, worries that Camilla might be going over the top.

Charlotte is understandably miffed. It looks as if she is going to be thwarted. 'Darling! I had no idea it was that bad. This is scandalous! You are upset! Are you quite sure you don't want me to pop round? I could, you know. No prob. I could be over there in half an hour.'

'No, really, that's kind, and it's good to think that somebody cares, but I need to be on my own.'

'Kids okay?'

'Oh, the kids are fine.' Caroline, in the guise of Camilla, refuses to be drawn.

Deeply disappointed, Charlotte slyly goads, 'Well, okay sweetie, if you're sure ...'

Still being painstakingly, frighteningly careful, but with the end so longingly in sight, Camilla goes on, 'I'll get back to you as soon as I can. Under the circs I won't say Happy Christmas.'

Charlotte cackles. 'And I won't say Happy New Year. Those greetings are loaded with bad vibrations ... just you go back to bed, have another drink and don't worry, there's plenty more fish in the sea. You just have to dive deep and sharpen your spear in order to find them.'

'Goodnight, Charlotte.'

'Bye, Caroline.'

Vanessa has to ease the phone from Camilla's rigid hand. She leads her to her chair where she slumps; her white-tighted legs sprawl in front of her, she runs shaking fingers over her cheeks and hair and she looks like an accident victim awkwardly arranged on the road by a passer-by. 'Oh! Oh!' she cries. 'Oh, I was awful!'

Dominic wears an expression of worship as he stares straight at Camilla, a lock of dark hair curling damply over his forehead, the skin on his temples almost translucent. 'You were not awful. You were wicked, brill – amazing. No one would know – *I* didn't know! By the end of all that, honestly, even I didn't know!'

'If you can keep that sort of performance up, Camilla, we are going to be fine!'

'Really, Vanny? Did it sound okay?'

'Camilla, it was absolutely perfect. Mother would have been so proud! You didn't just change your voice, you switched personalities! How I wish we'd recorded it so we could play it back. I'm sure you wouldn't recognise yourself.'

The first phone call has been dealt with more successfully than anyone could ever have expected, but the twins are upset. They didn't like the searing tension, the keeping quiet, the nervousness in the room that burnt cold fear like an opened freezer. And they are not enjoying their Christmas dinner. Quite obviously nobody wants it.

Poor little things. All this is disturbing enough for Vanessa and Camilla and Dominic, who are still trying to come to terms with the last awful visit to Daddy's gym, but for Sacha and Amber, who are tired, who wanted to stay with Daddy, who are bewildered by the speed of the changes of the last twenty-four hours, for them this must be terrifying.

'Come on you two, let's make some cocoa and go and sit for a while by the fire. And then it's bed.' If only Vanessa could give them a loving home, a mother, security ... all the blessings that make Suzie so smug, that Suzie takes for granted. She wants to remove the blight of this childhood ... give me a child until it is seven ... well, there's only a year to go for the twins before they are doomed forever, before it's too late.

'*The Skin Horse*?' Amber's request is a pitiful plea.

'Yes, of course, *The Skin Horse*. What else?'

'Shall I clear up?' Camilla is still shattered and shaking after her gruelling ordeal on the phone.

'No, let's all go. We'll clear up tomorrow morning. Mrs Guerney's not coming in until the day after and I doubt if Ilse will be back in the evening. Any excuse.'

'But when will we have to go down and visit Mother again?'

'Mother's all right for tonight. I don't want either of you to think about that ... you'll have bad dreams. Mother is not your responsibility and you are not to worry about her. Mother is perfectly all right.'

'Screaming. With her bosom out!' But Amber's giggles are more like sobs.

The drawing room is warm and familiar and the twins cuddle up on the hard leather sofa as best they can, one either side of Vanessa who takes the ragged book down from the shelf. The book is given prominence in the drawing room, not because it's a favourite book but because it is old and therefore valuable, but Mother says it must go for re-binding and then it must not be used. The Victorian book, which has pages of thumbed fluffy cardboard, smells of age. It was given to Mother's mother when she was a little girl – her childish signature, Elizabeth May Scott, is in the front – and even then it was old. Dominic and Camilla, on chairs by the fire, pretend not to listen to the story. They are far too old for *The Skin Horse* and everyone knows it off by heart.

'*Once upon a time there was a skin horse.*'

'What sort of skin?' Sacha is always alarmed by the fact that the horse is made of skin; annoyingly, she never fails to ask this same question. But tonight, because her sister is upset, Vanessa is prepared to answer. 'Lots of toys are made out of skin ... nowadays we call it leather.'

'Why?'

'Because the word skin is not very nice, I suppose. When you say skin, these days, you think of human skin.'

'But the skin horse was not made out of human skin, was he, Vanny?'

Vanessa groans. 'No, it certainly was not.'

'It might have been.'

'Dominic, I thought you weren't listening!' It is already late and she is not prepared to tolerate any of his gory interruptions.

'They might have made it out of native skin, like they made umbrella stands out of elephants' feet and rugs using tigers' heads. They used to make purses out of Indian women's breasts ...'

'Well, the skin horse was made out of leather which probably came from a cow. So shut up.'

'Ugh!'

'Like your shoes, Dominic, for goodness sake.' Vanessa assembles her patience. *'And the skin horse lived in the nursery that belonged to the parents of Amelia Ann Hunter.'*

'Who was lonely.' Sacha is half-asleep. With one hand she twists a piece of hair, and the other thumb is in her mouth. Amber behaves identically sleepily on Vanessa's other side. She yawns and judders, replacing her thumb.

'D'you want me to read this or don't you?'

Sacha gives an emphatic nod.

The tale is a hackneyed one, told in a thousand books in a thousand different ways. *'Now Amelia Ann Hunter had lots of toys. She had a beautiful china doll with hair of gold and the biggest blue eyes that closed because of a clever metal hook in her head. The doll, called Jemima, had a suitcase which was full of the most wonderful hand-sewn clothes, clothes which were every bit as good as Amelia Ann's own. She had a pair of wonderful Punch and Judy puppets carved from the finest wood and there was no chip to be seen, not even on Mr Punch's fierce long nose. And among all the toys in the nursery cupboard there was a mechanical, musical merry-go-round with a flag on the top and an awning striped in the pinks and whites of seaside rock ...'*

'... and then there was that old skin horse,' quotes Sacha. Vanessa frowns and obediently shows them the first picture before she turns the page. She has never particularly cared for this story, but it has always been Sacha's favourite. She studies her sister for a moment and knows why. There is something wrong with Sacha; there is something wrong with all Mother's children. The old skin horse is a sad-looking thing, forlorn as Eeyore, with a grave expression in his beady eye and a few ugly tufts of hair. It is hard to see how anyone could love him, other than an antique collector. It is hard to see how any right-minded child could favour such a dull brown thing over the other toys in that splendid nursery, and yet the rather haughty-looking Amelia Ann

Hunter loves it, takes it to bed, trails around with it everywhere even when she is invited to go down to bid goodnight to her mother — a papery-looking lady who languishes feebly on the chaise longue in the drawing room, and her stiff-collared father who stands before the fire rigid as the poker, looking angry.

And in the nursery at night, lit by the dying fire, that old skin horse comes alive and explains to the other superior toys that you become REAL when most of your hair has been loved off, when your eyes drop out and when you become old and shabby. Vanessa reads on, brisk and breezy. '*It is something that happens to you when you are* REALLY LOVED,' he says, '*and it doesn't happen all of a sudden, it takes a long, long time.*'

It is slightly unfair on the other toys who can't help being sharp, smart and elegant — and Sacha pulls out a wet sticky thumb and says, 'What the other toys could do is make holes in themselves and scribble felt pen on their faces ...'

'No, Sacha, the skin horse is tatty because it has been loved. It wasn't shabby to start with. It was probably quite smart when it came from the shop, like everything else.'

'Like Suzie's mother. But we're making our mother all tatty and old now, aren't we, Vanny? We have got her trapped in a cupboard. Perhaps we are going to make her real at last. Real and fat and homely.'

'Homely? But we're not giving her lots of love, not like Amelia Ann loves that skin horse.' Mother would not be amused to be compared with the old skin horse. Surely Mother is far more like the posh china doll, hard and cold with sharp fingers. But then Vanessa pictures Mother at her bad times, without her wig and her make-up. No, Sacha is right. Suzie is the doll, while Mother is only pretending ...

Why?

Sacha is silent for a while, sucking and thinking. She will pull that piece of hair right out of her head in a minute. She tucks herself more comfortably in beside Vanessa and she says hesitantly, 'We're doing it in a different kind of a way only because we have to.' She has always been an odd, illogical child. 'The skin horse didn't DO anything to make himself loved. He wasn't nice or kind or anything, he just had it DONE to him.'

Sacha is tired out. She must be put to bed before she becomes quite impossible.

Sixteen

'W-I-G-H-T — Wight!'

'That's no good. You can't have Wight — it's a capital noun.'

'Not always.'

'Of course it is, Isobel!' Suzie is the only one who dares to pick Isobel up at Scrabble. Robin would just as soon let her play her own game for the sake of peace and quiet, and Eileen doesn't care either way.

But Suzie, of course, plays to win.

Suzie would dearly love to fling open a window and breathe in some of that fresh, icy air. She wants to fill her lungs with some of that silver cold and wake herself up from this stupor. Overfed, overstrained, overstretched, they are crouched round the coffee table with eyes flicking about like surgeons at a dangerous operation because competition can be extremely stressful. It is overwarm in the drawing room with the curtains closed and the fire at full blast, but Isobel feels the cold so the heating has to stay on. Since the children departed, the time at Ammerton Mews has crept slowly along. They left an atmosphere of strain that cannot be sprayed away with a can of Suzie's lavender ... and when he returns from Camberley Road, Robin's gloomy face just adds to the general sense of unease. As Eileen quite rightly observes, 'Christmas is a time for children, and if children aren't happy, then who else can possibly be?'

Eileen's upset, coming to terms with the fact that she'll have to sell her beloved cottage. They've been talking about it for most of the evening and Suzie finds the concept of losing her childhood home almost too painful to bear. It's just one more frightful thread that has woven itself through this intolerable day.

'We had to do it.' Isobel showed no sympathy. 'Everyone has to do it. It's called coming to terms with age. Oh dear me, those poor children!'

'Oh, the children will be right as rain when they get home. The twins always play up when it's time to go. I'm quite used to it now.' But Eileen's sharp, disapproving glance tells Suzie she's been far too glib; she sounds cruel and heartless, not at all the sweet little Suzie her mother knows and loves, not at all like that happy girl who used to be so gentle and caring with her cats and her dolls.

'I don't know why you and Robin didn't arrange to have them here for the whole holiday.' Eileen regards her daughter speculatively as she props her glasses on the end of her nose in preparation for her turn. Her cheeks are a happy Father Christmas hue. Joe didn't want to play. He has abandoned his solitaire and now he is happily absorbed in a jigsaw puzzle at the safer end of the room. 'It's nice to have children around at Christmas-time.'

Because Robin is obviously not going to answer, it is left to Suzie to defend herself. 'We would have had them here, but it's not as easy as that, Mummy. Caroline would never have agreed to let them come.'

'But did you ask her, lovey?'

'No, precisely because there would be absolutely no point in asking her. You really don't understand, I'm afraid, Mummy.'

At nine o'clock Robin is going to run Joe and Isobel home to the bay-windowed suburban bungalow she chose to move into when she could no longer maintain a tight enough control over her Tudor country home, but Eileen is staying the night because there are no trains to Somerset until the morning.

'Well, I thought they were lovely,' says Eileen, needlessly protective, as she clacks down her double-word score with aplomb ... O-Z-O-N- E.

'Well, that's a capital noun!' Isobel bridles so the cameo brooch moves sharply on her hard flat chest. 'It's a brand name – I use it in my lavatory.'

'It is a gas, Isobel,' says Robin shortly, after wavering for only a second. 'And therefore perfectly acceptable. And it would have been difficult for them to stay on because after tomorrow I'll be at work, on and off, getting ready for the big New Year's Eve edition of the programme.'

'Suzie wouldn't have minded entertaining them I'm sure, would you, Suzie?'

'Well, I shall be doing other things, Mummy. I won't be exactly moping here indoors for the whole week waiting for Robin to come home. The children would be bored to tears here, there's not enough room for a start.'

Eileen raises her eyebrows mildly and Isobel purses her lips in reply – Isobel, who has no sympathy for the times in which she lives and no interest in putting anyone's mind at rest.

'If Caroline was different there wouldn't be any problem.' Suzie, infuriated, badly wants them to understand. 'She, after all, is their mother, not me. And anyway, you heard, we invited them to stay the night and they chose not to do so.'

'I thought that was rather strange.' Robin always wins at Scrabble and Suzie wonders why they ever bother to play. Now he casually adds W-E-I-G-H-T to W-A-T-C-H-E-R and lurches further into the lead with a triple-word score. He leans back, crosses his legs, and takes a triumphant sip from his glass.

Suzie is angry. Everyone is blaming her. Is Robin secretly blaming her, too?

Suzie sneaks a glance at the clock without anyone noticing. They can relax as soon as Isobel has gone. She might even have a bath and get into her dressing gown. She might even get drunk. Damn, damn, damn and blast Isobel!

When Robin first took Suzie to meet his parents, the freezing atmosphere in that spotless bungalow with the fireplace of red brick – hoovered each morning, she'd never heard of anyone hoovering a fireplace – could be cut with a knife.

Robin and Suzie had been seeing each other, of course, for a good year before they finally agreed to live together and Robin decided the time was right to brave the consequences and move out of 14, Camberley Road. He spent the night at Suzie's flat whenever the opportunity arose and for weeks before the move Suzie urged him, 'You'll have to tell her, Robin. You'll have to talk to Caroline some time soon. I mean, surely she already suspects that something's not right?'

But Caroline, so self-absorbed, so busy with her own games, had not suspected and when he moved out of Camberley Road the shock came like a bolt from the blue. By then Suzie and Robin jointly owned the mews flat; it was furnished mostly with Suzie's antiques – she'd moved in a few days earlier – and it was all ready for him to come home to.

And on the day Robin left Camberley Road he phoned Suzie from his office. 'Have you told her?' Suzie asked, holding her breath.

'No, I couldn't. I just walked out in the end.'

'And the children?'

'No. No. I haven't said anything to anyone.'

'But what about all your stuff?'

'I've just taken my personal papers ... no clothes, no books, no records ...'

'But Robin, you can't move out like that! You can't leave all your things behind – a whole lifetime's worth of belongings. You will have to return tonight and tell her; you will have to fetch them.'

'There's nothing there that I desperately want,' he told her defensively. 'There's nothing that can't be replaced.'

'So what are you going to do? You can't just not return! You must let her know where you are! She'll think you've had an accident and start phoning round the hospitals. She'll ring you at work ...'

'I was going to leave a note but I decided that wasn't the way. I am going to ring her in a minute.'

'Well Christ, you'd better make sure that you do! And the children – you'll have to see them and explain yourself. You can't let Caroline tell them!'

'I'll see you this evening and I'll tell you what happens,' he said hesitantly, and hung up. It should have been a happy day but he sounded fatigued and defeated like a traveller lost in the catacombs.

What happened was that he arrived at the flat shuddering with relief, and after he closed the door he stood defensively against it, breathing hard like a cartoon mouse. 'She doesn't know where I am,' he squeaked. 'I wouldn't tell her.'

Shocked, Suzie cried, 'But you did ring her? What did she say?'

'She said that I'd ruined her life, she said that she'd never find herself again and she said that she'd dedicate the rest of her life to the task of paying me back.'

'Oh? Is that all?'

Robin threw down his briefcase. The day was gloriously hot, the sun streamed through the newly cleaned windows turning the air the colour of marigolds – you could smell the freshness of the curtains – but Robin noticed none of this. He stretched out on the sofa and kicked off his shoes. He flung his arms over his head and groaned in anguished despair. 'She was totally unreasonable, Suzie. Beside herself. She was exactly as I knew she would be. But I am seeing the children the day after tomorrow, I insisted on that.' He turned to her almost pleadingly, but surely he didn't need reassuring on this – he'd always been a wonderful father. And Suzie gazed at him thoughtfully, as a cat looks at a king. She saw how handsome he was, how he handled the fast, exciting pace of his life. With that early trace of silver on those side-wings of hair, the high, thin bones of his face that look so well on television, the wide, intelligent brow and the neat, narrow nose, he was arrogant and handsome. But cowed by that woman as usual, as if she held something over him. The throb within Suzie slackened slowly ... she re-buttoned her blouse, she had hoped to make love on this their first evening but alas ...

He believed he had covered his tracks so well, he was so careful to take a devious route home, to check in his driving mirror in case he was being followed, to tell no one save for his most trusted friends about his new home, and it was a fortnight before Caroline's detective managed to track him down. That's when the banger went off in the hall, a mean little banger which was pushed through the letter box one Monday morning. It did no damage except for a small brown burn on the carpet.

'Ring the police! We must take out an injunction! She will kill somebody! First she tampers with your car and now she is attacking your home. She might have caused a fire! She is rabid and must be stopped.'

He sighed. 'She'll stop in the end. We just have to allow her to get this out of her system. She is a highly-strung woman, Suzie. She's always been highly-strung and given to dramatics.'

Suzie was truly frightened. 'Christ, Robin, I don't believe this! That woman will get away with murder one day and no one will turn a hair!'

Robin was desperate to convince her. 'Please believe me, Suzie. I know her, you don't. Let her burn herself out. Please, please!' He smashed his fist into his hand.

'Wait till she finds out that I live here, too. She is quite likely to kill *me*!'

'Just let's give her time,' was Robin's only answer, hardly reassuring, and so Suzie took to creeping about, keeping the curtains drawn when she was home, and making sure the oak door was locked and bolted when she went out into the garden, only coming home through the back way and inconveniently parking the Peugeot down the road at the bottom of the mews. It was all quite absurd. She never opened the door without peeping through the spyhole first. She always listened in before she picked up the answerphone. She felt like a fugitive. She had not met Caroline then, had only been shown some pictures, and they looked daunting enough ... a tall, lean woman in leather aggressively astride a powerful motor bike advertising some macho brand of aftershave ... 'but that was taken years ago,' said Robin carelessly. 'She doesn't look quite like that now.' Suzie was not comforted. Caroline had looked like that once – she couldn't have changed *that* much.

When Robin's children visited the flat Suzie was forced to move out.

And then, one day on the telephone: 'Why do you want a divorce, Robin?' Caroline screamed over the wires. 'There's someone else, isn't there? Why are you telling me lies! There must be somebody else.'

'There is someone else.' Robin was ashen-faced, the phone was a knife in his hand, he gripped it like a dagger, 'and we are going to get married.' Suzie stood at his side blowing out air like a bugler, urging her champion into battle. Robin kept his voice steady. In his best television tone he said, 'It really doesn't matter whether you agree or not, I'm afraid, Caroline. I intend to divorce you and that is what is going to happen whether you agree or not.'

'What about Isobel?'

'Isobel?' Robin stuttered.

'She will never speak to you again!'

'Don't threaten me with my own mother, Caroline. It will make no difference what Isobel says either.'

'You cowardly tosser!' Caroline's voice was a rusty blade. 'And what about that God of yours? How are you going to tell Him about your broken marriage vows? But then ... you can go through a priest, can't you Robin, it never needs to be face to face, not with you. Always from a distance ... that's you to a T, isn't it, you wanker, always on the phone, never face to face with anyone ... not me not God not Isobel not the kids. I hope your soul rots in hell!' and her voice rose to a screaming scrape. It was embarrassing. Such misery was horribly distasteful – how could Caroline expose herself so?

'Caroline, listen to yourself! Can you honestly blame me? I needn't have told you at all, I could have communicated through a solicitor.'

'And you fucking well would have done if I hadn't just bloody well asked you! Who is she? WHO IS THE BITCH?'

Robin put the phone down, unable to take any more, and Suzie, who felt that a contract had suddenly been taken out on her life, eased a stiff scotch into his shaking hand.

'I've told her!' he said quite needlessly, like a child who has swallowed his medicine. 'I've done it! And now you will have to meet Isobel and Joe.'

'And the children,' Suzie reminded him gently. 'No more moving out when they come.'

'Yes, of course.' But he sounded so wary! Caged in! The truth finally told had not brought anything like the relief for which Suzie had so desperately hoped.

As they drove towards the prearranged meeting with Isobel, along the identical streets, wet and dark, with their identical box hedges, bay windows and security alarms, the yellow road gleamed ahead of them through the rain. Robin's voice came to her through the soft rushing sounds of the downpour. 'Surrey was too much for them. The garden was too much for Joe and the house was too much for Isobel.'

How could they bear to live here? 'But surely they could have paid for some help?'

'Isobel doesn't trust cleaners.'

Suzie peered out of the window and saw no litter; every tree was the same shape, there was not even the messy clutter of anything so normal as a bus-stop. Her own family home was a rambling Somerset long house, and here Eileen lived on after Daddy's death six years ago in a dreadful, happy muddle amidst jars of pickle and magazines, amidst tall reeds and grasses and the collapsed woodwork of Suzie's old dens. She was beginning to wonder if she should move – she couldn't keep on top of it, but Suzie dissuaded her. 'You'd hate it. How could you leave all the memories behind? There is so much of Daddy still here and it doesn't cost much more. And then of course there's the cats.'

She couldn't bear the thought of Mummy moving, of never being able to go down to 'Poppins' again, as if that's where her strength was.

Picking up cups and straightening magazines, sitting up and down, clearing throats . . . Feeling slightly sick and shivery, Suzie noticed the knees as they all sat so squarely in Isobel's sitting room. Rows of dented, frightened knees all pointing to the middle. There were parrots on the chintz. There was a photograph of Robin in a gold frame and a small, faded one of Joe and Isobel. That was discoloured. There were fly specks on it, no one had noticed the fly specks . . . the only disruption in the room. The one of Robin was not a good likeness. It showed him in his wedding suit and spoke of a lost age. But he looked Suzie square in the eyes from that shiny piece of glass and even now she recalls the gaze of those tiny miniature eyes.

They stared at the fan of paper in the spotlessly empty red-brick hearth. A hoovered hearth.

'This is Suzie.'

Isobel's hand was cool and dry, like her greeting. Robin had told his parents about his impending divorce. 'They were quite shocked, of course, but they'll get over it. I am sure they will like you. Isobel never got on very well with Caroline.'

Now Suzie could see why.

Isobel's pink-rimmed eyes, her mildly disapproving stare flicked over her, Isobel, with her withered throat and her steel-grey hair. 'I believe you intend to marry my son, my son who is already married.'

What was going on here? Suzie, nervous now and taken aback, looked to Robin for rescue before she nodded cautiously.

'And I expect he has told you that I find divorce unacceptable — yes, even in this advanced day and age. I suppose you think that's peculiar.'

Suzie, a prisoner in that dreary little room, shook her head in disbelief. Could this really be Robin's mother? What hold did this woman have over him that he seemed to wither beside her, hoping for approval like a little boy. Suzie swore she would never see this woman again and Robin would just have to put up with it. 'I hadn't really given it much thought. It is Robin I am involved with, not his family.'

'A fact which is glaringly apparent.'

Suzie grimaced at Robin, preparing to rise and leave. 'I think I've already had enough of this, Robin. Shall we go now?'

'Isobel.' Robin sat forward, wringing his hands. 'I couldn't have gone on any longer. You know that, Mother.'

'I daresay. But that does not mean you have to abandon all restraint and leap straight into an unholy union with somebody else!'

Suzie flared. 'An unholy union? Robin, I will wait for you in the car.'

She sat in the car, listening to the rain, wondering and waiting. What sort of childhood had Robin had? He never spoke of it. What was he doing in there? And how dare he allow his mother to address her like that! He should have sprung to her defence: it was Robin who should have insisted they leave. Suzie was shaking with fury when he finally came out and slid self-consciously into the driving seat.

'She says she's sorry, darling. You have to understand, Isobel can't bear any sort of chaos and she sees divorce as totally calamitous ... it is nothing to do with you personally, in fact, I think she approves of you.'

'Approves of me! So what did she think she was going to achieve by that vicious performance? She was trying to drive me away!'

'She's a very direct person. She says exactly what she thinks ...'

Suzie stared, astonished and then she burst out laughing and went on, laughing and laughing. All Robin's women seemed to be allowed to behave however badly they pleased. He spent his life making excuses for them as if he was somehow to blame. He must pander to Isobel because his morals fall short of hers, he must put up with Caroline because he's responsible for her bad behaviour. She pulled herself together and cut off his misguided ramblings. 'You realise, of course, that after we marry I refuse to have anything whatsoever to do with your mother.'

'She'll come round eventually, once she sees I'm determined.'

'Oh? Oh? Just like Caroline will calm down if we wait long enough, if we're prepared to put up with anything? Well, I am NOT prepared I'm afraid, Robin – and you are being incredibly unreasonable if you expect anything else after what you've just put me through.' She looked at him hard. 'Perceptive,' they called him, and 'shrewd'. It is said that off-stage, comedians are often the saddest people, so perhaps the hardest investigative journalists are soft as butter underneath. Over dinner that night, amazed to find herself still with him, Suzie told Robin, 'I think that I really must love you very much.'

Though disapproving of their marriage, Isobel accepted Suzie in the end, just as Robin said she would. She sent her an Easter card — Christ rising, embossed, with arms outstretched, in a sickly glow of Cartland pink. Suzie's relationship with Robin's mother is as brittle as the tail of the glass hawk that stands on the mantelpiece over that red-brick fireplace.

'Mummy, I wish you wouldn't go on so much about Robin's children, especially when Isobel's here. It's difficult enough as it is.' Suzie is packing the Scrabble away. Robin is off running Joe and Isobel home at dear last. It has gone ten o'clock and she feels exhausted.

'I don't see what's difficult about it, lovey.'

'It is a struggle for me to have them here. They don't like me, Mummy, especially the oldest girl, Vanessa. I am constantly on edge when she's around. She watches me. She watches everything I do, every move I make.'

'I didn't notice. Are you sure you're not being paranoid, Suzie?'

It is unusual for Suzie's mother to contradict her; it is unusual and unpleasant.

'And Dominic undermines me whenever he gets the chance.'

'I doubt that. But even if they are, you can't really blame them. After all, it's far harder for children to criticise the people they love. They can't blame Robin so they have to blame you. It is up to you to deal with it sensitively.'

'And you don't think I'm trying?'

'I am sure you are, dear.'

'If Caroline was different there wouldn't be a problem.' Suzie travels uneasily round her drawing room, pummelling cushions. 'Robin feels so guilty, you see, knowing what a disastrous mother Caroline is. When we have our own child he'll feel easier.'

'But Caroline will surely still be a disastrous mother, won't she?'

Suzie confronts her with slipping control. 'You think I should have them here, don't you Mummy?'

'I think that's what Robin wants — certainly until Caroline improves. Perhaps, while she's away at this place ... Broadlands. They should not be left alone in that house for a fortnight. Even with the paid help it is not a satisfactory arrangement to my mind.'

Suzie's response is a sharp one. 'I'd never have married him if I'd known I'd be expected to play mother to his string of disturbed children.'

'You must work it out in your own way, lovey. The last thing I want to do is to interfere.'

Suzie wants to cry out – 'But you *have* interfered, Mummy! Everyone is interfering with the order of my life and my garden and my attitudes and I *just can't stand it any more.*'

Who can that be at this hour? Probably someone for Robin. Suzie removes her earring automatically as she picks up the phone.

'Ah, Isobel. I expect you are ringing to say that you've arrived safely and that Robin is on his way back now?'

'Well no, actually,' Isobel replies, 'although, yes, he has started back. I am really phoning to tell you that I looked up the word wight just now and it means a human being, a person, and it also means, by the way, courageous and brave. I thought I'd just ring to let you know, and you can tell Robin from me that just because he's on television that doesn't mean he knows everything.'

'Well, thank you, Isobel.' Suzie bats her cat-slit eyes as she regards herself in the wall mirror. 'Thank you for ringing to tell us that. Goodnight.'

SEVENTEEN

T IS FOR TINSEL and S is for good old Santa but they also stand for trouble and strife . . .

'Damn it, what did you say to him, Ruby? Lot has been sending me malicious looks all day and he's gone all distant and silent.'

Ruby Dance feels absolutely rotten; the room is swimming round and her eyes must surely be filled with straw. The children are bathed and in bed, sleeping by the sound of it, even Damian, thrown by Bart's fumbling attentions, fell straight to sleep tonight. Ruby feels sick. She should not have drunk all that wine. She should have refused the liqueurs. She is lying down flat on her back on the sofa in a cleared space between softly wrinkled balloons, a cup of black coffee on the table beside her, made by the clucking, anxious Bart. She lies there sinking, smothered, lost, obliterated by the depths of Bart's betrayal but it's easier now. Everyone has gone.

Everyone said they had a lovely time but Pat Dance sidled up to her once during the afternoon and whispered with deep understanding, 'Everything all right, Ruby?'

'Yes, of course Pat, everything's fine!'

'Only Lot is behaving very strangely, and he always picks up disturbing vibrations.'

'Really, I don't know what's the matter with Lot, but I am just fine.'

But already she regretted the way she had broken down when they'd all gone out to play in the snow. She wished she hadn't spilled the beans, the moment after she'd done it. It hadn't mattered that Lot was there – she would have talked to the wall at the time only Lot was there instead.

And afterwards, when they all traipsed in, wet and raw-skinned from the cold, Lot was perfectly silent. But gradually Ruby noticed that if Bart came anywhere near him he edged away, throwing black looks over his shoulder. If Bart actually came to sit beside him, then Lot got up and moved immediately. Bart asked him innocently, 'What's the matter, Lot? Have I said something?'

Lot clamped his lips tightly but his eyebrows beetled together like brushes and he hunched his shoulders right up to his ears. He turned his face to the wall. He would not allow Bart to touch him; he flinched when his well-meaning older brother laid a concerned hand on his shoulder. 'Well, I can't make it right if you don't tell me, now can I?'

Lot sniffed frostily and stared at an invisible spot somewhere on the ceiling: a prophet in turmoil communicating with Heaven.

'Leave him alone,' comforted Pat. 'He's in one of his funny moods. He'll be all right in a little while. It's probably all the excitement of the day.' She talked about her youngest son with a peculiar mixture of mischief and sorrow.

But Pat could afford to be proud of her Bart. He behaved himself impeccably all day. There was nothing he would not do to make life easier for Ruby. But she would not look at him, either. She would not catch his eye although she stared at him when his back was turned, asking herself over and over, driving herself to distraction: 'How could you, why would you, what did I fail to do for you, *and was this the first time*?' Her fondness for Bart felt like a photograph – she knew what it had once looked like, but no matter how she tried she could not recall it.

She even agreed to play charades after tea. Once Bart, grave and awkward in the face of her hilarity, sent her a strange look which seemed to ask – how can you laugh? Ruby flinched but laughed harder. She giggled with Elspeth who flirted with Kurt, who was a nice boy despite the fact that he had no job, no money, and no qualifications. He was good at clowning around with the children. If anyone looked in from the outside and ignored Lot's morose expression, they would say that the Dances were having a perfect Christmas, like the adverts showed ... happy people with glowing faces although Lot refused to play any game. He would not even pull his cracker. He would not throw his streamer.

'Will you kindly tell me exactly what you said to him.' Bart is clearing up. Bart is worried. Lot is notoriously unpredictable.

'I told him I was upset – well, hell, Bart, he knew I was upset, I was crying into the washing-up water. So I told him that you had been seeing some other woman.'

'Oh God, no! Did you tell him her name?'

'Probably. Poor Lot. I don't remember much about it but I think I told him her name.'

'And where she lives?'

'I don't know! Leave me alone, Bart! I'm sick of this. Do you really think it matters?'

'And what was Lot's reaction? I'm sorry, Ruby, I know it's hard and it seems unimportant just now, but you really must think!'

Ruby closes her eyes; she gives a deep, sickly sigh. 'I don't think there was any reaction. Not at the time. I don't think he said anything much. He just sat at the table looking pained and beautiful and he didn't comment at all. He went very quiet.'

'I wish you hadn't said anything to Lot.'

'Don't take that bossy tone with me, you bastard!' But Ruby's outburst exhausts her. She is not strong enough to attack yet. She sinks back with a groan.

'He doesn't understand, you see.'

'And neither do I. Not really. You try to be sophisticated, you try to tell yourself you'll be different if it happens to you. Was it the sex? How many times did you lie? Did you shower at work, before you came home?' Bart is her husband. She thought she knew Bart. But Bart has startled her in the way you are startled by a knife that is unexpectedly sharp. *If he can betray me then he can abandon me also, and one day he can forget me* ... an experience that Ruby associates with death and old age, not motherhood or wifehood ...

'I've told you it was nothing and I'd give my right arm to be able to say that it didn't happen. What more can I say? How can I make it right?'

'You can't. That's the trouble.'

'What are you going to do?' Bart sounds afraid.

'Do?'

'Do you want me to go?'

'Where would you go?'

'Well, I could have gone back with Mum and Dad.'

'Don't be silly, Bart.'

'If you'd rather I wasn't around ...'

'You have to be around, Bart. I can't cope with the kids on my own. Not now.' This conversation is becoming absurd. What are they talking about with their circling voices?

'Elspeth would have stayed with you.'

A sudden sighting of her reddened knuckles, of her workworn hands, makes her burst into anger. 'Oh Bart, for God's sake shut up and just get on with the clearing up. Everywhere is a mess, I'm a mess ...'

'I am worried about you and I am worried about Lot.' Bart crumples, he wipes his eyes with the back of his hand, he looks lost, he looks as puzzled as Damian does when he's about to cry.

Ruby says, 'Lot'll be all right. He'll have forgotten all about it by tomorrow.'

'You don't know him. You just see a handsome man, an innocent, but Lot is different. He doesn't let things go, he carries his resentments around with him and when he was small, if he didn't talk about them to anyone, these feelings got bigger and bigger until they exploded in terrible temper. When he was seven he smashed up a neighbour's garden shed with a mallet and that was because he thought the man had insulted my mother. We're always encouraging him to think out loud.'

'Well, he's not small any more, Bart. Lot has a gentle, sweet disposition, much nicer than most other people I know. Trusting and simple. You see him as a child, still. You all do it, particularly your mother, and I think that's a big mistake. Lot is a grown-up man now and he doesn't need anyone's protection.' Ruby thinks for a minute, and adds, 'And he's not stupid, either, he's misunderstood. He knows the birthdays of every single resident in that hostel.'

'He has always been able to do that. He remembers bus time-tables and train time-tables ...'

'And yet he's wasted, buried away folding boxes. Sometimes I think that Lot is pretending, that Lot is inspired ...'

129

'He is not inspired, he is mad. Crazy. Drugged to the eyeballs. Enclosed in his alternative world. And he *enjoys* folding boxes. He feels safe folding boxes.'

'Well then, maybe I should try and get a job folding boxes because I don't feel safe any more, not at all.' She feels like she feels when she's giving birth, in pain, in need of help but desperately alone. And at the last birth, Bart had said to her, 'If only I could bear the pain for you, I would.' It was just thirteen months ago and he meant it. But now?

Bart hovers uncertainly, wearing his stricken look. 'I want to hold you, but I daren't touch you Ruby, in case you push me away.'

'Oh Bart!' Ruby wants to scream and beat at the air, she wants to be destructive, like Lot, but she hasn't the strength. It's no good, Ruby cannot hold back the tears. Bart kneels beside her and holds her tightly in his arms while she whispers wetly into his neck, 'You bastard you bastard you bastard ...' She flies to a pain more compelling than gravity.

'I know, I know,' and he rocks her gently. He strokes her hair from her forehead but the mess of daffodil yellow will not go back, not completely. 'Let me carry you upstairs and put you to bed like a baby.'

'You can't get round me like this, Bart. It's not as simple as that. You have made your bed ...'

'Please don't punish me. I am not trying to get round you. I am trying to look after you.'

'You have hurt me, I'm dying ...' her face crumples up and she knows how ugly she must look. 'And if I asked you if you'd done this before you wouldn't tell me, would you?'

'Whatever I said you would not believe me.'

She shakes her head. She feels as out of control as a drunk. 'I wouldn't. I couldn't. I won't be able to trust you for years.'

And if Ruby cannot trust Bart, then why should she tell him the truth? If she is embarrassed to remember, then why does she need to pass on the facts which are already fuzzy and faded, thank God. She'd been unaware of Lot, then. She hadn't considered Lot's condition; she might have been all alone in the room, she had cared so little about anything, save for her anger and pain. She'd paced the kitchen in front of Lot, her head bobbing up and down like an agitated seabird as she shouted out loud, 'I wish she was dead! I wish she was dead or in pain or frightened or tormented. I wish I was a man so that I could go round to her house and drag her out by the hair and batter her head in.' Insane behaviour. Crazy words ... none of them meant to be taken literally. And then she'd picked up the rolling pin and smashed it down into the butter. A ritual blow.

Ruby frowns to remember. It is hard, with all the swimming going on in her head. After her performance Lot got up, he picked up the butter, still in its wrapping but dented down the middle — it was just out of the fridge so it wasn't soft. Effortlessly strong, he took it in one of his delicate, tapering hands and squeezed it until the yellow sludge bulged out of its wrapping and oozed between his long thin fingers. She noticed the length of his nails and it was at that same point that Ruby realised how Lot's distress had clouded the pure love in his eyes and she decided she had to stop. It was then that she turned to confront the washing up, it was then that she told him she felt better, that it takes two to tango ...

'They were dancing?'

'No, Lot, I'm afraid they were fucking.'

He did not say any more. Ruby thinks hard ... no, that's right, after that he fell silent.

When Christmas is over she must go and see Lot to make sure that he is all right.

Ruby allows Bart to carry her up to her bed. Well, what the hell? She doubts that her own rubbery legs will take her and with a bit of luck his back will go and he'll convulse with a fraction of the torment she's suffering. But it's awful — she knows she still loves him because of the way she pulls in her stomach before he lifts her, to try and make herself feel lighter. More appealing.

Eighteen

And now, on this endless, nerve-racking, unnamed day after Boxing Day, Vanessa Townsend is convinced that her mother is going to die. She is not going to die of any ordinary illness, like broncho-pneumonia, angina, coronary thrombosis, meningitis or Legionnaire's disease, oh no, none of these mundane afflictions. Caroline Townsend is going to die because she has been murdered by her children. She will find a certain kind of grisly fame; she will appear in a horrible grey way on the front pages of the newspapers at last.

Of course they should have called a doctor. They could call a doctor even now, and get it all over with. All they'd have to do would be to ring Daddy or confide in the comfortable Mrs Guerney.

As far as Vanessa knows, there have been no more manic outbursts from Mother. For a carefully monitored thirty-six hours, Mother has been lying on the floor of the sauna, half-hidden under the bench, shivering, calling out occasionally for a drink — sometimes her cracked voice is so mumbled they can't understand what she wants and at other times her lips are pulled back into an ugly, soundless scream — and sleeping. Down there in her throbbing, humming wooden cage, Mother has become, like an Aga, the heart of the house in a way she never achieved when she was free. The black wig has been left exactly where Sacha pushed it. Mother hasn't eaten a thing and she hasn't spoken to them again, not directly. She hasn't even been aware of their visits; she cannot have heard the dong of the tubular bells, Amber playing the first bar of *The Snowman*, very slowly each time, with her tongue twisting studiously over her lips.

Vanessa and Camilla paid two harrowing, secret visits to the gym during the night, determined not to let the others know how worried they were. When they finally shared their worst fears over breakfast this morning, Vanessa had already decided they should tell Mrs Guerney the truth as soon as the cleaner arrived.

But, 'She won't die!' scorned Dominic, dead against the idea.

'Well, she's not messing about any more, Dominic. Any fool can see that.'

'Even I can see that,' said Sacha.

'I don't know how long we can let her go on like this.'

Camilla said, 'Next time we're going to have to unlock the door and go in.'

'Oh yes, and then she'll spring on us.' After a hoarse, gulping sob Sacha started to cry quietly, pushing a tired spoon through her Ready Brek.

Maybe Vanessa should call for a priest. There might still be time to save Mother's soul, although Mother, in her right mind, would shriek with horror at the very idea. Mother does not believe ... in anything. 'When you are dead you're dead,' she says with scorn, 'and when you're alive you're bloody well dead most of the time anyway.'

'That Bart fellow of your mother's has just been on the phone,' says Mrs Guerney, 'so I read him her note.'

'Bart?' Vanessa frowns and catches Camilla's astonished eye – men! What a nerve – so the anonymous phone call hasn't worked, after all. No doubt Bart's wife will be interested to learn about this latest development.

'I must say I'm quite surprised he didn't know where she'd gone. He did sound bemused when I told him. After all, they were that close ...' Mrs Guerney's jowls tighten and stretch. 'He wanted to make arrangements to meet her! He didn't ask to speak to her. I think that's rather strange, don't you?'

'That's because Mother split up with Bart on Christmas Day.'

'Well, there you go then. That's why she departed so suddenly,' and Mrs Guerney's lips come together in a conclusive smack. 'And that's why the note is so hastily written. I daresay she was lucky to get into that place at such short notice.'

'That's why she had to go early this morning.' Camilla is quick with an explanation. 'If she hadn't gone at once the sudden vacancy they offered her would have been filled. You can see on the note ... she said she was sorry.' Once you have started to tell lies it is almost impossible to pull back.

'At least your father knows all about it so someone round here is accepting the responsibility for all this mess. He's bound to be round each day keeping an eye on everything. Ilse can't be trusted. Poor soul,' and she doesn't mean Ilse. Mrs Guerney switches the subject to Mother as she eyes the polished banister rail and gives it a final vigorous rub. 'To suffer like that. My sister-in-law was just the same, only ever could cry when she'd had a drink ... the rest of the time she went round pretending to be brave when really she was a very frightened person.'

Mid-morning, and they follow Mrs Guerney with her fast manly stride downstairs to the kitchen. 'Mrs Guerney, did you know that nine out of every ten men married to women alcoholics divorce them, while nine out of ten women married to men alcoholics stay loyal?'

'Well, you can understand that in a way.' Mrs Guerney is never daunted by Dominic's statistics; she holds unshakeable opinions on most aspects of life. 'Some women like to mother hopeless men but there aren't many men prepared to put up with a hopeless woman. And drunken women are so much more of a problem. Drunken men are funny or frightening but drunken women are always considered disgusting. But anyway, Dominic, who told you that your mother was an alcoholic?'

Dominic says no more but he raises his knowing black eyes to the ceiling.

Mrs Guerney picks up her Pledge in a large hand as, with a heavy sigh, she moves on. When she is in the house life feels much more normal. She brings normality with her in the same brown-paper-bag, unthinking way in which she carts her slippers about. 'My sister-in-law had to make do with the National Health.'

Although Mother doesn't know it, and although Mother would pour scorn on the concept, Mrs Guerney, is, in fact, Mother's most loyal and genuine friend. She's had a hard life. 'I am perfectly prepared to treat triumph and disaster just the same,' she says, 'but how can I prove it when I'm still waiting for the triumph?' Mrs Guerney enjoys taking her mind back to the early days when she first met Mother, to that time when Mother worked at a photographer's studio, when she was sought-after and work was plentiful: 'When that woman had the world at her feet if only she knew it. You just don't know how lucky you are,' she'll say, 'compared to some poor children I know.'

If she saw real cruelty, this bustling body would never stand by and watch. Although Mrs Guerney lives alone with her lady lodger (whose contributions to her income go undeclared) she loves children; she would wade into the breach with her hat at a combative angle and firmly put a stop to anything smacking of unkindness.

'Your mother has had a great deal to put up with in her life,' Mrs Guerney will say mysteriously. 'She could have been anyone! She could have been a real star! She has the creative temperament, and those of us who have not been blessed with such talent must make allowances for those who have. To succeed you need a man behind you – you just have to look at the poets and they were all men! No, your mother is one of those women, unfortunately, who should never have fallen in love and got married. But there ... she fell head over heels in love and wouldn't be warned, so what can you do?'

Three times in her life Mrs Guerney has allowed Mother to get under her skin. Three times she has threatened to leave, and on all three occasions Mother has been forced to back down. Life without Mrs Guerney's regular comings and goings would be as strange as living on a seashore without the rushings and sighings of an in-and-out moving tide.

It only takes a few moments after Mrs Guerney's arrival in the morning to tell what sort of mood she is in. Sometimes her face, tightly pleated, signals the very soul of discretion; she refuses to be drawn, she rolls her eyes instead of speaking. But this morning she signals a willingness to open up, electrified into confidences by the drama of Ilse's skulking man. Ilse returned soon after nine looking the worse for wear as usual, bursting with apologies and full of her short but perilous journey from the tube. 'I 'ave been followed all the way up the road by this most suspicious-looking man who 'az been skulking behind the bushes in the park.'

Mrs Guerney peered worriedly out of the window. She rubbed at the glass with her squeaking duster. 'There's no sign of him now, Ilse. Are you quite sure?'

'There is no doubt in my mind but that he was following me. He was, how do you put it ... a fanatical – a striker or a protester, tall and lean and lanky with black straggly hair dangling down over one eye and the other, the eye I could see, was staring madly out of his head.' The excitable Isle hurried on, exaggerating madly because the uglier he was the more sympathetic Mrs Guerney was likely to be. 'He watched me enter the house. He stood perfectly still and he watched. He stared hard at the house as if he was counting the windows. Believe me, I make no mistake.'

'Ugh!' exclaimed Mrs Guerney in a voice choked with outrage, who dips into scandal with the glee of a glutton delving into a box of chocolates. 'Nobody is safe. These beasts are everywhere, undeterred by seasonal goodwill, or the weather. They should pick these perverts up in a van like they do stray dogs; they should take them off and castrate them. Even on your own lounge couch there's no getting away from it, you see it in every wild-life programme you watch ... sea lions, coyotes, wildebeests, preying and coupling. They're exactly the same when it comes to that.'

'You'd do it yourself, wouldn't you, Mrs Guerney?' Amber has heard these awesome threats before.

'I would do it with my own bare hands and a sharp vegetable knife.'

'Or a cheese-grater. Let's go and see if we can find him. We could track his footprints in the snow.'

'Let poor Ilse get her coat off and unpack her bag first, Amber. And it is not a good idea for anyone to go searching in the park. If anything is to be done it is for the police to do it. That's what we pay our taxes for.' But everyone knows that Mrs Guerney does not pay taxes – that's why Mother pays her cash, weekly – and she's on income support. Mother says it is one of the ways, apart from her hats and her penchant for picnics, in which Mrs Guerney mimics the Queen, and if you look at Mrs Guerney sideways on there is a definite likeness, except that Mrs Guerney's hair has been allowed to go grey and there is not the merest suggestion of a curl in it. Mrs Guerney is such an excellent cleaner that on one occasion Mr Morrisey next door came round to ask Mother if she could spare her for just one morning a week at his house. Mother refused. She said, 'I certainly don't want all our private goings-on broadcast to the entire neighbourhood. It's bad enough that she also works at Safeways.'

'He didn't *do* anything, did he, Ilse? He didn't *show* you anything . . . or maybe you didn't notice,' Mrs Guerney asked in a low and terrible voice, deflated when Ilse shook her head.

'What would he show her?'

'Take Sacha and Amber upstairs, please, Camilla, while I get down to the root of this.'

Camilla burst out laughing, Dominic blushed and sneered, but Vanessa bit her lip and looked away. Vanessa was on Mrs Guerney's side when she snapped cryptically, 'Well I'm glad you can see a funny side, Camilla, because I can't. I find it absolutely revolting myself.'

Ilse looks bored and resigned when she comes downstairs in her powder-blue shell suit prepared for a long day's work.

Mrs Guerney looks up, annoyed, from her place at the grate and accosts her. 'You look washed out, Ilse. Are you ill? Have you had any sleep at all over the last two nights?'

'I 'ave been badly upset by the experience of the man, Mrs Guerney.' She picks up a magazine and listlessly heads for the sofa.

'There'll be some ironing to do when that washing's dry and Mrs Townsend's room could do with a good clear-out while she's away. You're in charge here now, Ilse . . .' But Ilse's eyes are already glued to the antics of Mario on the television screen. Her mouth falls stupidly open as she watches Dominic's expert performance from his nest of buttons and wires on the floor. If Dominic will let her, then Ilse will do little else but play Nintendo until the next time she has to eat or sleep or until she can sneak out for a couple of hours on some pretence. Ilse will do anything to wangle a few hours on her own with Paulo.

A rush of spidery worry crosses Mrs Guerney's face as she eases up from her kneeling position and expertly pushes a piece of newspaper over her bucketful of ashes. 'I think I'll phone Mr Townsend before I go, just to make sure . . .'

'There is no need for you to do that, Mrs Guerney. We are perfectly all right.' Ilse quickly defends her position, nervous of unnecessary interference. She prefers to be left on her own. 'If we need anything I know where he is and the children are very responsible.'

'I am concerned about that man, now that he knows where you live. If he should decide to ring this bell . . .'

'Mrs Guerney, I would never open the door without seeing who was there first. I can look after myself. I was only so nervous because I was out and he came with such sudden surprise.'

'If you see him again you must telephone the police, Ilse, you understand that?'

'Of course.'

But Mrs Guerney's decided that Ilse was probably behaving cheaply. She prefers the pregnant Welsh girls; she used to bore Mother to death with her nagging: 'Ilse is immature and irresponsible and I shouldn't be at all surprised if she's not here when she ought to be, but having a high time down at the Plume of Feathers with those Greeks.'

'The children would say something,' said Mother, trying not to listen, trying to move to another room where Mrs Guerney wouldn't follow her.

But Mrs Guerney was not so easily diverted. 'Not necessarily. They're not so stupid. The children can wrap Ilse round their little fingers. She's such a drip that they're probably far happier if she's out rather than drooping around indoors waiting for the next opportunity to escape. I know children, and I'm just warning you, Mrs Townsend, that's all. At least the Welsh girls had nowhere to go and were too large to want to be off flaunting themselves all over London getting up to God knows what.'

'They were too depressing to have around, sobbing and sighing all over the place. And you know how easily I get pulled down. Ilse's here now and Ilse will have to do.'

So Mrs Guerney would relent, but she never bothered to hide her disapproval of poor lovelorn Ilse. Now, quite understandably, she is reluctant to leave the household in Ilse's charge. She hovers, she spends too much time arranging her hat and packing her bag and all the while Vanessa watches and considers. Mrs Guerney would be horrified if she knew what they'd done with Mother; Mrs Guerney would be on Mother's side; Mrs Guerney would not sympathise with their reasons, she would refuse to understand.

What should she do? Oh God, what should she do? Where are the tears that might save her? Finally, at dear last, Mrs Guerney's cliff-like bosoms disappear behind the zip of her army surplus flying jacket. 'I wonder if there was a man at all, or if it was a figment of that girl's wild imagination. Or, of course, she could have been using it as an excuse for her lateness.' Vanessa is willing to agree with anything. If Mrs Guerney is going she wants her to go immediately, not hang around here in the hall where Mother's cries will be heard if she rouses herself from her torpor at this fatal moment.

But Vanessa half-dreads and half-hopes for some sound. She wants to be found out; the strain of this terrible crisis is proving too much for a twelve-year-old child to bear. She longs to go down to see what is happening but at the same time the thought of creeping back to that gym, the thought of what they might find there is repellent and terrible.

If Mother would only make a sound then Vanessa would know that Mother was still alive.

NINETEEN

HER FIRST, REAL AWARENESS comes along with the scratching at the window. At first Caroline thinks she is in bed and that birds are scuffling in the ivy outside her window ... the light is so bright it could be a warm, spring morning. Where, for God's sake, did she go last night? Her eyes are stuck together, her lips are parched and her whole head is rumbling hotly like the inside of a tumble dryer. Where the hell has she been and what has she done to make herself feel so rotten?

My God, she is down on some strange floor, hardly dressed. She moves every limb and muscle with care, easing her head from her cramped arms, wincing as the blood rushes back and she feels the pain shoot sharply through every vein in her body. Her bleary, bloodshot eyes automatically search for some kind of reviving drink. They rest despairingly on the wooden bucket of water. The habitual curse is there; natural to her as a heartbeat it comes without thought: 'Fuck this.'

Is she alone? She clears her throat in case she might be required to speak but the result is similar to ripping a plaster off a raw and open wound. She drags her body heavily behind her as she makes for the bucket of water. Moaning for moisture, she thinks of a lizard moving across the dunes under a scorchingly red Sahara sun. Her tongue flicks like a lizard's tongue and her hands are withered and dry, claws for nails, no eyelids ... God help me.

The searing heat which she first imagines to be emanating from her own wretched body is surely coming from the coals in the corner ... if she narrows her smarting eyes she can watch the atmosphere shimmer above them, mirage-like on the air. What the hell? She rises on her hands — an exhausted sort of press-up, the movement is all she can make — and she dips her entire head in the bucket, shivering at the stale, lukewarm thickness of the water. It's like dipping your head in a bucketful of silk ... dipping into nothing mixed with the smell of wood chips. And then, as she gasps harshly for the next breath, she lets herself slump back against the bench behind her, catches the bucket in both her hands and lifts it over her head.

'Will somebody turn this bloody light off, for Christ's sake?'

She smooths the stuck hair from her face, and then carefully, in case it might hurt her, she brings her knees to her chest and folds them in her wet arms. Slightly safer now, she dares to edge her eyes to take in the high sauna window and the rest of her bewildering surroundings. Have they put her in some weird high-security rehabilitation unit? Did she do something unlawful last night — and where *was* she last night ... Are there guards out there disguised as nurses in starched white, waiting for her to find some bell and ring it? But isn't there a faint familiarity about this place that she really ought to recognise? Damn the booze ... damn it, damn it, she has to sort this out before someone comes in and the battle begins ...

Or has she been taken hostage by terrorists?

Caroline Townsend fights sheer panic as she rises up stiffly; every muscle in her body screams out as she moves towards the door, terrified. And pushes. And gasps. And pushes again, cursing her pain and her weakness. And takes her frightened eyes to the window, screws them up to see through, licks her parched lips as she digests the stark basement room which is Robin's gym, as empty and cold as Robin is, as calculated and uniform as Robin is, as unsympathetic to her and all that she stands for as Robin is, with a love as rusty as a tin-can alley. 'There'll be nothing left of me soon,' she used to say pitifully, in the bad times, alone again, staring into her mirror, 'but my eyes and my laugh.'

Her attention is seized by a movement at the window over there in the far wall ... scratchings against the pane, only just noticeable, as if someone is attempting to scrape away the white paint with the edge of a coin in order to make a hole to see through. So that was the noise that woke her from a sleep that was more like a death ... no dreams.

Caroline is at home. Safe. At home. In her own house. This is not a hospital and there are no waiting syringes.

What day is this? There must be people upstairs who might hear her if she calls. But she knows she can't call with the kind of throat this heat has given her. No, all she can do is bang the empty bucket up and down against the pipes and hope there is someone responsible upstairs who will come, at once, to rescue her before she loses her mind.

She bangs. Every deep dong of the bucket assaults her brain, and her arm is achingly weak. She keeps on banging with a desperate regularity, her eyes closed against every sound. Caroline cannot bear to be shut in closed spaces. She imagines she cannot swallow or breathe. She listens … she has to know who is coming to get her. She has to fight, she daren't lie down in case she's not ready when they come with their strong arms and their punishments. It is a childhood thing; she really should have conquered it by now.

How could anybody hate her enough to lock her away in here like this?

And then she remembers that Robin is gone. Robin would have stopped them … Robin is the one she can count on to keep her safe whatever happens, but Robin has gone to live with Suzie now and there's absolutely nothing Caroline can do about it. Oh, falling in love with Robin was easy and wonderful. She remembers the delicious languor of the first time, her body under the thin sheet, the sheen on the pretty porcelain cups, the heady scents drifting through the green blinds; the day swam past and they drifted along it from morning to evening in a burning dream whose fever increased as the sun went down. And when the crimson and gold had faded, when the moon rose, then … they attained madness.

He's gone. It was atrocious enough when she realised he'd left her, but when she discovered he was in love with somebody else she thought she would lose her mind. They all say there's nothing worth doing but to work on oneself, work ceaselessly, work defiantly, laboriously, go against every habit, every craving, every fear, every hope and every pleasure … to what end? For the purpose of breaking through the pain. But all that is beyond her. She can't seem to do it – can't even understand it. And there's no reward at the end, or if there is it's too awful to contemplate. Childish things, that's what she wants. She wants to believe childish things told in such a way that she can believe they are true. Because, without Robin, life is so dark … because everything is lost and gone into darkness. And Caroline is only a crumpled flower pinned to the shoulders of many lovers.

Robin, fuck him, the prig, the cold-blooded fish, the intellectual with no time for hilarity, warmth or carelessness.

Caroline bangs stoically on, feeble bangs becoming progressively weaker. One for Mummy, one for Daddy, one for Robin, one for Caroline ... dear God, and all in this crippling, mind-blinding heat!

Nobody's going to come. She can bang as hard as she likes for as long as she likes. Nobody's going to answer and it's no good crying. She has to try and pretend she is not locked in. She has to use her imagination and pretend that she hasn't been abandoned here, maybe forever. She has to try and work out what has happened. If only her head would clear, so that she could remember ...

She should not have poured away all that water. Is there any way she can turn this heating down? Listless, more thirsty than she has ever been in her life, and with lips that taste more briny than any ocean, she folds her fur coat and lays it on the bench to make a thicker cushion to take her aching body. There are blankets, too. Someone must have worried that she might catch cold! Hah. Her laugh is brittle; she wishes she could take it back. That little laugh tore its way out of her throat and she is sure there was blood behind it. While she's stuck in here, laughing is out of the question: she cannot use laughter in her efforts to pretend. And anyway, there is nothing remotely funny about any of this. Why does she always have to make painful things funny? Or soak them in gin as if they are diamonds that need cleaning.

What time is it, for God's sake? Shouldn't the children be home from school? When she looks at her watch Caroline remembers and catches her throat ... it is Christmas! Vanessa, Camilla, Dom and the twins must be at home now, probably upstairs and wondering where she is, and the presents she's hidden might be wasted – the presents that would have to try and make up for last year's neglect when just to hear the word Christmas rent her, just to pass a shop where a carol was playing made her cry.

She'd remembered the presents this year but not the decorations. She'd been angry when she got home ... angry with Bart for being such a prat, angry to find that Vanessa had outwitted her again, Vanessa, solid and awkward as a kitchen chair, making her guilty again, somehow managing to make her fall short again. Vanessa seemed to be screaming, *'Why can't you do things quietly, live quietly and die quietly. Why does there have to be all the laughing and crying?'* And Caroline would have loved to scream back, 'I am *not* your monster, Vanessa! I used to stare at the soft sky with my mouth open, stupidly, like you, as if I was a stupid woman. But I was not too stupid to enjoy it, to love it, to sink into it. I have watched our lovely world, too. I have even found myself on my knees for all the enchantment of it ...'

They were proud of their efforts. They'd stood around, watching her, innocent in their dressing gowns. Beautiful, every one. Caroline remembers with difficulty, frowning, taken to some other world as she tries to bring back just how it was. She had teetered on the edge of some terrifying cliff then, and how many times in her life has she been to the edge of that cliff, staring down into the massively frightening awareness that there are things to live for, after all — that, with a mighty effort of will on her part, she might actually be able to reclaim the shattered shreds of her life and sew them together, give herself another chance. With Bart's cruel words still ringing in her ears, when she'd walked into that drawing room and so suddenly caught sight of the Christmas tree it felt as if someone was mocking her, trying to unravel her determination to create a Christmas this year. Drunk, she'd been rearranging the clumsily draped tinsel but it must have looked frightening to them, frightening and quite, quite different. When she heard the children come into the room behind her, she looked round and saw their fear ... fear over what she might do, what her reaction might be. Fear as if they were waiting to see which way the monster would pounce and the monster was *her*, vulgar and foul.

She stared at dear, skinny Vanessa, so alien, preposterously fastidious, docilely miserable with her monstrous deep wide eyes. Her full face was candid, downright and honest, but her profile was impertinent and her mouth was ... sensual. For all that she is so painfully thin Caroline's daughter's a warm little animal. She carries enchantment. Something in her hums. She saw her then as a drummer boy, very small and rather ragged, marching to the battle of life with her head up, whirling her brave little drumsticks. Caroline stared at her child and teetered. She desperately wanted to laugh, to hug them all to her, to breathe in the drowsy, talcumy smell of her children and laugh, to tell them to go upstairs and see what was waiting in her cupboard, to go and find the pantomime tickets, to look in the back of the pantry cupboard. She wanted to tell them the hell was over, that she was going to stop drinking. She dearly wanted to do that ...

Why couldn't she do that?

Oh, why couldn't she promise them that?

Why would that have been so much more dangerous than pushing remorselessly on, grimly stripping the tree in a kind of clumsy fever, behaving like the hateful creature she had become. She'd stared at her own reflection which was bright in her children's eyes. She'd wanted to stretch out her arms but knew that her children would recoil from her touch.

Caroline Townsend, frightened to make promises in case she can't keep them, terrified of her children's love, scared to betray such a precious thing, doesn't know how to beg for love, cannot cope with rejection. How much easier it is to be feared and hated. How much simpler it is to keep company with those who don't really matter, to fall so swiftly into meaningless love so that when you lose them it doesn't really hurt. And yet every passionate experience seems to have been a sort of death, every sexual intimacy a kind of murder.

Shit. Just another tomorrow gone up in smoke. And then what happened? Ashamed again, she forces her sluggish brain to remember. Did she have another drink? She must have done; she must have given in and followed the pattern – loud, ugly, uglier, demented, turning in dread from her children's touching needs. Had she staggered down to the gym in some misguided attempt to find Robin in his lost, secret world, had she turned on the sauna and somehow managed to lock herself in?

How else could she be here? How long *has* she been here?

But she hadn't been wearing her black wig when she went out on Christmas Eve, had she? She had been wearing the chestnut. So somebody else must have put the black wig on the floor – and what else? What are those crispy pieces of paper?

Her hands are trembling as she reaches down and brings the pages to a comfortable eye-height. It is an effort to move her head, unbearable to let it drop down; any extra weight on her neck is purgatory. She holds the menus as steady as she can and it doesn't take long to read them.

Christmas Day lunch. Boxing Day lunch. Christmas Day tea. Her smile hurts. Her skin is tight as a layer of dry parchment. Caroline used to write menus once. She drew them out carefully, just like this, and put them in front of her dolls as they sat on the chairs at the table. It was a large table and you could hardly see the dolls' heads even though they were raised as high as could be, on cushions. Really, there should have been people at the table but more often than not, as a child, in those long-ago rooms where memories lie, Caroline Heaten ate her meals in the company of crimped-haired dolls with puckered pink lips. When you are little you don't have the privilege of choice ... whether to be loved or not.

Her children know she is here.

Well, why on earth haven't they let her out?

Who else knows she is here?

For Christ's sake, this is bizarre!

Maybe she should bang again but she hasn't the energy, and a creeping dread is swamping her. Doubt and fear are cooling agents, protecting her from the fierce sauna heat. She doesn't want to bang any more; she wants to keep very quiet, to be left on her own to think and prepare – but for what? Will her children come, or have they decided to leave her here to die?

Can she honestly blame them if they have decided to do that? After what happened upstairs, after she, the weary old whore, tried to destroy their happy Christmas in a stupid contradiction of feelings. As a child Caroline often wanted to kill or destroy those that hurt her most. All of a sudden Caroline wishes she was merely waiting for men with syringes: at least she could fight and curse, at least she could kick and hurt. But if her children come, what then? If they won't let her out, what then? But there's Ilse and Mrs Guerney ... Christmas Day is obviously over and Boxing Day has gone by without her being aware of time passing. If it's later than that then Mrs Guerney will be in the house every morning and Ilse ought to be there, too.

How is it possible that no one has missed her? There must, at least, have been telephone calls.

Mrs Guerney cannot know. The stolid, sensible Mrs Guerney would never take part in anything as extraordinarily sinister as this, whatever the reason. And then there's Bart, Bart with his swooningly marvellous fingers and his frenzied, half-manic: 'Let's fuck!' But Bart doesn't want to meet any more, Bart has decided to stay faithful to his wife, poor cow. Caroline remembers the row, lets her head fall into her hands and groans. What a mess what a mess what a mess.

Oh God I feel so sick.

The scraping at the window has ceased, overtaken by the lightly rumbling sauna. She starts when she hears the tinkling sound, unmistakable; even the words of Sacha's favourite song, so familiar, spring to mind: *'We're walking in the air ...'* Caroline tenses. She stops breathing. She can smell herself – cornered animal. Her fists clench so hard that her nails dig into the flesh of her hands. Her eyes are wide now, and startled to a feverish brightness. A wintry shiver runs through her bones as the Christmassy sound of bells comes again, reverberating with a miniature sorrow, oddly unreal in the bleak wintry expanse of the gym.

'We're walking in the air ...'

They put her here, with their smooth, innocent skins and their impassive faces, with their short-cut nails and their heads that smell of sweet green shampoo. With their impossible expectations. Her jailers are coming and she cowers, while a perilous tingling shoots through her limbs like the pricking of millions of needles. She knows very well that they are coming, but what are they going to do? Caroline is frightened. She is terrified of her five children and totally dependent upon them. There are no shadows in this wooden cage and no hiding places, only the bench, and she can hardly crawl on the floor and try to hide under that. Achingly sad, vulnerable, she doesn't know what to put on her face, she has nothing, no refuge, no means, nothing to allow her to cover up, nowhere to hide.

No defence against this.

And no drink in her hand.

TWENTY

WALL-EYED WITH WONDER, Lot Dance catches a snowflake on the finger of his glove and, using the utmost delicacy, deposits the tiny flake in his mouth. He closes his eyes the better to taste it. In order to see more clearly and to react more quickly, he has ceased to take his daily medication and this is why he can enjoy the snowflake so.

A hurrying stranger, passing on the other side, notices him, thinks he's a tramp and looks away. But the stranger carries the image of the man with the classical, tragic face and wonders, deeply moved, what dreadful things he has endured in his loneliness. He imagines him laughed at, jeered at, spat at, lying sick and untended beneath some ungodly arch. Or sitting in a stiff chair, too small for him, down in a charitable crypt. How many days does he spend like this, trudging the dismal streets? Perhaps it's all the same to him where he is.

Lot would tell the stranger not to be so ridiculous.

Who is Lot? What is he all about? Well, Lot is not a tramp. He has a home and a family and his mother, embarrassingly, still tries to hold his hand in the street, but the stranger isn't so wrong. There is Lot's life and there is Life — the monstrous power which charges over the earth, carrying out its plan which has no use for individuals, needs no individuals to exist. In its slathering jaws it got hold of beautiful Ruby, used her, then tried to toss her on the scrap-heap. Lot is tougher; it hasn't done that with him yet, bloody hell, not quite — Lot keeps his eyes open. But it's the enemy, that's the point. Everyone's enemy. Everyone's in the same fix. Sleepwalkers and the groping blind wrestling with a monstrous antagonist. Everything it does is an attack. Everything that happens is a trap. Everything that Life, that growling monster, gives, every experience, every pleasure as well as every disappointment, is a plot to foil, is a move against, against arousal from the dream. Life is an evil scientist mixing stimulants and sedatives in exactly the right proportion to keep human beings in the proper state of stupor for its own purpose.

So Lot must keep on his toes.

Sometimes, when he's upset like this, every day feels the same. There is no tomorrow. There's just a day and a night, a circle wheeling from light to dark, from dark to light – just alternating light and dark.

Oh yes, the world according to Lot Dance is a strange one, full of misunderstandings and false messages. He does not see things like you or I do, and his needs and his loves are relatively simple. But he is not harmless. Thoughts of retribution, when they come, capture his soul completely. That hateful Caroline Townsend had better bloody well watch her step.

So here he is now, outside in the darkening afternoon where the sky is a bruised blue-yellow, furtive yet with an air of mission about him. Although Lot tries to connect to this pure white world of bewildering snow, the icy wind, the frosted branches above him, they are like ghosts to him, piles of ashes or whirls of dust, not recognisable like the solid things that are his – like his boxes. They belong to the big world, they are nothing to do with him and he does not want to see them. So there.

His fury is manageable now, and smothered. The fiery convulsions of rage he suffered for hours, alone while he ripped blankets and towels to shreds in his room on Christmas night, are reduced to a mildly beating pulse. There is not a lot more he can do for today. It is time for reverse action; it is time to pack up and move on.

Since his very traumatic experiences of Christmas Day, Lot has been far from idle. It is very annoying when he is trying to plan, to find that he cannot see himself, for he remembers in pictures and can never quite spot himself in these pictures. Where has he gone? If he remembers a group round a piano, or in a garden, he can see the other figures but never his own. He takes to muttering, 'Why am I always absent?' The bar stool or the armchair he sat in is there, but it is empty. Look. Now he can see his glove, his sleeve, his boot if he puts out his foot. If he could once see himself from top to bottom, back to front, what a help that would be. How can he put these bits together? It is all so bloody unsatisfactory.

Despite these debilitating handicaps, after a few false starts he managed to trace Caroline Townsend's address and telephone number by consulting a friendly man in a frayed Afghan hat who was keeping warm in the library, and he phoned from the station after his arrival in Highgate this morning, fully expecting the telephone to be answered by a child because it is holiday-time and he has noticed how children, even when adults are around, generally rush to answer. Pretending to be Bart, he realised this method of communication – a hasty message – would sound strange, coming from a lover, but he had prepared a quick explanation – no time to talk ... somebody coming ... that sort of thing. But Lot was thrown into confusion when the telephone was not answered by one of Caroline Townsend's five children. The woman was abrupt with him on the phone. She read him a note, she said to him crossly, 'How come you didn't know she'd gone to Broadlands? I thought you two were close.'

Lot, confounded, unable to think of a quick enough answer and with his mind wheeling out of control, started to stutter and so he put down the phone, cutting out the sharpish, 'Hello? hello?' with an impatient frown. Damn it. The last thing Lot wants to do is to make things worse. He merely wants to punish the woman who has hurt Ruby so deeply.

His hectic drifts of thought led him to plan on an assignation. He wanted to lure her out of her house. He decided on the Fat Controller Café, the one with the sticky red seats and the plastic daisies and every petal smells of onions, the one beside the station. Not the sort of place which his brother, Bart, would normally frequent but the best of a bad job. Not many places were open because people were still at home enjoying their holiday. The last thing he'd imagined was that his victim might have gone away.

'Patience, Lot, patience,' he muttered sternly to himself. The next time he rings he is going to pretend to be somebody else. Lot does not like trying to be Bart.

She has gone to Broadlands. But where is this place, Broadlands? Is it a hotel? How can he find out and how much money will it cost him to get there? Worry worry worry, but his sense of justice resigns him to the chase.

When he gets cold, when his feet burn in his boots and his eyes stream in the bitter air, Lot dismisses the tempting picture of his own cosy room and his welcoming gas fire. He stamps flat pathways round the trees in the snow and remembers that tragic image of Ruby, the beaten creature she'd turned into on Christmas Day, huddled at her own kitchen table, swollen-eyed, red-nosed, as in her choking voice she broke down and confided in him, sharing her terrible problems.

'*No, Lot, they were not dancing, they were fucking.*'

He claps his hands. He blows out white streamers, fierce as a bull, and his eyes are as glittery-bright. Not red eyes, but navy. Ruby trusts him. He will not let her down.

He might as well check out the place as Starsky would, as he was here and so near. There was only one window Lot could reach in the tall, superior Camberley Road house and that was down the basement steps – a dark little window in the cellar. One day he is going to have a house like this – although this house is not Lot's sort of house at all, there is something prim and stiff about it – with a wife and children and curtains with dressing-gown ties round their waists. Lot's first glance at the house felt as if it was received with a snub, as if it disapproved of him – although why should it? Why the hell should it, carrying its turmoil of moral disorder as it did? But, after crossing the street with stealth, looking this way and that, as taught, he sneaked down the steps, stuck his hand through the bars and scratched at the blanked-out surface of the glass, only to discover that the white paint was on the inside.

Damn it.

Lot's head feels like a house; it feels as static as a room with four walls entirely crammed with inanimate objects. He hasn't even been able to see inside and Lot is interested in houses ... all sorts of houses and their contents. Especially beds – monster four-posters, brass beds and iron beds, camp-beds and airbeds. Stairs, too. They are aggressive, they climb and wind. And there might be lots of bottles inside this house, innumerable bottles which catch the light on the glass shelves of bathrooms, hundreds of jars of face cream and shoes of every description, enough clothes to fill an aircraft hangar and books and writing paper. Books full of print that were once read but are now forgotten, writing paper covered with scrawled lilac words, or emerald green, words someone once wrote but cannot recall. Pens, pencils, cigarettes and wine.

Lot can remember the things that belong to people, more accurately than the people themselves. Even Ruby, whom he remembers more vividly than anyone, her scarves and berets are more definite than her face. He can't see her separate from her clothes, her furniture, Bart or her four children. Always he sees her surrounded, embedded, mixed up with the smell of home-made marmalade and the other junky stuff of her world. To visualise Ruby, Lot must put her in a frame.

He is here for Ruby.

He had only just retreated to a safe vantage point in the park when a blond-haired lady in blue came strutting by with a silver airline bag. Who could she be?

She could be a bird pecking along.

Lot emerged from behind his tree, curious to see if this could be Caroline returning. Maybe Broadlands was a shop, maybe she'd just popped down the road for a loaf of bread or a cream horn. But this younger version of Marilyn Monroe, tossing her curls and pouting her lips as she minced along the road, staring at him nervously, checking over her shoulder to see if he was still there, she was not Mrs Townsend ... with her vastly padded shoulders she could well be a model or an actress, but she was not old enough to have five children and Lot didn't think she was Bart's type.

Lot realised with alarm that the lady thought he was following her.

He imagines Bart's type to be his type ... soft in motherly cashmere with curly hair, little pearl earrings, and wearing pretty, gentle dresses of a rosebud print. Doesn't drink. Doesn't swear. Ruby could be his type, if she tried, if she took off her jeans and her make-up and wore white shoes with tiny heels with bows on the backs. Princess Diana might make the grade. Lot has never actually met his type of woman yet, not precisely. He has only ever seen one on telly – and that was Angela Rippon. He is never out of the hostel on a night when they show *Come Dancing*.

Once again he retreated to a hidden place in the park. Once again he stood, still as a tree trunk and just as dark in his long black coat, watching patiently. At twelve-thirty an older woman left the house wearing a fashionable felt hat, an RAF jacket and carrying a Union Jack carrier bag. She reminded Lot of the bossy hostel administrator who comes in and puts the fire on in the office two days a week, the woman who counts the biscuits. But this one strode off busily, head down, watching for treacherous ice on the pavements. She bustled along against the gathering wind while every now and then she glanced towards the park as if she was expecting to see someone there, but she couldn't see him because Lot stood back, well out of sight.

No more can be done. He has successfully located his target's house and he knows some of the people that come and go. His telephone call was unproductive and he could not see through the cellar window. Caroline Townsend is not at home and so he must seek her elsewhere.

He is cold. He is hungry. There's no work today, the workshop has closed until the sixth of January and nobody knows what to do with their time till it opens again. Back at the hostel everybody will be hanging around gormlessly, sitting in rows down the refectory table, playing crib, drinking tea and fugging the reccy with smoke. Watching telly, faces as puckered and blank as the sad balloons. Depressing. If Lot returns, he will go to his room and finish some more of his boxes ... the sackful he specially requested to take home. He likes to have something to do with his hands and he's finished the sweater he's been knitting for months. He is wearing it now – a reggae stripe with a polo neck. Slightly itchy.

But he doesn't want to go home yet. He doesn't want to go back to the hostel. He checks in his pockets for change. He wonders if Ruby and Bart would be genuinely pleased to see him if he went there.

TWENTY-ONE

DUSK FALLS. Dusk is a haze of cries and whispers. Even in the basement with its sterile, melancholy landscape, there is a sense of dusk falling.

'*We're walking in the air* ...' sob the tubular bells.

Moving on soft, considerate feet, it is the contained quietness of the creeping children that makes them so sinister.

'You've woken up again then, Mother.'

'I haven't been awake at all. I have only just come round.'

'No, you're wrong, you spoke to us two days ago.'

Mother's impatient fingers tangle with her fraught fuzz of hair. 'Then I can't remember.' She shrugs twitchily. 'Vanessa, I'm sorry, I can hardly remember a thing.'

After a long, embarrassed hesitation Vanessa says, 'You said some bad things to us two days ago. You said some very cruel things to us then, to me in particular. You threatened me with all sorts of awful punishments.'

What can she answer to that? For a start she can't remember – and is that any wonder? She was suffering from violent withdrawal and she didn't have a clue where she was or what was happening to her. Caroline's caustic cynicism is her first line of defence, one at which she has become an expert. But it's hopeless, like lead suits are hopeless against radiation but yes, she probably would have said hurtful things.

Caroline's face is on one side of the plastic window, Vanessa's on the other, and each of them feels they are talking to themselves through a round, metal-framed mirror because this conversation is so inane for such a solemn occasion. Her four younger children stand behind Vanessa in a perfect straight line, awaiting their turns.

'How are you feeling now, Mother?' Real concern is absent from the question although Caroline detects a kind of relief on her daughter's ashen face.

While straightening the strap of her slip Caroline attempts a little laugh and immediately regrets that she tried it. 'I could murder a drink.' Vanessa's face disappears for a second and Caroline imagines the expression she is wearing, how her slim eyebrows will be disapprovingly arched in her high, white forehead, how her nose will be crinkling up with distaste.

Vanessa comes back. 'You have water,' she says very gravely.

Caroline, humiliated and helpless, cannot argue.

'And don't worry, we are going out to buy you some appropriate clothes tomorrow morning.'

Caroline, suddenly aware of her semi-nakedness, modestly crosses her arms although her daughter can see only her face, not her body. Trying to be playful but meaning business she answers, 'Appropriate clothes? There are clothes in my wardrobe, Vanessa, and unless you can turn down the heat in here all I'm going to need is a bathing costume.' And then she dares to ask, 'What's going on, Vanessa? Why am I here? What are you planning to do? Don't you think you had better let me out now? This is all very childish, after all.' But she's frightened.

'It is childish because we are children, Mother.' Spoken without the faintest trace of irony.

What the hell can she possibly answer to that? If she could only speak to Camilla she might be able to influence her ... Camilla has always been steadier than Vanessa, gentler, more understanding. Not so obsessed with religion and Robin, with right and wrong.

'I know you are upset. What happened was dreadful ... and with Christmas and everything. I can understand why you did this, don't think I can't understand, darling. But what you didn't know was that I had made plans this year, special plans. Everything went wrong, but ...'

An impatient sigh briefly mists up the glass. 'Everything always goes wrong, that's the whole point.'

'How long have I been here?'

'We brought you down here on Christmas Eve. Well, it was early on Christmas Day morning. You passed out. You were drunk again. You were disgusting.'

'You brought me down here?' Caroline's hot, clammy flesh crawls.

'We wanted to have a good time. We couldn't do that, not with you as you were. I'd survive, but Dom and Sacha and Amber, how would they feel with their Christmas all spoilt again?'

Mother painfully clears her throat. 'How are they? Can I see them?'

'Later.' Vanessa sounds defensive. Perhaps the others are not so firmly behind her after all. Perhaps, if she's given a chance, Caroline can persuade them to change their mind.

'How long are you planning to keep me here?'

'Until you change.'

'Change?'

'Until you turn back into a mother again.'

Caroline feels tears threaten. She fights them hard. She does not want them to blind her eyes with their watery brightness. She wants to keep control so that Vanessa realises she is not in possession of this situation, she is not in command. 'But I *am* your mother, Vanessa. This is all getting rather silly. Already it's got way out of hand, hasn't it, darling? Be honest.'

'We have control, Mother. Everything is decided. You can't threaten us any longer.'

There is a long, difficult pause during which they study each other in the imaginary two-way mirror. After what feels like years of avoidance, for once they take on each other's eyes. Mother's turn suddenly wary; there's a danger that she might crumble away utterly. She says, 'They'll miss me at work.'

'We have sorted all that out, Mother. We're not stupid.'

'And Robin? I suppose you have smoothed that little hiccup out, too.'

'Daddy thinks you have gone to Broadlands.'

'You told him that? And he believed you?'

'Why wouldn't he believe us? It's exactly the sort of thing you might do.'

This is worse, far worse than Caroline has imagined to be remotely possible. Vanessa is so cold ... as if she hates her. As if all the resentments over the years – the tiny resentments of children, like refusing a lollipop or a television programme, or making Vanessa put on her cardigan ... all those furious little glances she remembers receiving and dismissing are summed up in this freezing cold stare.

'Vanessa, listen to me, darling. You can't force people to change. You can't take people prisoner at whim and turn them into what you want them to be! For God's sake child, you're not thick ... you're not a toddler. You must realise ...'

'If we can't make you change we are keeping you here. If you won't change we don't want you back.'

'But it's not so simple!' For Christ's sake! Just because you've managed to keep your secret for a few days – and God knows that's incredible enough – don't imagine you can incarcerate me here for weeks on end without anyone finding out. You must be out of your mind ...'

'Don't say that about me!'

'I'm just trying to make you see that this naïve idea of yours cannot succeed. Camilla! Camilla, are you there?'

'Camilla does not want to speak to you just now.'

'No, because Camilla knows better ...'

'Mother, can't you see that you are saying everything wrong? *I* am the one you must talk to.'

'I know, I know! But what the hell am I expected to say, given these extraordinary circumstances? I'm not going to beg you, Vanessa. You know that whatever happens I am never going to do that.'

'We're going to buy you some suitable clothes and some shampoo. I remember, and in the photographs, you have pretty hair.'

Strangely embarrassed, taken aback, Caroline brings her hand to her hair, and on the way up she passes her cheek. With a shock she remembers slapping Camilla when everything was so black. It was the only time she has raised a hand to her children, and something in Vanessa's expression not inches away from her gaze must have reminded her of that. Vanessa saw the slap and has not forgiven and her memories are probably as clear as crystal. Vanessa had no idea, when they played that ancient Electrolux ad. as Christmas drew nearer, how the horror had flooded back, how those great rollers of grief had pounded down and drowned her – and why should Vanessa know? Why should the children have to know? Isn't life bad enough that the past has to be endured as well? There she was, Caroline Heaten, so full of hope, pushing the gadget along the carpet, all dolled up and stiff with mascara and promises. Camilla smirked and laughed. She covered her mouth with one pretty hand and she laughed ... Camilla, with that sort of future so easily within her grasp – money no object, media connections, talent and beauty. *Camilla laughed*. It was unendurable. And so something snapped inside and Caroline slapped her. Immediately afterwards she had felt sick, but by then it was far too late.

And there's more, oh God so much more. There was, 'What have you done to my room, Mother?'

She recalls the horror on Dominic's face when he saw his new wallpaper.

'Don't you like it?' She'd been genuinely astonished.

'I hate it! I wanted it kept exactly as it was!'

'But how can you hate it? I chose the colours you like best. I spent hours choosing. I even went back to change my first choice because I know how you loathe fussy things.'

'You have spoilt my room and the whole house. I'm surprised you haven't taken my toys and my books and changed them, too. You should have put them on the fire and burnt them with the rest of Daddy's stuff.'

At the time Caroline groaned. Why on earth would she do that?

Couldn't they see? She was trying to make it a new house, a fresh start, free from the memories of those unhappy times. She could only curl up on her hurt, take another sip of her gin and say, 'Well, Dominic, I'm sure you will get used to it if you try.' And then, stabbed to the heart by the row of miserable faces, 'You will all get used to it if you try. This isn't easy for any of us. Can't you understand?'

'Why don't you talk to us, Mother?' That was Camilla, the child of the tender rosiness. 'Why can't we share this together?'

But what the hell do you say to children? How can you tell them you're contemplating taking your own life because you just can't cope with the scalding anguish any longer ... for them ... for anyone. All they wanted was Robin to come back. Well, what the hell did they think she wanted?

They worshipped Robin. They still do. They were cold and offhand with Caroline. They believed she had driven him away, and that's certainly how it must have appeared. Robin looked like – he still looks like – a man who can slouch round the course of life with a long, loose easy stride and never make a mistake. While she, with that demon of need inside her which she could not control … all that storming, raging, accusing him of caring nothing for her.

He'd insisted she be the perfect mother, and to start with, feeling safe with him, she'd trusted him and tried.

During the bad times she had to get out of the house or die. Sick with fright, she had to surround herself with friends who talked loudly about themselves and spent exciting evenings in brightly lit places. She went among them like a blindfolded woman playing a frantic game, bumping into costly stereos, tumbling into mountains of pillows, caught in the arms of one man, then another who sucked on her nipples, men whose faces she could not quite see. And home in the morning with silver tracks inside her knickers, wetting black leather car seats.

Where did her children fit into this? How did Vanessa fit in, with her black and white views, no shades of grey allowed to show through? Guilt, guilt, guilt. And how could she help them to understand?

Caroline makes a great effort to sound normal, to sound brighter. 'Hey, why don't we all try and relax here. If this wasn't quite so crazily funny it would be obscene. Well, if I'm not going to be allowed a drink, how about some cigarettes? I've run out.'

'I would rather you tried not to smoke. You haven't smoked for two days. You haven't had a drink for three days, either, and it made you very ill. Soon, you won't even want a drink or a cigarette. We'll have cured you.'

'But Vanessa, hell, my hands are shaking.'

'Don't worry, Mother, we'll look after you because we love you.' And this is said with such vehemence that Caroline recoils with a gasp.

'So what am I supposed to do while you decide whether or not to let me out? Am I going to be provided with something to read? A television set? Some knitting, perhaps?'

'You wouldn't get a picture down here. And yes, of course we'll let you have books. A pack of cards so that you can play Patience. Wool, too, if you want it.'

For Christ's sake she was joking. On a bubble of frightened anger she fumes, 'I could make Mrs Guerney hear me if I banged on the pipes. I could scream and someone would hear me.'

She doesn't like Vanessa's tone, quick and high with distraught emotions. 'The sauna heating is quite high at the moment. Before we leave we've decided to turn it down. But if any of us hear any noise from down here, the slightest sound during the day or night, Dominic's going to come down and turn it up. And don't think we'll all be going to school every day. Someone'll stay home to listen. Soon you'll be happy, Mother. Soon you won't want to make a noise. You won't need anybody's help but ours. Mother, we are going to make you much happier than you were. And don't worry that we'll ever leave you. We'll come and see you regularly at the same time every day. Otherwise you will not be disturbed.'

'But you wouldn't really hurt me?'

Fiercely uneasy, for there is madness in this. Could it be that Vanessa, Caroline's most serious, high-minded child, is unbalanced? Not just troubled, but possessed? Is it something to do with her age, and all that eerie religion?

'Vanessa,' Caroline starts carefully with a new tremble in her voice. The scant clothes she wears feel heavy and damp. The atmosphere inside the sauna is sticky-thick. 'Can you tell me what you think is going to happen in the end?'

'I think that in the end you might not want to come out. We might, in the end, have to coax you.'

Only half-listening, for this is all quite beyond her, Caroline, with her eyes clenched tightly shut, hangs on to the door for support. 'Right. Okay. If you're determined to stick to this peculiar attitude. So just for curiosity, what sort of timescale are you talking about?'

'Weeks, months, years, we can't really say yet, can we?' Vanessa's insolence is almost discreet. So close to panic she can almost taste it, like silver fillings touching foil, Caroline can't stand up for much longer. She wants to go and sit down on her bench. A feeling of terrible loss and regret tells her it's too late to try and touch Vanessa now. Surely her daughter knows that she, so fragilely balanced, is incapable of existing alone for a day or an hour? Vanessa turns round as if to consult the others and her face seems to turn on the air, separate, unsupported, naked. My God, oh God help me, she is being perfectly serious! Caroline knows this with a sickening certainty because Vanessa can't act as Camilla can act, as she herself can act. She'd wanted so much for Camilla, so much she had lost for herself.

'Daddy, I want to be an actress.'

Severe and cold. 'Over my dead body.'

Caroline was lucky. She was beautiful and talented. With a passion like a fire she got a place at LAMDA but she needed a grant. No matter how hard she begged, Daddy would not pay the fees. How hopeless it all seemed then. So she lived in a grimy bedsit and worked her way up, modelling for a pittance, then was taken on by an advertising agency and given small parts in three of those early television adverts, and she thought she'd made it. You had to be tough. There wasn't much dignity. So many of her friends lived like that then, lonely, no money, scant hope, grabbing and seizing, clinging and clutching, waiting for their chance in a world where men chose, assembled, worked out the scheme and set the pace. She swore that if she ever had children of her own, she would make anything possible. No matter what they wanted to do she would put all her power and influence behind them. At DOTS, where she found the job that saved her, she watches so many unlikely kids pushed by ambitious parents, encouraged, supported. But every so often one comes along, that special child comes along, and Caroline wants to puff them off the flat of her hand like a thistledown, wishing with her eyes squeezed tight and whispering, 'Go! Fly! Make it to the stars. Make it ... Make it, for me!'

The big time beckoned when William Moore, a stiff old man in a swivel chair, asked her to do an audition for a part in a television play which was topical and daring. 'You'll get it, you're perfect for it. He likes you,' the bespectacled secretary said. She was pregnant then, only just pregnant with Vanessa, two years married to Robin who was rising, a budding star in his own right, already working for the BBC. A kinder version of Daddy, he wanted to take care of her. Caroline was in love. Her romantic ideas about love didn't fit into this new experience with its subtle sickening excitements, its sensations of hunger and thirst. The thing crept into her body, interfered with her breathing and poured a delicious and dreadful fever into her blood. Caroline's ambition turned soft just when it ought to have turned hard as stone, and she never found that strange, dauntless self-confidence again – she never, ever found it again.

'How can you possibly risk your child for the sake of your own selfish ambition,' carped Isobel. 'Haven't you got enough?'

Risk? What risk? So Caroline, when offered the part, accepted it gladly.

Robin stayed silent.

She can't bear to think about that any more.

If only her mind was clearer, if only she could think. There must be something she can say or do to persuade them to let her out of here. What promises can she make . . . what do they want to hear?

Owlishly, stupidly, she stares through the glass while her unclear mind continues its racing. 'And what if I tell you that I've learned my lesson, that this action of yours has shocked me so much that things are bound to be different, that after these three days nothing can possibly stay as it was.'

Vanessa says simply, 'We would not believe you.'

'I don't normally tell lies. You must give me that, Vanessa. I'm honest.' She bites hard at the inside of her mouth in order to keep her composure.

'But we're not ready to have you back yet. And we can't see any positive changes.'

Caroline's heart sinks fathoms further. 'No make-up, no wig, no soap, no drink, my skin is cracking and my eyes have gone raw . . . and you say you can see no changes! Christ! If you let me out now I swear I'll say nothing. I won't tell a soul.' The intensity of her protest sounds like whining. 'Ask the others, don't make this decision yourself. The others are there, why not discuss it? Why not end this charade?' She senses a twinkling chance and takes it.

Vanessa's smile is sad and distant, not without compassion. She is not impressed. Damn it, she holds all the cards.

'Camilla's going to make a turkey curry and we wondered if you'd like some. That's really why we came down. We didn't come to bargain or to talk. Not yet. Anyone can see you're not ready yet.'

At the thought of food Caroline's stomach lurches. God knows when she last ate, God knows when last she felt genuinely hungry. Now, extraordinarily, in this intensely threatening situation she knows she wants food, and badly. It's the lack of fags, it's because her body is free of the booze and it hasn't been free for … mortified, she can't remember. Must be the last time she booked in at Broadlands. Against her will she is forced to accept the offer meekly. She turns her face from the window as she adds, 'And perhaps you would be good enough to turn the heat down.'

'If you eat your dinner we will turn it down because that's what we already decided. Don't worry, Mother, there is really nothing for you to get anxious about any more. Nobody's going to hurt you. We are all here, we love you, and we intend to take proper care of you.'

Oh dear God.

Please don't leave me!

She ought to laugh. She really ought to be able to laugh at this farce and she would – Caroline would throw back her head and laugh with that old raucous laugh of hers that has rattled behind her through time like a tin tray falling down a staircase. Oh yes, she would laugh – if she didn't feel so frightened, if she didn't feel so despairingly low, so ashamed and horrified by the threat that has plagued her for most of her life: the terror that she might, alone and unloved in the dark, alone with the terrible burden of herself, go mad.

TWENTY-TWO

FROM THE VERY BEGINNING Vanessa bewildered Caroline. She could not believe the baby was hers. Caroline could not believe that she was a mother. She looked at the other women in the ward, big and smug and satisfied. They smelled and they smiled like roses.

She looked down into the plastic cradle, at the pink bundle of blanket, and sometimes it stared back at her out of dark, eternal eyes, as if it saw for ever, into the depths of her soul.

She was frightened to pick her up. She felt that her baby was made out of glass.

Glass, like ice, is a supercooled liquid – not a true solid.

Imagine how you'd feel if you broke the *Mastermind* trophy, that Caithness vase, so spectacularly fragile, and how much more aghast you would be if it wasn't your own but somebody else's. How would you tell them what you had done?

You might resort to writing a note.

You might even run away.

Why award a prize so ephemeral, why give something which wouldn't stand a hope in hell if it drifted to the floor or to thick pile carpet? Are they trying to say that winning doesn't really matter, that you shouldn't need a prize? That the point is that success is all in the mind? If you dropped it, there'd be nothing left. You could go round saying you'd won *Mastermind*, but after a few years nobody would believe you. Do any of the winners or their spouses ever summon up the courage to go within yards of that vase? Is it ever brought out of the safe to clean or put on display? You must have seen it so you know as well as I do that not one shard would survive intact if it was dropped, and every trophy's a one-off job — it cannot be replaced.

Someone, some day, is bound to break every one of those Caithness vases because glass rarely lasts for hundreds of years. Some hapless cleaner, some rumbustious child, some doddery, drunken old uncle ... but most likely it will be the wife trying to bring back the sparkle, trying to wash the damn thing up.

It started before Vanessa was born. Robin had won the Caithness vase and Caroline was carrying it in her stomach. It wasn't hers but she had the care of it.

Eight months pregnant and Caroline grated the chocolate and melted it slowly, without allowing it to boil.

A cover of pink crocheted rosebuds, too stiff for a baby Caroline thought, was given pride of place in the nursery upstairs because Isobel had taken such pains to create it. The nursery was a little-girl world, paid for, designed and ventured into with awe, by Robin.

'What if it's a boy?'

'It won't be a boy.' In excellent spirits, he knew everything.

No wonder it was a difficult pregnancy, a time of unease which increased under the strain of waiting, made worse because of the inescapable heat and the difficulty she had with her breathing.

'It's nerves,' said Isobel knowingly, sticking her angry needles into a ball of grey wool.

'It's because I suddenly haven't got anything to do, nothing but think about this, and Robin is so intense about it ...' Caroline's eyes, shadowed and confused, settled on Isobel's hard face and she felt afraid for herself. She was behaving unnaturally. How could she talk about disappointment, bitterness and sorrow — how could she grieve when she was about to experience the most precious event of any woman's life — the birth of her first child — for Robin? To whom could she confess that losing her chance in the play after such struggling beginnings felt, unhealthily, like a miscarriage? How selfish she was and how shallow, with her pathetic urge for fulfilment. There'd been no real explanation for the director's change of mind, just a glib and easy telephone call made by the secretary, and this made it worse. She'd fought so hard to get there.

Birth! Birth! The word rang out like a church bell. She ought to be joyous, Robin said. In her frightful, matronly pastel dresses, in the ugly jeans with the stretch nylon stomach, in the huge white Aertex knickers which were the only ones that would fit, she ought to be fevered with happiness.

'Don't be too disappointed,' said Robin, when she told him about the play. 'Having a baby is much more important than any career, far more lasting than any transient success you imagine you might have achieved,' and he strode off to his important work.

She hated the loss of control, the slow but insidious manner in which nature took charge of her body, veining her massive breasts like a road map, taking her breath away. She hated the way Robin insisted on feeling the child with his hand pressed flat against her sexless bulge, taking such solemn soundings. She loathed the way he calmly removed a newly lit cigarette from her mouth with the warning, almost religious, 'That's not a good idea, Caroline, not now. You've more than yourself to think about now.' Every trifling wicked thing she did felt like a new drop of sustenance on which the lump could grow fat, the lump, and the developing guilt, the desperation. Because how could she do this to her own child, how could she bring her girl to the world unloved and unwanted, as she had been?

She dissolved the saffron in white wine. She needn't lay the table yet. She played her loud music and danced so that for a while she could forget all else save for her energy and her yearning. When she danced like this, with the curtains drawn, on her own, she was beautiful again, like a goddess, enchanted and suddenly anything in the world was possible. But there she was in the mirror, hideous, lumbering around the room with manic bright eyes and a body like a sow's so she turned down the sound and stood still again, legs throbbing, daunted by thoughts of the absorbed women in the relaxation class she must go to tomorrow.

No one she knew seemed to giggle any more. She used to giggle. She used to giggle till she wet her knickers.

By six-thirty she was ahead of herself; she had everything for the dinner party expertly organised. She skimmed off the excess fat from the juices in the casserole. What an interesting casserole – what a tasteful casserole dish. How lucky she was to be Robin's wife with a home any woman would envy, an intelligent, supportive husband, handsome and successful. How dare she mope her way round this beautiful house that she kept so clean, so proudly? (When the baby was born, Robin said they would get a cleaner but up until then he considered the gentle exercise to be beneficial.) When she'd left home and been cut off by her father she'd never expected to find this standard of comfort again. How fortunate she was that she no longer needed to take humiliating work in order to pay the rent, that she no longer feared the landlady's slippered tread on the stairs, that she no longer lived on tomatoes on toast, violently peppered for flavour, with the odd egg for celebration. Look at her now ... a dishwasher, washing machine and tumble dryer, all German. Yes, oh yes, and Robin loved her, certainly Caroline ought to feel grateful.

She had to be careful; she had to choose the menu imaginatively because Robin detested boring food, he'd been fed too much pap in his childhood, and the people he'd invited to dinner were favourite friends ... 'You will adore them, Caroline. Frances is such a fascinating woman, the sort of person you're bound to gell with.' He thought he'd 'discovered' Caroline, he thought he had plucked her from a life of despair as you might hoist a kitten from a fast-flowing river. They met in the BBC canteen, she after a disastrous audition she knew she had failed, he for a mid-morning rehearsal. She was impressed, you could even say she was overawed. When he offered to buy her a coffee she all but curtseyed, and she stuttered.

He didn't want the flotsam she'd mixed with spilling on to his own carpet – the first friend she asked home spent the whole evening toe-curlingly trying to get Robin to find him some work – and Caroline, she'd risen so fast and so high, she felt uneasy when she went back to her old bedsit world and the few friends she'd left there. 'Alternative types, hangers-on, ne'er do wells' he called them. 'You don't need people like that any more.' They wouldn't approve of him, either. They would be suspicious of his success and his luxurious lifestyle.

'Sometimes I wonder what attracted you to me in the first place,' she'd say to him, laughing carefully into his merry brown eyes. 'After all, in your own words, I was an alternative type and a ne'er do well ...

'It was your laugh,' he told her, slapping her bottom. 'And your fine, childbearing hips.'

Oh, how she'd loved him.

She removed the bones and the skin from the one and a half pounds of fresh salmon.

Immediately after their marriage she'd kept in touch with those early friends, but now she was pregnant it wasn't so easy, and Robin liked her to be waiting at home whenever he had a spare evening. He needed someone in whom to confide; he needed to discuss the stresses and strains of his day – and why not? Caroline's friends were still in pursuit of success, she had nothing to talk about but Robin's. 'But what do you do all day?' one of them once asked her, and although she always made herself busy she could think of no interesting reply. And Robin, well, surrounding his wife with the right sort of people, like eating the correct number of calories and wearing sensible, flat shoes, was essential for the wellbeing of his impending baby.

She beat the whites of four eggs until very stiff but not dry. She went upstairs to wash her hair and to soak in the bath until half-past seven.

'You look gorgeous!' She glowed. Robin patted her stomach and frowned at the drink on the dressing table, picking it up and sniffing it as though it was drugged or poisoned. He threw his suit jacket down on the bed and tore off his tie on his way to the shower. A busy, bustling, important man. And handsome.

'I was afraid you might be late again.' She cursed as she smudged her mascara but the water was gushing and he couldn't hear. She couldn't hear him, either, although he was shouting through the sheet of steam. Just lately, in these last few months, it often felt hard to hear what he said, or be heard. She lay on the bed and she waited. Smelling divinely of soap and hot water, she propped herself up on the pillows, untied her negligée ribbons and waited for Robin to come out. He shook the water from his hair like a bounding dog with the white towel sawing his muscled shoulders. 'Shirt? Shirt? Shirt?' he called – the beat of a certain, satisfied song.

'Darling, what on earth are you doing lying down? They'll be here in a minute.'

She stretched her arms above her head, feeling voluptuous in spite of her size. 'It's okay, there's no panic, everything's done.'

'Oh come on, Caroline, you're not dressed yet.'

'I've only got to slip my dress over . . .'

'And I'm not dressed either. Where is my white shirt?'

She shifted and slid on the bedspread. 'I want you, Robin. I've wanted you all day.'

And then he stopped. He turned and he looked at her with his most sincere television eyes. She could be a famine, an earthquake, a war, something heartbreaking and nasty. She felt cool and calculating, like a whore chasing business. 'And I don't think it's very wise, not at this late stage.'

'They say it's quite safe ...'

'They can say what they like, but I would rather not risk it.' And he came and bent over her nakedness and he patted her stomach possessively again. 'Come on, Mum,' he said. 'Cover up.'

She shuddered. 'You don't care about me any more, only the baby.' She started to sob.

'That's quite wrong. I do care. And it's because I care that I don't want to hurt you.'

Caroline sprinkled the nuts in a wild swirl over the top of the pudding.

Thin, suntanned Frances, in a kind of Armani battledress, sitting opposite, inspected a spoon when she said, 'But aren't you clever! This is gorgeous!'

'Well, I've got plenty of time to ...'

'It's always so nice to have a meal prepared without any fuss. And is it true, Robin, what they're all saying about Martin Reid ...'

Why couldn't she enjoy their conversation? Why couldn't she, like a good wife would, fit in, take an interest in the gossip from Robin's world? Surely all good scintillating stuff? But Caroline wanted to push back her chair and rest her head on her own knees, but she was too fat, she could never reach, and anyway she must not let Robin down. She interlaced her fingers tightly on her knee and listened to the conversation's ebb and flow. Nobody offered to help when she got up to take out the dishes, and she came to dread each compulsory exclamation as the next course was set on the table. She wanted to shout, 'You don't have to, really! Just carry on talking – you don't have to break off each time as if you are tipping the servant!' Giantlike, now, every time she got up she was more ungainly, she moved more clumsily, she slurped her wine. A grin like a facepack hardened her jawbones. While the adults talked she played messy games in the kitchen. Every now and again she was brought in as a kindness as someone who needed cheering up ... mostly by Sam, Frances' husband, who was decent enough to feel sorry that someone was being left out of the group.

Frances and Sam, Katie and Jasper, and how could Robin have ever imagined that she, haughty Frances and elegant Katie could possibly have anything remotely in common?

Nobody was interested in her and her baby and anyway, why would they be when she wasn't, either?

It didn't matter that what they were talking about was superficial nonsense, shoptalk, what counted was that Caroline was being so totally excluded. She wobbled and brooded for a good ten minutes, she licked her lips and asked weakly, 'Have you got a family, Frances? Or are you a workaholic, like Robin?' And she felt like somebody from *Woman's Own*; she might just as well have been offering a knitting pattern on the end of that long pale needle of a stare.

'I have two children from a previous marriage – they're both away at school now, of course – but Sam's not a father yet, are you Sam?'

As if to excuse her, Robin joined in: 'Caroline's not too sure about motherhood at the moment, are you darling?'

'Bit late for second thoughts.' Katie's profile was sharp-faced and thin as the Queen of Diamonds.

'There's nothing to it, nothing at all,' quipped Frances. 'Robin'll pay for the nanny and then you can go back to work. That's what I did.' Frances craned forward and Caroline could see that her eyes were weak. She was a woman who vainly refused to wear glasses and she must have left her lenses at home. Her stare was the one that she used when she sent her reports against the sun from Beirut, Belgrade, Bratislava. 'Didn't Robin mention that you used to act? Did you have a stage-name that I might know?'

Caroline slumped on her seat, her arms idly by her sides. 'Oh, just bits and pieces. I never managed to pick up ...'

'Well,' said Frances quickly, staring at her in amazement. 'Never mind. Not everyone can be a howling success. I should think that being Robin's partner is pretty much a fulltime job! Never a dull moment – lucky old you!'

'And she can certainly cook!' Jasper patted a shiny stomach before repositioning his limp lick of rusty red hair.

'Caroline's not interested in getting back to work.' Suddenly Robin was serious, leaning forward, and the rest of the room fell silent. His face was pale and his fist was clenched round his napkin. 'Motherhood has had to be different for you, Frances, partly because of your position – you could hardly leave your job at the moment, and Katie's never wanted children although, in her books, she gives advice about other people's. But it's not like that for Caroline and there's nothing worse than two people with careers in a family. I suffered from being an only child and I've always believed that there's nothing more satisfying than a proper family life . . . that's what I want for my children.'

'The little woman! That's your religion speaking, Robin, I'm afraid, or your mother . . . You've never really liked women.'

Everyone laughed at Frances with her hair as bleached as the desert sand and her bright red fingernails, but it wasn't funny. 'Caroline, why don't you fetch some water? You must have drunk too much, you're looking bleary.'

If only she hadn't fallen so sickeningly in love with Robin at the start, perhaps they might have worked this out. Perhaps Caroline would have been more forceful. Oh yes, she'd wanted children, but she'd wanted them in her own time. She'd wanted so much else, first. She was greedy, she wanted everything – but she'd never expected to lose her career and that wasn't Robin's fault, was it? Now, stout, placid-faced and big-breasted, the keeper of the Caithness vase and thus doomed, it was too late to find another identity. A wife and mother. Never to return to work? Never to use her talents again? If she waited until her children grew up she'd be too old to act. If she refused to have any more children then she would lose Robin. Caroline could stand up and argue, stand her ground and make a scene here and now at the table, or she could accept it. Shocked, she suddenly realised that either of these two women fiddling with their wine and their absurdly subservient men, would fall into bed with Robin at the drop of a hat – but he hadn't chosen them. Confident and successful as they were, he had chosen *her*. He didn't want competition: he wasn't even interested in sex any more. He wanted a wife and a mother for his children. A breeder.

But he doesn't know me! He doesn't know what I really look like. I am stuck in my own childhood, as far away from a mother as my own mother was.

Robin hadn't meant it but he'd made Caroline the joke, and when she dully got up to see to the coffee she knew, when she lit that secret, sympathetic cigarette, that the grin was still drilled to her face. She stood at the sink, dreaming balefully. Hell, things weren't as bad as all that. She would have something to do tomorrow, after all. She would fill the morning with the washing-up.

TWENTY-THREE

Of course he was with her at the birth, giving instructions and doing the breathing, as all good husbands are. The midwife, muscles straining and all powerful like a man, called Caroline a good girl. In order that he could be there, so that Robin could slot the event between the bulging pages of his filofax, the child was induced.

They gave her a monster sanitary towel with nothing to hold it on with. It lay there, trapped between her legs, like a sodden dead rat. She marked the sheets, a childhood horror which merited the direst of punishments – and she lay in a nest surrounded by flowers, rank with blood and freesia. There was no other way to travel, so she painfully made her way down the ward with her hand hitching the thing between her legs but half-hobbling. Caroline the model, wincing with every pull of the stitches, backwards and forwards she went.

Robin was enchanted. Vanessa was unique and quite, quite irreplaceable. Her skin was creased with the tiniest of wavering, cut-glass lines and she was downy with the soft fur of her packaging. Everything in which she was wrapped was white and delicate as the most expensive tissue paper, but the milk which dripped from Caroline's breasts was a kind of oily yellow.

Robin, noticing, asked the nurse, 'Is that natural?'

Caroline said, 'I have been thinking about this and I would rather bottle feed, if that's all right.'

'Darling, you can't mean that! Everyone knows that bottle feeding is second best.'

But bottled milk is sterilised and purified, while her own might be tainted ...

'Well, we have to know now,' said the nurse, pursed-lipped. 'You should really have spoken up earlier and then we could have started the process of drying up the milk.'

'She'll breastfeed,' said Robin firmly. 'Well, of course she will.'

'It's no good if Mother doesn't want to.' The nurses flirted with Robin, ignoring the silly billy on the bed; they knew who he was.

'Of course she wants to. She's just a little nervous at first. Well, that's understandable.'

'Isn't he gorgeous?' the nurse said to Caroline when, at last, Robin had gone, and she could have been talking about somebody's baby. 'Aren't you lucky?' A very lucky girl shouldn't be being so naughty! I mean, look at Mrs Vine over there, so blowsy and drab with her third draped round her neck, and no one to visit her yet. And look at sweet little Veronica, only sixteen, sobbing with happiness behind the curtains: 'A natural mother, it's quite amazing. What chance has she got in life?' said Sister.

And all the congratulations cards shouted down, they yelled at the face on the pillow:

'*A Baby Daughter ... how Wonderful!*'

And it was. It was wonderful.

That night, when all was as quiet as it could be, save for the squeaking of quick feet on lino and the muffled snores of mothers and children, Caroline, after watching for a while, rose from her bed and lifted Vanessa from her plastic crib. She took her into her rancid bed, she propped herself in a comfortable position, ungainly, ugly with her legs parted and her nightdress undone, and the stench of milk and blood and freesia and Body Shop coconut formed one heady, suppurating fragrance she knew she would never forget. And then she felt it come, in a redhot blast. The fierce surge of love was as powerful as the rush of milk from her breasts and just as uncontrollable. It was sexual ... charged with the heat of the body ... animal, not of the mind. To stop the love she would need tablets more powerful than milk-suppressants. She wept, she giggled with relief to find the love there, she'd read about women who couldn't, she'd read about them and felt it was just as sad as those tortured souls who could not bear children at all. She'd even been prepared to wait ... the love would come in the end, said the experts. But Caroline had no need to wait. In spite of her very worst fears, Caroline loved her child and compared to the tender thing she held in her arms, the part lost in the play sank into insignificance.

How lucky she was! She was normal! She was a natural mother. Thank God.

Wise, intelligent Robin, as usual, had been quite right.

There was quite a crowd to bid them farewell because Robin had his own programme now, and was already famous. Everyone wanted to shake his hand but he couldn't shake properly, everyone laughed about that, because he was carrying Vanessa so carefully.

How lucky Vanessa was to be Robin's child, to be brought to such a comfortable home, the cheerful nursery, clothes from The White House and a crib from Harrods, a beautiful mother – fulltime – an ambitious, adoring father and the richest God in the world looking down benignly upon her.

'Careful, darling.' Robin watched in case his wife arranged the carry-cot cover too clumsily. 'You go indoors and get comfortable. Put your feet up. Don't stretch over to the back of the car, you'll strain yourself. I'll do it.'

'But the case?'

'I'll bring the case in later.'

She had no one of her own to whom she could show the baby. The few friends she had left Robin considered unsuitable; he kept them away. Robin's friends were not the types to pop round and coo. No one had the time, for a start ...

The television play that she'd almost forgotten, *Hermione and the Fire-Eating Bear*, was a roaring success. Caroline couldn't bring herself to watch it, although she was spending the evening alone and there was nothing worth watching on the other channels. Robin brought Caroline all the reviews. He brought them to her in bundles. The unknown actress who had replaced Caroline was acclaimed and fêted by the critics. Why had she lost that part? Why had they changed their minds? Had she said something wrong, afterwards? Had something happened? But what was the point ... She told herself she did not care; she had Vanessa, and Vanessa was no nine-day wonder.

At one party they went to, Barry Kittow from the *Observer* said to

Caroline, 'How do we British manage to keep coming up with these astonishing talents? An unknown actress struts and frets on our airwaves, we're infatuated by her skills, she dazzles us all . . .'

'That part, the part of Hermione, it was offered to me, right at the start.'

'Sorry?' His ash trickled off the crusty bread and fell upon the Camembert. If he stood back now he would grind that grape. He thought she was lying! For some extraordinary reason this chubby-faced man thought that she was making it up.

Sometimes, alone and depressed, she dug out her old portfolio. She studied the glossy pictures and marvelled over the woman she once was in the days when it was so easy to giggle.

'Why do your friends ignore me, Robin? Why do their eyes slide off me? Why do I feel so unequal, as though I have nothing to contribute?'

'Most of them are extroverted people. You have to shove your way in, you know that.'

She stopped him. 'No, wait a minute, Robin. Please, please, think about this for a moment, take me seriously. If you were in my position, what would you say to them? How can I get back my self-esteem?'

'You are the one person I know who doesn't talk about herself, don't you see! That's why to have you around is such a blessed relief. Anyway, you have your opinions, your thoughts. It's not what you do that makes you interesting, it's how you interpret events and how you then put that interpretation over. What's happened to your acting skills? They're still there, aren't they? Tell them your opinions. You are being silly. You are being boring.'

When Robin was at work Caroline was left on her own with Vanessa. On her own in the lovely house with the hammock in the garden and the Silver Cross pram and the deep-freeze packed with good things from Fortnums. She wouldn't let herself dance. When she danced she seemed to make anger, a wooden spoon stirring the contents of some malevolent black stew, and she knew she should not be angry. Caroline was a lucky girl with a wonderful husband and a perfect baby. She ought to feel fresh and cool, pretty-green, like a salad.

'Perhaps we should get an au pair,' said Robin, passing through. 'You look tired. You must be doing too much.'

Caroline, bewildered, was doing nothing at all.

Caroline did not want some young girl around all the time to see her loneliness.

Babysitters were easy and Robin vetted them carefully. At least once a month they went to the theatre or a concert. More frequently than that they were asked to a party or out for a meal, or Caroline entertained for Robin at Camberley Road, but she never made friends with the women she met although a few, like her, were just wives. All they seemed to talk about was their own men – or Robin. A good number of them, she noticed, flirted quite shamelessly with Robin but if he was straying she realised with horror that, because of his peculiar hours, she would be the last to know.

She asked him outright. She said, 'Are you sleeping with Jayne?'

'I'm not interested in playing around. You and Vanessa mean the world to me and I wouldn't do anything to jeopardise that.'

On a Sunday, before he went to Mass, he brought her breakfast in bed and the papers and then he'd come home and push Vanessa through the park looking proud.

Caroline stayed in bed and slept in.

Oh Caroline was so very lucky. Caroline had it all.

If someone snapped at her in a shop she'd be unhappy for the rest of the day.

When she went for her walk with the pram she learned how to clear her throat quickly and say good morning in order to work a voice that rarely spoke.

Sometimes she dreamed about leaving, of walking out just like that. But she loved him too much and how could she leave her baby behind? She wouldn't have dreamed of taking it with her, it was far too precious and it was Robin's.

When he came home at night he was usually tired and most of the evening was already gone. He'd have a drink. They'd eat and they'd talk ... they'd talk about Vanessa; she'd said the word 'dog' for the first time today, she'd gone a bit red from the sun, she'd have to learn to keep that sunhat on. And then there'd be work he needed to do – the reading-up on personalities, histories and world situations, or he might have to watch a video someone said he must see. Caroline, exhausted for reasons unknown, was asleep most nights before Robin came up and it was he who got up in the nights to tend to the baby. Caroline slept so deeply she didn't even hear the child cry.

She rearranged the flowers. She liked to keep the house full of flowers. Flowers are flags. When Caroline was first in love she preferred the wild flowers she gathered herself, a riot of shape and colour; weeds didn't matter at all, they came complete with their bugs and snails, they warmed the house like bursts of laughter. Now she bought them in defensive bunches, forced flowers, their stems often cut by elastic bands, from the greengrocer in the market. How could she love her baby as much as she did, and yet be a mother badly?

'I need to get out of the house. I need a job. I have to make friends of my own. Surely you must see that I'm no good to Vanessa like this – bored, tired all the time. I think we should find a nanny.'

'Fine. Fine.' He sounded tired, pushed to the limits when confronted again and again with her whines. What a spoilt woman she was. 'But what would you do? I love to feel you're at home for me, for Vanessa. I think this is to do with post-natal depression. It might be better if you saw a doctor rather than went off at half-cock.' She'd be tarnished by the outside world, too weak, too stupid or too immoral, in the way that female paupers were viewed in the eighteenth-century workhouse.

'It wouldn't be half-cock, and surely there'd be something I could do. I'm not stupid. I'm not ugly. I'm not ill – I'm just bored. I could go on a course, train for something ... it's not the money, after all. I could do something voluntary, work part-time for some charity.' But she was wheedling, like a spoilt child.

'Most of the working women I know aren't terribly happy, Caroline. Actually, most of them would rather be at home, given the choice.'

'If you said that in public you would be lynched.'

Robin came to bed at the same time she did. Robin must find her attractive again – perhaps it was the new perfume she'd bought. She'd never used contraception because he was so fanatically against it. Within a month she was pregnant.

'Why don't you leave these ideas of yours until after the new baby is born? Give it some thought in the meantime. After all, you don't want to tire yourself out. We'll advertise for a cleaner.'

Oh I'm sorry, Vanessa, I'm sorry. Would her melancholy mood be absorbed, with her milk, into her baby's bloodstream? Would it mix with bone and sinew, turning the rest of her child's life sour? 'Very well, I'll leave it. And after the baby we'll look for a nanny and I'll make a start ...'

Etc. Etc.

And on and on and on and on and on it all went. Round and round and round.

Glass, like ice, is a supercooled liquid – not a true solid.

TWENTY-FOUR

HE KNOCKS. He waits. He knocks again before parting the dead bamboo-like shoots of lupins in the tiny patch of front garden and peering in through the kitchen window. By the time Lot Dance arrives at the canary house in Potters Bar – he has dallied his way here, as children do – he discovers his bright brother, Bart, sitting alone in the kitchen with his head in his hands, destroyed.

'It's only me, your brother, Lot. Open the door.' Lot takes off his gloves and taps. 'I'm like the wolf with chalk in his mouth, trying to get into the goat's house!' He chuckles. He presses his face hard against the pane so that his perfect nose is squashed flat. He widens his eyes to a hideous enquiry.

Bart raises a tired head. He stares at the figure at the window as if he is seeing a stranger, with his eyes half-closed.

'Open the door,' pleads Lot. 'I'm not the wolf and it's parky out here.' Then he goes back to the front-door steps, running his boots over the scraper while waiting politely for the door to be opened.

Inside, into the warmth at last – Lot didn't realise how cold he'd been, his face feels hard and slab-like – and the house looks as if a bomb has hit it. It smells of egg and cereal. Lot shrugs off his long coat and smooths the stiff wool of his crumpled jersey ... he wants Bart to notice it – it was knitted without one mistake completely by memory from an old pattern he lost long ago.

'She's left me.' Bart looks around with a hopeless sorrow in his eyes. His lips compress, his face looks as if it's about to fall in on itself. 'She's gone. She must have gone in a hurry because she hasn't cleared up and she never goes out without clearing up.'

After following his brother through to the kitchen, Lot sniffs again, grimacing at the vague but pervasive whiff of ammonia steaming from the cream-coloured kitchen pail. He says, 'The nappy bucket needs a lid. Where is the lid? And how do you know Ruby's gone?'

But even Lot knows that Ruby's gone. The house feels totally different this evening, as if someone's suddenly come in and rolled up the carpets. A sigh seems to come from the little green gingham curtains, the ones Ruby made, and old crusts of toast on the draining board waiting to be put out for the birds remind him of Ruby being there.

Bart doesn't answer. He just nods dully in the direction of the kitchen shelf.

The note, in Ruby's thin, loopy hand, gives no real explanation for the drama. Lot reads it slowly. Like almost everything he has ever read, it will imprint itself on his mind so that he will never forget it. '*What the hell's going on here, Bart? You managed to fool me once but you'll not get the chance to do it again. Why did you lie? I'm sorry I can't be more grown-up about this. I've gone to Esher. I've taken the car. Feel perfectly free to go to her now, if you still want to. Love, Ruby.*'

'I don't understand it,' groans Bart. 'That's what makes it worse. I just don't understand it. I thought we were beginning to work things through ... shit ... shit ... and when I phoned Ruby's house just now her mother said that Ruby refused to speak to me.' He opens his hands, splaying his fingers in a way that makes them look as if they're letting out water. He stares at his hands, as surprised as Lot is to see them quite empty. 'What am I going to do, Lot? That's the thing. I just don't know what to do and I don't know why she has gone.'

Neither does Lot. He is worried that Bart is not really pleased to see him, that he might want to be alone with his sickness as a dog crawls behind the hedge with his wound. Or it might be that he is glad. There is no way of telling and it just makes Lot feel horrible. He can't understand why Ruby left, either, and he doesn't know what to say to make things any better. He has never seen Bart looking so forlorn and dejected before. It is not in his brother's nature to succumb to misery and let it envelop him like this.

'I've lost my business, I've lost my house, I've lost my kids and I've lost my wife.'

'And the car.'

Bart's smile is the furthest from a smile that Lot has ever seen. An icy snarl would be a better description of the grim crack that cuts across his face, like a piece of metal twisted from a bumper. 'Oh thanks, Lot. Great. Yep, and the car, Lot, and the car. Ever been drunk, brother of mine? Ever been well and truly pissed right out of your head so you don't know the day let alone the time, so you don't know your own fucking name? Have you?'

Lot shakes a heavy head. Bart looks as if he's been drinking already. He sounds as though he has, too — heavy and slurred like the men who sleep on the pavements, although there is no bitter smell in the room, only the nappies. He fingers his rainbow pullover lovingly. Nope, he doesn't think Bart is going to notice it after all.

'Well, that's what I'm supposed to do, isn't it? Get frigging well pissed as a fart and then put the gun to my head.'

'Or we could have a cup of tea.' Lot inspects the selection of bottles, messily arranged behind the sink. 'Or lime juice might be better. Have you got a gun licence, Bart?'

The vehemence of Bart's anger is startling. 'The bitch ... The cunt ... the cow!'

Lot shivers all over; even his hair seems to stand on end. Slack-jawed with astonishment he pleads, 'No, Bart, no. Please don't talk about Ruby like that.'

'Not Ruby, Caroline!' Bart shouts desperately, his cheeks flooding flaming beetroot. 'Not Ruby, you arsehole — Caroline fucking Townsend! Why did I ever do it? What got into me? And who made that phone call, anyway? Who is stirring this shit?'

Damn it, Bart is absolutely right. He is not to blame for this in spite of Ruby's, 'It takes two to tango.' Lot is uneasy to see Bart vulnerable and self-reproachful, it's not right. That woman must have lured him like a wicked enchantress and bewitched him against his will. Lot knows how that happens to men — it's going on all the time on the telly, and look at that picture of Eve that hangs on the hostel wall! Bart is innocent and yet poor Bart is having to shoulder all the blame. Lot is desperate to help his poor brother. It is very satisfactory to hate someone together, especially someone who's wanton and vicious. Patently uncomplicated, Lot knows that there is nothing more potent than searing hatred or hopeless love — lovelorn scrawls and harsh stabbing, that's what Lot likes to do best with his pencil — and now he's got both he's upset, but there's a kind of harmony in hating and loving at the same time, like when a circle becomes complete. And Lot finds a certain wholeness in it.

Minutes pass. Miserable, uncomfortable minutes as Lot watches Bart's unhappy white fingers moving over the stubble on his chin. He thinks to say, 'Perhaps you've got enemies that you don't know about.'

'What's the point of anyone being my enemy, Lot?' Bart continues to stare at Lot but his gaze passes through; he does not see him — perhaps he sees Ruby still sitting in the chair. 'No one can possibly be envious of me. I haven't got anything of anyone else's, and I don't owe anyone, except for the bank and they have no feelings, like executioners.'

'Well, somebody must have done it.'

'Unless it was Caroline herself.'

'Caroline, phoning up to tell Ruby what was going on? Phoning up to get you into trouble? Why? Why would she do that?'

Bart sneers. 'A woman scorned! And a pretty hysterical sort of woman at that. I wouldn't put it past her. I wouldn't put anything past that bitch. And d'you know what I'm gonna do, I'm going to ring her up right now and find out.' Wildly excited by his rabid animosity, Bart thinks that doing something is going to ease his pain. He is trying to wiggle his way right out of reality.

Now is not the time to tell his brother that this device never works.

Lot, sighing, lets his guilty eyes slide round the room. When he is nervous he can't stop yawning and there's a yawn so huge coming along that his jaw will probably click. He tries to stop himself and his eyes water. He's not about to tell Bart that he's been stalking up and down Camberley Road all day seeking his own revenge. Not in the mood Bart's in. He's not about to get himself into trouble with Bart. It's up to Bart to discover where Caroline is and perhaps Lot can profit from Bart's investigations.

Lot fights his straining jaw while fiddling with the salt pot, pretending not to listen too hard to Bart's one-way phone conversation. The woman is out ... that is quite clear from the outset; whoever answers the telephone must be telling Bart that Caroline Townsend has gone away. Bart's hard voice softens slightly so Lot assumes he is speaking to a child.

'This is Bart. I wonder if you could tell me how long she'll be away?'

And then there's a pause while some sort of explanation is given.

'And what is this Broadlands?' He is listening intently now. 'When did she leave? Is there a number I can call her on? Oh, I see. It's like that. I don't suppose you'd know whether she telephoned my house on Christmas Day? No? No, I suppose not. That's okay. No reason, really. Never mind, it's not that important.'

Bart rings off and collapses once more. 'None the wiser. Ought to have known it'd be a complete waste of time. She's gone to some clinic in Sussex for a fortnight, and apparently it's not the done thing to contact anyone there. It's a kind of controlled retreat where these nutters can get their heads together. I think I was speaking to one of the older girls so I couldn't go into it too deeply. Damn and blast. She could well have been the one who phoned Ruby. Apparently she didn't leave home until Boxing Day and if she's crazy enough to decide to shut herself away for two weeks then she must have been pretty upset. Yes, Lot, it could well have been her.'

Pleased with the result of Bart's enquiries – he knows about Broadlands now, he can get the full address from the helpful man who shelters in the library – Lot proceeds gingerly. 'But Bart, it wasn't that phone call which drove Ruby away. Something else must have happened since then, something that Caroline couldn't have caused.'

'If only Ruby would speak to me! Hell, don't I deserve some sort of explanation, for Christ's sake?'

The look Lot gives his despairing brother tells him that no, he doesn't think he deserves a thing. 'Let's hope Mum doesn't find out,' warns Lot.

'What's Mum got to do with this?'

'Mum likes Ruby. So does Dad.'

'Lot, damn you, there's no need to make things bloody well worse! Ruby was going to ask for a loan, I don't suppose she'll be doing that now. I'm going to have to put the house on the market. I'm going to have to sell the house on top of everything else. I have lost everything!' He breaks off for an instant, there is a catch in the back of his throat, then a long hesitation and much helpless shrugging before he is able to continue. 'You read about people like me. I am a man who has just gone and bloody well lost everything.'

Lot takes a deep breath. 'You could come and live at the hostel with me, share my room if you wanted.'

Bart's head returns to his hands; they seem to be the only comfortable place for it.

'Bart! Bart!' shouts Lot, with a burst of childish earnestness. 'I know what! You could help with the boxes.'

Is Bart crying? Lot has never seen Bart crying before and it is an unpleasant sound. It is jerky and gurgling, like a sink that needs clearing. It makes Lot feel as if he is falling, as if he doesn't understand anything in the world any more because Lot is supposed to be the fool, Lot is the one who cries. When Lot was little Bart was the leader, he took care of Lot when the going got tough and sometimes he let Lot play with his friends. Bart taught Lot how to ride a two-wheeler. Bart showed him where the best conkers were and Lot made friends of his own when he gave away his biggest, most round, most shiny conkers. Once he gave a whole bucketful away to be allowed to bat.

But Lot is suffused with a new strength of purpose. With a passion that is more like a rage, nothing can deflect him now. For not only has Caroline Townsend destroyed Ruby's happiness, she has, with her cruel, vindictive telephone calls, managed to bring Lot's capable, successful brother to his knees. Well look at him, he's lost everything. And he's crying. Lot's two favourite people, broken and brought so low by the deliberately bad behaviour of one most exceedingly wicked woman.

Lot thinks about apples and serpents. She must be found immediately – and she must be made to pay.

TWENTY-FIVE

THEY'VE GOT TO keep going, there's so much to get done.

'Bart's still trying to contact Mother, can you believe it? That's lust for you. He doesn't care about his wife at all. I thought that second phone call would put a stop to all that, but I was wrong. We'll have to leave it now. We can't keep informing on him when that pitiful woman of his obviously can't do anything about it.'

Vanessa's voice comes breathlessly because they are walking quickly down Oxford Street where the snow is yellow and wet like a kitchen towel used to mop up spilt tea. Parted by crowds every now and again, they swim back together to form a pattern, like filings to a magnet, to continue their avid conversation. This is an important outing. Dominic agreed to stay home with Mrs Guerney. He is acting as watchman this morning. He emptied a jigsaw on the hall floor and was sprawled there, already starting it, when the bustling cleaner arrived.

'What thoughtlessness! Why have you put yourself here of all places? You've got the whole house, so why on earth choose this particular spot, directly under the feet of anyone who's coming or going. What a nuisance, Dominic! Your mother would make you move it, I know.'

But it was essential that he stay close to the cellar door on this first morning after Mother's revival. It was imperative that he hear every sound. And he's the one most likely to deal with trouble without any trace of sentiment. Ilse is out, supposed to be shopping for candles and light bulbs but she'll be hanging about for hours on Napier Road and then she'll probably see if Paulo's sitting in the Plume of Feathers. Luckily, when there's no one around for Mrs Guerney to talk to, she turns the radio on loud. If Mother decides to be difficult then Dominic will have plenty of time to slip through the basement door and turn up the sauna heating controls.

'Are you sure you wouldn't rather one of us stayed with you? As it's the first time?' Vanessa was worried to leave him with so much responsibility.

'I'd rather be on my own. I don't want to be influenced.'

First stop, and they gathered round Vanessa when she slipped Mother's cash card into the machine. It was hard to believe that getting someone else's money was so easy. Over the last few days they have been feeding the card into the machine, and they've accumulated enough cash to cover their immediate expenses.

'We'd have to go mad to spend that amount!'

'Still, we must be careful to stick to the list.'

The list is a long one. They're all going to have to help carry things back. 'We've got to remember that today we have to concentrate on essentials. There'll be lots of time to come back and get more as the need arises.'

With a surging army of others – the sales are in full swing – the four of them halt at a crossing. Sacha, clinging to Vanessa's hand, ventures quietly, 'I think you might have upset Mother yesterday, Vanny.'

Vanessa stiffens. She has tossed and turned all night, reliving the nightmare of the evening visit when she confronted Mother, head on, for the first time in her life. If she hurt Mother then she certainly hurt herself even more. 'What else could I have said? What other way was there to play it? If I had weakened she would have pounced. I know I was hard, but what we are doing *is* hard. It's not a nice thing to do you know, Sacha, to keep somebody locked up. It's not easy knowing how to talk to a prisoner, particularly when it's your mother.' Reassuring Sacha like this, Vanessa is merely running through the arguments she used to console herself last night.

The green light replaces the red and they move across the road, hurrying because everyone else is hurrying, caught up in the after-Christmas rush.

'I didn't really realise that we were meaning to keep her down there for so long.'

'Camilla, nor did I. None of us did. But now she's down there we have to see if we can make things better ... for her and for us. We'll never get another chance.'

'We should have talked about it first.'

'But there wasn't any time. She asked how long we were going to keep her there and I said that we didn't know. Anyway, there was nothing stopping you from speaking. Mother even asked to speak to you but you shook your head and I didn't think you wanted to.'

'Well, I'm looking forward to a new mother.' Amber, attached to Camilla's hand, tries to shake herself free. 'I'm on Vanny's side. It's much better being on our own. It's much better coming out like this to buy exciting things, to bring Mother presents that she's going to love.' The child in the bright red tights is forced into a skip to keep up.

Vanessa is grateful for any support; she feels guilty enough without Camilla rubbing it in. 'She won't love them to start with, Amber, we know that, but we just hope she will in the end.'

But Camilla still isn't happy. 'It's easy now, now that we've told everyone she's away. But what happens in a fortnight's time after she's supposed to come back? How will we get away with it then? I'm really scared. Sometimes, you know, I just feel so scared.'

'We'll have to face that when it comes. Nothing's so hard when it's actually happening. Nobody really wants to see Mother, that's why it's so easy to shake them off. I think, if we play this right, we could keep her down there for years – not that I want to. All I'm saying, is that it's probably going to be much easier than we think.' She stops in her tracks and faces Camilla. Her hand tightens firmly on Sacha's; she can feel the child's small fingerbones under the woollen gloves, like a bird's. 'The most important thing is that we keep together, as we always have. We might not have an enemy any more, but we still need to hang together. We mustn't fall out over this, Camilla.'

'Don't worry, we won't.'

And then it's straight in to Dickins & Jones where they look for a suitable nightie. They are as one when they make their choice. The prettily sprigged cotton with forget-me-nots on a pastel blue base, that's the one. Full-length and with long sleeves gathered to a ruff at the wrists, it buttons right up to its high neck. It is voluminous. It is beautiful. It is soft and cuddly and fresh.

'It reminds me of King Arthur. I thought you might go for pure white . . . the kind that you like yourself.'

'No, Camilla, we're buying for Mother now, not me. Pure white is too childish. And Mother, remember, is not a virgin. Mother has been married.' Vanessa, flushed, stands at the counter with her wad of notes and feels her heart beating fast because this is the first time they have used Mother's money in the big outside world. The corner shop doesn't count.

But the assistant doesn't bat an eyelid as she wraps the nightie in tissue before folding it into the bag. She is far too busy to make enquiries about the age of the customer. And anyway, Vanessa, in her severely adult buttoned-up coat, and her ageless hairstyle, looks far too stolid and sensible to be up to anything suspicious.

It's Liberty's next, and here the choice is more difficult. Something simple can be translated into so many different styles. The twins sit down on the carpet while Vanessa and Camilla look round, trying not to miss anything slightly suitable, but the pinafore dress is hard to beat. Floral again, it hangs softly down from above the breasts of the hard-faced model, softening even her with her coarse horsehair and her flat, flaring nose, and if it can soften that plastic woman it must surely soften Mother. And ideal underneath is a crisp, white blouse with a queenly ruff at the neck.

'Mother's going to look like someone out of the Damart catalogue . . .'

'Don't be silly, Sacha. These clothes are expensive – these clothes have style.'

'But nothing like Mother's normal choice.'

'Well no, of course not. That's exactly why we are doing this!'

'I don't think she's going to be over the moon.'

'They'll grow on her. They'll grow on her because she's not going to have anything else.'

This time Vanessa writes a cheque, her first forgery, and it's good. She's glad Mother's is a gold card. She was not prepared for such enormous prices.

For underwear they go straight to Marks & Spencer. They can hardly push their way through for the rough, eager crowd, but they are not interested in the sales items flopping out of tall baskets, they only want the best. The two packs of knickers are white; they look sensibly square, pinned to the cardboard illustration, with a fierce elastic waist and a simple frill round each leg. They've got Mother's bra size written on the list and Camilla consults it now ... 36A ... and there's a demure, serviceable garment, modestly concealing, with a band round the bottom instead of that other uncomfortable-looking rim. The petticoat they add to the pile is cotton, too – a bit like a child's summer dress: you could go out with it on and not attract attention. The last items they buy from Marks are three pairs of thick black tights, innocent because they are the same make Vanessa wears for school.

Books now. Lots of books. Having shared out the bags they struggle along the slushy pavement. They are hit by the heat as they push inside the store. 'Keep together. Keep tight hold of each other. It's a good thing Dom didn't come, he would have hated this.' Once through the foyer they move straight to the paperbacks where Vanessa hands her bag to Camilla and says, 'You stand over there while I look. It's essential we choose right. At the end of the day these could prove more important than anything else.'

She moves along the paperbacks, her bottom lip caught between her teeth and her tongue occasionally flicking in and out as her concentration grows. What to choose, what to choose ... If only she was older and wiser. She picks out two Daphne du Mauriers, two James Herriots and one Barbara Cartland before spying the Miss Reads further along the shelves. She spends some time reading the backs and looking at the jackets. Then she returns the Barbara Cartland with a sigh and takes three Miss Reads instead. She picks up a Lillian Beckwith on the way by.

'That ought to keep her busy,' says Vanessa, pleased, as they queue for what feels like hours at the till.

'But Mother never reads books.'

'She used to. She used to read all the time – but not nice books like these – books by that Fay Weldon and Germaine Greer, books by Nancy Friday and Marilyn French. It's only since Daddy left that she hasn't been able to read. It's only since then that she's stopped watching plays on TV and changed to those terrible game shows. She'll be very happy reading these. I bet you she'll ask for some more.'

But Sacha doesn't look convinced.

There's only shoes to find now and that would be easy, save for the fact that they are all struggling under the weight of the bags. They trail up the road, looking in shoe-shop windows, bored. Mother is fond of shoes. Mother owns hundreds of pairs, but they are all sharp, pointed and smart, and it's definitely flat ones the children are after. Amber points to a pair of summer sandals. 'Jesus sandals! Amber, I think you are probably going too far. She doesn't want anything huge and gawky. She wants to be neat and pretty, not hippy!'

Amber starts sulking. She hangs a finger in her mouth while hoisting the carrier bag high on her shoulder, protesting under the weight. 'I haven't chosen anything yet. It's all been you and Camilla.'

'But don't you approve of what we've bought?'

'Oh yes, I suppose so, but I haven't chosen, that's the thing.'

'Well, before we go home we're going into Boots and you and Sacha can pick out the make-up.'

'I thought we didn't want Mother to wear make-up. I thought you said it would be good for her skin if she stopped painting her face.'

'But she needs creams and lotions, and I suppose she could do with a pale shade of lipstick. And then there's the shampoo ...'

'Okay, okay.' Amber is mollified for a while.

'I don't like selling shoes without the wearer trying them on.' This is their first real obstacle, the large, coarse-looking woman in the shoe shop. The line of her knickers is showing under her skirt.

'But it's a late Christmas present.'

'It is not a good idea to give anyone shoes. Shoes tend to be a most personal choice. I don't want my customers coming back here to me and complaining that their shoes don't fit, having to have them changed because they haven't even tried them on.'

'All I want to know,' says Vanessa in her most haughty voice, 'is if this measurement is the equivalent to a five and a half?'

The assistant smacks her lips together but nods her head at the same time.

'That's all I want to know. I'll take them.'

'Well, don't say I didn't warn you.'

The lemon and white leather crosses over at the front, and there's a hole where the toe will poke out. In spite of what the assistant says there's a strap at the back so they must be adjustable. Neat, flat sandals like these need not be a perfect fit.

'But will they look all right with black tights?'

'They'll look all right with anything. They are just ordinary shoes, Sacha, for goodness sake. Even someone like Mrs Guerney would be perfectly happy to wear them.'

Everyone is close to exhaustion by now; everyone is near to snapping. It's not the distance they've covered, it's not the heat in the shops, it's the tiring drag of the huge crowds of people. And the worry of what they might face when they do reach home – a furious Mrs Guerney on the phone to the police, a pale, sad-looking Daddy forced to come round to sort it out and Mother at her most manic – cross-legged, drink in hand, towering over all the proceedings, enormous in her anger while she lets her ash fall on the carpet and they start the struggle all over again ...

'Oh please God let it all be all right,' Vanessa murmurs to herself as they finally climb to the top of the bus, Sacha and Amber sorting through the make-up; Ponds Cold Cream, Bronley lemons, cleansing lotion ... everything fresh in pink or white packaging, nothing dirtily strong or strident, and a bottle of gentle Vosene shampoo. Amber opens the box of talc and there's a soft puff of red roses.

'We must have spent hundreds of pounds.'

'We have. But it's going to be worth it.'

'What if Mother refuses to wear any of the things we've bought her?'

'She won't have much option. Her black dress is all damp and sweaty. Her fur coat is too hot. Her underwear needs washing and she won't be offered anything else.'

'She might choose to go round with nothing on, just to spite us.'

'Then we will simply turn the heating up.'

'Mother is going to start to hate us, Vanny. Who knows, maybe she already does.'

'Dominic says that prisoners kept in solitary confinement might start by hating their captors, but after a while they come to love them, no matter what they do. Even when they torture them, there's a kind of loving there.'

'I don't understand that.'

'Well you wouldn't, Amber, because you're far too young.'

'I don't think I ever want to be old enough to understand about that.'

As they trudge the last few yards along Camberley Road, every step feels heavier. Vanessa wants to rest and yet she doesn't want to reach home. She is relieved to see the road in front of the house free from police cars, from cameras and Black Marias ...

Dominic opens the door with a smile. It is the most wonderful smile Vanessa has ever seen. She wants to take it and keep it for ever, dried and pressed in a book. 'It's okay,' he says quickly, sensing her desperate anxiety. 'Ilse's not even back yet. Bring it all in and we'll take it straight down to her. There's no point in carting it upstairs first. She'll enjoy undoing the parcels.'

'Have there been any difficult phone calls?'

'No, none.'

'Have you been down?'

'No. I haven't needed to go down. She's been absolutely silent all morning. I've done the jigsaw three times. Mrs Guerney thinks I must be coming down with something so tomorrow she's bringing some malt.'

Amber insists on the tubular bells although Camilla tells her it's silly. 'It has to be done this way,' she insists stiffly. 'It feels better when we ring the bells, and it means that Mother knows we are coming and it makes it feel important.'

So, tired as they are, and eager to get on, they have to stand and wait till the ritualistic ringing is done with. Then, down they go, and Mother is not at the window, but sitting listlessly on her bench with her face towards the circle of plastic, waiting – just waiting.

'Does anyone else want to do the speaking?'

Vanessa turns to Camilla, but she shakes her head.

So Vanessa moves to the window again. 'We've been out to get you some things, Mother. We're going to push them through the pipe-hole now. Some of the bags are too big so we'll have to get the things out and send them through separately.'

Mother does not respond. She just continues to sit on her bench and Vanessa senses the twins' joint disappointment.

One by one, with the help of the hoover extension tube, Dominic pushes the various items carefully through the hole. They gather there, on the floor, not looking half so good, so interesting, or so fresh as they did when they were displayed in the shops. Mother watches their arrival without much interest.

When he has finished with the clothes, Vanessa signals for Dominic to start pushing the books through. Each one is in a paper bag so Mother can't see the titles immediately. The sandals go through one at a time, the make-up follows last of all.

'Aren't you even going to look at them, Mother? They cost a lot of money. The dress, for instance, was very expensive.'

'Vanessa, I'm afraid I just don't understand what this is all about. I don't understand what is going on or what sort of response you want from me. I have spent the night down here all on my own, not knowing what is going to happen, not knowing what is going through that head of yours ...'

'We just want you to look at what we've brought you, Mother, and then we will bring you your lunch.'

'Well, if that's what you want, I'd better do it.'

'Is she looking now?' Sacha spits with excitement.

Vanessa nods impatiently without removing her eyes from the window. She's never noticed before how Mother's shoulders are so childishly narrow.

Like an automaton Mother gets up and starts picking up the various pieces of clothing. She puts the underwear to one side and there's no way of telling what she is thinking. She unfolds the vast nightdress and glances towards the glass but there's still no expression on her face. She looks better than she did yesterday, but that is probably because she is eating. She ate all her curry last night, and the fruit, and she finished the grapefruit and toast that they offered her this morning.

Now, clammy and drab in her over-worn slip, she undoes the pinafore dress (they pinned it in the shop and Mother undoes the pins) and lays it out on her knee. Her limbs are thin and marble-white. Once again she turns her face to the window but this time there's a quizzical crinkling around her eyes. She can tell that the blouse goes with the dress because she puts them aside both together. She is neither approving nor disapproving. She looks kind of ... defeated. But she sorts through the make-up all the same, holding it up to the light the better to see the labels on the individual jars and boxes.

'Well, Mother, so what do you think?'

'I had better put them on.' Vanessa, taken aback, has never heard

Mother quite so submissive. Normally, when she's sad, when something disappoints her, she rages.

'There's still the books.' But Mother doesn't seem interested, or strong enough to tackle anything else. Vanessa tries to encourage her on. 'You've got lots of time to read now, Mother, and tomorrow we're going to bring your Walkman down, and some of your music.'

Obediently – she thought she had finished but now she knows she must go on performing – Mother stoops to pick up the scatter of books that are piled messily on the floor. One by one she slips them from their bags, and reads the titles before stacking them dully on the bench beside her.

'Who chose the books?'

'I did, Mother.'

'Yes, of course you did. I can see.'

'Will you read them?'

'I don't know. What will you do if I don't read them, Vanessa? Turn the heating up?'

Vanessa doesn't know what to say. She turns to Dominic for reassurance but he seems quite happy. He is waiting beside the hole for the dirty clothes to come through. Camilla, too, has a satisfied look on her face because, after all, they have accomplished what they set out to achieve; they have used the cards and the chequebook successfully. They have cash in their purses and Mrs Guerney has gone home with her mind fixed on malt, unsuspecting.

There has to be a balance, you see, especially with the reading. Mother has gone to such wild extremes! She is bound to be depressed – who wouldn't be depressed, locked up and alone in a basement sauna? But Vanessa could stand all this much more easily if Mother stayed angry. Coping with screams and curses is far more straightforward than dealing with this.

Vanessa needs to get out of here quickly. Something intolerable and new in the atmosphere is making her ache. Perhaps it is just that she is tired after her nerve-racking morning struggle around London.

But just as they're leaving, just as Dominic is closing the door and they breathe in the safe, warm sanity of the hall at last, the laugh that floats up from below, swirling up from the basement like coloured smoke in a bell-bottomed jar, is so shivery cold, so devoid of any kind of recognisable mirth, that Vanessa can't keep strong any longer. Her face rigid, her eyes enormous, she shudders sharply and bursts into hysterical tears.

TWENTY-SIX

HERE IS A blustery February morning with pavements slick and dark with rain; when the gusts shift it beats against the chilly windows of Bertorelli's. Suzie's here, warm and comfortable at a window table, and she is not laughing because what she is hearing is far too important merely to amuse her. There is pleasure to be had in watching the people battling along down Floral Street, grim-faced, wild-haired beneath warring umbrellas, longing to be home or whatever place, to them, signifies safety. Suzie's concentrating terribly hard; she's listening to Kitty Beavers-St Clair whose skin – minutely creased and tacked to seams hidden behind her hairline – hardly moves as she tells her guest that the world is her oyster if she wants it.

Suzie goes coy though deep inside she feels herself swelling with pleasure. 'I wouldn't get the job. They'd say that I was too young – not enough experience.'

'Rubbish. My, my, what a *careful* person all of a sudden! A year ago and you wouldn't have hesitated.'

Suzie clears her throat. 'Well, maybe so, but I've never been in charge of people before. I'm not sure I know how to get in touch with them any more. And I know nothing about running a business.'

Kitty scans the menu, taking it down to knee-level. 'Oh, fine! Be negative then. This job is nothing to do with running a business. All they want you to do is boost circulation and churn out the profits. It's just a matter of commissioning the right sort of people and giving the right sort of editorial input. You can't stand outside other people's lives watching for ever you know, Suzie.'

'Who else would be interested?' Suzie's not hungry for this kind of rich food any more. She wishes she was at home with something simple and hot in a pot, consoling.

Kitty Beavers-St Clair, columnist, society watcher, would turn this subdued luncheon into a frenzied feeding of famished piranha if she sensed the slightest whiff of a scandal. Kitty waves an elegant arm in the air to attract the waiter's attention. Her hand revolves like a ferret's nose, and her fingers could almost be sniffing. She is known at this restaurant; she is known at most of the most sophisticated restaurants in the squares and back-streets of London's West End. She has no trouble, absolutely no trouble at all, filling her column with gossip, and Robin, as a respectable celebrity with a cool eye for public opinion, keeps Kitty and her ilk at a healthily calculated distance. 'You know as well as I do who they are. Since your self-imposed hibernation from the big wide world nothing has changed that much. Daphne Frazer will apply because she applies for everything but she's not a journalist, she's a salesperson really, only knows about admin. She's so shrill no one can stand her and she doesn't have the languages like you. Then there's Bob Beevis, the walking accident, but somebody told me his old problem was rearing its ugly head again. Let's see ... Amanda Bracewell might apply, and Fiona Hawkins is being considered, but isn't Fiona pregnant? You'd have thought she'd be past all that, at her age. They don't want someone who's going to keep ducking off for childbearing and rearing – well, obviously they don't. I think the contract runs for five years.'

'I'd have to ask Robin.'

Kitty narrows her lilac-skinned eyes. They are merely a suggestive wink between two stretched linings. Her face looms closer over the table and her breath is a sweet garlic breeze. 'What did you say?'

Suzie sucks the slice of lemon that she slides from the side of her glass. 'Naturally I'll have to ask Robin.'

'Discuss it with Robin, yes, but *ask* him? Suzie, did you say *ask* him?'

'Slip of the tongue.' The lemon is more sour than she had expected. She winces, she wrinkles her pert little nose. 'What if they decide to appoint from inside?'

'Nope. I was speaking to Hilary yesterday and they want a new face, preferably pretty. They want someone with expert knowledge, a member of all the right organisations, someone who can write, and most important of all, they want that someone to be British, absolutely! That's when I told her I'd talk to you.'

'What did she say?'

'Not much. But she seemed satisfied.'

'When would I have to let them know?'

'Now. You'd have to say you were interested right away. Go and meet them, chew the fat.'

A little crowd forms outside. Someone important is coming out of the stage-door.

'It's funny, you know, Kitty, it feels strange telling you this, but it's made me feel quite honoured to even be thought of. Working from home, you know, I seem to have lost touch with the buzz of it all.'

'My goodness! This is new. You were never ... quite so modest! Good God, Suzie, I don't have to remind you that even the experts ring you up if they're stuck for a name or a piece of obscure information. Honestly, you're the one. Orchids have always been your passion ...'

'Tatty flowers, Robin calls them.'

'He would. He's jealous. You're his wife.'

'Oh Kitty, you were always so suspicious of men.'

'With good reason, and don't exaggerate.'

'I'd have to have some time to think.'

'What about? Just imagine the sort of salary it'll bring, and the lifestyle!'

'It's the five-year contract, really, and leaving London.'

'A mere hop from terminus to terminus. Not even the time to read a quick book. I honestly wouldn't leave it longer than a week. It's a vast organisation, Suzie — you make a success of this title so dear to the old boy's heart, and who knows where it'll lead? It was one of his first, you know. His first wife was very involved and he's just as obsessed with her memory as he ever was. It would be one helluva springboard ...'

Suzie laughs. And it's good, so good to shed some of the strain. 'Well, if you say so.'

'One phone call, Suzie, that's all I need to make to get the ball rolling,' says Kitty.

'Anyone would think there was something in this for you!'

'Nothing more, I assure you, than the simple fact that I think you'd be good and that at the moment I consider your talents are being wasted.'

'Tell Robin that.'

'Darling, be honest, Monday to Friday, would he notice?' Brittle hands, brittle face, brittle smile.

Suzie snorts disdainfully. 'He notices if the papers and magazines are out of order, so I think he might notice the space in the bed.' Yes, she's sure he would notice that. Suzie isn't quite so certain any more, Suzie's not half so convinced, but Robin seems desperate to beget a child from their union, and how can she backtrack after so encouraging his early desires? How can she possibly, in the face of his unflagging passion?

And now this! This fateful, unexpected lunch with Kitty, a bolt from the blue. Perhaps it is fate stepping in (and fate has always smiled upon Suzie) in time to prevent some major catastrophe.

Because does Suzie really want a child? Were any of her reasons genuine ones, or were they to do with gaining possession? Bored, unchallenged, she paced around her perfect flat arranging the fall of her perfect drapes, placing her perfect arrangements of pansies. But what would she do without a baby? Time, she'd discovered, tends to pass slowly when you are efficient and quick, when you finish your work as effortlessly as she does. Sometimes she reads, she rings her friends ... those few that are home in the day, but Robin has never been keen on her friends and she's caught him eavesdropping on her conversations. She doesn't really need to go out. She enjoys entertaining for Robin. She looks forward to the evenings he comes home early.

Since Christmas Suzie has been taking stock; she has had the time and the peace of mind to take stock. Just recently his children have been less of a problem, to Robin as well as to her. The old habits have been changing but the initiative hasn't come from Robin's end, it has, quite clearly, been coming from theirs.

'But are you quite sure you're all right, Vanessa?' Robin asked, the last time they cancelled a Sunday. And he seemed quite satisfied with the reply. They were going to the zoo with some friends, 'While it's still open,' Vanessa explained.

'We could have taken them,' said Robin, morosely.

'Don't take that attitude, Robin, for goodness sake. They're getting involved with other people, and surely that's far better for them than moping round here every weekend, causing scenes and getting upset. Encourage them, please!'

'I just wish I'd known sooner, that's all. I could have made other plans.'

They'd have the day to themselves now – a whole day without interruption. Suzie was pleased and couldn't disguise it. She draped herself over the back of his chair. She circled his head in her arms. 'You're hurt!' she said, gently mocking. 'Don't pretend. There's no need to act, it's only me. You're hurt, go on, admit it. You were hurt the week before last as well. You are always hurt when they ring up and cancel.'

'God, you annoy me sometimes!' And he shot forward suddenly out of her reach.

'Robin! Christ, for goodness sake!'

'I'm so sorry, Suzie, I'm sorry. Perhaps you are right.' He picked up the supplement and went off with it, but his apology did not reach his eyes or his smile.

The whole business was all rather perverse, odd enough to worry her, because the less she was bothered by Robin's children the less her desire to replace them with her own, whereas Robin's need for a child by Suzie seemed to increase for the very same reasons.

'But you're not *losing* them,' she went off to find him and say. 'Just because they are occupied happily you don't have to feel threatened. Why do you act towards them in this manner?'

'I don't act towards them in any manner.'

'Oh yes, you do.'

He wanted them to need him, that was his trouble, and Suzie saw that as rather sick. I mean, it's nice to be needed and all that stuff, but couldn't he see that that would make them vulnerable? How traumatic it would have been for Robin, had Caroline been a speckledy hen kind of mother, pushing him out like some women do. In some ways her failure as a mother had given Robin his biggest gift ... the adoration and, as Suzie sees it, the crippling needs of his children. Well, there'd be none of this nonsense if Suzie got pregnant. With two balanced, caring parents Suzie's child would grow up to be independent and strong. Like her.

Wasn't it lunchtime yet? Christ, she could do with a drink.

Ten minutes later, when Suzie had only just cooled down, Robin put his head round the door and suggested, 'Perhaps, as we've nothing organised, we ought to go and see Isobel.'

'If you can't come up with anything better than that, then why don't you go back into your study. I'm quite happy pottering, Robin, perfectly happy to spend the day in the greenhouse.'

'That greenhouse is becoming an obsession with you,' said Robin, only half-joking.

'It gives me something to talk about,' she snapped before she could stop herself, and her voice buzzed like a stinging bee. 'It means I can turn the conversation when I'm stuck with your boring, conceited friends.' She softened when she saw how far his face fell. She hadn't meant to say that. She liked most of his friends, it was just that, whenever they left, she'd started to feel inadequate just lately. Ridiculous. So silly. And not like Suzie at all. 'You go and see your mother,' she said, miserable, unwilling to endure the feeling of being presented yet again. 'I'm quite happy to stay here.'

He didn't bother to argue. They rarely actually argued. Robin tended to listen and then he faded away, to church, to work, to a book, to indifference. But on several occasions Suzie managed to make her position quite clear. When faced with his mother Robin withered like a small boy and his wives were of no more consequence than little friends he brought with him. Sometimes Suzie wondered if his single-minded ambition, his constant striving for success and yes, even his children, were nothing more than gifts to be offered at that bleak childhood shrine. Intelligent, shrewd as he was, couldn't he see that whatever he achieved that woman, that zealot, would never be satisfied? They'd argued for hours, Robin glum, Suzie shouting, while she tried desperately to explain. 'She's never let you go, don't you see? Why do you let her do this? Why do you allow her to play any role in your life at all? It's all mixed up with religion and guilt, that's quite obvious and the most extraordinary part is that you haven't grown up hating women ... all women ... trying to destroy them in revenge. I'm quite surprised you're not a batterer, Robin, a sick abuser of women, and yet you go on and on, allowing her to dominate you just as she did when you were small. She can't have shown you any love ...'

She said, 'Why don't you answer me?'

She said, 'Why won't you talk about this?'

She said, 'Why won't you face it? If you disagree with what I'm saying, why don't you tell me why?'

But there was no point in arguing. Whatever went on between Robin and his mother was so deep-seated that nothing Suzie could say would make any difference.

'I'll get you a drink,' he suggested, and it was exactly the right thing to say just then. It was precisely what Suzie needed in order to calm herself down. Damn it, was her hand shaking? No, surely not.

'Is everything all right, Suzie? You seem to be only half-here. Everything's going well, isn't it, with you and Robin? You haven't had some silly kind of quarrel? Have another drink.'

Suzie pulls herself abruptly together and tries to stare truthfully into Kitty Beavers-St Clair's fishing eyes. This woman, this scandalmonger and gossip-swapper doesn't need anything more firm than a feeling in order to sell her thoughts to the world.

With her sharp little nose, with her piercing eyes, has she sensed there is something wrong? 'Is that why she really asked me here,' thinks Suzie, 'nothing to do with the job but to poke and pry into our marriage?' But there *is* nothing wrong – Suzie doesn't need to be so defensive and anyway, the state of Robin's marriage is not important; no small scandal could possibly damage his career. With carefully cultivated friends in high places, it would have to be something like sexual deviation, cruelty, fraud ... and he's squeaky clean, there's never been anything like that. What a disappointment he must be to people like Kitty.

Publicly, Caroline's performance was the worst thing that ever happened to Robin and that time the columnists came down firmly on his side. Well, there was no doubt that the woman was mad. Nobody liked drunken, embarrassing, angry Caroline.

Suzie's voice is softly reassuring. 'We are both very happy, Kitty, and it's time Robin found a little peace and happiness in his life.'

'What a ghastly business that was.' What a sweet smile.

'Yes, it was, but all over now.'

'Do you hear from her still? Are you pestered? I know it was all pretty nasty for a while.'

'Not really, but Robin is still very close to his children.'

'Oh yes, I remember. They're with her, aren't they? And at the time everyone expected Robin to take them, responsible half and all that. And what about you, Suzie? Not ready for motherhood yet, I presume? I must say it's hard to picture you dandling children at your knee.'

Oh? Suzie can't help but feel hurt. 'We have never seriously discussed it.'

'So that wouldn't prevent you going for the appointment?'

'That would not be an obstacle. No.' Suzie sits back and sips more wine and her hopes fizz like the bubbles inside her. 'The more I think about this marvellous chance the more I'm convinced I should take it.'

Kitty smiles back. 'I'm so glad. I'd be astonished if you didn't. And surely Robin would be thrilled on your behalf once he got used to the idea. No man really wants to live with a cabbage.'

A cabbage? Was that how people saw her now? As a cabbage? Was that what they were saying behind her back? 'You needn't have bothered to do this for me, Kitty. You know, of course, that I'm grateful.'

The silvery laugh frosts the glass and the tip of her tongue dips the wine like a cocktail cherry. 'You haven't got it yet, darling. And it's always nice to see you. The information fell into my lap, I certainly went to no trouble.'

'No, no, let me pay. My treat. You must come to dinner, soon. I'll invite some amusing people. Bring Aiden with you.'

This will be difficult. Robin can't stand either Kitty or her lover.

'That would be nice. Thank you, Suzie. I haven't seen poor, dear Robin for absolute ages.'

TWENTY-SEVEN

MOTHERTIME — Christmastime — springtime — and an Eastertime when yellow islands of daffodils spangle against the undergrowth and the unbroken blue of the Somerset sky stretches to the breathless place where the fresh sun blazes. And do iridescent dragonflies still hover over the crystal stream?

It is a day to fire the most miserable soul with those bursts of exhilaration and delicious well-being. In London the privets are golden and the lilacs are heavy with blossom. The cherry tree in Suzie Townsend's mews garden is dusted with pink and white, and when she left the city this morning the sweet, fresh fragrance of spring was resting on the air.

She passes through the gate of her childhood home and it creaks a protest at her entry — cross to be so long abandoned? She moves slowly, but it's not that her bag is heavy. She hasn't been here for a long weekend since she first met Robin ... this is the first time she's been away from him, the first time she's felt the need for somebody other than him. From some hazy childhood habit she pauses to straighten her hair and brush her skirt, as if she's been playing in the garden. As if her mother is going to send her upstairs to tidy up. She walks up the path and opens the door.

In the hall she passes the row of wooden pegs, still cluttered with warped tennis rackets and old straw hats. Eileen is in the kitchen washing up her few breakfast things, and why does the fact that she's still in her dressing-gown disturb poor Suzie so? Perhaps it's because that comfortable, well-worn garment is none too clean and a marmalade cat sits purring, preening itself on a draining board that ought to be sterile. Blue and white bowls of yellowing milk are set on the questionably clean kitchen floor, milk with skin on. But the window is open and the warm scents of April are bowling through from the garden, a wild smell to stir and freshen the senses.

Two months have gone by since she broke the brilliant news to Robin – the news they'd been waiting for – the fact that she, at last, after all their efforts, is pregnant. And of course pregnancy goes well with Easter and frisky things ... with cuddly white rabbits and lambs and ribbons and eggs.

Eileen twists at the sink to look round at her daughter. 'Suzie, darling! You're so terribly pale! You don't look like you ought to look. I'd imagined you blossoming ...' and then, as if suddenly aware that this overprotective role is not hers by right any more, she falters, peels off her red rubber gloves and asks, 'Suzie, what's the matter?'

'Nothing, Mummy, nothing. I just felt like a rest, that's all.'

'And why on earth not. You work so hard, that's no wonder.'

So they sit and they talk round a pot of tea, Suzie, settling into the chair, settling into the familiar house, telling Eileen all about the prestigious new job she's been offered, editing the specialist European magazine *The Garden* with a readership, all over the continent as well as the USA, of millions. They discuss how she managed to get the job – she never believed she'd actually be offered it, and they debate what ought to happen next, and how pleased all her friends have been.

'It means I would have to work from Brussels – that's where the company have their headquarters.'

'Do you want some food?' asks Eileen. 'Shall I get you something to eat?'

'No, I only want to talk and relax. The traffic out of London was dreadful.' And her eyes stray to the open window, to the wild, hidden garden where happiness has always lain. She won't be able to come here soon. The house is on the market and Suzie hopes it won't sell.

'And Robin,' ventures Eileen. 'What's Robin doing this weekend?'

'Oh, Robin is fine. He is working.' Suzie nods, again and again, as she smooths her skirt with her neat little hand.

'And Caroline? And the children?'

'Caroline is amazingly happy. Her last stay at Broadlands did the trick. She's not drinking. She's got a new job – in some art gallery in Knightsbridge, apparently, but nobody quite knows which one and Robin doesn't like to pursue it. He's just so relieved that she's happy at last and out of his hair. They're working her terribly hard ... she goes out early in the morning and comes back, sometimes, at all hours. Mrs Guerney says she hasn't seen her for months and neither has Robin, but everything's very calm and the children are fine.' Suzie has to keep talking. If she stops the tears that are threatening might fill her eyes. What was her mother's secret? She and Daddy were always so close! 'We don't see them quite so much but they are more accepting of me now. Ilse's most reliable, she's there all the time, of course. And as far as we know there've been no new men in Caroline's life. No, it's incredible, she really seems to have found peace at last.'

'And what about the baby? How did she accept that piece of news?'

'She was very sweet! She sent us a congratulations card!'

'What a turn about!'

'I know. It's wonderful, really, isn't it?'

But Suzie's news is given automatically. She doesn't even listen to what she is saying. Her brain is working these days, always working. Round and round the question that should not have posed itself at all, the question she never remotely imagined would raise its ugly head, not with her. Not with Robin. Not in this day and age.

He was over the moon about the child and Suzie laughed and accepted his concern. She felt rather special when he cancelled their skiing holiday because he said, 'It's the first three months which are the most dangerous and you're not the most dependable person on the slopes.' So although she'd been looking forward to getting away from a chilly, miserable, dark-grey London, she lit her false-flame fire, she sat beside it surrounded by cushions, feeling cosseted and cared for. When Suzie talked about the job Robin was a bit grudging. She sent off her CV, she had lunch with various useful contacts. When she went for her first interview he took her to the airport, fussing like a mother hen. 'I don't know if you ought to be flying at all.'

Suzie's irritation gathered force and erupted. She grabbed her bag from his helpful hand and she snapped, 'For goodness sake, don't be so silly! What's happening to me is perfectly normal and you of all people ought to know that. After all, you've been a father five times!'

Sitting in the cafeteria waiting to be called, Suzie on tomato juice because that's the first thing Robin did, to forbid alcoholic drinks, and Suzie, flattered by his sweet concern, was humouring him, he said, 'I think I'm only reacting to Caroline's irresponsible behaviour. I'm sorry, Suzie, but you'll just have to bear with me.'

'But Robin, there was never anything wrong with Caroline's babies.'

'No, but only because I took care of things.'

She watched the chunk of ice creaking up through the gritty red flecks in her glass. He said, 'In this sick world it's so easy to get carried away and put money and ambition before anything else, when it's what's happening inside you that's truly important.'

Suzie laughed. 'Robin! This is terrible! Now you're beginning to sound just like Isobel!'

And he looked at her gravely as he sat on that red plastic chair with his copy of *The Times* sticking out of his jacket pocket, his legs crossed and his hand wrapped casually round his glass as if he was discussing something just as mundane as the state of the plastic cutlery.

'Mummy, I never realised that it was Robin who interfered directly when Caroline was first pregnant. Do you know that he went straight to the director of the play Caroline was going to do, and he managed to stop her from getting the part?' Her neck feels stiff. Suzie stands up and moves towards the door. She opens it and stands on the step, breathing deeply as she stares out at the untended garden and her voice comes more quietly, mingled with the birdsong and the breeze. 'Can you believe that? Caroline didn't know anything about it! He went behind her back and he told them she was pregnant and that it would be dangerous for her to accept the part. He knew the director of the play. Caroline had got it, Mummy! She'd managed to get this fantastic part – even Robin admits she was brilliant – she would have been made ... a star for ever! She lived for her acting, Mummy. He went behind her back and ruined it for her. I only found that out a few days ago. He told me. He came out with it as if it was something that was perfectly acceptable, as if it was almost something to be proud of, and just told me. I didn't know what to say. Eventually I asked him why. He seemed to think the answer was obvious: she could have damaged herself and the baby working long hours, staying in hotels and travelling to different locations. It could have been his dreadful mother talking. I didn't realise how influenced he was by all that religious crap. I've hardly been able to speak to him since. I was trying to discuss our arrangements – you know, after the baby's born. I'd decided to hire a nanny during the week and come home at weekends.'

Suzie holds her hand towards the garden in a gesture of despair. The grass is high and needs cutting before it gets right out of hand. The garden hedges are festooned and tangled with bellbine, the flowerbeds which Daddy kept with such care are shaggy with dog rose and brambles, and down in the hollows where Suzie played, the willows stand feathery and neglected.

Suzie's mother is fat and homely and her hair is tangled in kirby grips. Her cosy bun has slipped and hangs precariously on one side of her head. Under her dressing gown she's not wearing slippers, oh dear, she is wearing wellington boots.

'Oh Suzie, that wouldn't be ideal at all.' The discomfort in the atmosphere grows.

'I know it wouldn't be ideal, Mummy, but this is a chance I know that I'm most unlikely ever to be given again.'

'Couldn't you have the child with you in Brussels? Just while it's little? The poor little thing wouldn't know you!'

'During the week my life would be far too hectic. I'd be trying to entertain, trying to work, having to contact people in the evenings. Mummy, don't look at me like that ... this new job is going to be terribly demanding and I don't know if I want a baby with its nanny and all that entails to be around me and interfering, just at the very time when I'm going to be under such pressure, just when I need to try and get it right.' Suzie stares down at her hands. She sounds subdued when she goes on, 'And here was I, thinking you would support me.'

Eileen looks uneasy. She doesn't want an argument, she is anxious to be kind. It is clear that she doesn't understand. 'You don't have enough confidence in yourself, Suzie. A baby is not a raving monster.'

'I know, Mummy! I've been through it, I do nothing else but go through it, over and over. I know what it looks like. I feel guilty and selfish. . .'

Eileen's response shows exactly where her real thoughts lie. She keeps her eyes firmly fixed on her daughter as she speaks and she tries to touch her hand. 'To me it looks as if you shouldn't have decided on a baby at all!'

Suzie watches Eileen's hand. She won't move hers towards it. It's encouragement she wants, not commiserations. 'But I didn't know! How could I tell that this job would come up? How could I have guessed that Robin would take this attitude?'

'Well, you needn't have applied for it. You needn't have accepted it.'

'Just gone on as I was, you mean?'

'Why on earth not? You seemed perfectly happy to me.'

Suzie wishes she was not pregnant at all. She wonders why she wanted a baby so badly. She was influenced by Robin's devotion to his children and yes, she was jealous of that. She suffered as he suffered, during the times he was silent and abstracted, she was quiet and understanding, believing that a replacement of their own would be the answer, and she's a normal woman, isn't she, and every woman, deep down, wants a child. Hell, Caroline managed to have five! 'I was bored! Bored, damn it! Doing the same old thing every day for the last five years! You are taking exactly the same attitude as Robin. I didn't want to hear this from you. I wouldn't have come. I can see now that coming here was another mistake.'

'What does Robin say?'

'He sulks. He sulks very effectively. It's quite hard to talk to Robin about anything important. What starts as a reasonable discussion turns into me shouting and screaming – something I've never done in my life, drat it. He's got this knack of withdrawing from trouble but he doesn't back down like Daddy used to, it's not at all like that. He puts up a barrier, and it's strange, I feel that he doesn't really see me or hear me. He's got that sad smile; when he smiles at me that way I begin to think I'm going mad. And he stays much longer at work these days.'

'Oh, Suzie, I'm sorry. But you wanted my opinion. I've only told you how I honestly feel. We were lucky, I suppose – we didn't have these problems in my day.'

Suzie's voice rises with angry doubt. 'You think I should do what Robin wants and turn down the job? You think I should tell them I don't want it, after all this? You are saying that I ought to turn down this chance and spend the rest of my life waiting and hoping that something else will turn up?'

'I wouldn't be so presumptuous as to tell you to do anything. You are going to have to make up your own mind. You're not dependent on

Robin – presumably you could ignore him, take the job, install a nanny, do exactly what you want.'

Guiltily, desperately, Suzie pours out in a passionate stream the arguments she has been forming in her head for weeks. But whenever she pauses to look at her mother, Eileen still wears that same look on her face, implacable, the one who knows best. 'It's not so easy as that. Robin feels very strongly about this, but why can't *he* have the baby during the week? Why can't he let me go? He knows how excited I am, and why can't we put a nanny in the flat? It'd make much more sense because all our belongings are there and Robin's so marvellous with children. Mummy, it just seems so crazy that the baby can't stay with Robin and I could come home at weekends relaxed, able to give it my proper love. I just fail to understand why it always has to be the mother who has to disrupt her whole life.'

Eileen adjusts the dingy cushion and pushes it lower in her creaking chair. She sighs unhappily. 'It doesn't have to be the mother, Suzie. It's just a fact that most mothers want to be close to their babies.'

'Well, thank you very much, Mummy, now you have said it all! I wanted your support but instead of that you tell me that I'm abnormal. I'm unnatural. Perhaps I should have been born a man!' Suzie does not confide to her mother that since she's been pregnant Robin has not wanted sex with her at all.

'Oh dear, this shouldn't be so awful,' moans Eileen. 'This ought to be such a happy time. I had thought we might paint some eggs like we used to . . .'

But Suzie just wants to go off and sit in the garden alone while it's still hers, while she still has the time.

TWENTY-EIGHT

AT LAST! AT LAST, Lot's endless patience has paid off. He has seen her! He has caught his first glimpse of Caroline Townsend – a tiny little person – and it was only accidental, he hadn't planned it, he'd arrived at his watching post early because he'd buggered up his alarm.

Most days he comes here now. Back at the workshop they say they're not happy with his low output of boxes – they say someone else will soon take the record off him and have their name stuck on the top of the chart, but they know he's busy doing something else so they don't really mind.

Oh, he spoke to her weeks ago, when he discovered she wasn't at Broadlands after all his clever detective work … getting the address, travelling there in a freezing cold bus, finding the place, going to the grand reception lounge and asking for her directly. The trip was such a big project in itself that halfway to Sussex Lot almost forgot its purpose.

'Mrs Townsend is not registered with us at the moment. I'm sorry, sir.'

'She must be,' argued Lot. 'You've made a mistake. Check again. Let me have a look at your list.' And Lot dumped his half-eaten picnic down on the counter.

The alert woman in the white coat grew distant and haughty as if he was having one of his worst crazy spells. She had small ears and she was a woman but she looked very much like Mr Spock. 'I am so sorry, Mr—?'

'Dance.'

'Well, Mr Dance, I would know if Mrs Townsend was here. I don't even have to check my files, and my list is far too private to be handed over the counter to strangers. We know our clients personally, and there are never more than twenty residents here at one time. We are not a hotel, you know.'

Lot fingered through his picnic. He eased a slice of cheese from a half-eaten roll. He might fancy that on the journey home. 'But I've come all the way, by bus, from London.'

People were staring but Lot's used to that. He has sometimes been treated with attitudes akin to reverence by people who don't know him, those that are captivated by his extraordinary, dramatic good looks, his piercing eyes, his perfect features.

'May I enquire where your interest lies? Are you a relative by any chance?'

'By marriage I am a relative of a friend of Mrs Townsend's.'

While the wary receptionist tried to unscrabble Lot's claim his eyes followed her forehead; he watched as it was gathered up like crisp hospital stitches.

'I am afraid you have been mistakenly informed, Mr Dance, and I cannot help you any further.'

'I'm not going back without speaking to the boss.' And he stood beside the potted palm ... used to standing and staring. Her ploy — hoping that leaving him waiting around, untended, would send him away didn't work. They called the director down in the end and Lot had no alternative but to accept the fact. The director swore, he crossed his heart. Nope, Caroline Townsend was not at Broadlands. Bloody hell.

Perhaps she'd got wind of him. Perhaps, knowing he was after her, she'd gone into hiding.

He fumed all the way back from Sussex and went straight to see Bart, sad to see the familiar house half-hidden behind FOR SALE signs. But his brother had other, more important things on his mind than listening to Lot's longwinded report. He didn't seem interested in contacting Caroline again. The bank was taking him to court, and Ruby still wouldn't speak to him. He'd gone to seek her out but her mother refused to open the door. 'They wouldn't even let me see the children. Oh God, oh God,' cried Bart.

Lot misses the children, too. And he misses Ruby. He can hardly remember what she looks like and trying to remember is a torturing business. When he tries to think of her the shadows in his head turn fluid. His head becomes a dark flooded cave with tides sweeping in and out, and if he manages to catch her it is only for one exasperating second and then bang, she's gone again. He can see the top of her head, and her hats, but he cannot see her. His love was hopeless and innocent, nothing to be done with it, but until now Ruby was always there, very near and very far away, so close, but just out of reach and he'd thought that beautiful state would last for ever. Doesn't she ever think of Lot? Lot has done nothing to hurt her.

He knows that Ruby is angry with Bart — he can understand that up to a point — but she's gone far enough and she's being very stupid to go on upsetting Bart like this. After all, Bart needs his wife now. He needs her love and support, and although Lot is averse to criticising the love of his life, with her sweet, kind disposition and her chaste nature, although he feels wretchedly disloyal, his admiration slips a little and he has to stoke it to maintain it. Without someone to love he's afraid he might find himself with no one in sight at all. There's a great beauty inside Lot and he has to spread it over someone, or he might not find it again.

'She's not gone to Broadlands,' Lot insisted. But Bart looked at him blankly as if he'd forgotten who Lot was talking about.

'Why did she say she'd gone to Broadlands when she hadn't gone there at all?'

'She never said she had.' Bart was too abstracted to bother with much of an answer. 'It was one of her children who told me. Leave it alone, Lot, will you? What the hell do I care where Caroline's gone?' His voice was laden with gloom, and distant.

And Lot came away from the lost little house with Bart's agony stooping his shoulders. Just as determined as ever. And on his way home something snapped inside him. There was an empty bottle of lager on a wall and he picked it up by its neck and hurled it. He didn't wait to see what happened but he heard it crash against stone and he hurried back to the hostel, flung himself on his bed and took out his misery on the bedclothes.

A few days later, disguising his voice, he rang Caroline's house again and the answerphone told him that she was away. He did not leave a message. He wanted time to think. I mean — why was everyone saying she was away? Where was she?

He tried all sorts of different tactics. Pretending to be a garage mechanic he rang and asked to speak to her personally. He was told that Mrs Townsend didn't have a car so what did he think he was playing at? He discovered that the phone was always answered by this same gruff voice in the mornings. In the afternoons a foreigner answered — not all there, thought Lot to himself, tapping his forehead, but this girl believed him when he said he had a personal message to deliver. In a lisping voice she informed him that Mrs Townsend would be home at the end of the week. Aha.

'Where is she?' asked Lot.

And the girl replied, 'She's gone to Broadlands.'

And in the evenings the phone would be answered by one of the children. By this time Lot was beginning to recognise them all.

They said that Caroline Townsend was back, but still nothing changed. She remained unavailable.

He took to watching the house. He knows when the children leave for school and when the older woman arrives ... they change places around about quarter to nine. The young girl who looks like Marilyn Monroe is a drifter, you can never be sure when she's in or out. It's the same in the evenings. Most of the time the children are left in the house on their own, and the young girl doesn't get home till the early hours. Lot sees it all, always taking care to conceal himself.

But still no sign of Caroline Townsend. And now the phone calls are telling him that she's at work.

'But it's most important that I contact her,' said Lot, the last time he rang. An evening call.

'She's terribly busy at the moment and I don't know what time she'll be home,' said the child. 'She might not come home straight after work, she might well go to see a friend.'

'Well, this is absolutely essential,' Lot insisted.

'Are you the same man who's been trying for some time?'

'Yes, I am Mr Walsh,' lied Lot. 'And it's private. It's to do with tax matters.'

'Can't you write?'

'No, it's important that I speak to Mrs Townsend personally.'

'Well, I'm sorry, I can't tell you when you'll get hold of her. She goes to work early, you see.'

'Hasn't she got a number at work?'

'She can't use the phone at work. It's against the firm's policy.' And then, after a slight pause, 'If I take your number perhaps she could call you back ... if she gets home in time, Mr Walsh, that is.'

Lot is stubborn. He persevered. By that time he knew very well that Mrs Townsend did not leave the house for work every morning, nor did she return home at night. Ever. He would have liked to discuss the situation with Bart but Bart seemed to have no time for him any more, and anyway, Bart would wonder why he was still trying to trace Caroline. Bart would not understand.

Come to that, why *is* he trying to trace Caroline? What does Lot intend to do once he has finally tracked her down? Well, he spends hours thinking about that, mulling it over in his head, and he's decided that once he's got her alone he is going to confront her with what she has done. Apples and serpents. It won't be any good her denying it. Lot does not intend to be swayed, he's far too single-minded for that. Protesting her innocence won't do her the slightest good. He doesn't particularly want to hurt her, Lot doesn't like watching pain. He is going to put his hands round her neck, gently and firmly, and squeeze until there's no life there any more, until the dreadful look of surprise goes away and her wicked eyes close and she drifts to the floor at his feet and all the while he's going to try and remember Ruby's face ... not just the hat or the chair, but HER FACE.

And then he is going to fold her up and put her in one of his boxes.

'This is Mr Walsh again. I rang last night, and the night before that, and I also rang last Monday.'

'Hang on a moment, Mr Walsh. My mother will speak to you now.'

Disbelieving but hopeful, he gripped the receiver. After a pause he heard a cough before the new voice came on the phone. 'Hello, can I help you?'

Lot's heart beat like a hammer. 'Is that Mrs Townsend?'

'Yes, speaking.'

'I've had a terrible time trying to get hold of you.'

'I'm not often in, I'm afraid. I'm very busy at the moment. How can I help you?'

'There are some important tax matters that I'd like to discuss and I wondered if I might make arrangements to ...'

'I do not deal with tax matters, Mr Walsh. You'll have to get in touch with my accountant for that, and anyway, who are you? What department are you from?'

'It's a matter of urgency and I feel we should meet.'

'What is this? Who are you?'

'Where have you been all this time, Mrs Townsend?'

Damn! He'd gone too far, too quickly. The phone went dead and he was left hanging on, so near yet so far ... but wait a minute − if he knocked on the door now he would find her in!

He battered his way out of the booth and hurried down Camberley Road, hanging on to his hat and clutching his coat tight around him. He cursed the slippery pavements. Up the steps he went, the steps he had watched with such patience over so many days and nights. It was evening-time, the pineapples, one either side of the door, shone out a pale, pallid light and heavy rain obscured all but the pool of porch-light he stood in. He pressed the bell. And again. Each time water ran up his sleeve and he shivered. Lot stepped back when a small boy opened the door, very composed and in a grey uniform. Very polite, he said, 'Yes, can I help you?'

If he stretched and stood on his toes, Lot could just see the other children, bunched there, further up on the stairs, watching and listening. He tried to step inside but the boy kept the chain on the door. 'I have come to see Mrs Townsend.'

'She's not in,' said the good-looking boy with a stubborn tilt of his chin.

'But she must be in. She *is* in! I've just been speaking to her on the phone, not two minutes ago.'

The boy pushed the door further closed so Lot was forced to listen through a crack. 'She had to go out, in a hurry. Why did you want her?'

'Important matters I have to discuss. I have been trying to explain for weeks now.'

More than a spark of interest then − unease? 'Are you Mr Walsh?'

He did not want to alarm the child. Lot excitedly moved his hat from one side of his head to the other. A hard drip of rain was hitting his ear, leaking from the porch gutter.

'Yes, I am Mr Walsh.'

'I will tell her you called.' And the door was closed. If he hadn't removed his hand in time his fingers would have been cut off. Lot found himself standing there feeling silly with his mouth still open, foiled once again. Why were her children hiding her? Why was the woman so afraid to venture out into the world?

But he'd spoken to her! He had managed that. He went home that night disappointed but hopeful.

And that is the nearest he's been till this morning when he made the mistake with his damnfool alarm.

He's given up arriving early because he has learnt that there is no point. At Camberley Road the morning routine hardly varies. The children set out together and they split when they come to the end of Camberley Road. Sometimes the cleaner uses her own key, sometimes the children are still there to let her in. But this morning he stands and he watches beside his tree and he sees four children come out of the house ... sometimes this happens ... and when it does he assumes one of them is ill. Children are like that, after all − colds and snuffles. He used to try all ways to get out of going to school himself. It's the second child, the second eldest, who's missing. And he's hanging around hardly taking any notice when he sees the cleaner turn the corner and approach the house with her Union Jack carrier bag as usual. And just as Lot is about to turn away, the navy door opens and out comes Caroline Townsend. It must be her − it must be her ...

She carries a briefcase. She's so small! Her head is wrapped in a scarf and her trenchcoat is swinging behind her; she walks with a confident stride. She glances back down the road, sees the cleaner and raises her hand in a brief wave before hurrying on.

The next-door neighbour, coming out of his house at the same time, tips his hat to her but although she smiles she does not pause.

Way down the road the cleaner stops and screws up her eyes. She raises her head like a hunting dog and she calls, 'Cooeee! Mrs Townsend! Mrs Townsend! Just a sec.' And then she clutches her hat, lowers her head and flops along on her stout, stumpy legs. She wobbles all over as she goes, looking up every now and again to avoid the dangerous lamp-posts. But she's too old for running and Mrs Townsend's almost round the corner by now. The older woman grips her chest and stops and pants dangerously; her shoulders droop and her bag hangs heavily at her side. She hasn't been able to keep up and Mrs Townsend's gone. She's going so fast, striding out so briskly that she must have caught up with her children.

The cleaner calls out feebly, 'Mrs Townsend!' But it's no use. She hasn't got much of a voice left and her employer can't hear her.

In his excitement Lot almost forgets to follow his prey. He is tempted to go to the aid of the cleaner because she's standing there puffing, close to collapse after her brave athletic effort. But pulling himself together just in time Lot comes out of hiding and, going at a pace that's closer to a run than a walk – he doesn't want to attract too much attention – he hastens up the road after Caroline Townsend and it takes him about four minutes to reach the corner.

It's too late. There are not four children at all ... but five. There they go, sauntering along the road, three going one way and two the other as if it's any other morning, as if their mother had not, just a moment ago, been rushing along behind them.

Lot stands on the junction, baffled, scratching his head. Strange though, very odd, because as well as an overstuffed satchel, this morning the second child, the one who he thought was originally missing, is carrying what looks like her mother's briefcase.

This is too much for poor Lot to bear. Frustrated and angry, he can't give up now, not when he's come so close. He knows Caroline Townsend exists, he knows she is there, and so that's why he's going to come back to Camberley Road tomorrow night after dark and break in through the cellar window.

Twenty-nine

She sits quietly for a long time, and then, 'You call yourself a Christian and yet you can do this to me! Three months and God knows how many days you've kept me here ... not knowing what's going to happen next, never knowing what ridiculous game you're going to play, robbing me of everything, leaving me with nothing, no dignity, no pride! You seem to think that you're going to get away with it, well screw you, Vanessa. *Screw you!*' She weakens again, ready to cry while her words ricochet madly about in her head and she realises dimly that if she goes on much longer at this pitch she's going to fall into a faint like she did last time. She will wake up with that disgusting odour cloying the air all around her, a rancid stench she could not identify until gradually, feeling the soggy stain down the front of her dress, she became aware that she was lying in a pool of her own sick. 'Last week you said you were going to let me out but you lied! You lied! I'm *talking* to you Vanessa, damn you, I know you're out there! Can you *hear* me? I *know* you can hear me so why don't you speak?'

She should sound powerful in her rage but she doesn't, not any longer. By the time she stops yelling the world is topsy-turvy, her words are disjointed and she hardly knows who she is any more.

She doesn't even know if she means what she says.

'I should break your neck, you fucking little shit,' Caroline Townsend trails off in a voice that is full of contempt and revulsion. Weakly she returns to sit down on her bench while she winds a piece of new, softly curling hair round her finger. 'And so help me when I get out of here I am going to do that.' But this last sentence is murmured so low and despairingly it cannot possibly be heard outside the walls of the sauna.

There's nobody there to hear anyway. Caroline is alone. The children aren't due for another half-hour. She weeps until her body aches.

She continues to whisper to herself; on and on her own voice goes, a gentle monologue lulling and soothing, infusing herself with a sense of repose because she knows from experience now that this is the only way to get by, the only method of staying sane. She even strokes herself with her hands, pretending that they are somebody else's, long, gentle strokes that are cool and calming on her brow. 'You're all right, Carrie, you're all right. Nothing's going to happen. Nobody's going to hurt you. Now why don't you go over there and fill your cup. Try taking a sip of water.'

It's not that she's suffered any violence in her long, warm months of solitary confinement. It isn't that she's been starved, or abused, or deprived of light, books or music. In a weird way she has acclimatised to it very well, a life without any pressure. She doesn't have to pretend to be anything other than who she is. And her children have never threatened her with anything more than a rise in the temperature of her cage. They didn't have to do that. She took great pains to do everything she was told. Apart from the occasional unpreventable outpouring of rage — and only when she knows it is safe to do that — she has obeyed their every command. You cannot trust children . . . not in the same way as you might trust an adult. She feels like Gulliver, bound and held down by little minds. And she'd soon learned she had nothing with which to bribe them, or to threaten them, or to fool them.

Quite often she weeps like this when they leave her.

But she felt she had been attacked. Day after day, night after night she lay in her prison licking her wounds, ashamed of the grotesque crime committed against her almost as though she'd been raped. She squirmed at the idea of ever telling a living soul. Whatever else, what has happened between herself and her children must forever remain a secret. She felt befouled, even though she was encouraged to keep herself clean, even though they brought medication for the ailments she complained about — her aching bones and her headaches, her mouth ulcers and her sore throats. Oh yes, and true to their word they allowed her her Walkman, with a boxful of carefully chosen tapes, vetted by

Vanessa — classical music only, none of her old sleazy Tina Turners or the wonderful Marianne Faithfull.

She has become possessed by food. It is fun for her, a pleasant game trying to guess what they're going to bring. Every time it arrives, pushed in through the pipe-hole, she must eat it, she must finish every last crumb on her plate. She has become fat, cherubic, like a Rossetti angel or one of those ancient, languishing Madonnas with a revoltingly white, slug-like child at her breast. Her hands, which used to be long and sinewy, have become chubby — even her finger-ends look square. She has set herself time for exercise. Four times a day, after food, she paces her cell, fifty times across and back, and she does step-ups on and off the sauna bench but even so she is fat, but she is not unhealthy. She is not unhealthy in the way she was before she became a prisoner.

Caroline Townsend never thought she would ever be free of alcohol. But now, the thought of a drink makes her shudder; the thought of a cigarette in her new, sweet-smelling mouth seems foul. Over and over again she's asked for a mirror but up until now the children have refused her permission. 'You're not vain like that any more, Mother,' says Vanessa. 'It's not what is on the outside that counts, you have to feel beautiful from within.'

Caroline cannot bring herself to reply to that sort of inane remark.

Sometimes, at the very beginning of her captivity, she cried, pleading hysterically, but her children refused to come near her when she was doing that. At a regal nod from Vanessa they cut short their visit and left her alone. She thought about slicing her wrists with the bits of glass from a broken bowl, but something warned her that, even if she succeeded, even if she was very brave and cut through a vein, they would not let her out. They did not care if she died, but that was not their intention. They did not want her dead.

At first she prayed every day to a God in Whom she did not believe. She prayed that Robin would come and save her. Even then, even in those first slow weeks, she believed she loved Robin, and thoughts of him hurt her heart. But slowly and relentlessly in her lonely hours she gradually began to see that her pursuit of him was not a need any more, but a habit, so deadly precise, so predictable that it was obscene. She gradually began to understand that Robin and everything about him had become nothing more than an evil storm in her own heart.

Calmly rising to his full height he used to say to his friends, 'Excuse her.' Wagging a sarcastic, hypocritical finger he used to scorn, 'Why don't you have another drink, Caroline. It'll help you become more interesting and that is obviously what you want.' There was a hard metallic edge to his voice – a new edge. The house was full of flowers then, she used to make sure it was always full of flowers ... and how was it possible that no one but she could smell the stench of the sickroom under the blossoms?

It was true – from the moment she first got pregnant, he immediately embarked on a subtle mission to destroy her. She'd had her fling and now that he had made her a *Mother* she must settle down to looking after her children and be *Good*. She was such a child that the very word 'Mother' frightened Caroline. There were so many examples of Robin's incongruous behaviour, all the more sinister because they were so commonplace. And Caroline saw how influenced he was by the whip of religion held over him by his mother.

Having had no family life of her own, Caroline made an awkward mother; with no model to base herself on she was vulnerable. In spite of the milk she couldn't breastfeed though she tried at first, for Robin's sake. Too ashamed, too confused, she couldn't tell him why. She was a model, an actress – her breasts were as important to her as Robin's craggy television face was to him, and in this world of men she might have to depend on them one day. If she had told him this, the scorn in his eyes would have slain her. So she tried. She struggled with a great reservoir of love which she did not dare release, unable to understand her own anger. It was horribly painful. She ended up like a cow, milking herself with an ugly machine while waves of misery swamped her, transferring her milk to Tupperware bottles which were kept stacked up in the fridge.

What was she born for?

The answer was plain in Robin's eyes, so baleful and accusing. At the end of the day she was born, as all women were, to give birth.

She could not bear the way she sounded. Yes, oh yes, it was perfectly true, it was as her own mother told her – she was a person impossible to love.

Even their lovemaking changed and she was afraid that Robin was being unfaithful. Ordinary and boring as she was – perhaps her hair was wrong, or her face – she tried all ways to make herself more appealing. Sex was not for pleasure any more – it should only be enjoyable when it was part of a nobler scheme, to procreate. His glib insults over anything she did when it came to the kids, oh God, why did she try when right from the start she was doomed – and she soon became apprehensive. If Robin was around she hardly dared pick up her baby. A light sleeper, Robin woke instantly in response to a baby's screams and by the time Caroline dragged herself out of the deepest slumber, chilly, miserable and indecisive, he had warmed the bottle and was rocking the guzzling child, tightlipped. 'I've got to be up before seven,' he would say, cold and blaming. And there she was, standing at the door in her negligée, not like a mother at all but more like a slut, slick with face-cream.

'I was on my way, don't worry. It just takes me longer to get going, that's all. You go back to bed, I'll do it.' But jittery, frantically trying to do well, she was rough. She didn't dress them correctly, she couldn't manage money, she couldn't even get up in time to take the kids to the park with Robin on a Sunday. But then, one morning, she was shocked to hear him whisper, 'Don't disturb your mother, she needs her sleep.' Poor, hopeless, inefficient Mother. Such an innocent start to that slow, insidious conspiracy. And they'd creep around the house getting dressed and they'd go out wearing unsuitable clothes and laugh about it together when they got home.

She began to feel like a child to her children.

At twenty-five, there she was with modest attainment and thwarted ambition, nothing very much to say except that she was pregnant again. Robin's media friends, some of them the most awful, conceited people, were not Caroline's friends ... she realised she didn't have very many friends of her own any more, they'd been driven away by Robin who called them embarrassing. The arguments started. She'd interrupt his conversations just to let people know she had views of her own, and he would pause politely and raise his eyebrows and say, 'Well, that's certainly another way of looking at it, Caroline, but as I was saying, Alan ...' Everyone started to take that attitude – oh, don't worry she was always invited – she went everywhere with Robin but among the witty women she was the one with nothing to say and nothing in her head worth listening to. Pretty and amusing, she could talk about people and things but she didn't have a clue when it came to the larger issues and the starved and undeveloped side of her sat at the table struggling for words.

If she grumbled she was a dissatisfied wife and a nag. 'Darling, you make no sense,' he'd say. 'You are making a fool of yourself.'

If she strayed into his study while he was working she immediately knew she was a nuisance, so she never stayed long. His real interests lay with himself — his work, his children, his house and his furniture — and now she'd given him the children (he'd obeyed his promise to God) his wife was only a piece of that furniture, a piece full of unfortunate flaws. His passion found its release in his work and going to Mass on a Sunday.

'Why must you look so hurt all the time?'

So that's pretty much how it was. But it was like that for a very long time. They stopped calling her Mummy — she can't remember either of the twins ever calling her that — because Robin so often referred to her disparagingly, using that freezing cold title 'your mother'.

And Isobel watched with delighted eyes and sent her daughter-in-law pious verses at Christmas, illustrated with bloated Madonnas. The cardboard itself smelled of churches.

And yet she still loved him ... *can you believe it!* And she still wanted him. There was something she could not understand going on inside him, and the more he withdrew, the more precise and fastidious he became, the more desperate was Caroline.

Courteous, understanding and considerate, nobody could call Robin insensitive and anyone could see that he was the world's most wonderful father. 'Aren't you lucky, Caroline? He's absolutely marvellous with the children!' You don't leave husbands like that, not unless you're mad you don't.

Caroline said, 'He has very firm ideas about family life, about children.' Perhaps she was paranoid, filling her head with imaginary fears. It must be so, because everyone thought he was wonderful while they made sure Caroline knew that she was a mess. She was beautiful, but a mess. Oh, but she ached for love. She longed to find someone to play with. She pushed her pram through the park when the great solitary trees were decked in their reds and russets and yellows. She walked through the streets when it was dusk, when the shopfronts were ablaze with lights and illuminations, and then back to the park again where she'd try to get lost in the spindly woods, she'd try to identify the birdsong when the rust was on the bracken, as another day led to another, and another. And another. And once she ran home to the waiting house, pounding on the door like a terrified woman, feeling herself trapped, unable to get in or out, forgetting about her key.

'If you're going to tear around madly like that, you'd better leave the pram behind next time,' said Robin, appraising her coldly. 'Why don't you let Mrs Guerney take them? After all, that's what she's paid for.'

She was out of control and disgraceful.

Thank God for Mrs Guerney. That bulwark of common sense arrived just in time. She came to scrub, to beat and to sweep, she came in time to prevent Caroline Townsend from losing her nerve completely. When she'd heard that Caroline had given up acting, given up everything, she called that a 'monstrous occurrence'. Remembering the Caroline she used to know when they both worked in the photographic studio, the girl with such hope, such beauty, such poise, 'What on earth has become of you?' she asked, her big face almost rammed against Caroline's own. 'What have they done?'

'I want something to do,' cried Caroline. 'I'm no use here any more and I'm desperate.'

'Leave him,' said Mrs Guerney firmly. 'Take the baby, pick up your bags and go.'

'I love him, and where would I go?' *And I am not fit to look after my baby.*

'Then fight,' said Mrs Guerney, her eyes dark and casting themselves suspiciously around. 'You were never a timid woman, Mrs Townsend. You were tough once, I remember. You'll just have to get tough again.' She sucked on a plastic cigarette. Mrs Guerney had only just given up smoking. 'I hope you are up to it.'

'Fight against what?'

'You have married a man who does not like women. He is in love with the Virgin Mary, he is in love with his mother.'

But it was years before Caroline dared pluck up the courage to go out to look for a job. By then she was steel, honed, shiny metal, tempered in the fire of humiliation and loss. But as fragile as a tiny little baby.

'Mother, do you know anyone called Mr Walsh?'

'I've never heard of Mr Walsh. Why?'

'He's been trying to get hold of you. He keeps phoning up and this evening he came to the door. Dominic thinks that he might be a plain-clothes policeman.' Vanessa is pale and nervous. She cannot continue for very much longer.

'Perhaps he is.'

'Or he could be a pervert. Ilse is worried. She says he sounds like the man she's seen lurking in the park.'

Last weekend, home from school, Sacha and Amber played down in the basement for most of the day. It was amazing ... Caroline felt absurdly proud! Sacha brought down the tubular bells and Caroline taught them some French songs. The twins pushed a book through the pipe-hole and Caroline read them *The Skin Horse*.

The children have taken to eating their supper down in the basement now and Caroline adores their company. Three weeks ago they brought down two standard lamps, five deckchairs and a round Chinese rug. Occasionally Vanessa lights a candle and leads the children in embarrassed prayer. They chat together now, as a family, except for the locked door between them to which they hardly ever refer because it would be too impolite. They come down to tell her what they've been up to during the day, they bring her their little problems and Mother listens. While Sacha and Amber are playing, while Dominic builds himself up on Daddy's weights, the older girls listen to the radio play sharing toast and porridge with their mother.

Caroline tenses and holds her breath when she hears Amber whisper, 'Vanny, don't you think that it might be a good idea to do what you said yesterday and let Mummy out? I think that I want to touch her.'

Caroline says very gently, 'Oh Amber, I would like it very much if you did.'

THIRTY

Is mr walsh a policeman?

And who is the strange man who watches the house?

'There he is again,' Dominic would say, annoyingly excited, looking out into the night almost as if he welcomed trouble, peeping through the curtains, and Vanessa's heart would drop, her eyes would go bright and frightened as she joined him at the window. She'd do her homework badly again and she might have to stay behind tomorrow.

'Maybe we should just go right out there and ask him.'

'No.' Dominic was firm about that. 'He looks like a nutter to me.' Since Mother's been a prisoner Dominic has, extraordinarily, stopped wetting the bed. More than any of the others he seems to enjoy the feeling of being in control.

Dominic's difficult. Out of all her four siblings Vanessa would have guessed the twins would cause the most concern but it hadn't worked out that way – apart from the few times they nearly blurted out the truth, that is. When their little friend Jessie came to tea Vanessa, horrified, heard them discussing the matter quite calmly right there on the bedroom floor. They'd got out their tatty paper dolls; they had hundreds of them, in a box, cut from Mrs Guerney's catalogues – a bizarre mixture of types and age groups: middle-aged women in bloomers and long, bone-ribbed corsets, men with peaked caps, in golfing gear, children in frilly swimsuits, and teenagers clad in jeans and leather.

'Here's Mother,' Vanessa heard Sacha say in her dreamily soft play voice. Her hand hopped up and down as she moved Mother along by the neck, into the empty shoe box which stood upright on the carpet. Vanessa waited at the door and watched her sister fix the lid. 'All safely locked away. Look, Jessie, she can't get out. Even if she tries. Even if she jumps up and down.'

'What have you locked her up for? I wouldn't like to lock my mummy up,' said little wide-eyed Jessie, poking a trembling lip with a finger.

'Why not?' asked Amber defiantly. 'You can look after them much better. This is fun!' And she went on in her elderly way, 'Look, here comes a friendly child with some sweets. Think how pleased Mother will be to see her after such a long time all alone. And if she's not pleased she can be punished.'

'How? Punished?' Jessie, alarmed by the frightening turn in the familiar game, went into a sulk and said, 'Well, I don't want to play it like this. If we let Mother out she could go and sit over there with Daddy, quietly. She could watch the telly. Look, here he is, waiting for her.'

'Don't you dare let her out! Don't you dare! You'll get into terrible trouble, my girl!'

Jessie cried steadily – that was the sort of child she was – but Amber giggled to hear such a perfect interpretation of Mrs Guerney, and when Vanessa strode into the room the twins looked up with open mouths while comprehension dawned.

'That's enough of this game!' Vanessa bore down on them, bending to clear up the mess. 'Jessie doesn't like it and you know you shouldn't be playing it. What have I told you, again and again,' she said in a firm, knowing voice, while for Jessie's benefit she added, 'You let your imaginations run away with you, you two! If you don't behave yourselves better than this, Jessie will not want to come again.'

Everything's falling apart. *She just isn't old enough*! And how can Vanessa be on the watch for this sort of thing, day and night? Time is passing her by. Tense and watchful, she daren't go out in the evenings to the cinema with her friends, and she excused herself from the school play because of all the rehearsals. She is thirteen years old now, fourteen next March the tenth; she will probably never marry, she will probably never be a missionary now, or a doctor, or a nun. She has given up trying to be wise. She will hide under the stairs while sniffer dogs search the house. She will end up in a prison cell, shunned and scorned by the whole world.

Last week, along with a cardboard swan on a string, supposed to be a mobile, the twins brought home their finished drawing books. They sit together at the same table in the classroom but, even if they work apart, the results are always eerily similar.

'Amber, what's this?' Vanessa flicked through Sacha's book and found the almost identical picture. Underneath was the ill-formed caption, *Mummy's room*. 'What did Mrs Brightwater say when she looked at these? Did she ask you what you meant?'

Mummy's room was a black, square box with a single light dangling like Miss Muffet's spider – the hanging legs illustrated the width and length of the beam. Mummy was in there of course, standing up, with her multi-striped triangular skirt and her splayed, red-block feet. Her face was big and pink at the window and her upside down smile was scribbled in like a tunnel. She looked as if she was screaming. And hard black lines made the bars which banged vertically down the page.

'But Mother doesn't look like that any more!' Vanessa could have sobbed with frustration. 'How could you draw her like that? How could you?' She wanted to shake them. They hadn't done that to Mother, had they? They'd never been so cruel! 'What did she say? *What did Mrs Brightwater say when she saw this?*'

Amber, upset, taken aback by her sister's angry reaction, stuttered, 'That's an old picture. We wouldn't draw Mummy like that now, would we Sacha?'

Sacha clutched her sister's arm. She plucked the sleeve for extra support. 'No, we'd draw her smiling.'

'*But what did she say?*'

Sacha frowned, remembering, and her glasses glinted dully. 'She said it was a novel idea, didn't she, Amber? She said she wondered what our mother would make of it when she saw it. Oh yes, and then she asked you, didn't she, Amber, if you sometimes found it hard to get close to your Mummy.'

'I didn't know what she meant,' Amber nodded emphatically. She kept nodding. On and on, until it became a game and she tried to make herself dizzy. It looked as if she might wobble her head off her neck. Vanessa grabbed her shoulders and stopped her. Shaking her head now, in lively defiance, Amber said, 'I told her that of course we couldn't get close because of the door.'

Vanessa sank down on the sofa, letting her head rest in her hands. Where was God in all this? Where had He gone? When she couldn't watch over the twins, why wasn't God taking over? She couldn't cope with this all alone, not any longer.

'I'm sorry, Vanny. It could have been any door. Mrs Brightwater wouldn't know it was *that* door. Everyone's house has lots of doors. It could have been the lavatory door for all she knew. Couldn't it, Sacha?'

Life used to be full of doors but now Vanessa's afraid to peer through any of them for fear of what she might find there. There's nothing good. There's nothing nice waiting any more.

And school's difficult. She is falling behind in her work and last week Sister Agnes called her in for a talk. 'Is there anything wrong, dear? Are there difficulties at home? You know you can confide in me.' Sister Agnes knew about Mother. Well, everyone knew about Mother in her heyday, everyone knew about the bad things Mother did around about the time Daddy left her. Mother flamboyantly told the world that she didn't care but she wouldn't have got herself splashed all over the papers, or done all those terrible things unless she had really minded. Everyone read about her behaviour and Vanessa's best friend, Hazel Ledson, used to bring neat little cuttings to school, folded over in a long brown envelope. 'You could make a scrapbook,' she told Vanessa, enviously.

'Perhaps I should have a talk with your mother.' Was that a threat? Did she know? Sister Agnes sat at her desk and between her hands she rolled a thin black pencil. The nun's eyes were grave and grey and Vanessa feared they could see right through her. 'Or your father. We have his number. Well, I don't believe you're suddenly finding the work too hard,' she went on in a cold, scornful manner. 'You've never had any difficulty keeping up with the class before, so there must be some other explanation.' But she didn't really want to know. God was the one to be burdened, not a busy nun with a school to run and gall to apply every night, every morning. For an awful moment Vanessa imagined Sister Agnes' reaction if she told her the truth. She'd recoil in distaste. 'This is a very important year for you, Vanessa, you do realise that? Are you allowing enough time for your homework? Three hours a night, you know, at least three hours, Vanessa.'

Vanessa did not care about Sister Agnes' opinion any more and it was suddenly, horribly obvious that the nun had never liked her. Not as a person, she hadn't. All she cared about was having a pupil who handed in good work and the minute something went wrong she imagined it was deliberate. Vanessa didn't want it to be like this. She'd be working if she could ... she'd be pleasing her if she could. Sister Agnes smelled of mothballs and chalk and she carried too many burdens. Let Valerie Anderson be her favourite now, why should Vanessa care?

Concentration of any kind is difficult. Every time Vanessa leaves the house for longer than an hour she panics, well aware of the horror she's left behind her, and how easy it would be for someone to discover their secret.

If the central heating broke down Mrs Guerney would ring the company. They'd be down in the cellar with their little toolbags within half an hour – and how could anyone stop them?

Mr Walsh could knock on the door with a warrant and demand entry at any moment.

If the water froze (and it's cold enough these days), the cleaner would contact the plumber. He'd be bound to go straight down to the basement.

Daddy might even decide that the time was right to sell his equipment. Vanessa wouldn't know. He could be deciding it right now. His hand could be on the telephone this very minute, organising the whole thing.

Then, when she found the money gone, she was mystified. For the life of her she couldn't work out what had happened. She kept the petty cash – sometimes they accumulated well over a hundred pounds at a time – in the back of her musical box. The back was held on by two easy screws and she'd often kept secret things there, stories she didn't want Mother to read, poems for Daddy.

She trembled when she discovered that twenty-five pounds was missing, because it wasn't the fact that the money was gone, it was because someone must have discovered their secret. It had to be Ilse. If Mrs Guerney found it by accident, dusting, or maybe she'd drop it on the carpet and perhaps the screws weren't in there securely, she would call Vanessa and demand to know why she was hoarding such a huge amount. Mrs Guerney would never steal it! Thieves should have their hands chopped off as far as she was concerned.

But Ilse needed money. She needed it to buy all the clothes that made her attractive for Paulo – she'd only just bought herself a pair of new Timberland boots. She needed money to go to her raves and to buy rounds of drinks at the pub.

Wearily, feeling old and tired, Vanessa came downstairs, turned off the TV and told the others. 'It's gone. I've checked and re-checked. I don't know what this means . . .'

'I took it!'

There was a stunned, loaded silence as everyone absorbed this. 'You took twenty-five pounds out of the kitty? Dominic! What for?'

'A remote control boat, like the one Josh Collins' got.'

Camilla said, 'Why didn't you ask us, if you wanted something so badly?'

'I didn't know I had to. I didn't know the money was yours!'

'Can we all have money?'

'Shush, Amber. No, of course we can't help ourselves and spend money when we feel like it. For one thing, we have to be careful to use it sensibly, and for another, if we start filling the house with new toys and books people will get suspicious. Surely you don't need to be told these things, Dom. Surely you understand. Where is the boat?'

He was quite unrepentant. His huge brown eyes were calm and sure and the lashes swept his cheeks dismissively. 'I went out with Jonathan last Saturday morning. That's when I bought it. I keep it at his house because it's next to the river.'

'But why didn't you say?'

'I didn't think it was that important. And I don't see why we shouldn't have money to spend. After all, it belongs to all of us.'

'But it's Mother's money.' But Vanessa wasn't getting through. Dominic, impassive, uninterested, was propped in a corner of the sofa absorbed in his Gameboy, considering the whole discussion a boring waste of time.

'If it's Mother's money, not ours, then it means we have stolen it and we shouldn't be spending it at all,' he said. 'But it's ours.'

'And what about the Gameboy?' Camilla demanded to know. 'You said you were given it to borrow by someone at school and I thought that was a bit funny. You've had it a long while now. When have you got to give it back?'

'I swapped it.'

'What with?'

'My Walkman.'

'How could you! Daddy gave you your Walkman!'

'I can do what I like with my own things and you're silly the way you are about Daddy. Just because he gives us presents it doesn't mean anything so special. Daddy should never have let this happen. Anyway, we can buy our own things now, we don't have to wait for birthdays or Christmas. We don't have to be nice or good any more.' The machine on his knee bleeped loudly and Dominic gave a heavy sigh. He regarded Vanessa vaguely, like someone coming out of a trance. 'And I don't see why any of you think you can tell me what to do. No one can tell me what to do any more. I can do exactly as I like. No one's in charge.'

'Vanessa's the oldest. Vanessa's in charge.' Vanessa sent the supportive Camilla a grateful look.

'Who said so?'

Vanessa replied reasonably, 'It's not a question of anyone being in charge. It's to do with sticking together so that everything turns out all right in the end and we all want that, don't we?' But she didn't feel reasonable. She felt like screaming. And she didn't feel hopeful either, nothing like her calm voice sounded.

'How can it be right? You're all so silly sometimes! *How can anything ever be right any more, can't you see?*' And he stood up and marched through the door. They heard him take the stairs two at a time. They heard him shutting himself in his bedroom.

There is something the matter with Dominic and for this, and so many other reasons, the sooner they let Mother out the better.

But is she ready? What will she do? Oh dear God, Vanessa wishes she had someone at hand with a voice, someone more substantial than God, to tell her, to help her, *to hold her*.

THIRTY-ONE

VANESSA WOKE UP last night with pains in the palms of her hands. This was not stigmata, it was her fingernails, because of the tight fists she'd been making in her sleep.

Is Mother really ready, or might she be only pretending? It is all up to Vanessa because there is still no one else.

There is one more extremely important thing they must do before they let Mummy out, and Amber knows it. She should not have suggested the possibility, she ought not to have raised Mummy's hopes like that until they had carried this last task through.

Time is against them now, especially if that Mr Walsh really is a policeman and if Mrs Guerney's unease hasn't been calmed by yesterday's little performance. She's been nagging on lately; like a dog at a bone every time they meet her she worries. 'It doesn't seem possible but I've been thinking about this and I realise that I haven't seen Mrs Townsend for months now.' When she said this, she sucked in her cheeks and whooshed as if she was going to blow up balloons. 'Yes, it has been months . . . not since before Christmas!'

'But you've had her notes. She's apologised to you in her notes. She's explained about this new job.'

'I know that, Vanessa, but it still seems queer. Something around here's not right but I can't for the life of me put a finger on it.' The cleaner lifted her heavy tweed skirt and scratched at her garter marks before hoisting her pop socks over her knees. Even her clothes had the vague smell of her tin of polishing rags. 'But you've spoken to Daddy on the phone. Daddy knows there's nothing wrong. He told you that when you last rang him up. And Ilse's perfectly happy. Ilse has seen her.'

But Mrs Guerney wrinkled her nose, shook her head and said dismissively, 'Oh, Ilse.' So they dressed Camilla up yesterday in an attempt to reassure Mrs Guerney. She didn't want to do it. 'All you've got to do is come out of the house and walk down the road . . .'

'But I'm much too small. I don't look anything like Mother!'

'That's why we're going to make sure you come out when she's still miles away. You can't make out sizes from a distance, Camilla. And it won't even cross her mind that Mother is somebody else. You've just got to get the walk right, and do the little wave, that's all.'

It seemed to work.

Everything they've done so far seems to have worked. Even when they rang DOTS to say that Mother had taken a temporary but profitable acting job and wouldn't be coming in for a while, there wasn't much of a hassle. 'Tell her that's real fine, honey, we're quiet at the moment anyway.' All this is not merely good luck but the result of Vanessa's prayers. God is on her side because what she is doing is right. She is doing it, not for herself, but for Sacha and Amber, Camilla and Dom. Mother is growing quite beautiful, gracious, with her rich brown curls and her fresh skin; even her voice has gone smooth and gentle. It is hard to stay upstairs when you know that she's down there, all on her own. Now, all of them want to be with her but it's important they regulate the visits so she remains eager to see them.

Ilse had to be threatened, of course. That was one of the hardest parts because none of them was quite certain that their methods were going to work. They lied. Even Ilse, however desperate she was to remain in this country, to be near the love of her life – it was obvious the boy didn't want her – even Ilse would balk at the thought of her employer being kept as a prisoner so they told her that Mother had gone away but she didn't want anyone, even Mrs Guerney, to know.

'Sorry? Tell me again. I do not quite understand. I thought you said that Mrs Townsend was now back from Broadlands.' They caught her one night on the stairs, late again. They caught her on the hop.

'Ilse, Mother came back from Broadlands but she had to go away again, in a hurry. She asked us to explain this to you; she was in too much of a rush to tell you herself. She's had to go away . . .'

'For reasons of her health?'

'Yes, for reasons of her health. But it's essential that nobody else knows, not even Mrs Guerney, and you are going to have to assure Mrs Guerney that Mother is still here. You are going to have to make sure Mrs Guerney believes you when you tell her you've seen her.'

Ilse narrowed her eyes. 'But why? Why should I do that silly thing?' She looked totally bewildered.

'Because we're asking you to, that's all. And because Mother herself would have asked you but it all happened in such a hurry.'

'It sounds most strange to me. I do not know if I want to be part of this very odd arrangement. What are you really up to, you children?' She stared at them with incredulous eyes. She looked very foreign all of a sudden, and alone, as if wasn't on the stairs but standing in the middle of a big cold space.

Dominic gazed hard at his fingernails. 'Ilse, I think Mother has been quite worried, lately, about the hours you spend away from work.'

'What hours?' Her pretty face flushed. Her eyes widened, horrified. She looked more of a fool than ever and the children stood round in a hard little circle and watched her.

'The nights you're supposed to be in when you're not. The times you go creeping off down the back stairs. Those hours, Ilse, and if we told her the truth you'd be sent back to Sweden without even being allowed to say goodbye to Paulo.' Hah, let her wriggle out of that!

Vanessa pushed on, dangling the carrot. 'While Mother is away we won't need you here in the evenings. We wouldn't worry if you went out – we wouldn't even care if you stayed out all night, as long as you were back by the time Mrs Guerney got here in the morning. And the fact that your work permit is about to expire doesn't disturb us at all, does it, Camilla?'

'But where is Mrs Townsend?'

'She's gone to a clinic in Switzerland.'

'And how long will she be there?'

'For as long as it takes her to get well – or as well as she can. Poor Mother. I should think she'll be back by Easter.'

'I shall need to think.'

'Well, I wouldn't take too long about it if I were you,' said Dominic, significantly, and they were able to watch as Ilse's natural resistance wavered.

237

'Oh dear,' she said, and again, 'oh dear.'

But now is the moment for which Camilla has been practising long and hard. Speaking to Caroline's friends — Mother was ever a fair-weather friend so it's easy to brush them off — acquaintances, people at work, is one thing, but this is going to be quite another. She's got to telephone Daddy and pretend to be Caroline, and she's got to convince him of something so big, so essential to the overall plan that, if she fails, they might as well not have gone through all this heartache; they might as well have not started. They gather round the phone in the drawing room like robbers round a safe.

'I bet he's out. That would be typical.'

Camilla, shaking, moans, 'I don't know that I could attempt it a second time.'

'You'll be fine. You know exactly what to say and you'll be fine.'

'Yes, but what if Daddy brings up something personal, something that we could not know about? What if they have a special way of speaking?'

'Well they don't, we know that they don't. You are getting yourself into a state. Stop it before you ruin everything.'

Sacha steps forward and plants a kiss on Camilla's pale cheek. 'Please, Camilla. You're going to be brilliant. And you're not only doing it for us, now, you're doing it for Mummy's sake, too.'

They rig up the telephone so the conversation can be heard in the room. Daddy answers, surprised when he hears Caroline's voice on the other end of the line.

'Caroline? I haven't heard from you for so long I thought you were going through one of your anti-telephone phases.'

'No, Robin.' Camilla is calm. 'I've just been amazingly busy, that's all. So busy that I've worn myself out completely. And I've not only been busy working, but I've been spending a lot of time lately searching for somewhere else to live.'

'Oh yes, the children mentioned something about that the last time they came over.'

'Yes, they are excited about the idea. We all are. And now we've made our decision so I'm ringing to say that I'm ready to sell this house. I've seen somewhere I like and want to make an offer.'

'This all sounds terribly amusing. I never imagined you'd ever want to move. Tell me more ...'

'I need to get out of London,' Camilla adds a little belligerence.

'Well, lots of people are trying to do that.'

Dominic gazes out of the window but sees nothing. There's a hole in the sock that has fallen down.

'And I've settled on a cottage in the West Country.'

'Say again?'

'You heard me, Robin. There's no need to be facetious.'

'Well, the children were suggesting ... but I put it down to their imaginations. They've been listening to too many stories about Suzie's childhood. Suzie's mother's been forced to put her house up for sale, you know. Can't really cope. It's all very sad, because a house is much more than a house when you've been brought up in it. Poor Suzie, she's very dejected. She even tried to get me to buy it as a holiday home. But you – buried away in the middle of the country! Hours from the clubs and the theatres, without a car ...'

'I am not a child, Robin. I am quite capable of making my own decisions without expecting to be grilled by you.'

'I'm sorry. It just seems so sudden.'

Sacha's got her eyes tight shut and her fists are hard balls at her side.

'It's not sudden at all, I've been mulling it over for months. It was only a question of finding the right place. Well, now I've found it! I'm not ringing for your approval, Robin. I am ringing to ask you to start the ball rolling. I want to be able to make my offer and I need to know that everything this end will go smoothly. There'll be no problems as far as selling this goes. Mr Morrisey next door has often told me that if we ever move he wants to be informed. He's had his eyes on this house for years because of the garage and the larger garden. So Morrisey needs to be contacted and the solicitor needs to be instructed.'

'I think we should meet ...'

Vanessa wills Camilla on with all her heart and all her soul.

'Not interested, Robin, I'm afraid. Far too much on my plate and anyway, there's nothing else to be said. My mind is made up.'

'And you want me to make all the arrangements?'

'No, I just want you to deal with this end of things. That would be easier for me. You just clear the way and I will cope with the purchase. I imagine you'll be glad to see me out of London.'

He's taken aback, yet there's nothing Daddy can do but agree. 'You'd better make your offer and tell me when you want to put Camberley Road on the market.'

'I'll do that tomorrow morning. I will also arrange for a survey.'

'Is everything all right, Caroline?'

'Why should it be otherwise?'

'You just sound ... firmer than usual, I suppose. More purposeful.' Funny, Daddy sounds rather sad when he says that. 'Are the children still coming over tomorrow evening?'

'As far as I know, Robin – why? As you know, I prefer them to make their own arrangements. I am far too busy to bother.'

When she has finished Camilla falls into Vanessa's arms. She is trembling all over and she can't stop laughing. It's infectious. The magazine they haven't dared leave open, the *Country Life*, is quickly found through their wild tears and shrieks to be thumbed through yet again. And there it is, the cottage that every child draws, the cottage of every child's dreams, the fiction and fantasy tangled up in its five-acre paddock, its thatched roof, the trickling stream and the diamond-paned windows. It beckons with love from a fragrant valley, half-hidden there with its wriggling staircase, its old cream Aga and its ancient beams.

And only Vanessa knows whose house it is. She's been buying magazines for weeks, not entirely sure which one Suzie mentioned. 'Don't let it be sold, God, oh please don't let it be sold. Don't let it go to anyone else.' Only Vanessa, who hasn't had a childhood, understands the effect this is going to have on poor Suzie.

They will no longer be different. They already have Daddy in a way that she never can. They've nearly got a mother like hers and now they'll have her dreams and her happiest places. Let his new bitchy wife hate Daddy's children properly. Let her despise them on equal terms.

They'll be able to invite her down – Suzie, and Daddy and the new London baby. They'll be able to picnic on rugs in the garden and when Suzie's baby gets older they'll be able to play hide and seek and leave it, crying, on its own ... or be terribly nice to it, be sickly kind to their stepmother, rubbing in the fact that *she* is the stranger.

Suzie will see them so happy together, so will Daddy. He might even want to come back, but Vanessa's not too sure about this. Let things stay as they are for a while – they've been through hell to get hold of a mother, perhaps things should slide for a while.

Fresh eggs, hens and sponge puddings. Log fires, ponies and daisy chains – all these combine to give Suzie her superiority, her confidence and her arrogant nerve. Anyway, they have to move Mother out. Mother can't stay in the sauna but nor can she survive in this house. Not now. She has to live somewhere else and before they saw it, everyone knew exactly what it would look like.

Vanessa stares at the picture of the house, so frightened to let herself believe, scared of hoping too hard.

'Let's take it with us tomorrow and show it to Daddy!'

'No! No! He might think it strange that Mother has chosen a place so secluded. He might start interfering … the price is too high or the roof looks dodgy. And we don't want Suzie mauling it, making her bitchy comments. No, not yet. It's not time yet. We must keep this, as we are keeping everything else, strictly to ourselves.'

'So when are we going to let Mummy out?'

'Not tomorrow, because we'll be out all evening and I wouldn't want to leave her alone. You do realise, don't you, Sacha, that once she's out of the sauna and roaming free in that basement we can't put her back?'

But the longing in the small child's face is so poignant – it's a yearning of years and years – that Vanessa is moved to commit herself.

'What does everyone else think? Shall we let her out on Saturday morning when we've got the whole weekend to stay with her? The solicitor will make an offer tomorrow and if it's accepted we'll know about the house. We'll be able to tell her about the house and watch to see how she behaves.'

No one but Sacha and Amber seem brave enough to make a decision. They have made such a sweet dream, it's tempting just to let it continue. Breaking it feels such a violent act.

Dominic says very carefully, 'I suppose that if she hasn't changed by now she isn't really going to. We've got to face that. It's been a long time, nearly four months, and there's nothing much more we can do.'

'I want her to be with us. I don't want to be cruel to her any more.'

'Have we been very cruel, Camilla?'

And then Sacha puts in, 'Oh yes, we have, but only to be kind.'

THIRTY-TWO

FRIDAY NIGHT, and the evening clouds are darker than the distant pines. Flocks of London starlings fly low over the park in wild arcs and eclipses before coming to rest in a neat line on the telegraph wires, settling like an audience to watch him.

Lot Dance prepares for entry. This is better than he ever could have hoped. There is nobody home except, of course, for the mysterious Caroline Townsend.

Damn it, she's in there somewhere.

Dressed all in black he flows like a beardless wizard. There is nothing Lot can do to camouflage himself, although he alone doesn't understand that. His night-black hair and his angular cheekbones are the first anomalies to attract attention, and after that no one can help but focus on those brilliant, startling navy-blue eyes. Crouched in the shadows, stealthily smooth and intensely purposeful, in a different part of London, in a different age, he might be mistaken for Sherlock Holmes. But luckily for Lot there are no pedestrians about when he crosses the road and slinks down the basement steps with his precious glass-cutter in his pocket. He wants to do this properly. He doesn't want to make a mess. He bends back one of the rusty old bars and he sticky-tapes up one of the panes. He should have done this long ago, and not wasted so much time making stupid telephone calls and hanging around.

But perhaps he's been enjoying himself. Perhaps he's getting fed up with boxes, and there's no fun going to Bart's any more. In Lot's eyes to go home to Mum, somewhere he's always sure of a warm and genuine welcome, is an admission of failure. In some ways he hopes he doesn't find Caroline; he hopes that the house might be empty so that he can continue his search, because it gives him such a definite reason for getting up in the mornings.

With a torch between his teeth — a tricky business because he finds he can't swallow and he's in danger of dribbling — he starts work on the glass. The flakes of paint impede his progress, clogging his fierce little blade, but it doesn't take long to cut out a square large enough so that he can insert his hand and snip the catch on the window. It's a jolly good thing the house is not protected by any alarms.

Lot steps into a twilight darkness. The stale air down here is static, as if it hasn't been disturbed for a very long time, like in a supermarket where everything's packaged so nothing smells, nothing's allowed to age. There's something tinny in the atmosphere and there, square, at the back of the room stands what looks like a 1950s fridge, glowing softly, dimly lit from within, although when Lot directs his torchbeam he can see that it is made out of wood and there's a glass window in the front.

The clouds pass over the moon outside as he crosses the room with stealth, emotionally quite unprepared for the most enormous trauma of his life. He has to stoop to see through the window and then he stiffens with shock; he stifles a groan, because he's not been expecting anything like this. There before him, draped impassively on a fur-covered seat (and the fur is arranged like you'd see in a famous painting), dressed in ivory, with the light playing silverily with her serenity is a fairy-tale woman. By her side sits a vase full of primroses and violets, and her concentration is centred entirely on her music.

She's got headphones on her head.

Lot's mind ranges madly over the length and breadth of his experience ... films, books, bill-boards, adverts on telly, but he comes back to the same, intolerably sweet sensations ... bluebells, wild garlic and soft, silver shawls ... never has he seen such a complete woman. Mother, lover, wife and child. A vision. A small smile plays round her gentle mouth. And, as he watches, when she raises a hand to disentangle one of her curls, he remembers the fallow deer browsing under the branches in the park, and the way that they have of flicking their tails at the flies. Human voices scare them.

It seems like hours, but it's for only seconds that Lot stands trembling, rooted to the spot. His longing is like a hurricane and he's going to be blown away by it. And is this the woman he's come to kill? Shaking with remorse and tenderness, his eyes feel sharp, like a jackdaw's eyes viewing something shiny that the bird must risk its life to possess. He spies the padlock with alarm: the door is locked! She's a prisoner here, just as Lot's been a prisoner for most of his life, and she's come to terms with her fate just as he has.

Lot steps back and bursts straight into tears.

Deep inside himself he experiences a burst of beauty so immense that he feels as if he is dying.

He must have cast a shadow on the ceiling, or maybe she caught his short, strangled cry, because seconds later she is at the window, staring out into the moonlit gym and her eyes shine a grey-green sea spray.

'It's all right! It's all right! It's quite all right!' Oh please, please, she must not be afraid of him.

'Who is there?'

Even his name, given so coarsely, feels like a blasphemy in her presence.

'Well, Lot, what are you doing in this house?'

He can't think of anything clever to say save for the straightforward truth. 'Are you Caroline Townsend?'

When she nods her head he says, 'Well, I have been trying to find you.'

'Couldn't you have come to the front door? Could you be the mysterious Mr Walsh?'

That's the second time he's been asked. 'No, I am Bart's brother. What are you doing in there? Who has locked you in?'

Caroline does not reply. Ignoring his question she says, 'There's a key at the top of the basement steps. Perhaps you would be good enough to let me out.'

Ashamed of his overwhelming desire to keep her locked up, safe in her cage like the rarest, most beautiful of butterflies, like a priceless relic which might crumble and disappear if it was exposed to the air, he overcomes his reluctance to move and leaps to obey her request. Lot, more clumsy than ever, falls over himself in order to obey.

'There's a light,' she calls. 'Put it on. It'll make things much easier.' And flaming hot in the chill of the basement, Lot finds the keys and hurries to comply.

She smiles at her saviour, disarmed, as most people are, by his extraordinarily compelling good looks, not knowing, as most people don't, about the cruel quirk of nature that has made him so perfect without, so complicated and tumultuous within. When she was little Caroline shuddered at the sight of old women, grimacing through their painted masks at divine young men ... she feels herself doing that now. The man looks stiff with shock, and no wonder he's shocked after so dramatically discovering her here. Caroline doesn't feel too calm herself, disturbed in her sanctuary by an intruder.

'You let me out and I'm grateful. Let me shake your hand.'

He winces when she touches him, tongue-tied with wonder. She puts on her negligée, she floats in it, it's cotton smooth as silk, paler than the moon. She tells him: 'Well, I frankly don't care who you are or what you are doing. You can take all the silver if you like.' She smiles again. He's like a dog when he follows her as Caroline Townsend takes a deep breath and prepares to return to the rest of her house.

Lot goes first. She's determined to see everything, to touch everything, to reassure herself that it's real and no dream. She moves into her house as if through the foliage of a dark forest and Lot is the prince, chopping through fearful memories – the tangles of shame – leading the way. She reaches the hall mirror and pauses, turns to it and stands staring with fascinated eyes, absorbing her own reflection. A film of tears mists her eyes as she leans towards it and traces the shape of her face ... not hard and lean any more but rounded and smooth. The sharp lines she tried to cover have softened as the leanness has left, replaced by a natural fullness. Why has she hidden her hair all these years? She straightens the coils of deep brown, wonders over the few strands of grey, touching it lightly, smoothing it lightly, trying to shape it but it goes its own way. It's still short, of course, not more than three inches long all over, but it frames her face and it's shiny clean. She looks so much younger! Innocent even. She seems disconcerted by her own breath on the glass, tries to pull back, appalled, like a mother accidentally smothering her own baby. She tries for that old sarcastic smile but it won't come and she's not going to force it. The smile that confronts her is genuine, sweet!

She whispers, 'Who can this be?' And Lot watches her, full of awe.

It is all happening so fast, too fast for poor Lot to make any sense of it. Caroline turns on the lights and paces backwards and forwards through every room, picking up stray bits and pieces, digesting small details with strokes and sighs. But the house is not like her. He'd never have guessed, having seen her, that her house would be furnished like this – hard, brittle like a glossy magazine, with overpriced refinement, nothing homely here. 'It's just as I left it.' She sounds quite mystified. She turns to him with the whispered question, 'I don't know why, but I imagined it would have totally changed, but it hasn't, has it? It's just me that's changed. Nothing else. It is all exactly the same.'

Her stricken admirer brings himself to say, 'Well, I wouldn't know anything about that. It's just how I imagined it would be, but that's before I met you.'

'Strange, how I feel so much smaller in it. I suppose it's all those months locked away in that tiny box. Anyway, why would you be trying to imagine the inside of my house?'

'Don't worry, I do that all the time.' But he'd rather stay silent, afraid to displease her. Falling in love at first sight is the name of this sort of thing and Lot has done this before, but never quite so totally. It's a curious phenomenon, a chemical process in which billions of atoms rush together and communicate to the heart, brain, stomach, and everywhere else. For Lot the world has turned magical again, just when he thought he was losing it. She must never know about the violence he came here to commit, she must never suspect that he hated her. Oh God, is some deep instinct even now – his breathing, dilated pupils perhaps – sounding a soundless alarm? No, there's no sign that Caroline is afraid of him, and why should she be? He is determined to protect her from harm for the rest of her life. If she'll let him.

She is dismayed to see her own stale room messy and disturbed. There is a violence here, a wasted place, an eerie lagoon of sexual energy gone stagnant. 'Why do things seem to last forever here?' She closes her eyes tightly, though trying not to flinch from the pain. The dressing table is strewn with half-used bottles without their lids and, tinted with make-up, imprinted with lips, muddled old tissues fill the bin. Lot does not recognise the large, brassy photograph of herself that's standing on the windowsill. She sees him staring and smiles. 'I was pregnant. That was taken just before the twins were born.' Old clothes, a mess of ruffles and flounces, hang limply on the back of a cream calf-skin chair. Even her bed is rumpled as if she's just thrown back the duvet and there's her discarded dressing gown on the floor. There's pity in her eyes when she exclaims, 'The children have deliberately kept it like this, haunted by a slatternly old ghost ...'

If Caroline hadn't told him, Lot would never have imagined the room to be anything to do with her. Anyone could see that she hasn't been here, anyone could sense that the smell in this room is of dust. What is more extraordinary is that, apart from a few neat toys and bookshelves, there is hardly a sign that this is a house where children live. And just as he's finished thinking it she puts it into words. 'There's nothing of the children in this house. I'm sure you noticed. I wouldn't let them. You see, I just couldn't let them.'

It's extraordinary, it's flattering, the way she assumes he understands.

They come downstairs and it's as though she has just remembered who he is when she asks, 'And how is Bart?'

'Bart isn't very good at all. He's run out of money and Ruby's left him.'

'Ruby?'

'His wife. The one you telephoned.' The one who used to make Lot's life wonderful but Ruby's disappeared now, she's lost behind the haze and Lot cannot even remember her hats.

'Not me. I've never even heard of anyone called Ruby.' And then, slowly, wistfully, 'I knew he was married, of course, but Bart never mentioned her to me.'

He must get this right, although it no longer matters much and Lot feels himself delving into one of his baffling distances. 'But you had an affair with Bart? You were with him on the nights when Ruby was alone?'

'Yes, I had what you call in your old-fashioned way "an affair" with Bart. But that seems like another life now.'

Lot knows all about other lives. You go into another life each time you change your mind about something big. You have to refocus and start again while your old life settles and forms, once more, around you.

In the kitchen she heads straight for the cupboard beside the fridge. She's after the gin, never mind the tonic. She brings out a bottle in the weary, practised way of the addict, in the impatient, brutal way that smokers take their cigarettes out of their packets. She gazes at it for a moment before putting it back with a smile that is wonderful, full of delight, pleased and yet frightened by her newfound composure. 'Even the booze,' she says, more impressed than astonished. 'They have even been pouring the booze away and replacing it in order to fool Mrs Guerney.'

'They fooled everyone. You must be very angry.'

'Angry?'

'They must have kept you locked up for a very long time.'

'Locked up?'

'Yes!' Lot gapes at her, emotionally electrified, trying to keep control over his emotions while he feels he has strayed into a magnetic field. Why is she being so obtuse? She knows very well what he's talking about. He's only just let her out . . .

Her eyes meet his and hold them levelly. 'Nobody locked me up, Lot,' she says positively. 'And no, I'm not angry.'

'But I broke into your house and I found you down in the sauna! There was a padlock on the door.'

He holds his breath and listens hard, trying to understand what she means when she says, 'If that's what you think then it's obvious that both you and I have been dreaming.'

'I suppose we have.' Baffled, he feels obliged to agree. And then comes the warning. 'They'll probably be back soon. Everyone will be back. Look at the time — it's almost half-past ten.' Whatever has happened here, and Lot isn't quite sure what it was, surely Caroline must be dreading the first encounter with her children?

But she doesn't seem nervous. Perhaps she realises that Lot is here to protect her. 'How do you know, so absolutely, the comings and goings of my house? I think you're probably a private detective.'

And perhaps Caroline is right. Perhaps Lot ought to agree with that because he quite likes the concept and it's not quite a lie and he doesn't want to tell her that he folds boxes. Why should he do himself down? So he's just about to nod eagerly when she shrugs and says, 'But it doesn't matter anyway. What matters is that we're here, sitting in this kitchen, and I haven't got a drink in my hand and I'm talking to you quite openly and frankly without being afraid and do you know Lot, I haven't had this experience, I haven't been able to relax with people for . . . years without a sense of suffocation, of being diminished.' She finishes with brilliant eyes. 'It's quite unbelievable. You know, I just can't remember the last time I felt so natural with anyone. Is it you or is it me?'

'It's a spell that's been cast by someone,' says Lot, who rarely deviates from the truth – his lie about being Mr Walsh proved tremendously taxing – because it's all too confusing. 'And when I get home I'm going to wash my hair.'

THIRTY-THREE

EVERYONE'S SO EXCITED. She wishes they weren't quite so hyped-up. Before Daddy arrived to collect them, Vanessa had to make Amber calm down. She had to stop her jumping up and down, yelling over and over again, 'We're going to let Mummy out in the morning!' And even now they've arrived, despite all the warnings, Vanessa watches how the twins keep nudging each other, breaking into secretive smiles.

They think it's going to be wonderful, but what if it's not? What if it all goes terribly wrong? There's no way of telling what's going to happen. If it was only herself then Vanessa could bear it, whatever the outcome. But the thought of the younger ones being hurt again breaks her heart.

Daddy's pleased. 'There's cause for celebration this evening. Incredibly, Suzie's mother has managed to sell her house!'

But Suzie doesn't seem too cheerful just now. She's not her normal competent self. Vanessa's been watching and Suzie's been weakening for some time lately. She feels she's been sucking her up, bit by bit, pieces of Suzie sucked up through a straw.

'Whoever's buying it didn't even bother to look round it,' she moans while preparing a nasty, healthily green-looking salad. The stable door to the garden is open and as long as the rain keeps off they're going to eat their supper outside – first time this year. 'Probably some rich Yank – all done through a tight-lipped solicitor who refers to the purchaser as "my client" when he's asked.'

Daddy is perched on a kitchen stool, watching Suzie's efforts impatiently. 'Suzie, you shouldn't complain. Eileen's very lucky the house has been sold and with no inconvenience to herself. She hasn't even had to show anyone round. It's all been very painless.'

'It's probably a developer,' says Dominic slyly. 'Planning to knock it down and build an estate.'

'Don't,' Suzie wails. 'Please, don't even joke like that.'

Robin quickly deflects any trouble. He eyes Dominic warningly. 'And you're going to tell me all about the house that your mother has her eye on.'

'It's much more than that. She made an offer this morning and it looks as if it's going to be accepted.'

'Did she choose it herself or have you all seen it?'

'Oh, we've all seen it.' Dominic's lies are always convincing. 'We've been round it several times. We've even decided on our own bedrooms.'

'Come on, describe it to me,' says Daddy. 'Haven't you even brought a picture?'

Sacha, who's buttering the bread, looks away and nudges Amber, reminding her to keep quiet. They've been warned they must leave this part to Vanessa.

'Well, it's very old,' their sensible sister starts.

Daddy has taken the knife from Suzie, driven to take over the task as she seems to be all fingers and thumbs these days. Daddy is quicker, more efficient, and he doesn't make such a mess. He clears up behind him ... he always used to blame Mother for the chaos in the kitchen and the number of unnecessary basins and jugs she used. 'Yes, go on.'

Suzie takes a deep gulp of her brandy: it's a little display of temper.

'And it's what you would call picturesque.'

'With a garden?' Suzie asks.

Is she jealous? Is she already jealous? And are they going to have something that Suzie wants, at dear last? She cannot treat them with the same degree of contempt any longer. Soon *they* will have all the power ...

'Oh yes, it's got a large, wild garden. Mummy says it's probably glorious underneath.'

'*Mummy?* That's new! And since when was your mother interested in gardening? She managed to make quite a muddle of ours until Mr Broomhead took over, remember?'

'She thinks she might take it up again in all the spare time she's going to have once she's finished work.'

Robin glances at Suzie who's staring out over the top of the door at hers. It's dark out there and not too warm; eating out so early was a stupid suggestion of Suzie's. 'That makes two of you with time on your hands all of a sudden. What a pity that neither of you have managed to get on.'

Suzie swings round. 'Why, Robin? Oh, jolly good! You're about to suggest that we could have spent some of our spare time together now, are you? My God! My God! After everything that woman's put us through . . .'

'She's all right now. She's over it now, just as I said she would be. When I spoke to her yesterday morning she sounded like a completely different person.'

'Robin, why are you always making excuses for Caroline? You've always defended her. You've never once come out in total condemnation! Could it be because you feel guilty?' Suzie's given up her job. She doesn't work any more, not even part-time. Well, first there was the demanding task of turning the attic rooms into a nursery and playroom. 'Let's get this straight, Suzie, are you honestly telling me you're quite happy to allow an interior decorator to take over?' Robin asked her, astonished. 'And that you wouldn't find any enjoyment in picking out the materials and wallpapers yourself?'

'That's not going to take me very long, is it Robin, for God's sake.'

'But it's not just that,' he went on. She'd already turned down the offer from Brussels; she realised in the end what a selfish move that would be. After all, she didn't want to be a bad mother, hard and uncaring, like Caroline. 'I want this whole process to be meaningful and enjoyable for both of us. This is our baby. Such a special child deserves a mother full-time, don't you think?'

She laughed at first. 'What on earth would I do with my spare time? And I enjoy working. I don't work very hard, Robin. What I do is scarcely taxing!'

'But it takes you away from me, don't you see?'

'No, frankly, I don't.' And Suzie thought about Caroline. She remembered the play and the part she had lost. And Suzie slept uneasily in her bed; she fretted about the child she carried, she felt it sucking at her already like a parasite in her womb, and she worried that she might not love it. If she gave up something she enjoyed, she'd be proving something, wouldn't she?

'You're looking tired and pale,' everyone told her. 'Why don't you ease up a bit.'

'You can always start working again afterwards,' said Suzie's mother sensibly. 'Pander to Robin a little bit, dear. Men like that. He loves you too much, that's his trouble.' And Robin fusses and frets over her as if she's a fragile china doll. Suzie pretends to be happy with this but she's not. Vanessa has never seen her pour a second brandy before and Daddy is hurt. He knows that, being pregnant, she should not drink. He moves over as if he's about to . . .

'Damn you!' shouts Suzie. 'I need this! I need it! So why don't you bloody well leave me alone, or have you a sick compulsion about correction on top of all your other sodding hang-ups!'

Everyone is embarrassed. This is not how it is at Ammerton Mews; this is far more like Camberley Road, and Amber jumps up and rushes to Daddy's side. She tries to fit her small hand into his but he's tense, he's angry, he won't let her in. For a split second, but only for a second, Vanessa feels sorry for Suzie because she can't fight him. No one can fight against Daddy. He's far too gentle and good, he just goes away. He just goes to God, or to work.

It's dark outside, and cold, and everyone secretly wants to go upstairs and turn on the fire.

'Where will Eileen go after she's moved?' asks Camilla politely.

Robin has to answer because Suzie's not prepared to cooperate. Suzie doesn't look too well, she looks drawn and nervous. The rug has been whipped from under her. 'Not far away. She is moving into a bungalow in the village. It's far more sensible for a woman on her own and she'll be able to take all her cats, although I don't know how long they'll last with the traffic going past the front door. And what about schools? Has your mother given any thought to where you will go to school? You'll be sorry to leave the convent, Vanessa. I need to know much more about that. I don't suppose your mother has bothered to find out if there's anything suitable in the vicinity? She certainly didn't mention anything to me on the phone.'

Yes, Vanessa will be sorry to leave the convent and the magnificently religious Sister Agnes, although she is not the nun's favourite any more. As a child she is safe but Vanessa knows that when she becomes a woman she is going to lose Daddy. But she no longer wants to become a nun, not any longer. Being a nun won't stop her growing up; her face might remain like a child's, framed by that stiff halo of plastic but even under a nun's habit her body will be all rude and hairy. Her breasts are growing, one much faster than the other, and there's nothing she can do to stop them. Binding them in bandages every night only makes her feel sore in the morning and they're still coming through. Prayers don't stop them.

No, there's no getting away from the fact that Daddy loves Suzie. He likes the sort of hard-faced woman that Suzie is, and the only way to achieve that is to follow as firmly as she can in Suzie's footsteps. Absorb all the influences. It's not too late. 'The younger ones are going to the village school and Camilla and I are going to what used to be the high school. Mother's found out that the old high school has a very good reputation.' She's accumulated all this information from the estate agent's brochure. And she knows that Suzie went there before she left home to go to university. Vanessa's going to try for the same university as Suzie, too – Bristol, and it's got a name for being the most right-wing and snobby.

Suzie looks peeved while Daddy is still concerned. 'You're going to find it all very different after London.'

'You won't like it,' says Suzie nastily, and Vanessa detects the first suggestion of a respectful, honest kind of dislike showing through at last. There'll be less of the biting sarcasm now, less of the mocking laughter. Dominic flips back with: 'Well, are you offering to have us stay here?'

'I think that is what your father would like,' says Suzie, drily. 'He is good with children. He knows all there is to know about children and their care.'

'We've been through all that, Suzie, and now is not the time, nor the place.'

'Whatever you say, dear,' and Suzie mocks but Suzie is almost in tears.

Robin refuses to rise to the bait. That's funny ... Caroline used to say that with that same, sarcastic tone in her voice before she reached for another drink. Suzie's doing the same thing now. There's definitely something wrong.

Daddy goes on, 'You'll have to come and stay with us during the school holidays. You can always come at weekends, although where we'll put you all I don't know, now that we are converting the attic.'

'I used to think it would make an ideal study, a nice, peaceful place to work with a lovely view.' But nobody's listening to Suzie any more because she's just being difficult and silly, excluded and chilled, reduced to such childish behaviour to attract Daddy's attention now.

'And you must come and stay with us, Daddy. You must bring Suzie and the baby. I'm sure Mother would like that.'

Daddy smiles at what he considers to be Vanessa's little joke. 'At a pub down the road, perhaps. I doubt very much that your mother would want us any nearer than that. Where, exactly, is this place? Caroline told me the West Country but she didn't say where.'

'We will probably be allowed to have a cat.' Amber can't stay quiet any longer and Daddy is so annoyed with Suzie — you can see how annoyed he is underneath — that, to Vanessa's enormous relief he forgets the difficult question. Somerset is a large county but it might come as too much of a coincidence were she to mention that now. Suzie's much too defensive.

It's nice not having to be sullen here; it's nice not having to be sullen and sour when she's with Daddy and Suzie. For the first time ever her secret hopes give Vanessa the sense of equality that's always been lacking when she visits Suzie's house. Vanessa wants to wrap up her hope into something hard, like a stone, and throw it at Suzie to hurt her harder. 'We are all very excited indeed. We can't wait to move to the country.'

Suzie says, 'It can only be a whim of Caroline's. It's a silly whim. It can't last. She won't fit into the country at all. She doesn't even drive a car — and what about men?'

Daddy says, 'Don't spoil this for them, Suzie, please. Can't you see how much they all want it?'

'Are you having one of your bad days, Suzie?' Amber asks the question in the same innocent manner she used to ask Mother.

Suzie smashes a plate. It shatters noisily and the slivers fly out in a circle. It's hard to tell if it is deliberate or accidental ... but Vanessa knows how much Suzie wants to shout, 'You little bitch!' and she smiles with a bittersweet pleasure as Daddy bends to pick it up tiredly.

By now the night is thoroughly dark. It's a relief to be safe inside Daddy's car after the tension of the evening. Always the best place to be, Vanessa sits in the front beside him, sad because he's unhappy but pleased to see Suzie so riled. Oh dear, maybe tomorrow all this will be different. Maybe tomorrow Suzie will be laughing her head off when she hears that there's no house in the country after all, when she discovers that Vanessa has been taken off by the police and the children are to be split up. Suzie will gain such strength from that! Suzie will tower on her pinnacle again. Wincing, Vanessa can even hear Suzie telling Daddy she'd always known there was something wrong with her, 'sitting there staring, peculiar, withdrawn. We should have done something earlier – it was obvious there was something psychologically wrong with the girl.'

When Vanessa sees the lights shining on to the street her heart beats with hot, sickly thumps and she feels such shock it is like being punched in the stomach. *What has happened?* The curtains have not been drawn, and every room is lit up like a lantern, but there are no signs of anyone moving about – there's nobody standing there waiting or looking out. She turns to Daddy, so afraid that for a dangerous instant, she is about to give the whole game away. But he merely looks out and says mildly, 'Your mother must be home for once. I really think I should come in and see her.'

'But Suzie's upset,' is the first thing Vanessa can think of to say. 'You must get back.' She can hear Sacha about to start whimpering. She must get them out of the car before they start asking stupid questions. 'And Mother'll probably be in the bath, anyway. If she's just got home that's where she'll be and she stays there for ages.'

'You are probably right.' But he isn't totally convinced. It's a great relief when the children scramble out of the car, without any fuss for once, and he drives away.

They stand in a frightened bunch at the bottom of the steps, looking up. Dominic sounds so sinister. 'Somebody must be there. What if it's a burglar, or Mr Walsh?'

'We should have made Daddy come in with us. I don't like it,' whines Sacha.

Camilla asks the question slowly. 'I wonder how she got out?'

'We don't know it's Mother yet, do we?'

One more night, God, one more night, that's all I asked from You! It wasn't much, was it. Why did You have to let me down, why did You have to go and spoil everything?

But quite unaffected by any such dark misgivings, Amber's away and dashing across the pavement. With her duffle coat swinging behind her, she's up the steps and jumping up to stab at the bell. 'Come on! Come on! Bring the key! What are you all doing standing there? Come on, hurry up, let's all go and find Mummy!'

Dominic marches deliberately towards the door with the key in his hand. He opens it and disappears inside number 14, Camberley Road. Camilla is next; with a protective arm around Sacha's shoulders her golden hair catches the gleam of the porchlight as she steps over the threshold. They do not look back. They do not return for Vanessa. It's so easy for them to go, it's so easy for them to trust ... they are children, they've done nothing wrong. But Vanessa, paperwhite, cannot follow. Mother will be in there waiting, dishevelled, wild-eyed and completely insane. Truly a living nightmare. Vanessa's head has grown so enormous that she holds it carefully on her neck so it will not fall off and burst into scarlet pieces on the pavement. She stands there twisting her hands, biting her lips, staring up at the drawing-room window, caught so obviously in an act of such cruelty, such unmitigated unkindness that suddenly she knows absolutely that Mother, let alone God, will never, ever forgive her.

All of a sudden the fun house has switched off all its lights and turned into the house of horrors.

When she kissed her it was softly, not touching anywhere else save for raising one hand to her daughter's cheek. The tears with which they met each other were like rain on their faces.

THIRTY-FOUR

IT WAS SOMETHING so wild, so savage. Vanessa had been mad, hadn't she, obsessed by something which was not quite wholesome. No one's ashamed, it's just that they choose not to mention it. *Ever*. The kiss seemed to seal it; it seemed to say – put it away till I'm dead and then you can get it out, but only if you have to.

But whichever way you look at it, Mother has been saved.

Autumn, winter, springtime, Mothertime – she is the one that everybody wants. She's not all milk and honey, though. She can be stern when it's necessary, and although they've not quite been down at Poppins for one full year yet, she's already a member of the village fête committee, she organises the speakers for the village hall debates and she's on the junior school PTA. She's made new friends now and it seems that she's very popular – properly popular. People are always popping in for her homemade lemonade and her brown, sugary biscuits, crisp and crumby from the Aga. People are always commenting, 'What a remarkable woman you are!'

She has started to play the cello. She plays it in the garden, at night, when it's dark. When it's full moon she swims naked in the lake on the hills – she says she knows what it's like being inside a diamond.

How small her world is now. But she doesn't appear to mind. You can get close, you can nuzzle her, you can *breathe* her.

She is the mother to whom you could send one of those curious cards that read *'Mother is another word for love ...'*

She is the mother from *Swallows and Amazons*, *The Railway Children* and *Little Women* rolled sweetly into one. A slightly tragic figure, she looks as if she's been hurt, as if she knows that the struggle she fought against this will mark her for the rest of her life. But her beautiful, faraway smile holds such wisdom, such understanding, that whenever he sees it, poor old Lot loses his heart all over again.

She looks like the statue Lot found, drowning beneath the fountain.

The pagan Lot is useful here like a dog on a lead, and wanted, in his baggy trousers, his open-toed sandals and his striped, Victorian collarless shirts, bleached and tattered. He keeps other, more dangerous men with primitive urges, at bay, to the children's total approval. All Lot wants is to be close and to please her. With his strong, agile hands he built a house for the hens. He has sawn out a flap in the kitchen door for the cats. He looks far more 'normal' in Somerset, and that's what he reckons was wrong with him. 'It's the country life that suits me. I am obviously a man of the soil and I needed to be closer to the earth.' He flexes his muscles. He brings Mummy bunches of flowers and soft fruits, strange arrangements, sometimes. He seems to imagine she is a kind of tree goddess. He changes plugs, he chops the wood, he carves flat-bottomed boats for Dominic and he works on the garden stolidly, sweating and bronzed, in a soil that wriggles with earthworms, with his shirt like a flag proclaiming his happiness hooked on the handle of the spade. He sends lavender bags to the people he loves – Mum and Dad, Bart and Ruby. Well of course she came back, she was only trying to teach Bart a lesson. Behind the scenes Ruby's Dad saved the house and the company, Bart lost his casting vote, but he couldn't care less about that. This is a tapestry garden, with its tall hedges and narrow green pathways, with its bower of roses propped up again, renovated from olden days. Its old-fashioned flowerbeds are full of Mummy's favourite flowers – hollyhocks, lupins and Canterbury bells. When they sit outside in the summer evenings with a jug of lemon barley water, the swifts whoosh low overhead.

It is riddled with dens, new and old, and every so often the children discover neglected toys – little bits of a doll's dainty teaset sitting among the weeds, and the rusting wheels of somebody's go-cart.

Mrs Guerney didn't come with them although Mummy asked her.

'You don't need me now,' she said, but she wasn't cross. 'Any fool can see that. I was getting worried about you, I have to say it. I wondered what was going on but Vanessa is such a reliable child that I thought to myself, "you silly old party, don't be so darn soft." That spell at Broadlands and that last job of yours, whatever it was and I don't like to pry, well, Mrs Townsend, what can I say? You've matured, that's what you've done. You don't need me and at dear last you don't need HIM. Saints alive, Mrs Townsend, you don't need anybody any more. And I've got my lodger to look after and besides, Mr Morrisey needs me here what with his wife, poor old soul. Are you all right, Mrs Townsend, dear? Are you really, truly all right? There's nothing wrong, is there?'

It was a touching moment. And Caroline kissed Mrs Guerney ... they all did. They hugged her and they kissed her and her lips smacked tight together and her great bosom quivered, but you could see that she loved it. Before they moved they clubbed together and bought her a bust of the Queen.

Ilse's gone back to Sweden but before she departed she made quite sure that Paulo put a ring on her finger. It is questionable whether she'll qualify to come back to England ... it is questionable whether Paulo was a British Citizen in the first place, but Mrs Guerney proved her largeness of spirit by giving the sobbing girl a brand new Union Jack flight bag.

The sun wakes the children on these golden mornings; it peers in through their clematis-tangled windows, kissing them with its fluttery light, settling down on the patchwork quilts which Mummy helped them to make. Sacha and Amber won't be parted but the others have their own rooms. Vanessa's is in the attic: its two tiny windows are embedded in thatch, it runs across the top of the house so it's more of a den than a bedroom, and she's done it up exactly as she likes it.

In this weather it's a bit too hot to be travelling, especially with a squalling baby in a carrycot on the back seat. Suzie drives. They have taken the Peugeot because, if Holly grizzles on the journey, Robin is so much better at calming her down than the nervous, uptight Suzie. 'It's probably because I'm used to children, unlike you. It'll come, Suzie, you'll see, if you persevere. The trouble with you is that you are trying too hard. Holly does love you, you know, it's just that babies feel so much safer if they are treated with confidence.'

Suzie hangs her head like a child.

Of course the journey would be more comfortable if they had taken the Jag, but think of all the stops, searching for suitable lay-bys so that Robin could stop the car, get out, and comfort the baby. Robin won't let Suzie drive his car. 'It's not that I don't trust you, darling. Everyone knows that women are better drivers than men. I think it's to do with the legacy of Caroline. God, you should have seen her trying to handle a car. The roads are much safer since they removed her licence.'

It was all extremely fraught. They can't put the roof down because Robin says that Holly will catch cold and Suzie's scared to open the window too far in case he goes into one of his long, laborious sulks. Suzie feels guilty because of his moods. She wants the weekend to go well so that, at long last, he might be able to come to terms with the fact that his children no longer need him ... not in the desperate way that they used to.

'We're a family now,' she says. 'Your new family. You've got to let that other one go.'

'They are still my children.'

'Of course they are, Robin. Of course they are.'

'And I have to make sure they're being raised properly.'

'That's a funny, old-fashioned way to put it.'

'Caroline cannot be trusted. She never could be trusted. Oh, by the way, Suzie — did you put the spare feeding bottles in the box as I asked you?'

'I only brought the one. I thought we could wash it afterwards.'

'You forgot! I specifically asked you, and you forgot! Sometimes, I know it's extraordinary, but sometimes I think you do it deliberately. Proper sterilisation is so important. Children of Holly's age are so susceptible to germs — surely you don't still need to be told.'

Suzie stiffens but says nothing, there's no point. Robin is watching her every move, his right foot is directly connected to an imaginary brake on the passenger floor, his jaw is set as he stares before him and his arm is lodged rigidly across the back of the driver's seat. Every now and then he breathes out, which is deeply disconcerting, as if he's emerging from a dangerous dive only to take another breath in order to return down under. Suzie touches the kerb, something she's never done in her life for she was always an expert driver, and fear shoots through her. She winces, she grips the steering wheel with hot, sweaty hands. She used to enjoy journeys but now even her choice of car is wrong. 'There's just no room in this to stretch out properly. When we make a change perhaps an estate would be more sensible. Caroline used to drive an estate, much handier to fit all the family gear in the back – prams, and the shopping.'

She wanted to wear jeans but Robin reminded her she'd be too hot. 'You want to get your legs brown, don't you?' She didn't protest although no, actually, she didn't particularly. She wanted to wear jeans because she always used to wear jeans at Poppins – she can never remember being out of them.

Neither of them realised that Poppins was the house Caroline was buying until she had actually moved. There was no contact between Robin and Caroline, only a strange and rather unnerving silence coming from Camberley Road as moving day approached, as if Caroline had suddenly ceased to care – the game was finally over. They moved out of London in July and it was Vanessa who sent Robin the card, responsible Vanessa – she would, after all, be the one to handle the change-of-address cards. Caroline wouldn't be bothered to think of anything like that. She'd ring up her friends on the spur of the moment when she realised they didn't know where she was.

'What's this, Robin?' Suzie waddled to pick up the post on her way through to the kitchen. She was heavy then, clumsy like a penguin, not quick, not deft any longer. She screwed up her eyes as she read the card and her fingers fluttered around her lips. The kitchen was darkened, shiny with yellows and greens, and she held the card to the natural light. 'What does this mean, d'you think? It must be Vanessa's attempt at a joke!'

'Let's see.' Robin sat at the breakfast table shuffling the rest of the mail. He leaned on the cheerful, fresh green cloth while Suzie squeezed his orange juice, while Suzie prepared his coffee. 'It says they're at Poppins! That's strange. It gives the same telephone number, too – your mother's old number.'

Suzie's hand flew to her mouth. 'You don't think ...? Surely, it can't be ...'

Robin's laugh was caustic. 'No, no. Why do you always have to jump to the wrong conclusions? Why must you be so damn dramatic?'

She shouted, 'Well, what am I supposed to think?' She leaned forward and beat the card with a desperate finger. 'That's what it says, damn you, it says they are at Poppins! Caroline could easily have bought it, we wouldn't know! And Mummy never knew who the purchaser was. Oh my God! Oh my God! This is just too awful. This is the end!' And Suzie sat heavily down on her white kitchen chair – bang – and began to shudder and dribble, calling out unpleasantly for help.

Robin said, 'Suzie, don't cry! Please, don't cry. After all this time, after all this time and we had such good reason to think that Caroline was over the worst. Now we see that she has been conniving all the while, determined to hurt you as deeply as she could. She has bought this house for no other reason than to try and upset you. Even I, knowing her as well as I do, even I am horrified that the woman I once loved could go to these malicious lengths.'

But no matter how he sympathised he couldn't conceal his gratification, as if this was the proof he'd been waiting for, proof that the woman still loved him. Because for what other reason would she do this? Why else would she do anything so cruel? Why else would she continue to hate poor Suzie so?

'Well, she's clever,' Suzie sobbed, hugging her little unborn lump. 'I've got to give her that. She's clever and she's far more sensitive than I ever gave her credit for, because she understands how much Poppins means to me, and there's only one way she could ever have worked that out. She must have been listening to the children. They have come, like little spies, to my house, carrying back messages for Caroline to decode. I can't believe it! I just can't believe the slyness, the viciousness of it all!'

'Poppins was going to belong to somebody else, anyway.'

'I know, I know,' wept Suzie. 'But to them! It feels as if they've finally won.'

'It was never a battle, Suzie.' Robin picked up his fat, overflowing filofax, prepared for work.

'Not to you it wasn't, no.' Suzie had nothing to do all day. Not even the dentist. Nothing at all.

'She won't stick it for a week ...'

'Oh, I hope not. I so hope not. They're not coming here for

Christmas, Robin, I'm warning you now. I'm never going through that again.'

But while the vengeful Caroline sticks it out at Poppins, Robin still knows that he hasn't lost her. And he hasn't lost the children, either. He's always sending little gifts to Vanessa – mostly religious things, a leather bookmark, some incense sticks, meaningful verses he has found. Suzie knows Holly will be brought up in Robin's faith; she never imagined otherwise, and until lately she didn't really mind. But now she sees it's a kind of subtle collusion, not deliberately done, she's sure, full of so much secret mumbo jumbo it's designed to create outsiders.

She asked him once, only once, way back at the very beginning: 'Would you prefer it, would you like me to convert? I only ask because you've never mentioned it and sometimes, you know, because your religion is so important to you I feel a little bit excluded.'

He gave her a wry, disapproving look. 'That's the worst reason for changing faith that I have ever heard of.'

So she didn't mention that again.

But now they are nearly there. After waiting for the invitation that never came, Robin has invited himself to stay at Poppins for the weekend.

'You haven't! Without asking me? How could you! If Caroline had wanted you she would have suggested it. Well, I'm not going. Surely you can't expect me to go into that den of thieves. There is no reason for me to go and I refuse. They are nothing to do with me, never have been. You go.'

Quite naturally this was Suzie's reaction, but Robin was adamant. 'Think of Holly, Suzie, please. And grow up! It's time you came to terms with the situation as it is. These are Holly's stepbrothers and sisters and although you don't approve of them for reasons of your own – some deep-down insecurity perhaps, which is quite understandable – they are sweet, intelligent well-brought-up kids, you won't find better, and of course they've got to know each other. And it's time this feuding between them stopped. You're a mother now, Suzie, not a little girl. When I spoke to Caroline she said they were all longing to see you again, and Holly. They haven't seen her yet and she is already eight months old.'

She ranted and raved, to no avail. He was determined that they both should go.

It is all very odd. Since the move Robin's children have not asked to come to London for a single visit, not even for a weekend.

Oh, how poor Suzie dreads seeing her old home being lived in by somebody else.

THIRTY-FIVE

'I WONDER IF Caroline's cooking's improved?'

Suzie turns and stares at him sharply.

'And how on earth is she coping with a garden? She doesn't even know what a spade looks like!' Robin chuckles knowingly.

When they pull in beside the gate, Suzie is forced to close her eyes. The memories swim behind them, borne on the scents of the breeze. Last time she came here she sat in Eileen's kitchen; she watched her mother's sensible hands, she drank from familiar blue and white tea cups, she found a sense of time and place that was healing.

'I can't bear it,' she chokes, clutching at Robin's sleeve.

Robin says, 'Now Suzie, don't be so silly. You bring the bags and I'll take Holly. You can take her for a walk if you need to get away, if you can't stand being with Caroline. I'll put the wheels on the carrycot, but do take care. Remember, in these narrow country lanes there aren't any pavements . . .'

He gets importantly out of the car but stops dead in his tracks when he sees Caroline. She sails down the path with her curls springing shyly from under the brim of a huge straw hat. She's tanned, in a sky-blue dress that's almost flimsy enough to see through. Her smiling eyes are the soft green of the weeping willow she passes. She holds out her arms in what can only be a genuine greeting and it's all so . . . perfect. 'Robin,' she says, 'at last! Suzie, thank you for coming, it must have been very difficult for you. It must have been agony but we're all determined to make that right, if you'll let us. Would you mind if I picked up your baby?' And she stoops to reveal a curve of soft breast; she cradles Holly in her bare, comfortable, motherly arms.

Can this creature possibly be Caroline? Suzie attempts to hide her astonishment but it's difficult. Very difficult. Over the gate she can see the twins, naked, splashing about in the paddling pool. The fierce plastic blue is just one more patch of colour in this cradle of luscious greens. There's a man over there who looks like Adonis in a sunhat bringing some sandwiches out on a tray and putting them in the shade, on the old wicker table surrounded by baggy, bent chairs. Dominic hangs from a rope-ladder halfway up a tree-house; he watches their arrival intently like a sturdy beast regurgitating while Camilla's narrow, pixie face grins down through the branches. That delicate child, that pretty ballerina, looks like Tom Sawyer, more like a boy than a girl.

'Daddy! Daddy!' The naked twins rush towards Robin, but they do not cling as they used to; there is something different, like pride. They tug at his hands and they shout, 'Come and see! Come and see!'

Robin clears his throat as he's dragged along. 'Hang on! Hang on a minute.' He is forced into being falsely jovial. 'I wanted to take you out for tea. I told you. I thought you'd be all dressed and ready.'

'It's too hot, Daddy. It's much too hot and we've got all this food here we must eat.'

'Perhaps this evening, then. We could all go out for a meal, give your mother some peace. First we must put all Holly's things in the kitchen, away from the flies.'

'Oh Daddy, don't be so fussy, just give them to Lot.'

Robin frowns. 'To whom?'

'Lot will look after them. Come on, Daddy, watch how we jump!'

If this is a show put on to confuse them then it's been expertly rehearsed. There's no way this could be a show. Suzie stares, confounded, because it's just how it used to be when she and Mummy and Daddy were there, and her little friends. It's glorious, it is perfection, such a faithful representation ... and the change in Caroline is startling. She glows with satisfaction. Suzie is moved to say without thinking, 'Caroline, I don't think I would have recognised you. You look so happy! You look so stunningly beautiful.'

'Oh, I am.'

'Oh, she is. This man down the road who does adverts on TV asked her if she'd do some sessions for a lot of money but she didn't want to, did you, Mummy?'

And there are no wiles about her. She's an actress, but nobody could act as naturally as this. Nobody could act the way that Dominic comes to idle by her side, his little brown hand in hers, gently waiting. Nobody could act the way Camilla pushes so confidently forward. 'Can we start the sandwiches now? Shall I bring out the blackberry wine, or the beetroot?'

'No dear, tea will do.'

Nobody could have baked that sponge cake, that enormously topply, creamy, swirly sponge cake with anything else but love. And nobody who didn't like children could arrange Holly so sweetly, could have suddenly thought up the parasol and the natural windchimes of leaves and branches. The baby knows. The baby chortles. 'Oh she's gorgeous, Suzie. You must be so proud. She's wonderful! Look, Camilla, hold her little fist. I'm so sorry, Suzie, I'm quite dotty about other people's babies.' And Caroline closes her eyes and absorbs her.

Is Holly wonderful? Is she? Suzie has nearly forgotten. Suzie sees her baby through eyes cobwebbed with worry and all sorts of difficult questions.

Robin stands alone, blinky and owl-like, his hands gripped behind his back as he watches the twins' mad splashings. You could almost imagine they've forgotten he's there.

'Where is Vanessa?'

Caroline's face saddens suddenly and the shadow's a drift of pain that lightly brushes her eyes. She takes off her hat and she fans herself with it and then they're aware of the terrible beat of the drums. Robin looks up towards the top window — you can only just make out the blasted words: 'INJECT THE VENOM'.

'How ghastly,' says Robin, frowning, his hands to his ears and pricked by a hot, suspicious sweat. All is not right here.

'That's AC-DC,' Dominic explains with an eager half-smile, telling tales. 'She doesn't listen to anyone but AC-DC now.'

'Heavy metal,' says Caroline shortly, cramming that hat back on her head. 'She knew what time you'd be coming. She's really very naughty. She should have come down. I'll call her if you like, but maybe we ought to just wait until later.'

But everyone can see that Robin is hurt. His little girl should have run out to greet him. 'I told her to come down. I called her earlier, when I heard you arrive.' Caroline repeats herself stupidly. She looks slightly nervous. 'I'll just go and see ...'

Caroline disappears into the house and she's gone for a good five minutes while Robin waits, glancing at his watch, smiling weakly at the twins, at Suzie. It's all so strange — he is so out of his depth in this alien place.

Suzie sinks apprehensively into one of the old uneven chairs, just relieved that her difficult baby is contented and silent for once, sucking her tiny fist. She gazes around her wonderful garden remembering those happy old times. She wants to put up her arms like a boxer, to shield her brain from the force of them. None of this is hers any more and it feels as if it's been stolen away.

It's such a shock! Vanessa is dressed all in black. Her hair is a row of tall purple spikes, gelled into place, like the back of some prehistoric beast. There's a silver ring through her nose. Her skin-tight jeans have holes in the knee and her boots make her feet ugly and duck-like. Robin walks towards her uncertainly. 'Darling?'

Vanessa glowers out between thick black lashes. She does not even deign to reply.

'What's all this?'

There is no response, none at all. Just a fierce, bored look and she is tapping one of her monstrous feet on the grass. Why is his daughter wearing workman's boots?

'Well, you've changed! Just look at you! How long has this been going on?' He stares at his daughter with all the solemnity of a judge passing sentence but he blames his wife. It's his first wife who must give him an explanation.

Caroline contributes an uncertain laugh. 'Oh, it's just a phase, Robin. She's fourteen now, you know. She's been responsible for so long, she had to let go of it some time, don't you see ...'

'But like this? Vanessa?' He slaps his forehead. 'I just don't believe it. The girl must be ill.'

'No, Robin, no.' Caroline laughs, but softly, sadly. 'What Vanessa needs is to be left alone to sort her own self out, without anyone interfering.'

'How can you talk this way, Caroline? You were always impossibly stupid and irresponsible as a mother but I never thought I'd see the day—'

'Robin, please don't! You sound so—'

'Be quiet, Suzie, please. You do not know what you are talking about.'

'But you sound so unpleasant, Robin.'

'I'm grown up now, Daddy. I'm a woman.'

'I know, and you look disgusting!'

Vanessa's smile is the smile of the clown under that chalk-white make-up. It is not the smile of a child. She turns away on her two-inch-thick, black rubber heel.

Caroline flushes. 'Shall we all have some tea? It's ready, I think. The children will bring the rest of it out. Sit down, Robin, it's far too hot for a drama. Just sit down and try to relax.'

But Robin falls angrily into his chair, glaring at his daughter's back as she disappears into the cooler shadows, as she stomps through the open door, under the rustic eyebrow of thatch. Is it possible that the sound of that terrible music has now been turned up even higher?

The hills are silvery in the sunlight and buttercups spread the fields with gold. 'Well, it's certainly all very nice. You've done jolly well, Caroline,' says Robin, trying, as he waits for his tea to be poured.

From the window the drums beat down, there's an air of voodoo about the heat as Caroline passes his cup and says, 'It's a difficult time for Vanessa. She's changing . . . Go on, help yourself to a sandwich.'

'How can you talk this way, Caroline? *You* haven't changed, have you? Still exactly the same pathetic—'

'Robin, please!'

'It's all right, Suzie, I'm quite used to this. Vanessa is lovely in her own way, Robin, if you look hard under all the black.'

'I will not look hard – I should not *have* to look hard. She is my daughter and I was looking forward to taking her out, but I don't really feel like a burger and chips at some road hut . . .'

They look round, astonished, when they see Suzie laughing. Perhaps it's the heat and the terrible journey, perhaps the fact that she's in her own garden, combined with the fear of Caroline and Robin's crass behaviour – maybe these things have helped to unhinge her. But the silent laughter's infectious. Suzie is shaking, wiping her eyes and Caroline, made nervous by Robin's fury, can't control herself any longer. They look at each other as they sit there exhausted, absorbing the feeling of changelessness that comforted Suzie as a child. It's a healing balm. With the drumbeat pounding down from above and Robin's cross face, his angry words cutting the breeze, they collapse in their chairs and they laugh, flapping their hands to cool themselves. Suzie finally manages to cry, 'There's no competition here, Robin! Your women, your children, there's nobody vying to be first with you any more!' She chokes and wipes her eyes again. 'That's why you wanted to come, isn't it? That's why you made me come with you!'

Robin, silenced, stares at his wife in clenched amazement.

'Suzie, let's go inside. Bring your tea, it's too hot out here and the children can entertain Robin.'

'What about Holly?' Suzie, still giggling, still hysterical, hangs back nervously.

'Holly is far better off here with me,' says Robin, tartly.

'Or Lot can look after Holly, or Vanessa might have her upstairs for a while . . .'

'Vanessa?' Robin is horrified. 'You are mad, woman! You must be completely crazed to think that I'd be so irresponsible as to let a child of mine alone with that creature.' Sweat pours down his face. He waves his arms, making futile stabs at the air.

'But Vanessa is not one of your wives, Robin. She is your loving daughter, made in your own image. Surely you trust Vanessa? Surely there's someone you can still trust, besides Isobel and God?'

The younger children have stopped playing. They stand and stare, astounded to see such fury here in this safe place where it is normally only house martins that slice the still summer air.

Caroline tactfully tries to be cheerful. 'While I show Suzie inside, maybe you lot would like to take Daddy off for a walk – show him the lake in the trees, perhaps, or the badger set?'

When no one responds, when they all hang back, Robin hisses to Caroline: 'I can't believe it – you've done this! You've secretly been working towards this and now is your little moment of triumph. That's it, isn't it? You have turned my daughter, you have turned *all* my children against me. Look at them all – just look at them! Running wild like savages!'

'They're not used to scenes like this, Robin, that's all. They're not used to atmospheres of this kind any more. They don't know how to deal with them. I promise you there's been no secret scheming.' Caroline watches his fury for a moment, fascinated, horrified, as you might watch a lion tearing away at its scarlet kill, before she smiles and tells him, 'Don't be so idiotic. Suzie, ignore him, come with me.'

'And who is that man, might I ask?'

Both Suzie and Caroline ignore his rudeness but Robin, hot and bothered, calls out after them, 'Balls, ball, balls.'

'He sounds as if he has finally gone stark staring mad!'

'It's the atmosphere – he poisons it!' Suzie's whole body is trembling now and she cannot hold back the tears any longer. She wants to hit him or spit in his face. It's a good thing Caroline brought her indoors, away from the fury, away from the heat. It is cool indoors. Suzie's bedroom is much the same as it always was. It welcomes her back with its gentle pastels and that same squeak of the bed; there's that vague smell of new-mown hay or is it ironing? It seems to be part of the curtains, like the red hem of cross-stitch she sewed years ago while she learned to be a woman, and the breeze flutters a welcome familiar and sweet. 'I don't want to share this bed with Robin. Not this bed. It's mine, isn't it? My old bed?

'It's such a subtle destruction.' She sits down heavily on the bed and confesses timidly to Caroline, to the one who was always the enemy: 'I could have been laughing out there, I could have been crying, it's all the same. I know how irrational I'm sounding now but whatever he did to you, Caroline, whatever happened, I think that he is in the process of doing the same thing to me. I know it. I've been so blind! I didn't want to see but it was so obvious down there in the garden, staring me in the face. Poor Vanessa! There was only one woman in his life who ever made Robin unhappy, and it wasn't you, Caroline, it was never you. It was Isobel. I've thought about it. I've stayed awake nights, I've watched so many dawns come in, wondering. What did she do to him, Caroline? Dear God, what did she do?'

'You're emeshed in it all, as I was. You need time alone, away from him. You need time to think.'

Suzie's face is a picture of misery. She delves in her basket and brings out a packet of cigarettes. Her hand trembles as she lights one. Robin would frown with disgust and say, 'Oh Suzie, must you!' 'I was so strong once,' she sobs distraughtly, 'but you wouldn't think it to see me now! I'm afraid of my baby! She's never been mine and I seem to have somehow lost everything else. How can I leave him when I'd have to leave Holly behind because, Caroline, I hardly dare touch her! I'm not like a mother, Caroline. I'm not like a mother and yet I love her! Can anyone understand that?'

Caroline moves to look out of the window. Robin sits in the garden alone, slumped in an attitude of stunned dejection. 'Vanessa knew. I suppose her childish instinct told her; she knew long before I did. She was always so frightened of growing up. Robin's never liked women, and when you consider Isobel, is that any wonder? He has to try and reduce them, turning them back into children again. Robin adores his children.' She goes to sit down beside the miserable Suzie. 'I'm not even sure he's aware that he does it. He's not a cruel man. How he must have been looking forward to this weekend, to hearing his children whine to stay with him just as they always used to. And you and me, Suzie, how we would have fought over him once. And I whined in my own way. God, for years, how I whined.' Caroline turns to survey the woman crying softly on the crumpled bed and there's a lost sound in her voice when she says, 'But the trouble is, Suzie, the really awful thing is that I don't think there is any way out of it. Robin will not let go.'

Caroline's eyes are like two wet stones. 'He would get custody of mine, or yours if you dared to leave him. He's a powerful man with friends in high places. He would get it!'

Thirty-six

She is competent. Vanessa knows that she is. Well, she managed to carry the weight of a household on her shoulders but what's going to happen now? The atmosphere's suffocating! They'd planned a barbecue so at least Robin was busy. The younger children helped him through the sticky twilight, so at least there were things going on last night to relieve some of that terrible tension.

He and Suzie hardly spoke and Caroline played the motherly hostess, intercepting those flying emotional shards, glossing over the difficulties. In the end she came straight out with it. 'Suzie might be staying here for a while, Robin. And Holly. She needs a rest.'

'Suzie can stay here if she likes but I'm not leaving Holly in this madhouse if it's the last thing I do!' And he went back to turning the sausages.

And how is Vanessa, crouched under the crushing heat of thatch in her stuffy darkness of a den with her cupboard full of hair gel, a wide selection of acne creams and stubby tubes of coverup – how is she taking this, her old arch-enemy welcomed into the warm bosom of the house? This is not how she planned it during those difficult times, all those months ago.

She stares at herself in her bedroom mirror, a long, cool, unperturbed look. Neither ashamed nor frightened, she arches her back and places her hands on her hips. Her mauve lips stiffly unstick before they come apart again and form the shape of a whore's blown kiss.

Vanessa understands at last. Perhaps she had to reach fourteen before she could see it so clearly — through a glass darkly and all that. She is quite prepared to accept poor Suzie. There was never any point in competing with Suzie ... they have both already lost the battle because they are grown-up women. All Daddy ever does is to try and turn women back into little girls again. Perhaps he thinks that little girls are innocent and lovely.

Vanessa listens to them down in the garden and her stare conveys just a mild distaste. God, why are they all so boring?

Last week, shifting from foot to foot, Amber asked her, 'Have we made Mummy happy, d'you think?'

Vanessa thought for only a moment. 'No, I don't think she's actually happy, but she's not in love with Daddy any more so I think she's probably contented.'

It was Camilla who put their fears into words. 'Why don't we say what we're all thinking? We've been as bad as Daddy, haven't we? Worse, even. Everyone's been trying to turn Mummy into something to suit themselves.'

Is Camilla blaming Vanessa? That's not fair. 'But at least she's got a chance now.'

'What kind of a chance?'

'She's got a chance to find out what she wants to be. Just for herself.'

'But how can she do that when she is stuck here with us?'

Vanessa scoffed at the ignorant child. 'She loves us. She has always loved us. She is not stuck here at all — this is where she would choose to be.'

And what about poor Daddy now? Who is going to save him from himself? He looked so pathetic this morning, sitting bewildered as a sun-bleached gnome, balanced on that spindly chair in the garden.

Why would Vanessa want to go out for a meal? Why was there such a great fuss? Don't they all realise that half the world is starving? Anyone would think the world would end if she, Vanessa, refused to change out of her black string vest and into a dress. Nobody in this family has their priorities right. None of them care, like she does, about vivisection and the future of the whales and the shooting of elephants or the scandalous rape of the North Pole by the all those greedy oilmen.

Jesus, how can there possibly be a God? Vanessa's not conned by the opt-out clause, man's free will, any more. Why would you give free will to a vicious animal? So it's all much easier now, not at all like it was. Sod the lot of them, frankly it's as simple as that! Let them make what messes they like of their lives. Before she leaves for school each morning Vanessa stuffs tights inside her bra, for she has moved on from God and Sister Agnes, and yesterday at break Carl Baker, hunt saboteur and perfectly bald, told Nicky Morgan that he fancied her. Did she want to go with him on the animal rights march next weekend? If so, could she please make and bring her own banner?

But with Daddy so upset like this, what's going to happen to them now? Vanessa does not want her world to change; she's happy for it to stay as it is.

It was Dominic who overheard them talking long after the others had all gone to sleep. He reported back in the morning. The night voices from the garden seats drifted, like a mist, through his window.

'I mean it, Caroline. I am not prepared to leave Holly in this household for one day and I feel so uneasy about all this that I'm getting on to my solicitors just as soon as I get back to London. The children need to be with me – there is plenty of room at the flat. You know I would have had them from the start but Suzie was so stubbornly against it.'

'You know I would never agree to that!'

'Caroline, stop and think for a moment. Just let a judge know the sort of unstable woman you are, just give him a hint of your past. He's only got to read the papers, he doesn't need to hear it from me.' Daddy lowered his voice then so Dominic had to strain to hear. 'He wouldn't hesitate for a moment.'

'The children would refuse to leave.'

'Their minds have been poisoned! The children will do as *I* say. And where would you live? You haven't got a penny of your own. You could never afford a place like this without my total support.'

'Think of the publicity, Robin.'

'There is nothing in any of this that could possibly do me any damage.'

'People will wonder why you didn't insist on taking your children with you before,' Suzie interrupted. 'Your wife was an alcoholic, and I would have headed in the same direction. Why reclaim them *now*, when everything's so much better?'

'Better? You call this chaos better? Living in turmoil with a man half her age, running naked across the hills ...'

Suzie seems to realise the magnitude of what she is saying. Her voice stays low. 'While Caroline was ill you pulled the strings and that is just what you wanted. Your children were so dependent on you they were putty in your hands. You didn't need to live there to wage your twisted war. It were quite safe to leave her and start on somebody else. It's so sick, yes – *sick*. Can't you see it?'

'Oh good heavens! You talk like that to a judge and he'll call you raving mad.'

After a long pause – there's just the sound of a cricket somewhere, and the soft strike of a match: 'And if I agreed to go with you, would you leave them alone?'

'I'm afraid not, Suzie. Look what has happened to Vanessa. Think of the others, so young and vulnerable.' His tone was an easy banter.

Caroline cried, 'Suzie, think about what you are saying. I wouldn't let you make that sacrifice!'

'Oh Robin, why don't you just go away and leave us all alone?'

'Because I'm responsible, and my children need me, that's why!' And in the darkness his voice trailed away.

Robin slept on the sofa downstairs with his unpacked bag on the floor beside him.

Caroline cooks breakfast. They eat it in the garden which is breathtaking, hung with cobwebs of dewy lace. But nobody speaks much and the twins are sullen and shy, sensing danger.

'Suzie and I will be leaving soon.' He must be hoping that she won't have the courage to contradict him, too intimidated to cause a scene.

Caroline says, 'Your father's mistaken. Suzie and Holly will be staying here with us for a few days.'

Robin says, 'I'm warning you, Caroline!' and all the children's eyes are cast down; they are all completely absorbed in their eggs.

But Mummy just goes on buttering her toast. She shrugs and smiles at him sadly.

'Where is Vanessa?'

'Oh, still asleep, I'm afraid. During the holidays she doesn't get up much before one.'

'Does nobody want to know why I am going? Does nobody want to know what's going on?' he asks on a note of exasperation. But they don't. It's awful. Flushed and embarrassed, they don't even answer. There is nothing more to be said. Eventually Dominic fetches Robin's bag and it's like a dismissal.

'Thank you, Dominic,' his father says stiffly.

'They will ask us, Daddy. They do these days. They ask the children.'

'What?' Robin's astonished. 'They've been listening – or you and Suzie have been talking to them already. This is beyond belief! This is nothing to do with you, Dominic, so please don't interfere.'

'Just go home, Daddy.'

'What did you say?'

The boy's soft eyelids don't even flutter. 'I said why don't you just go home, Daddy.'

Vanessa's not here, but the four younger children stand in a semi-circle to watch him; they form a primitive nursery-rhyme moon, a judgement. Robin sticks it out for as long as he can; he jangles the loose change in his pockets as if he is handling prayer beads. Several times he starts to speak but it's useless, his words trail off aimlessly, taken up to the hard blue sky which is clear and cloudless and sure of itself.

'I've had enough of this,' he says, inviting contradiction. Straightening. 'I'm off. Give me the car keys, Suzie.'

It's with a kind of lethargic weariness that he starts off down the path, expecting one of his children to follow but there is only the one. He follows his father to the gate. They pass through, one behind the other, and Robin sits in the driving seat of Suzie's car, fiddling with the keys, while Dominic stands at the door looking down at his father through long, feminine lashes.

'Well, at least one of you cared enough to come and say goodbye to me.'

'Daddy, did you know that a polar bear's skin is really as black as his nose? And the fur is a pure, clear colour – it just reflects the visible light.'

'Sometimes, Dominic, I wish you would just come out and say exactly what you mean. There are times when this habit of yours, talking through stories, can be quite infuriating and this is one of them, I'm afraid.'

278

Dominic, so easily cut by Daddy's impatience, moves not one muscle in his face. 'Nothing is quite what it seems, is it, Daddy? And it never really has been. I heard about a family who lived in London. There were five children, four girls and a boy. And d'you know what they did?'

'No, Dominic, what did they do?' Tortured by the turn of events it is all Robin can do to muster this last shred of patience, but his pretty little son has always been such a sensitive child and it's so important . . .

'They didn't like their mother much. So they kept her prisoner for four months, down in the basement, down in their father's sauna. He wasn't there. He was a very important man with no time to waste. He'd gone away and left them.'

As Robin stares up, the sun glares into his watering eyes. 'What an extraordinary imagination . . .'

'And I was just wondering, Daddy, what would happen to this famous man if people got to hear about what happened. The mother wouldn't mind – the mother's happy now. The children wouldn't mind – they're safe and looked after. Nobody would mind about people finding out – except the father. Anyway, that's what I think.'

'Are you trying to tell me . . . are you honestly expecting me to believe . . . This is absurd!'

'I have even taken some pictures with the Instamatic you gave me, and they're very good, sharp. I focused it just like you showed me. I think some people would call them scandalous pictures. But what I would really like is a darkroom of my own and some proper photographic equipment. Mummy says that it's far too expensive, but she wouldn't be able to do anything if you insisted that I had it.'

'This is quite unbelievable! I don't know what's going on here, Dominic, or quite what you are getting at, but I'm going to go back and have a long talk to Caroline about this *right now*.'

Dominic's smile is sugar-sweet. 'If you do that, Daddy, I think you'll find that the newspapers have those pictures, probably by next Tuesday. Because wouldn't they be interested to know, wouldn't people like Kitty Beavers-St Clair love to hear all about it – and wouldn't they wonder what sort of person you really were, with your children doing that while you were there, talking to them all, telling them about the world on TV. I think it would make a wonderful story. Whose side d'you think they'd all be on, Daddy?'

Robin's voice is thin, tense as his mouth. Can this sweet-talking boy be just ten years old? *'In the sauna?'*

'In the sauna.'

'For four months?'

'For four months.'

'Locked in?'

'Locked in.'

'And Mrs Guerney? What about Ilse?' Robin feels trapped, shut in, imprisoned – surely this cannot be true – and if it *is* true, where will this leave him? Never to be free for the rest of his life, from childish demands, from fear of exposure? Powerless – dependent on this child? 'It's not true – I would have known!'

Dominic shrugs. The thin white T-shirt strap slips over one bronzed shoulder. 'I think I might like to be a photographer when I've seen the world. And I'd like to sail. I'd like a yacht of my own one day. I expect Vanessa and Camilla and Sacha and Amber will all have their own dreams too, when they're older. Loving us all as much as you do, you'll want to know what their dreams are too, Daddy, won't you?'

See, Jane, see. Look, Jane, look. Here is Mummy. Here is Daddy. Perfect mother. Perfect father. Just like books.

'He's gone. Bloody hell,' and Lot surfaces, wiping his brow, from where he's been scything the nettles.

'That was nearly a terrible scene!'

But now it's all peace, perfect peace at Poppins.

With the drumbeat pounding down from above, Robin's two wives collapse in their chairs. There's so much to say but it's much too soon; it's much too early to speak yet.

As she flaps a hand to cool herself, Caroline, who has despised herself for so many years, gazes across at her children fondly. She flicks a leaf from the hem of her skirt. A dragonfly hovers over the checked tablecloth and all the air is a soft summer buzzing. She tilts her straw hat and closes her eyes as Suzie leans forward to pour the tea.

She smiles with relief when she hears the car pull away. Dominic was gone a long time. She wants to weep when he comes to hold her hand, a dry, firm, warm little paw in her own. For an awful moment she feared she might lose him to Robin, such an oversensitive child, in tune to the pain of other people and wise beyond his years. Not so impulsive or impassioned as poor Vanessa. With tender loving care he will go far.

She sighs. There is nothing else for it, they will just have to cope with Robin's attack, and be ready whenever it comes. At least, now, she is not alone. She and Suzie can fight him together.

She brushes a moth from her cheek. This morning she woke up to discover a note on her pillow. The notepaper said Save the Whale. '*I have been thinking. When I get through this, if I get through this, I think I might like to be your friend. Sincerely yours, Vanessa.*'

In the soft dawn light Caroline crept up the twisted stairs and returned it, after first crossing out the signature and replacing it with her own - *Caroline.*